LOVE'S WARM EMBRACE

"You," he grinned, reaching out for her. Her eyes opened wide, playfully fearful, and she started to run. Quanah caught her in two strides, turning her around by the arm.

She was still laughing as his mouth closed over hers, his arms pulling her body tightly against his. She molded herself to him, her arms entwining around his neck. His lips traveled over her cheek to her neck . . . He kissed her again as his hand inched up her back to her shoulder, bearing pressure there, pulling her downward. Yielding, Nalin knelt, then allowed him to lay her back on the grass. The ground was cold with the coming of winter, but she hardly felt it as another kind of warmth spread through her . . .

CAPTIVE OF THE HEART

KATE DOUGLAS

AVON
PUBLISHERS OF BARD, CAMELOT, DISCUS AND FLARE BOOKS

CAPTIVE OF THE HEART is an original publication of
Avon Books. This work has never before appeared in book
form.

AVON BOOKS
A division of
The Hearst Corporation
959 Eighth Avenue
New York, New York 10019

First Avon Printing, October, 1982

AVON TRADEMARK REG. U. S. PAT. OFF. AND IN
OTHER COUNTRIES. MARCA REGISTRADA. HECHO EN
U. S. A.

Printed in the U. S. A.

WFH 10 9 8 7 6 5 4 3 2 1

TO SEBASTIANA

Prologue

A MOONLESS night provided the stalking forms with a blanket of darkness. On hands and knees, five of them moved over the hard-packed ground, dragging buffalo skins behind them. Their leader stopped to listen, raising a hand, palm outward, for silence. Only the woman behind him saw the signal; she passed it on.

She waited, watching her husband's motionless black shadow, all her eyes could make out in the ebony of the night. Her companions were camouflaged by the copper shade of their skins which blended into the scene of rocks and grass-strewn prairie. She had covered herself in a coating of mud; without it, her fair white skin might give away their position to the posted sentries.

While she waited for his signal, her hand reached down to check the security of her sheathed knife, the only weapon she carried. For a moment she felt a twinge of apprehension. This was not the best time to be accompanying him on a raid. Riding horseback at a fast gallop had caused her to lose every other pregnancy. This baby must survive, and it could do that only if she stopped riding, stopped raiding. Yet she was reluctant to tell him until this matter was settled. After tonight, if all went well, she would tell him that until the child was born she could not go with him any longer. Quanah would be glad of it. It was by her choice that she rode beside him in every encounter.

His hand dropped, and he moved off to the left. As they had done before, she moved off to the right, clutching her

1

buffalo skin, keeping her body sheltered from sight along the ground.

Harrison Parker tried futilely to make himself comfortable on the ground. Every time he thought he had cleared his spot of debris, his back found another rock the moment he stretched out. The army issue blanket was completely inadequate for his six-foot frame. Apparently Supply thought soldiers came in sizes five feet tall and under. If he covered his shoulders, his feet stuck out. Irritated, Harry reached down to tuck the blanket beneath his bare feet.

"Shouldn't ought to sleep with yer boots off, Major," Sergeant Ryker advised from the place beside him.

Harry glared at the twenty-year veteran, and Ryker shrugged before turning over. Ryker knew that the hills were filled with Indians, that camping out under the stars meant sleeping fully clothed and ready just in case. He tried to impart that knowledge to Parker, but the major insisted he should be safe enough with Colonel MacKenzie's entire detachment camped out around him. Born in Texas twenty-nine years before, Harry had spent most of his life in the East, in boarding school and then law school. Fort Smith was his first assignment in the West. He was clean shaven, which was unusual for an army officer of 1867; he good-naturedly ignored the jocular advice of subordinates who said that a beard or moustache would make him look more like an officer and less like a lawyer. His dark blond hair was short even by military standards. Light blue eyes reflected warmth and compassion, while a quick, disarming grin gave his features a boyish charm that concealed a formidable intelligence.

Until now he had never slept in anything more uncomfortable than an army-issue cot. He had missed the Civil War by mere moments, sworn in the day Lee surrendered. Harry's father had felt the war would last until he finished school; as far as his son knew, it was the only time Isaac Parker had been wrong. Impatient at missing out on all the action, the new captain made major before his transfer west came in. He suspected Senator Parker had had something to do with the delay as well. Harrison hadn't seen Texas since his boyhood. Now he was seeing too much of its flat, arid desert. Since Colonel MacKenzie was going the same way as Major Parker, it was only logical, by army standards of reason, that Harrison should travel along.

Colonel Ronald MacKenzie had been sent out with orders to subdue the renegade Kwahadi Comanche, and en route to Fort Smith, he was to look for his quarry; consequently the trip was taking days longer than it would have if Harry had gone by stagecoach. As the fort's new resident attorney, camping out on the prairie was hardly what he had had in mind. All the way he had listened to MacKenzie boasting about how quickly he would take care of Quanah and his band. He referred to the warring Comanche as if they were misbehaving children who simply needed a firm hand. MacKenzie intended to provide that firm hand.

He was qualified to do it; he was a recent veteran of the Civil War and had engaged in several skirmishes with the Sioux. But Ryker, Parker's usual traveling companion along the trail, muttered his own doubts about the colonel's ability.

"He won't do it," Sergeant Ryker had predicted as they rode side by side. "Hell, I'll bet that asshole colonel . . . oh, 'scuse me, sir." Ryker flashed a grin at Major Parker.

"I didn't hear you say that, Sergeant. Nor did you hear me agree with you."

"Yes, sir, Major." Ryker's grin broadened.

"What about the asshole colonel," Parker prodded.

"Oh, well, he wouldn't know a Comanche from a Tankawa, or a 'pache from a Pueblo. He thinks long as they're Injun they think alike, an' they don't, not by a long shot. See, he's us' ta fightin' Sioux and Cheyenne. They have a diff'rent outlook from Comanche. You kin call 'em out an' they'll meet ya right there. Lots of courage, them uns, an' they're hard ta beat, sure enuf."

3

"Then what about the Comanche?"

"Oh, well," he drawled, smiling slyly. "They got a diff'rent way a' thinkin', that's all."

"Different how?"

"You'll see, Major. You'll see. I just hope we keep our scalps when you find out."

That bit of news hadn't helped Harry sleep peacefully either. Quanah, the one MacKenzie was after, had made a name for himself all the way from the Mexican border to Colorado. While some of the Comanche tribes talked over peace terms, Quanah and his Kwahadi band refused to even discuss the matter. Though invited to the Medicine Bend Peace Treaty Conference, Quanah had not bothered to come, relaying a message that he would surrender only when the bluecoats came and defeated him. MacKenzie was sent for to do just that.

Grumbling out loud, Harry had just settled down again when a shrill cry tore through the camp, followed immediately by the sounds of gunfire and stampeding horses' hooves. Parker jumped to his feet just behind Sergeant Ryker, who was already moving at a dead run for the edge of camp, where the horses were staked.

While chaos reigned around him, Parker had to pause to put his boots on. Cursing himself for not listening to the Sergeant, he at last scrambled to his feet only to discover that he was the only one left on his side of camp. He could hear shrill war cries from the Indians, the loud report of rifles and pistols, and curses and shouts from the soldiers all about him. Trying to decide where he could do the most good, he was jumped from behind and knocked to the ground. A blow stunned him but failed to leave him unconscious as it no doubt had been intended to do. Harry turned around just in time to see an Indian leading five U.S. Cavalry horses through the unguarded section where he had been standing.

The horses were panicked by the sounds around them, and the brave could barely hold on to the severed lead ropes. Shooting the Indian would have been easy, but Harrison Parker never believed in using guns when two strong arms could settle the matter. Harry tackled, bring-

4

ing the Indian down. He was just about to smash a hard right into the Indian's jaw when his upraised arm froze. The form beneath him wasn't a brave at all, but a woman. Even more startling, the eyes staring back at him in a mixture of fear and anger were light—green or blue, he couldn't be sure, but definitely light. Her face was streaked with mud to darken the light skin; her lips were wide and full, the nose sharp and long. Her hair, bound in a leather headband, gave off a reddish glow as the firelight cast sparks off the top of her head. Not only wasn't she a warrior, she wasn't even an Indian. She was white!

Harry gaped just a second too long, not hearing the muffled sound of moccasins behind him. He was barely aware of a moment of sharp agony before he plunged to the ground in complete oblivion.

Though few of the soldiers wished to talk about it, MacKenzie had no choice but to report what had happened. They were camped on the trail, searching for Quanah's band, when a pack of Comanche raiders sneaked in, split the lines tethering the horses, and then, waving buffalo skins and screaming like the devils they were, drove off or stole every single horse in the camp, leaving the Cavalry sent to subdue them to walk the many miles to the fort. MacKenzie was livid with rage at the "sneaking, thieving red devils" who had caused him this embarrassment. Harrison listened while the discussion over Quanah reached a fever pitch. In attendance were General Beaumont, commanding officer at Fort Smith, Colonel MacKenzie, and another officer, older than Parker but at the same rank, Roger Nash, a man Harry had only met briefly that afternoon.

"We're going to have to do something," MacKenzie was in the midst of saying.

"If you can't handle it, MacKenzie, say so," Beaumont suggested from behind his desk. "Your friends back East can find something else for you to do, I'm sure."

"General, sir," MacKenzie snapped tightly, "I was sent here because you failed to bring Quanah in on the treaty.

5

He's gaining influence with the entire Comanche nation. The hotheads from all the other bands are deserting their chiefs to follow this half-breed bastard."

"Sir, perhaps a delegation specifically sent to talk with him on a more personal level—"

"Are you crazy, Parker?" MacKenzie turned on the lawyer. "Five words wouldn't be out of your mouth before he had your scalp in his hands. You've already met his wife the *hard* way. . . . How much more proof do you need?"

"His wife?" Harry parroted, staring at MacKenzie. He had reported everything that happened, not expecting them to believe what he said.

"That woman wasn't a hallucination, Parker. She's as real as the bump on your head."

Harry still looked dumbstruck. "The Comanche call her Warrior Woman, but most everybody else calls her Quanah's woman . . . she's real."

"But she's white . . . ," Harrison exclaimed, as if he were the only one to have made the discovery.

"You bet she is." Beaumont sat back. "On the outside . . . inside she's all Comanche. Don't make the mistake of thinking she's a hostage or prisoner. She's as much a Comanche as that husband of hers."

"Sir . . ." The voice came from Major Nash, who, until now, had been sitting quietly. "May I make a suggestion?"

"Go ahead, Nash," MacKenzie grumbled. "That's what you're here for."

Beaumont glared at him, but let the usurpation pass.

"Sir, I'm wondering if the way to strike at Quanah isn't right before us . . . Quanah's wife." Nash glanced from one officer to the other, pausing to let his words sink in. "It's known fact that she rides with him on every encounter. And it's known fact she isn't Indian. If we could . . . take her back . . . capture her . . . perhaps he would be more inclined to listen to peace terms."

"He'd be more *inclined*," Beaumont stressed, "to fight harder than ever."

"Perhaps, if we simply held her as we did his mother,

6

he might go on trying to free her. But if he didn't have that kind of time . . ."

"What are you talking about, Nash?"

"If she had a price on her head, technically, we can consider her a traitor. It would be a simple matter to have her tried and convicted."

"Hang a woman!" Beaumont shouted. "That's preposterous."

"I don't think it would go that far, sir. I happen to know, on good authority, how much this woman means to him. If Quanah learned she were about to be executed, I think he would be more than willing to surrender his *principles,* shall we say, in exchange for her life."

"We can't do that!" Parker stared at the major, disbelieving his ears.

"Why not?" MacKenzie said, thinking as he spoke. "She's white, isn't she? She kills whites to help the Indians. Quanah has declared war on the United States, and she's part of it, isn't she?"

"But surely there's a reason for her being there. . . . The whole idea of calling her a traitor is highly—"

"Look, lawyer." MacKenzie frowned at him. "Leave the Indian Wars to me. You just shuffle papers or something. . . ."

MacKenzie turned back to Nash. "The biggest problem is how we're going to get our hands on her without taking on the whole Comanche nation. She never leaves that half-breed's side."

Parker gazed at General Beaumont, who gave him a sympathetic shrug. There really wasn't much he could do about it. MacKenzie was on orders to subdue Quanah in any manner he found feasible. How he did it was out of the general's hands.

Parker leaned back in his chair in disgust.

Nalin began to smile as his expression changed. "You are pleased?" she urged, wanting to hear the words from him. He was already in high spirits from the success of their raid against the bluecoats. Her news could only add to his pleasure.

"You well knew that I would be." Quanah's dark eyes glistened with pleasure. In the two years of their marriage she had become pregnant several times—how could she not with such a man as Quanah?—but the pregnancies had all ended before her body even revealed its hidden burden. Red Eagle Feather, the Kwahadi medicine man, had told her what he had heard from a visiting doctor of the whites, that the reason Comanche women lost so many children unborn was due to the length of time they spent on horseback. For her it was truer than for most.

Quanah lay down on the bedroll, urging her to lie beside him. "Perhaps I am wrong to deny the white man's peace." He looked vaguely troubled. "Perhaps we should try—"

"No, Quanah." She pulled out of his arms far enough to look at him. "We will do as you have decided, my husband. If the Kwahadi are to fight, then your sons shall follow you."

His slow smile returned at her answer. "I have been too long without you. . . ." The dark eyes turned lusty, his fingers massaging the back of her neck. Nalin moved away to remove her clothing while he watched. Already her breasts were fuller than before, her usually flat stomach was slightly rounded. He reached out and placed his hand over the bare midriff. "We would not hurt the child?"

"No, my foolish warrior." She shook her head. "I will not break." She leaned forward into his arms. Quanah lifted her face and kissed her, drawing her tightly against him. Nalin clung to him, her passions ignited by the heat of his kiss, her body already responding to his gentle and ardent caresses. Anxious for him, Nalin mounted him in growing urgency, relishing the moment when he entered her, his strong lean hips thrusting against her.

She knew the name the bluecoats called her—Quanah's woman, nameless except for her connection to him. As Comanche names should be, the bluecoats' name for her was right and fitting; it pleased her to be so known. She was Quanah's woman proudly.

8

Later, as she lay beside her sleeping husband, deeply buried memories began to stir. Nalin's pregnancy troubled her. She had no fear of bearing Quanah's child; for two years she had prayed for this miracle. Nor were her fears centered on her husband's refusal of the white man's peace. Had she not told him that though the white man's wagons were now heavy with gifts, they would soon desert their promises? Nalin's unhappiness involved memories of long ago. So many years. Ten winters had passed since she had last seen her father. Not her Indian father whom she had just told of the grandchild she would give him, but her true father, also a gentle, kind, and loving father, who would no doubt have equally welcomed such news.

Nalin touched the slightly swelled abdomen. Quanah's joy at his impending fatherhood, her own experiences carrying the tiny life within her, had made her think differently; she was more aware of the feelings parents must have for the children they bear. Always impulsive and headstrong, she began to wonder if her judgment of the man who had sired her had been too harsh.

She closed her eyes and tried to sleep, but her mind drifted back over the years to the time when she had another name, a barely remembered name. She saw again the small, dusty town she had been born in, so different from the life she had now. She didn't for a moment regret the course her life had taken, only the hurt she had caused along the way. People had died for her; some by her hand. Some she regretted, and some had deserved it. Death was so close to life; such a thin line separated the two. Now, since her mind refused to be stilled, it was perhaps time to think back over the ten long years that had so radically changed her life. Nalin *was* white, though she could hardly remember what it felt like to *be* white. The name she had been born to was a distant memory, clouded with pain.

Chapter 1

"LISA!" Mrs. Thompson called from the doorway. "Lisa Thompson, you come in here when I call you!"

"In a minute, Ma," she shouted from across the yard.

"Right now, young lady!" Maureen shut the door resoundingly. "Land sakes, can't that child stay away from that horse for a minute? She's beginning to smell like one."

Henry Thompson peered over the upper half of his newspaper. He'd rather have stayed out of this running battle between his wife and child. Maureen had stomped back to the stove, and was now stirring the pot with a vengeance. Lisa was the spitting image of her mother. Her unruly flaming red hair would darken in time to match her mother's lovely auburn tresses. Both of them had eyes that made a man's heart jump in his chest. Their skins were creamy and flawless, except that Lisa's had a light scattering of freckles over her nose from her refusal to keep a sunbonnet on her head. Lisa took after Maureen Brannigan Thompson's side for sure, having an Irish temper that flared as easily as her mother's.

"Hank, you're gonna have to talk to that girl." Maureen cast another glance out the window at her daughter, who was obeying finally, but slowly.

"Why me?" Hank murmured from behind his paper. "She's your daughter."

"And yours." The green eyes flashed in his direction. "She spends too much time with that horse. And I don't

10

like her galloping all over town like a wild Indian, riding bareback, too. She'll kill herself for sure. Did you know she nearly knocked poor Mrs. Maples down as she was carrying her wash to the line yesterday? *Your* daughter had to jump the fence between our yard and hers. She could have killed that poor woman."

"I'll speak to her," Henry sighed, hoping Maureen was through.

"It's time she started to act like a lady. She's getting too old to be straddling a horse, her dresses pulled up near to mid-thigh!"

"You could buy her a pair of britches, Mo." Henry retreated behind the paper to avoid the fiery glance his wife gave him. Maureen was dead set against any daughter of hers wearing britches. She insisted on frilly dresses and hair ribbons in spite of the fact that on Lisa they looked a mite ridiculous. Not that Lisa wasn't pretty enough in them—everyone agreed she was the prettiest girl in town—but she was a tomboy, happier climbing a tree than playing with dolls. In fact, the last doll she had been given for her birthday a month ago had been found swinging by the neck from a tree branch. "Hung for cattle rustlin'," Lisa had explained.

He supposed a lot of her attitudes came from him. Can't be town sheriff for eight years without some of it rubbing off on your offspring. He might have encouraged, also, the boyish tendencies toward rough-and-tumble play. He had treated her like the son he had hoped for, teaching her to shoot, taking her hunting—over Maureen's protests. He liked having her hang around the jailhouse to keep him company; the child showed no fear of the outlaws detained there, and often struck up conversations with them. God only knew what she might be learning from them. He would have to stop that.

Henry, however, had not gotten her the horse. It had been brought into town by a band of cowboys who had caught him in the wild. They had been unable to break him, and the animal had been covered with the cuts of spurs and whips. Lisa had used her usual charm to beg the animal from them. They weren't quite willing to part

11

with him, especially into the custody of a sweet-faced seven-year-old. Somehow, though, Lisa had her way, as she always did.

She nursed the horse to health, and, in what seemed like gratitude, the "unbreakable" young stallion allowed her to ride wherever she wished upon his unsaddled back.

She was a natural with horses. She seemed to mold herself to the animal as if the two of them were a single entity. Maureen didn't care for it much. Henry peered over his paper at his wife now staring out the window, hands on hips, impatiently waiting. Mo didn't like the breakneck speed Lisa took on her mount. She fretted over the chances the girl took, setting up kegs to race around, creating jumps for the stallion to overcome; Mo was often pale with fright as Lisa entertained herself. Henry was beginning to believe Mo was right. It was time the girl began acting like her sex.

Lisa popped into the kitchen, the back door slamming behind her. At the sound of the loud crack she froze, awaiting her mother's ire.

"Don't slam the door! Did you wash up?"

Lisa nodded and offered her hands, palms up, for Maureen's inspection. Maureen turned them over and scowled. "Get back out there and wash proper!"

"Yes, m'am," Lisa mumbled.

"Lord, you stink, child." Maureen's nose wrinkled. The girl's blue calico dress was filthy, wet with horse sweat. "I don't know what I'm gonna do with you."

The girl turned up an innocent face, smiling at her mother.

"Wait a minute." Lisa's mother frowned. "Turn those hands back."

The smile vanished as she complied.

"What is that?"

Lisa's gaze followed her mother's to the sparkling ring on her left hand. Far too big for her, Lisa had to hold the finger crooked to keep from losing it.

"That?" Lisa queried.

"Yes, that! Where did you get it?"

"Hugo Brady?" she offered, looking a bit sick.

12

"That's his poor dead mother's ring. How did you get it?"

"Hugo gave it to me."

"And why would he do that?" Maureen's hands came up to her hips as she glared down at her daughter.

Lisa grinned nervously. "We're engaged."

"Engaged!" her mother echoed incredulously, while Henry snickered behind the newspaper.

Lisa started chattering wildly. "But Momma, Hugo said he loves me and wants to marry me when we get older. I told him I would. So we needed a promise, and he gave me the ring so everybody in the whole world would know it."

"Lisa Thompson, that's the craziest thing I've ever heard. You're only ten, and he just turned twelve. His pa will have a fit when he finds out."

Crestfallen, Lisa hung her head low, slipping the offending hand behind her back.

"Now you listen, young lady. You go out and wash this very minute. Then you change your clothes and go straight to Mr. Brady's, and you tell him what Hugo did, and you give that ring back. You get no supper till you're done with it."

"Can't I give it back to Hugo?"

"No, you take it straight to Mr. Brady, and I better hear no more 'bout you being engaged, you hear me?"

"Yes, Momma." Lisa trudged back outside.

"Did you ever hear of such foolishness? Hank, you better talk to her."

" 'Bout which problem, Mo?"

Jesse Sutton stood outside the brown frame building under the sign reading "Public Baths, 50¢." He was clean and freshly shaven and smelled better than he had in weeks. Tall, good-looking, with black curly hair and deep blue eyes, his golden tan showed how much time he spent under the western sun. Finely sculpted features made him look the exact opposite of his dead pa's brother, Sam.

Sam was short and squatty. Not even in his younger days had he been the ladies' man that Jesse was. His hair

13

was almost pure white now but still showed traces of its original yellow. His weather-beaten face had a long scar from an Apache warrior's tomahawk, but his brown eyes had a strangely youthful and excited look, like a young boy taking his first rifle in his hands. They didn't quite fit his fifty-seven-year-old frame. Sam's body was still as muscular as it had been in his youth, though he did have a small pot belly. Though Sam was getting a bit old, his name still sent a chill down the back of many an honest citizen. The Sutton name was famous—or infamous, depending on how you looked at it. Most folks chose to look at it according to the latter term.

Jesse reached down and brushed off his black trousers, working his way up to his black shirt and vest with the silver spangles, though they were as clean as he was and didn't need the effort. He was completely dressed in black except for the silver on the vest and on his hat band, and the delicate handiwork of silver stitched into his boots and gunbelt. He was a tough-looking character and proud of it in spite of Sam's disapproval. Sam said the clothes made him look like an outlaw and it was dangerous to look like what you were. He had warned him many times that he could be recognized by what he wore, but Jesse was much too vain to give up the striking figure he made in the outfit.

He walked over to where his new horse was tied to the post in front of the saloon and stroked the silky black mane. He was a magnificent animal. He had thought so the moment he saw him on the range of the San Diablo Ranch. He and Sam stole the gelding along with a dozen other fine horses, which brought them a tidy profit on the other side of the border.

Jesse looked up to see the buckboard coming down the road toward him. It was Sam. He pulled up in front of Jesse and hopped lightly off the wagon.

"How was the trip, Sam?"

"Good as can be, I guess." They strode through the swinging doors together and took a table in a dim corner. "Two beers," Sam called to the bartender.

"When?" Jesse asked.

"Right when the bank closes."

The bartender interrupted by setting down the foamy beer. Sam took a long swallow.

"Awful small town," Jesse commented after the bartender left. He wasn't so sure about this job, whether the risk was worth it.

"Awful small and awful rich, son." Sam winked slyly.

Jesse shrugged and drank his beer, figuring Sam knew what he was talking about. He always did. "Okay, Sam, if you say so."

In a fresh dress and with new ribbons tying her hair back, Lisa peered into the bank's darkened interior. She had purposely walked slowly, stopping along the way to chat with old Mrs. Maples. She knew the woman's feathers were still ruffled about the jumping incident. She deliberately applied a bit of little-girl charm to make sure the old biddy would sing her praises next time she saw Ma. She was also hoping the bank might have closed before she got there and it seemed it had. The shutters were down, and Mr. Brady's "Closed" sign hung in the window, but the usually locked door was slightly ajar. If Ma checked and found out Mr. Brady had been in the bank when Lisa had said he wasn't, she'd tan her for sure.

"Mr. Brady," she called softly, peeking inside. The bank was empty, which was very strange. "Mr. Brady," she called again, louder this time. She heard a thump from the back and started toward it. Suddenly she was grabbed from behind, a gloved hand over her mouth. Her hands flew up, the fingers spreading wide, and Hugo Brady's engagement token came off, rolling under the teller's cage. Then she was yanked up into the crook of an arm and carted toward the alley, where a man was throwing sacks into the back of a buckboard. Throwing a blanket over the pile, he looked up. A kerchief was wrapped around the lower portion of his face, and she had no further doubt as to what was happening.

"What the hell . . . ," the man began, but the one holding Lisa's mouth in a tight, suffocating grip interrupted.

"It's a goddamn kid. Walked into the back. I think she might'a seen the old man."

Lisa frantically tried to shake her head to tell him she hadn't. The one facing her looked a bit like Papa; maybe she could get him to understand.

"Shee-it!" Brown eyes glared down at her from above the kerchief.

"If I let her go we won't be five minutes outa' here till the whole town knows," the one holding her said.

"Better kill the brat." The other one turned away with finality.

"Christ, I can't do that. . . . She's a baby!"

"A baby with big eyes and a big mouth," the first one countered.

"We'll take her with us. Give me some a' that rope."

"You crazy? What the hell—"

"We're wastin' time arguin'. We'll throw her in the back and turn her loose outa' town."

"Look, if you ain't got the stomach for it . . ." The man started toward her, and Lisa fought in panic.

"Leave her be, Sam. We ain't killin' no kid, goddamn it! Now give me that rope."

They stared at each other for several moments with Lisa between them. Finally the man went to the buckboard and fetched a rope. The one who held her said harshly, "Don't scream, kid, I mean it, or I'll let him have you."

Lisa nodded her head, eyes wide on the other outlaw, who wasn't a bit like Papa. A bandanna went over her mouth, then her hands were tightly tied behind her.

"Legs too." The older man handed her captor another length of rope. A securely tied Lisa was tossed into the back of the buckboard.

"Help! Someone help me!" Mr. Brady staggered out of the bank, blood streaming down his face from the gash on his forehead.

Sheriff Thompson pushed aside the people who had begun to gather around the sobbing banker. Thompson took him by the shoulder, leading him back into the building, and deposited him in a chair. "Calm down, Brady." The sheriff went into the back for a wet cloth. When he returned, the banker had stopped sobbing, but was still shaking uncontrollably. Thompson pressed the cool, damp cloth over the cut. "Now tell me what happened."

Brady jumped up quickly, the words tumbling out of his mouth. "The bank's been robbed. . . . Aren't you going to go after them?"

"Them who?" Thompson pushed him back into the chair. "I got to know who I'm lookin' for. How long you been knocked out?"

Brady checked his pocket watch. He had closed at four. " 'Bout twenty minutes or so, I guess." He was calming down.

"Now, I doubt you know what direction they took, as you was laid out on the floor," Thompson continued. "And since they headed out twenty minutes ago, just where you expect me to go after 'em? Now, Bob, you just start tellin' me what happened."

In a few tense words, Bob told him how he was closing up when two men walked in with guns drawn. "I gave them all the money in the teller's desk. What else could I do? Then they said they wanted the money in the safe, too. It was the miners' payroll they were after. They got all of it."

"What'd the men look like, Bob?"

"Oh, I don't know." Brady rubbed his forehead. "An older man, maybe mid-fifties. He had a bandanna on, but I saw a scar on his face. The other was younger, dressed all in black."

"Sam and Jesse Sutton." Thompson started to stride out the door. "Okay, at least now we know who we're after."

A crowd was gathering, summoned by news of the robbery. "Listen," the sheriff shouted. The crowd stilled, waiting. "I'm gonna need a posse. Any of you men who can, the town will be beholden to ya. We'll leave tonight, got two hours of daylight left. Saddle up and meet me in front of the jail. We're after the Suttons, and I'm obliged to warn you they ain't gonna be easy to bring in. Mean-

17

while, any of you seen two men leaving town 'bout half an hour ago, I'd appreciate you comin' forward. It'd be a man about fifty-five, sixty, ridin' with a young one wearin' black."

"Ohh." Mrs. Maples covered her mouth, startled.

"Sophie?" The sheriff looked down the steps at her. "You see somebody fits that description?"

"Yes, Sheriff," she replied nervously. "They were riding a buckboard and went in that direction." She pointed south. "I had seen the same two pass through the alley earlier, as I was talking with Lisa. When they came by again I was inside Mr. Cameron's dry goods store, and this time there was a bundle in the back of the wagon."

"Good girl, Sophie. That's real helpful."

"That's the bank money." Johnny Petrie nodded.

"No, I don't think so." Sophie Maples paused. "I'm sure I saw it move."

"Move?" Thompson echoed.

"I'm sure whatever was beneath that blanket moved. I remember that it struck me as strange . . ."

Thompson was no longer listening. Instead he was searching the crowd for a small yellow dress or a swatch of red hair. "Bob, did you see Lisa afore you closed?"

"Lisa? No."

He surveyed the crowd with mounting foreboding. Lisa would have been right here . . . "My God, Bob, I think they got my daughter."

Lisa felt sick, sicker than she had ever felt in her life. Her head ached, and her stomach churned with every turn of the buckboard's wheels. The younger one in black had turned her loose and set her on the buckboard between them, fearful that she'd smother in the back, but he wasn't ready to let her go. "I'm gonna be sick," she moaned from between the two outlaws.

"Don't," the older one said without looking away from the road.

"I can't help it!"

"Help it, girlie, help it!"

18

"Sam, that posse will be after us soon. Where the hell is that grove?"

"It ain't much farther." Sam snapped the whip at the horses' backsides. The pair quickened their pace only slightly. "What we gonna do with this kid?"

"Leave her with the wagon, I reckon."

"Too bad she ain't older. I'd have other ideas," Sam said with a sideways glance. Lisa paled, thinking he meant he'd kill her, and Sam burst into laughter. "Don't worry, kid, you ain't my type. Now, my type's got to have the big . . ." He started to demonstrate with his hands.

"Sam, not in front of the kid."

"Stop calling me a kid."

"Well, what are ya, eight, nine?"

"I'm ten," she shot back as Sam pulled the horses to a stop in a grove of trees that concealed the wagon from view.

"You'll be sorry. Both of you," Lisa said haughtily, trying to salvage some dignity. There wasn't anything that could make a hot-tempered Irisher, as her pa called her, mad faster than reminding her she was still a child. "When my father gets through with you . . ."

"Yeah, and just who's your father?" Sam parried. "That wiggle-worm son of a bitch at the bank?"

"No," she sneered, her nose up in the air. "My father is Hank Thompson. *Sheriff* Hank Thompson."

Sam stopped still in the middle of transferring the stolen payroll to his saddlebags. "Your old man is Hank Thompson?"

Lisa nodded, not so sure now that she had said the right thing.

"Aw shit," Jesse swore from the ground behind her. Lisa turned back and forth, looking at both men.

"Of all the dumb-ass things . . . ," Sam finally said. "You had to go and take the sheriff's kid hostage? Of all the dumb-ass—"

"Shit, Sam, how was I to know? You think she was wearing a badge says 'I'm the sheriff's kid' on it?"

"Goddamn!" Sam stuffed the rest of the money into his

saddlebag. Two more sacks would have to be tied across the saddles. "That man's gonna comb this territory for his kid and them that took her. And that *them* is us!" Sam glared at his partner.

"So, we'll leave her right here, and the sheriff will pick up his brat and go on home with her."

"Maybe." Sam began to take a horse out of the wagon harness. "Then again, maybe not. He just might keep it in mind about that bank money. As well as the fact we took the kid in the first place."

"Sam, what the hell you doin'?" Jesse turned from tightening the saddle on his own horse. The idea was to leave the wagon, the rented horses, and the girl in the grove.

"Well, seems to me we might have a good thing here after all," Sam explained, rigging a rope harness around the horse's head. "That Thompson is a pretty set lawman under the best a' times. Now, I don' think he'll be any too likely to give up if we leave the kid or no."

"So you're gonna take the kid with us?" Jesse asked in disbelief. "Sam, that'll make sure he follows us clear into Mexico."

"He prob'ly has it in mind anyhow, but as long as we got his kid he ain't gonna try nothin' 'at might put the little darlin' in danger, is he?"

"I don't think that's a very good idea."

"Mebbe, mebbe not, but my brains has got us this far. Seems to me it's your brains what got us into this mess in the first place."

Jesse's answer was a deep scowl.

"Get the kid, Jesse."

Lisa did not care for the turn the conversation had taken. Jesse reached up for her, and as he did Lisa kicked. Slightly missing her target, her foot caught him in the shoulder, sending him reeling backward.

"Sweet Jesus, Jesse, can't you do anything right?" Sam stormed.

Jesse grabbed for her as she jumped from the wagon. Lisa screamed, fighting and kicking for all she was worth.

20

"Shut her up, Jesse!"

Jesse tried to hold the struggling girl, but she connected with a well-placed kick to his shin that forced him to release her, and then she sprinted for the woods. In a few running steps, Sam Sutton caught her by the hair, twirled her around, and slapped her with an open palm. The girl's head snapped to the side, then she slumped forward into his arms.

"Did you kill her, Sam? If you killed her so help me—"

"She's awright." He scowled. He had seen the small foot move beneath the yellow dress. She was propped up on the front of Jesse's horse, the younger outlaw holding her to keep her from falling. He had insisted there was no way he would trust his partner to hold her since they had to ride hard to out-distance the posse, sure to be following them by now. They had finally slowed to a walk to rest the horses.

"You shouldn'ta hit her so hard," Jesse scolded.

"Yeah, well I guess I coulda let her beat the shit out a' ya."

"She's a kid, goddamn it! I don't go for hittin' kids!" The outlaw's hands clenched convulsively on the small waist he was balancing. Inadvertently, his grip pinched her, and she moaned, lifting her head from his chest. "You okay now?" he asked as she shook her head to clear it. Lisa nodded.

"Good. Now you can ride your own horse. You do know how ta ride, don't ya?"

She was about to nod again, then changed her mind. Maybe if she couldn't, they'd leave her. "No." She shook it instead.

"Then you dang well better learn quick." He lifted her onto the unsaddled back of the extra horse. Instead of handing her the horse's lead rope as she had hoped he might, he led the animal behind his own. For the moment, escape was out of the question.

21

Chapter 2

"MY butt hurts!" Lisa complained loudly.

"Will you shut up about your damn butt already." Jesse only half turned toward her. He couldn't quite believe this kid. She hadn't cried once, but she sure complained regularly.

"I'm getting blisters," she continued to wail from behind him. "I've been riding bareback for two whole days. I can't *stand* it anymore!"

"Well, what am I supposed to do about it? You want me to give you my saddle?"

Her eyes brightened at the prospect.

"Jesse, shut that damn kid up," Sam yelled without turning.

"You shut her up—if you can . . . if anything can." His eyes rolled heavenward.

"Jesse," she pleaded. "It hurts!"

Jesse stopped his horse and jumped off, muttering, "Damn, damn, damn," as if the repetitions might help the situation. "Awright, get down."

Lisa jumped into his arms, and he eased her gently to the ground. She moaned, her hands reaching for her backside. As Jesse followed her to his horse he saw two wet stains darkening the seat of the yellow dress. He had had plenty of saddle blisters before and knew how much they could hurt. Hers must be pretty good size to ooze like that. He felt a rush of guilt over not believing her when she began to complain. "Get on up there," he said gently,

22

helping to boost her into the saddle. "We'll get some bear grease to put on 'em later."

"Bear grease!" Lisa grimaced.

"Yeah, bear grease!" Jesse stomped back to the other horse. He put both hands on the horse's bare back then kicked up and over with ease.

"I never could do that," Lisa commented, watching.

"It's all in the arm muscles," Jesse answered. "I don't think you'd need to have arm muscles like mine, though. 'Sides, you gotta grow up some more." He smiled and winked, forgetting his irritation.

Lisa smiled back. "You're nice when you smile."

"You ain't so bad yourself."

"Will you two shut up." Sam's voice was stern but low. They had been traveling through a narrow path scattered with boulders. Sam had just come to the end of the upward turn, and the path would now take them downward onto the sagebrush-strewn plain. In the ensuing silence, Jesse could make out the sound that had caught Sam's attention. Sam got off his horse and leaned over the edge of the rock wall. It's the posse," he whispered loudly.

"Did they hear us?"

"No, too busy talkin' theirselves. 'Sides, sound travels up."

Suddenly, one voice from below sounded out above the rest, issuing orders to mount up. Lisa had dismounted, taking a step toward the edge. She was about to shout when Jesse's hand clapped over her mouth. She struggled, but his grip only tightened. Hot tears burned her eyes. They spilled onto her cheeks and over the outlaw's hand as she heard the horses' hooves pounding away from her.

When the sound faded entirely, Jesse released his hold. Lisa was openly sobbing now. Jesse's hand had left a white imprint across her sunburned features. "I'm sorry, kid," he said gently. "I'm real sorry." She only began to cry harder. Uncertainly at first, Jesse touched her shoulder, then, with a whispered "Oh damn," he pulled her to him, letting her cry on his shoulder until the sobs turned into whimpers. Jesse searched with his free hand for his handkerchief. Sam thrust one at him from his own pocket.

"Is it dirty?" Jesse glanced up at him.

"No, it ain't." Sam scowled, stomping off toward the horses.

Jesse put the handkerchief in her hand, and Lisa dabbed at her face with it. The front of Jesse's neat black shirt was soaked.

"I'm okay," she sniffed, still dabbing at her eyes.

"Blow your nose." Jesse grinned. "Sam." He got up and walked toward him. "Let's let the kid go."

"She's our insurance inta Mexico."

"We ain't that far from the border, and we know where the posse is now. We can stay behind 'em. Let's drop the kid off in Tucson. She can ride into town, and they can get her back to her old man."

Sam looked at Jesse, then at the kid, then back to his nephew. "Okay," he sighed. "Tucson it is."

Lisa would never know exactly when her feelings about Jesse began to change. Perhaps it was when he began to be nice to her, or it may have been when he held her as she cried. She no longer feared him as she still did Sam. He was becoming, to her inexperienced eye, a sort of Robin Hood. Not really bad at all, just misunderstood. She began to elevate him to a pedestal of first-infatuation as only the mind and heart of a precocious ten-year-old could.

Prairie Dog, in the Arizona Territory, was a town that had seemingly sprung up out of the desert. Hardly more than a trading post and stagecoach stop, the town boasted one hotel, a flea-ridden hole that sat over the saloon. Sam and Jesse didn't worry at all about bringing their young kidnap victim right into town. The town didn't have a sheriff, and the only law that had ever been there was four years ago when the territory's new marshal stopped in on his introductory tour. He had said if Prairie Dog ever needed him to send him a wire, forgetting that the town had never seen fit to install a telegraph. In any case, they had never had occasion to use his services. The town minded its own business and expected its visitors to do the same. If the guests happen to be wanted, like the Suttons, well, as long as they kept to their own, they were welcome to spend their money like anyone else.

"Now, you lock this door, and you don't open it for nobody, y'hear?" Jesse warned her sternly as he deposited her within the hotel room. "I mean nobody! This town ain't like your town back home. You can get hurt real easy."

"Can't I stay with you?" The large green eyes looked up at him beseechingly.

"I'll only be downstairs havin' a few beers. Now do as I say and stay put. If you need me later, knock on that wall. I'll be sleepin' in there."

Lisa nodded, pouting. "Aren't you afraid I'll escape?"

Jesse turned back at the door with a deep sigh. "No, I ain't, 'cause I think you got sense enough to know better. There's fifty miles of pure desert between here and the next town . . . and Apaches."

"You can't scare me with that. The Apaches signed a treaty."

"Some of 'em did. Not all. And you can bet your sweet little . . . hair ribbons that if they find you out there you won't be goin' home to your pa day after tomorrow." Jesse hurried out before she could come up with a new argument. He waited behind the door for several seconds before he shouted, "Lock it!" Moments later the key turned from the inside. Satisfied, he went downstairs.

Lisa waited quietly in the dark, covers tucked up to her chin. She had no way of guessing the time, and, though she strained, she couldn't pick out Jesse's voice from the others in the saloon below her. Once she thought she had heard Sam laugh, and a few times heavy steps had echoed on the bare wood floor of the hallway, sometimes alone, but more often accompanied by a light step and high, feminine giggles. She couldn't close her eyes and sleep until she knew Jesse was in the next room.

At last she heard the sound she had been waiting for,

the key turning in the lock of the room next door. She closed her eyes, ready for sleep, then he said something in a soft voice, barely audible through the thin walls. She heard a woman's laugh, and her eyes sprang open.

She crept out of bed and over to the wall, pressing her ear against it. Jesse spoke again, so low she couldn't make out the words. Then the woman answered in the same low whisper. The bed creaked, and Lisa backed up as if she'd suddenly been scolded.

Jealousy far beyond her years flushed the sunburned cheeks even redder, her emotions torn between hurt and anger. Jesse had left her alone because he had a woman in there. She didn't know what went on, specifically, but enough to know the meaning of the times Ma and Pa wanted to be undisturbed.

Lisa dressed hurriedly. The yellow dress was filthy beyond cleaning now, and both sleeves were torn. She carried her shoes to the door, quietly unlocking it. He probably wouldn't hear me if I clomped out of here and yelled good-bye, she told herself as she slipped out. At the stairs she put the shoes on, remembering only briefly his warning about going out. Her biggest worry was Sam. Had he, too, gone upstairs, or was he still down below?

Lisa edged down the steps until she was low enough to peek into the saloon. The place was not well lit, and a cloud of smoke added to the obscurity. She couldn't pick Sam out of the dozen or so faces below, so she continued downward. At the bottom she paused, expecting to be accosted at any moment, but no one glanced in her direction. She steeled herself with a deep breath and ran for the door.

Outside, she stayed in the shadows, making her way down the street to the stables. In minutes she had a horse saddled and had provisioned herself with a full canteen of water. Tears burned her eyes as she led the horse out and mounted. They started to spill over her cheeks as she galloped out of town.

Eventually the sun rose and then began to burn down on her. She had no way of knowing where the nearest town lay or even how far fifty miles could be. Papa's hunting lessons had not extended to finding directions in the desert. The terrain around her was dry, with only patches of saw grass, tumbleweed, and cactus. The rocky hills around every side only served to further conceal any sign of civilization that might be behind them.

The desert was taking its toll on Lisa's stolen horse. Ridden hard through the night, he was getting cranky, stomping his hooves in irritation and thirst. Lisa reined him into the shade of a hill and dismounted, then loosened the cinch of the saddle for him.

Last night her only thought had been to get away from the hurt and embarrassment. She still hoped it would hurt Jesse to think of her out in the desert alone. She hoped she'd die out there. That would serve him right. He could carry her on his conscience forever. Lisa leaned her back against a boulder, holding the horse's reins in her hand, dreaming of Jesse finding her body right there where she sat. In her dreams Jesse cried uncontrollably.

In fact, Jesse was angry, stomping out of her empty room and banging loudly on Sam's door down the hall. "She's gone, Sam," he announced as the bleary-eyed Sam opened up. "Get dressed. We gotta go after her."

Sam moaned, rubbing his forehead to clear last night's whiskey. A female shape stirred from under the covers of Sam's bed. "Aw, shit," he croaked sleepily. "Hell with it. Let the little bitch go."

"Sam, goddamn you, she's out in the desert. She'll die out there!"

"Better her than me. Rita tol' me some soldiers passed through here yesterday. Them Injuns is at it again. The kid prob'ly went north, thinkin' to head back home, and that's right into the arms of them Apaches. Me, I'm headin' south fast as I can."

"Sam, we're not leavin' her out there. I'm goin' after her. You comin' or not?"

Sam stared at him. "We bin together a lot a' years, Jess. You been a son to me. But if you're goin' after that brat then we're goin' our separate ways."

27

"I got to, Sam. You go on then, and I'll catch up when I got the kid in a safe place."

Sam nodded, pausing uncertainly, mouth hung open as if to say something, but he couldn't decide what. Jesse turned to go.

"Jess." Sam stopped him. "You sure you'll be goin' south, after you find the kid that is?"

"Yeah, I'll be there. Don't worry." Jesse laid his hand on the man's shoulder. "We're still partners."

Sam grinned feebly back at the only person in the world he had ever cared about. "Be careful, son."

The tracks of a single horse with a lone rider were impossible to see in the hard-baked desert. Jesse could only hope she had traveled north, as Sam suspected she would, and follow a zigzag pattern in that direction. He still wasn't sure why he was going after her. For a good many years now Jesse had avoided any kind of responsibility or attachment. Why, then, was he risking his most precious commodity, his own neck, for a spoiled brat? If Lisa Thompson had been full grown he might not have bothered. Chivalry was not built into Jesse Sutton either.

He turned the horse in a northeasterly direction, hoping the shadow of the hills might have drawn her that way. Why did the kid have to go and run off anyway? He had told her they would be leaving her in Tucson. Or, at least, why couldn't she have run off while they were farther north, in country where she might survive? Because she was a goddamn kid, he decided, and kids were goddamn stupid and a pain in the ass.

He saw something bright fluttering from a tall cactus. Now, something yellow did not belong on a cactus at this time of year. Jesse rode toward it, recognizing a piece of the yellow dress the kid was wearing. He surveyed the terrain ahead, then urged his horse toward the hills. "When I get my hands on you, kid . . ."

Lisa awoke into fright, discovering that her horse, along with the canteen of water tied to the saddle, was gone. She had just started to cry in despair, all desire to be found dead obliterated in the face of the reality of that possibility, when she saw the figure on horseback approaching.

"Jesse," she yelled, running toward him. More tears spilled down her face as she splattered herself against his horse, hugging his leg and muttering in a nonstop babble about being saved.

"Let go a' my foot, girl." Jesse finally managed to dismount, then scowled. "Well, you really did it this time, didn't you? Why'd you run off for?"

She only shook her head. There was no way she would tell him she ran off because of the woman in his room.

"I told you we'd leave you safe in Tucson in 'nother day or so, but oh, no, you gotta go marchin' off across the desert." Jesse looked about. "Lost your horse, too, huh? Stupid, goddamn stupid!"

He lifted her up onto his saddle. "Oh no, uh-uh." He motioned her toward the back. "You're takin' the back seat." Lisa lifted her bottom over the saddle rim to the bare, broad back. Jesse climbed on in front, swinging his leg over and barely missing her head.

He headed south again, this time directly for Tucson. He could feel the light weight of the child leaning against his back. She hadn't budged in at least an hour, and he was fairly certain she was asleep. He turned the horse into the path of some shading hills.

Since heading out after her, Jesse had maintained a feeling of uneasiness. During the trek north after Lisa he had been backtracking right into the path of the posse; as he headed southward he felt no better. Crossing Apache country was not conducive to restful riding at the best of times. The Apache had recently worked themselves up with some powerful medicine or other and had decided to try raiding a few white settlements. Jesse's gaze kept darting to the high bluffs that surrounded them. Suddenly his body stiffened, gaze frozen on a mounted figure in the distance.

"Lisa," he said softly, touching the small hand clinging to his waist. "Hey, kid, wake up."

She squirmed, and then her head rose.

29

"I want you to hold on to me tight, you hear?"

"What'sa matter?" she asked sleepily.

"Just do as I tell ya !"

She responded by grasping him tighter. Jesse kept his gaze fastened on the figure growing larger as he approached.

"Is Papa close by?" she said softly behind him.

"Honey, I half wish he was." Jesse pointed at the man on the bluff. "Indians," he murmured. "Now you be ready every minute, 'cause when I kick this horse in the side we're gonna ride."

" 'Pache?" Her voice was filled with girlish excitement. Kids for you, he told himself. Full of the childish assurance that nothing bad could happen if a grown up was around. He shuddered to think of what might happen to them both.

"Are they Apache?" she asked again.

Now several more riders had appeared on the bluffs to either side. "God, I hope so . . . ," he replied as a few more mounted riders appeared. He and Sam had spent a lot of time in the area from Texas to Arizona and north to Oklahoma. He knew well the locations of tribes as well as their appearances, and he was getting the awful feeling these weren't Apache. Too many horses for one thing. The desert-dwelling Apache couldn't afford to keep that many on the sparse grass, so many braves went on foot. All the horses Jesse saw now were immaculate, well-fed, magnificent beasts, their riders sitting astride them like pictures of centaurs he had seen in a book once. This was Apache territory all right, but that would hardly matter to the Comanche. They had raided their neighbors before, and nothing on God's green earth would keep them from doing it again.

Jesse would have preferred to face Apache. At least he'd have a slim chance of outrunning the puny Apache ponies. The Apache would as soon eat their horses as ride them. Comanche were another matter. The thought of eating a horse was, to them, as repellant as eating their grandmothers. He and the girl could no sooner outride Comanche than they could sprout wings and fly.

"Kid?"

"Yeah?"

"I'm sorry I got you into this."

"Are we gonna die?"

In spite of himself he smiled. "I hope not, honey."

At last one warrior started down the hill, riding slowly toward them. Jesse wasn't anxious to start the wild and futile ride. He kept going at a slow walk. Soon the rest of the horsemen began to descend from the hills, all meandering down the steep inclines. The lead Indian approached until Jesse had no further doubt—Comanche. His heart sank in his chest with a thump.

He pulled the horse to a stop as the Comanche surrounded him on all sides. He knew a little of their language but not much, since Sam had always done the talking the few times they had encountered them, trading their lives for guns, supplies, or whatever the Indians decided they wanted. This time he had nothing to offer. The leader pulled in line with Jesse's saddlehorn and stopped. The Comanche's gaze was fastened on the girl in back; all the Indians were gazing in wonder at the red-haired girl. They pointed and talked among themselves for several minutes before Jesse recalled Sam telling him red was their sacred color. Now they might have seen blondes, he surmised, but probably not too many redheads, especially not with Lisa's bright-copper-penny locks. Maybe he could get them out of this yet. The leader lifted an arm, reaching for the girl's hair. She cringed and clung to Jesse.

"Let him touch it, honey. It's all right," Jesse assured her as the leader tried again. The Indian lifted a lock of hair and rubbed it between his fingers to see if the color would come off. Lisa's hair glinted in the sunlight, not smudging the chieftain's hand. A murmur of approval arose from the group.

The chieftain released the lock and turned to Jesse. "I give five horses for girl," he stated in English.

Shee-it, Jesse thought, suppressing a snicker. He must

think I'm dumb. For a Comanche chief five horses for a woman was about average; if the chief was rich it was cheap. Jesse shook his head.

"Seven horses," the chief countered.

Again Jesse shook his head.

"She small woman," he protested. "Ten horses."

"Sorry, Chief, but she ain't mine to trade."

"She not yours?" The Indian scowled.

"Nope, I'm takin' her to her papa."

The chief's scowl deepened. "Ten horses good offer."

"You're right there." Jesse looked like he was pondering the offer for a moment. Obviously, to the Comanche mind, possession was nine-tenths of the law. Since Jesse had her he ought to consider a fair trade. "Naw, I can't do it, Chief. This girl here is powerful medicine. You seen the red hair. Much big medicine, even if she is kinda' puny. Her papa, he's a big medicine man. He'll lay a curse on whoever steals her that'll knock your eyes out."

Now it was the chief's turn to consider for a long moment. "Where is pa-pa?"

"North Fork." Jesse took one of the money sacks out of the saddlebag. "See this here? This sack is plumb full of strong medicine her papa sent with her. See that?" He pointed at the black lettering reading "North Fork Bank." "Them symbols say if she don't get there . . . big, bad medicine . . ." Jesse rolled his eyes skyward, as if dreading the consequences.

"You take girl to pa-pa?" The chief eyed him suspiciously.

"Yep."

"North Fork there." The Indian pointed somberly in the direction opposite to the one Jesse was traveling in.

Jesse paled. There was no fooling a Comanche on geography. They knew every square inch of the territory from Oklahoma clear into Mexico. He chided himself silently for not saying Tucson. The damn Indian couldn't read . . . or could he?

"Shucks, Chief, you know you're right about that. I

musta got turned around somehow. North Fork's north, ain't it?" He smiled innocently. The chief was waiting.

"North Fork, that way." Jesse pointed around behind him. "Right."

He turned the horse about and started off at a slow walk away from them. Any moment he expected instant death, fearing that would not be in store for Lisa but much worse, unless he had convinced them the girl with red hair was truly powerful medicine. Maybe they wouldn't dare harm her. The North Fork thing was stupid. Why didn't he say Tucson? Shee-it!

"Jesse," Lisa's small voice said from behind him. "Why did that man want to buy me?"

"Honey, that was a compliment because he likes ya." There was no point in trying to explain it to the kid.

"If I'm a pain in the ass, how come you didn't sell me then?"

Jesse smiled. "You're a pain, no doubt about it, but I like ya, too."

She didn't reply but hugged his waist tighter. Several minutes later Jesse peered behind him, and the Indians were gone.

Chapter 3

"HOW come we're still going north?" she piped up an hour later. From her weight on his back, Jesse figured she had been napping—she was quiet only when asleep.

" 'Cause we told them Comanches we were going north to take you to your papa."

Lisa's head flipped from side to side. "But they ain't here now."

"I won't bet a nickel on it, kid. You can't see 'em, but they're there."

"You sure?" She searched the countryside but could not discern a single hiding place. There were only hills and rocks and desert.

"Kid, I ain't gonna bet my scalp on whether they are or they ain't. We go north—clear to North Fork if we gotta."

"Are you taking me back to Papa?"

The question caught him by surprise. He hadn't deliberately thought about taking her back, but here he was doing just that. And what he said about liking her was true. She was an incessant talker and a big pain in the ass, but he did like her. The emotion was new to Jesse, who had taken to no human in his life but Sam. So far she had not asked to be returned, but the hope was in the question. "Yeah, kid, I'll take you back."

"But Papa would put you in jail for robbing the bank."

"Maybe not. I'll leave you outside a' town where you can walk in real easy, and I'll ride off for Mexico. Alone I can make it."

"I'll miss you, Jesse."

"I'll miss you, too, kid."

"Hol—y!" Jesse's cut-off curse woke Lisa from another nap. She looked up, stretching over his shoulder, trying to see what he saw. Straight in front of them and on every side men were pointing guns down on them; not Indians this time, but white men. Lisa recognized every one of their faces.

"Papa's posse," she whispered, as though the men one hundred feet in front might overhear.

"You don't have to tell me. Hang on, Lisa . . . I don't like my bargaining power from here."

Lisa's arm tightened, her body hugging his back. He spun the horse around, galloping for the shelter of a ravine he had passed. Shots were fired but came nowhere near them. He had counted on the knowledge that they wouldn't harm his small hostage. He jerked the horse to a stop and, in a single swift movement, jumped off, pulling her from the saddle with him, then ducking behind the rocks.

"Jesse Sutton, give yourself up."

"Papa! It's Papa!" Lisa's face beamed. She started to leap up, but Jesse pulled her down again.

"You stay down!" he ordered harshly.

"But Jesse, it's my papa. I can talk to him. I'll tell him to let you go."

"Honey, that won't work. You stay behind these rocks like I tol' ya."

"Jesse Sutton, you hear me? Turn her loose and come out!"

"Not a chance, Sheriff. We make a trade. You let me go, and I'll leave the girl."

"Jesse." Lisa tugged on his sleeve. "I can tell Papa you helped me. I'll tell him you're my friend."

"No deal, Sutton. Send the girl out, and I'll ask the judge to go easy on you."

"Yeah, easy like with a soft rope?"

"No, Jesse, Papa won't hang you if I tell him you're my friend."

"Lisa, for chrissake, sit down before they shoot you by mistake." He turned away from her. "Listen, Thompson, there's only one way you'll get your daughter back, and that's to let me ride outa' here." He was about to add more when Lisa's form appeared, scurrying out on the far side of the rocks. She was waving her hands frantically at the townsmen. "Goddamn kid," he muttered.

"Papa, listen to me." She stopped halfway between the two. "Jesse's my friend. Don't hurt him. Let him go. Please, Papa! He saved me from Sam and from the Indians, too."

"Lisa, run for that boulder." Sheriff Thompson appeared from the shadows behind several large rocks, his gun pointed at Jesse's refuge. "Run for it . . . now!"

"Papa, you don't understand. Jesse won't hurt me, he's my friend. Papa, please listen!" Hot tears squeezed out of her eyes as she pleaded.

"Lisa, get down!" echoed from either side of her, but as long as she stood in the line of fire neither could harm the other.

"No, Papa, you let Jesse go! He didn't hurt me. He was taking me back."

Sheriff Thompson turned to his daughter, a look of puzzlement on his face. She was crying, the tears leaving clean streaks down her dust-covered cheeks. "Please, Papa, don't hurt Jesse."

Gunfire exploded behind her, and Lisa spun around in time to see Johnny Petrie on a rise above Jesse's cover. "Noooo!" she screamed, running for the rocks where she had left him. Petrie stood up boldly now, gazing below.

Lisa reached the rocks and stopped. A shrill scream shattered the sudden silence. Jesse Sutton was sprawled on his stomach, his neck twisted around to the side, his black shirt covered in blood. His face was gone. She screamed again and again in an almost continuous stream.

Her father grabbed her shoulder, shaking her. "Lisa, stop it." Her mouth closed, glaring at her father's suddenly pale features with hatred. "You killed him! You murdered him! He was my friend, and you killed him. I

hate you! I hate you!" She began pummeling his chest
while Hank Thompson mutely bore his daughter's punishment. He had told Petrie to cover, not fire. He wasn't
to shoot unless Lisa was in imminent danger, which she
hadn't been.

"I'll hate you forever," his daughter screamed. She tore
free of his grasp and ran wildly. Hank paused a few seconds too long before he realized her goal. He raced after
her, but the child reached Jesse Sutton's horse, scrambling into the saddle.

"Lisa, come back!" He gave chase on foot. "Lisa, listen
to me, come back!" She disappeared from view over the
top of the hill before he turned back. "Petrie, climb
higher and watch where she goes." The words were un-
necessary, as the townsman was already scrambling up
the hill. The men trotted back to where they had left
their horses. Once mounted, they checked again with
Petrie.

"She went over the crest of that hill." He pointed. "I
can't see her no more now." The posse left his horse for
him and started off in the direction he had pointed, but
beyond the hill there was no sign of her; hard-packed desert left no trail, as if the countryside had suddenly swal-
lowed both horse and rider.

She had already used up the last of the water from Jesse's canteen and had nursed the meager supply, but even
so it had only lasted a day and a night. She had not seen
Papa's posse once since she had hidden herself and the
horse behind a pile of boulders and watched as they rode
past.

Lisa dismounted, then removed the saddle from the
outlaw's horse. She loosened the bridle but held it in
place to keep the horse with her a moment longer.
"You're a good horse, Blackie." She patted the ebony
neck. "I don't want you to die out here with me. You follow your nose and find some water . . . and sweet grass,
you hear?" Tears glistened in her eyes again, blurring
her vision of him, but she held them back. She had cried
once for Papa and her life in North Fork; she had spent

all of yesterday crying for Jesse. She'd never let herself cry again. Nothing would ever be the same again. Not now. She couldn't go back to North Fork after what had happened. There was nowhere else to go.

Jesse's horse had had no water or food for two days. He was tired, starved, and dying of thirst, yet the gelding's ears moved forward, listening to her. "Don't you worry 'bout me," Lisa told him. "I don't think I wanna live no more. You go on now." She removed the bridle, but the gelding didn't move. "Go on." She slapped the black rump. The muscle twitched, but he stayed still. "Go on, you hear? Get outa' here. I don't want you to die."

She waved her arms at the gelding's head. The head bobbed with each gesture, but the feet remained rooted. "You dumb horse, get on outa' here."

He turned his head and looked at her.

"Okay, stupid. You just stay and die with me, then." Lisa started walking for the flat, open desert. The horse trod wearily behind her. She turned briefly and scowled at him. "Dumb horse."

All she would later recall was endless miles of walking across the arid desert, her skin burned to bright red, her lips blistered, her tongue swollen and feeling as hot and dry as the sand beneath her feet. Her last memory was her collapse to the ground and the gentle nudge of the horse that had followed her.

She thought she had died and gone to hell for her sins. She could tell she was in some kind of enclosure. Strange smells assailed her nostrils, the acrid smell of a camp fire, odd cooking odors. She hadn't known they cooked in hell.

As Lisa opened her eyes in curiosity, the first sight before her was an angle that stretched upward and disappeared into darkness above. Smoke drifted out at the same spot. Yep, hell, sure enough . . . And yet she wasn't hot, only pleasantly warm, covered up in something that smelled awful. Her nose wrinkled in distaste as she gazed down at her covering. Yikes! It was an animal hide, all hair and smelling rank. She threw the cover off and sat up quickly.

A human body appeared quickly at her side, gently pushing her down again. She turned her head and peered into gentle brown eyes. A woman . . . an Indian woman . . . Lisa complied with the woman's soft force. Did Indians go to hell, too? Yet the dark eyes gazing down at her kindly didn't look deserving of punishment. The woman's face broke into a grin.

"Who are you?" Lisa ventured.

The woman muttered a string of unintelligible words as she went to the fire and ladled something into a bowl. Preacher Halstrom had said hell was plain fire and brimstone. He had said nothing about kind Indian ladies and warm tepees, therefore this couldn't be the place. Her trek across the desert must not have worked; Jesse was still dead, and Lisa was still alive, and there was nowhere to go and nothing to go back to.

The Indian woman brought the bowl to Lisa and motioned for her to drink. The appetizing aroma was tempting, but Lisa remembered she hadn't succeeded in killing herself yet. She closed her mouth tightly and shook her head.

Again the woman said something in what didn't even sound like a language. She offered the bowl again, and Lisa's hands firmly covered her mouth.

The woman looked puzzled but kept the bowl raised toward the girl. Finally she set the food down and left the tepee. A moment later she returned behind a warrior. Lisa recognized him as the same one who had tried to barter for her in the canyon: rich copper-colored skin and black hair heavily tinged with gray, parted down the middle and bound by a headband of beaded leather. His face was leathery and wrinkled from a great deal of time spent under a hot sun. The black eyes looked down at her, kind and warm. Inside the tepee he looked far less formidable than he had in the canyon. "You not eat," he admonished with an attempt at sternness that fell a bit short, being negated by the concern on his features.

"How did I get here?" Lisa ignored his gesture of pointing at the bowl beside her.

"We find in desert. Take back here. You eat now."

"You go to hell," Lisa shot back hotly. "I didn't ask you to bring me back here. Why didn't you leave me be? It was none of your business!"

The warrior's brow creased in a deep frown. The chieftain wasn't looking for gushing gratitude, but he didn't expect to be upbraided for his efforts on her behalf. "You die in desert."

"Yeah, if you hadn't stuck your big nose in. . . . You leave me alone."

"You want die?" he asked in disbelief. Deliberate suicide was not one of the Comanche solutions to any problem. In battle, yes, to offer one's life to save the tribe, but for a young girl, only a child, it was unthinkable.

The Comanche band had only chanced upon her, sprawled on the sand, the black horse standing patiently by her side. They had not followed Sutton, being too busy conducting a retaliatory raid on some Apaches who had attempted an unsuccessful raid on the Comanche recently. Having stolen a number of horses, they were on their way back to the war camp when they saw the riderless black horse in the distance. As they approached the horse, they saw the half-dead girl at his feet. "Where man that take you North Fork?"

"Dead!" Her eyes filled with tears again, but she forced them back for all she was worth. It wasn't easy, but she was set on never crying again. "My people killed him, and I'll hate them forever for it. They betrayed me, and I hate them!" Her voice filled with emotion, but still she refused to cry.

The chieftain gazed at her silently and long. The white man had been right, the girl was strong medicine, this child of red hair, brave and defiant. Too bad she was a girl; she would have made a fine warrior. Her values were strange perhaps, but she had strong will. He pondered what she had just told him. If it was true her people had betrayed her and the young man, if she truly hated them as she said, and these things must be true, then killing herself was not the Comanche answer. "Girl of red hair," he said quietly, choosing the words carefully from his limited stock of English. "Is revenge not better than death?"

Her gaze darted toward him. The smooth brow, blistered from the sun, furrowed.

"You die . . . they live?" He shrugged, indicating the futility of her plan. To him the proper route was clear. When one was wronged one fought back. Choosing death on the desert was courageous but foolish. He did something he had never done for a woman in his life. He picked up the bowl of buffalo meat and stewed vegetables and offered it to her. "You eat . . . make strong. Fight. Not die."

Lisa stared at him, the chieftain's words striking a chord within her—an inherited pack of Irish genes that weren't programmed for giving up. She recalled Jesse's form splattered with blood, the gaping hole where his face had been. Then she pictured Johnny Petrie, Jesse's murderer. All the men of North Fork, men who had been her friends, people she had trusted. They had not even bothered to listen to her pleas, had given him no chance to survive or surrender. Damn them! Damn them all!

He held the bowl up before her as the girl's face set with determination. Greedily, she accepted the offer, bolting the food until he was forced to slow her down.

For many days after he called her Hungry Wolf, only partially for the speed at which she ate and partly for the spirit of the wolf inside her. When the chieftain formally adopted her as his daughter he changed her name to Nalin, never having pronounced the name she had been born with.

The first day she was well enough to step outside the tepee, Manatah, her new father, indicated that she should follow him. She came out behind him, her eyes blinking in the unaccustomed sunlight. Copper faces turned toward them, staring in wonder at the white girl with the strangely colored hair. They had seen many odd shades of hair among the whites, varying shades of brown, some blonde, but red was rare, and they were in awe of it. Many wanted a chance to touch it or examine it. Lisa let them, until a few pulled too hard. Then she struck out at them, yanking her wavy tresses out of their grasps.

Manatah kept walking ahead, leaving her to settle her own accounts with his curious people. He was curious himself about how she'd handle it. He smiled in satisfaction and a trace of growing pride as she showed no fear, defending her right to unmolested hair.

Toppasannah, his wife, had spent the days of the new Nalin's convalescence making a dress to replace her torn yellow rag. She had done well; the dress fit the short, boyish figure perfectly. New moccasins adorned her feet, replacing the ripped, worn, ankle-high boots she had been found in, though she wasn't used to them yet. Each time she set her lightly protected feet on a pebble or stone she winced and made short hops as she followed him.

As he led her through the small camp, her eyes darted this way and that, taking in the sights and sounds around her. Although she wouldn't know it for a while this was only a temporary camp for a small war party. The majority of the residents here were male, between the ages of fourteen and fifty-five. Only childless women or those whose children had grown or died, as Toppasannah's had, accompanied the warriors on hunts or raids. This excursion had a bit of both in its plan: hunting meat to bring back to the main camp and stealing as much as they could make off with from the Lipan Apache or anyone else they encountered. These bandits of the Great Plains had never signed a treaty with the white man, thus making settlements fair game along with the rest. White children were occasionally taken as slaves or hostages, though rarely were they adopted into the tribe. Lisa had been because Manatah and his wife had lost their own children, one boy to the dangerous buffalo hunt and a son and a daughter to the white man's plague called small pox that had decimated the Comanche many years ago. His daughter had been just about her age, and her name had been Nalin. Manatah had seen the joy on his wife's face when he brought her the unconscious child. The sen-

42

sation felt good now, to be a father again, leading his daughter among his neighbors. She would be a good daughter. She had not questioned when he signaled her to come. He was pleased.

They crossed to the far side of the camp where the horses were grazing on the sparse grass, many miles west of where Lisa had been found. Manatah frowned, realizing they would soon have to move northeast, back to Comanche territory where green grass was more plentiful. They would move soon anyway, as it grew closer to the date of the reunion of the Comanche bands. Some of the lodges were already coming down in preparation for the journey to reunite with their own band, the Kwahadi, before the festivities began.

The newly christened Nalin stopped behind her father, looking over the vast number of horses, most stolen in the past few weeks of raiding. She heard a whinny behind her and turned toward the sound. "Blackie!" she squealed in delight, running toward Jesse's black gelding, arms outstretched. She hugged the horse's neck, burying her face in the silky mane. Though still skinny from the arduous trek, he had been well taken care of and looked wonderful.

She gazed fondly at the man who had rescued them both, then ran to him and hugged him tightly, her cheek pressed aganst his bare, hard stomach. "Thank you, oh thank you!" the child gushed.

Manatah was taken off guard by the sudden outburst. He laid a hand gently on her shoulder. The child, still holding his waist, backed up to look at him, her face brighter, happier than he had yet seen it.

"May I ride him, please? Right now? Is it okay? I'll come right back, I promise. Cross my heart." She gestured with a finger drawn over her chest in an "x" pattern. He didn't understand all her words or the gesture she used for her vow, but he understood her desire. He smiled down at her and nodded, about to add that he had only a warrior's saddle to give her, barely more than a piece of hide and blanket, but the girl was already bounding back to the horse. She unfastened the picket rope from Blackie's halter, and, before Manatah could reach her, she had scrambled onto the tall, broad back like a little squirrel. He watched in amazement as she did something he had seen no white person do before. Entwining her fingers in the thick mane, she kicked the gelding in the ribs and took off at a gallop, riding a large circle around the outskirts of the Comanche horses. A few of the unstaked younger colts took off in pursuit, whinnying and snorting as they ran.

Hunched over the horse's neck, her new dress of buffalo hide hitched up to the top of her thighs, she shouted a shrill "Yahoo!" as she rounded the farthest end. As she had practiced in North Fork on her own mount, she signaled Blackie's movements with her legs, creating a zigzag pattern on her last dash for the starting place. As she shifted her weight back, Blackie slowed into an easy lope, then stopped in front of Manatah. Both the horse and the girl astride him looked pleased with their accomplishment.

Everyone, including Toppasannah, had gathered around to watch the white girl who rode like a Comanche brave. They had never seen white people ride without a saddle. And no bridle? No reins? Warriors did so, but not young girls scarcely past ten winters.

Noticing her attentive audience, she grinned mischievously as she spied an old Indian pony half the size of Blackie tied into the traces of a travois packed solidly with supplies. Using the foot signals, she lined Blackie up. He knew what she asked of him, and, being fully as impish as his mistress, Blackie loped forward, gathering speed toward the pony. He sprang effortlessly over the pony's back, landing gracefully on the far side. The Indian pony's eyes shot wide open. He jerked in surprise and then took off, the packed travois bouncing wildly behind him as the startled animal fled across the open fields. Leather ties started breaking, and hide-bound packages began to shed their contents along his path.

She slowed Blackie, turning just in time to see the trail of destruction. She urged Blackie on to catch up to the fleeing pony. Pulling up abreast of him she cut Blackie in front of the charging pony, who stopped short only to take off again in a new direction.

"Oh, Jesus, they're gonna be mad." She shot a glance toward the watching Indians. A few braves were unstaking their own horses to begin pursuit. She had to get to the pony first to make up for the damage she had caused. She urged Blackie into another sprint for the pony.

All that remained of the travois by now were two long poles bouncing along behind him. She came abreast again, but now only desperate measures were left. Her mother would have killed her if she had ever tried this before. As Blackie galloped next to the pony at an even pace, Lisa lifted one leg over his back and jumped for the pony's back. She landed squarely but almost missed her grip for the pony's mane and leaned precariously before she recovered. The pony slowed even before she reached for his bridle. By the time she had the rope halter in her hands he had stopped. Angry at what she had put him through, the pony bucked, sending both hind legs out simultaneously, and the object of his grief went sailing over his head. The pony snorted in satisfaction, beginning a prance back to camp with an enthusiasm that he hadn't shown in years.

Her new foster father was in the lead of the warriors who had given chase. He pulled up short in front of the girl now picking herself painfully up out of the dust. She looked up at him sheepishly. Manatah's stern glare turned into a grin, then broke into open laughter that soon spread throughout the warriors. He offered his hand down to her, and Lisa sprang onto the horse's back with him. Only one warrior spoke from beside Manatah, in the language she did not, as yet, understand. "I was glad when Manatah found a daughter, now I am happy he has a son."

Chapter 4

BEFORE being found in the desert Lisa had known very little about Indians. She had seen them in North Fork, but had not known what tribes they came from unless she heard a name mentioned. Her first contact had been at age five when she asked a Mr. Cherokee to retrieve a ball that had bounced into a rain gutter.

To her they were people who dressed differently. She never understood the hostility in some of her friends who made bad remarks. Her mother had always sent her out of the room when the subject among visitors turned to Indian atrocities. When she asked Henry Thompson what a dirty redskin was, he had said it was stupid name-calling by people who should know better but didn't have the common a-hole sense to keep their opinions to themselves around little ears. Then the subject had turned to what an a-hole was, and Hank had told her to go out and play.

Since she hadn't seen many of them, and only in groups of five or six who might enter the town at any given time to trade, she had assumed there weren't too many of them.

What she saw as they neared the main camp in Texas looked as though all the Indians in the world had settled here in this lush green valley hundreds of miles north and east of North Fork. Acres of grass were covered with the triangular tepees. Although she didn't know it, there were around ten thousand Comanche in the midwest at the time, and a portion of that number were now in this single encampment. The scattered bands of nomads occasionally met in a designated area to renew friendships and visit kin. These reunions were met with a great deal of celebration and feasting, and many games between bands that had perhaps not seen each other in many passing winters. In this particular gathering there were several Comanche bands: the Mutsani, Nawkoni, and Yamparika, and the Kwahadi, one of the largest of the Comanche sub-tribes. There were also a few Kiowa and Cheyenne visiting for a short while. Omitted from the gathering were the Penatuhka Comanche, mainly because the strong Kwahadi band had refused to have anything to do with them since the equally numerous Penatuhka had begun parleying with the whites like a bunch of Cherokee.

For a few days or weeks while the pasture held out, the bands would visit together to renew old family ties and friendships, exchanging news and jokes, trading and racing horses, gambling on the results. Then each band would separate and head out in its own direction.

To Lisa's mind the place was heaven. She had not seen so many horses in her entire life, not even on drives that passed North Fork. Of every size, color, and description, her favorite animals were spread out in the thousands, grazing on the valley's lush pasture.

Wide-eyed with wonder she followed Manatah, watching the sights unfold around her. The single camp covered the hills and straddled a wide, clear stream. As she rode behind her newly adopted father they passed the cone-shaped tepees, most decorated with pictures that reflected the history and deeds of the owner. Worn paths in the grass connected each lodge to its neighbor, and women worked in the open over the cook fires or beneath brush-constructed arbors for cool shade. Previously she had begun to suspect Indians didn't have children her age and below, since she hadn't seen any within the war party she traveled with. Now she was relieved to see hundreds of them, boys, girls, and babies, running about, most of them naked. Almost all stopped in their varied activities to peer curiously at the small white girl with the sacred-colored hair.

Her adopted father kept riding toward the camp's center, even after his followers dispersed behind him. Lisa was surprised when she looked back to find Toppasannah had disappeared, too, along with the horses and travois she had led the whole distance. She faced front again in time to see Manatah stop before one of the largest lodges. He jumped off his horse and indicated that she should do the same.

By now several men had emerged from the largest tepee and her new father greeted each in turn. The talk was inflected with many gestures, much laughter, and some congratulatory pats. Understanding not a word of it, Lisa soon lost interest. Several boys around her own age, wearing only breechclouts, emerged from behind a lodge. Spying the young white girl they began milling around her, bursting with curiosity and vexed that they couldn't get her to understand them. One of the older boys of about twelve or thirteen years approached, fed up with the wild gesturing that was getting them nowhere. He faced the girl and pointed to the center of his chest. "Pecos." He pounded the slim brown chest several times, then repeated, "Pecos," and turned the finger around to point at her.

"Lisa . . . I mean, Nalin." She pointed at her own chest. "Nalin."

The boy nodded, grinning broadly, and she returned the smile.

Pecos soon took care of the language barrier, pointing out objects and giving her the names of each as he led her on a grand tour of the camp. She hardly knew what he was pointing to and explaining along the way but listened intently in hopes that some of his words would stick.

In the first few days of her voluntary capture she had entertained a faint notion of rejoining her own race in some other town or settlement. Though unwilling to return to North Fork, she still regarded the whites as her people. The Comanche camp would do until a white camp came along, but she never saw one as the first few weeks passed.

Manatah had never asked her if she wished to become his daughter; she never asked him if she could stay. Her real home, North Fork, was far away, and by now she wouldn't be able to guess its direction. And there was Jesse's death. She still too clearly recalled every second of the confrontation, reliving it in nightmares that awakened her screaming in the middle of the night. And now it was Toppasannah, the warrior's wife with the soft brown eyes, who rushed to her, held her, and comforted her sorrow. During the night, too, when the camp was quiet, or in the early morning as she watched Toppasannah stir the fire for breakfast, her mind might drift back to North Fork and her other mother who had cared for her and fretted over her much as Toppasannah did now. She might become sad for a while, wondering what Maureen was doing, wondering if she thought of her daughter, worried about her. Then her thoughts would fall to Hank Thompson, at first nostalgically, until Jesse Sutton's death reappeared, and clouded the memory with pain. However, her waking hours were filled with new interests and pursuits, and Hank and Maureen Thompson faded in her memory.

As she learned the language, the customs began to fall into place. In Comanche daily life there weren't too many rules to follow. The Cheyenne, she discovered in due time, made up rules to direct every facet of life. There was hardly a function that did not have a ritual attached to it or a prescribed way of doing it. Therefore she was glad she had been found by Comanche, who only made up laws when they were essential.

She found a part of their lifestyle that suited her perfectly: Their world revolved around the horse, and the first word she learned to understand thoroughly was the Comanche word for horse, God-dog. The Great Spirit, so Manatah told her, had given the Comanche God-dog to help the warrior bring down the buffalo and to lighten the burden of the wives and dogs once expected to carry the supplies necessary to their nomadic existence. It was the coming of God-dog that had given the Comanche dominion over the rest of the Indian nations. No other tribe used the horse as extensively as the Comanche. The Sioux were second in proficiency on horseback. The Nez Perce were the only nation that took more care in breeding than the Comanche. While other tribes might use horses, in varying degrees of proficiency, only the Comanche structured their entire existence around them. A man's wealth was measured by the number of horses he owned. His standing in the band was measured not only by heredity but by how expert he became in raiding and stealing horses or how well he could capture and train the wild mustangs that shared their land. From earliest childhood a Comanche, man or woman, learned to ride, first sharing his mother's saddle, then by age seven or eight getting a horse of his own from an indulgent father, grandfather, or uncle, and from there spending the rest of his life on horseback, even into his old age when he could expect to be placed in a travois pulled by a horse. For the newly named Nalin there would be no more bows and ribbons, or scoldings that her inclinations were not becoming for a young lady. Here, she was accepted as she was. Any idea of leaving began to fade.

Nalin's first fret was over Pecos leading her away from Manatah on his introductory tour. Hank Thompson might've skinned her for taking off from where he'd left her. Besides that, she had no idea of how to find him again among the forest of, to her, identical tepees. Those fears were put to rest at suppertime when her tour guide deposited her at Manatah's lodge door with assurances relayed through her new pa that he'd return tomorrow for more lessons.

Manatah, contrary to her notions, wasn't the least concerned about her absence, neither did he or Toppasannah take particular pains over her whereabouts in the following days. She was with the Comanche, and Nalin began to learn that anywhere in camp was within family bounds. At first she was lost in confusion over family ties, until she learned that there were biological ones and there were figurative ones. Any Comanche was considered a brother or sister. Then there were family relationships, which were confusing until Nalin found the key

50

when she asked why her own family was considerably smaller than most. A few short years ago Manatah and Toppasannah had had three children. He also had had a second wife who had succumbed to the plague brought by the white man. Manatah's father had lived with them until the old man figured he was too old and infirm to travel any longer. Nalin didn't understand for quite some time what they meant when they said he left one day, thinking he had just wandered off and no one had bothered to look for him, until she knew enough of the customs to understand that Manatah's father had wandered off deliberately, unwilling to hold the band back to care for his increasing infirmities. He went the way of many of the old ones, giving away his belongings, even his name, to the younger generation, then walking off alone onto the prairie to await death.

Toppasannah's mother had lived with them, too, until only the spring before, when she had been found in her bedroll, having died peacefully in her sleep. For that reason the old woman's name was never mentioned, since she had died without giving her name away.

From that time, the pair had lived alone and childless, until he found the white girl; he considered her a special gift from the Great Spirit to console them for their losses.

Nalin's adopted father was a major sub-chief and raiding party leader in the latter half of his prime. Because of his special standing and wealth he was in the upper echelons of the band's society. The girl with red hair whom he had adopted was allowed even more rein than other girls her age. Comanche children had very little responsibility; they were allowed to run naked and carefree, visiting as they might, playing at grown-up games from sunup to sundown. Usually by Nalin's age the girls began to follow and help their mothers with the never-ending chores of gathering food, tanning hides, and other domestic tasks.

But Nalin was not interested in such things. Word soon spread that the girl not only owned her own horse but could ride as well as many of the boys.

Everyone, including the adults, was interested in see-

51

ing how far the white girl's courage and prowess on horseback would take her. The boys began inviting her into their horse races, and the white girl on the handsome black gelding often won. They began to include her in other games, usually engaged in only by the boys in training to become warriors, but Nalin played the rough-and-tumble games right along with them.

When the reunion ended and the Kwahadi band moved off from the main camp, following their own direction farther north into Oklahoma, Nalin was pleased to discover her new-found friends, Pecos, Little Eagle, Broken Hand, and Red Fox, went with them. Only Toppasannah disapproved of the fact that her daughter's constant companions were boys, not girls, that through choice and ability Nalin spent her time in young men's pursuits, not those of women. It was always young warriors between ten and fourteen who called Nalin out to join in their pastimes. Toppasannah would have complained of this to Manatah, but his beaming face told her he was too proud of her accomplishments to worry that Nalin would grow up learning nothing of what women should know to find a husband.

Of all her new Comanche friends, Pecos became the closest. Two years older, he became her instructor in all the games. She spent as much time with his family as she did with her own. His father was civil chief and war chief and thus was the most respected and richest man in the tribe. He had three wives and several children, but of those sisters and brothers only one was a full brother to her best friend, and that was the eldest son, the somber and morose Quanah.

Years later she wouldn't recall when she first became aware of Quanah. She did recall that he, like his father, Nacoma, scared her slightly, being the exact opposite of the gay and reckless Pecos. Five years older than Nalin, Quanah at fifteen was not interested in the children's games they played. He was already going on war parties and hunts, allowed to hold horses and watch the temporary camps. What she remembered most about him was that he never smiled.

Now that her friendships had taught her enough to speak with her mother, she finally asked Toppasannah about the long-faced young man. At the time her questions had been no more than curiosity.

She was told that barely a year before Nalin came, bluecoats had raided the Kwahadi band. Quanah, his father, and his brother, young Pecos, had escaped onto the prairie, but Quanah's mother and baby sister had been captured. Because Quanah's mother was white the bluecoats had taken her away, and Quanah had not smiled or laughed since that day.

Nalin was horrified. She still wasn't sure just what separated her status from that of the few white slaves she saw in the camp; perhaps it was that she came by choice, and the others tried so hard to escape. Perhaps it was only her red hair that Jesse had talked about. Or maybe the whites were being punished for something, like Papa's prisoners. Whatever it was, Nalin took no chances and spoke with them as little as possible. But that could not have been the status of Quanah's mother, who had come as a prisoner but had married a chief. "Did she want to go with them?"

"Oh, no," Toppasannah replied. "We were close friends, she and I. She loved her husband and her sons and would never have left them."

"Why did they make her go then?"

"Because she was white," Toppasannah answered patiently. "To the bluecoats they had rescued her, but she had been taken as a young child, almost your age when she came. She grew up here. Her heart was here."

"Why didn't she run away from them then?"

"She tried . . . many times. Always they caught her and brought her back. Then a few moons ago we heard that her baby daughter caught the fever and died in the bluecoat fort. After that Quanah's mother would not eat. She starved herself to death. That is why, when the other boys took new names to call themselves, Quanah kept the baby name his mother had given him."

Nalin knew enough Comanche now to know the name meant *fragrant*, an endearing name a new mother might

53

choose for her sweet-smelling baby. It was not a name be-fitting a warrior, yet anyone who dared tease him about it soon learned to hold his tongue. Quanah was already getting a reputation for his aggressiveness as a warrior.

"I will never hear you tease him about his name, will I?" Toppasannah looked down at her daughter sternly.

"Oh, no, Mother, never," she swore, and meant it with her whole body and soul. She couldn't believe such an awful thing could happen; to drag a mother from her children, to allow her to starve rather than return her to those she loved. To Nalin's inexperienced mind this was the single most atrocious act she had ever heard of, except for her own betrayal. She was here because she wanted to be, her whiteness fading from memory as the months passed and her desire to find her own people waned. She was happy here, gradually settling into the new way of life, accepting Manatah and Toppasannah as her foster parents as fully as they had accepted her as their daughter.

Quanah's mother had been white, too. "Mother?" Nalin said in a startled whisper, having just thought of it. "Would they do that to me? Would they take me back?"

"They might," Toppasannah answered sadly. "That is why you must never be seen by them, my daughter. If they come you must hide."

Nalin's face darkened with determination. "I won't hide . . . I'll fight. They will never take me back. I will fight till I die, but I won't go back."

Toppasannah smiled at the childish bravado. "Women do not fight, my child. Warriors fight."

"Then I'll become a warrior . . . and I will fight them. They won't take me back!"

Toppasannah had laughed, rubbing the child's head, little realizing how firmly her daughter meant every word.

Nalin's friends, almost exclusively boys, were teaching her everything in their play that she would need to accomplish her end. They treated her like any one of the young braves in training. She hunted small game with them, mastering bow as well as rifle, and, in wrestling,

54

since she grew taller faster than they did, she occasionally beat them.

Such was the case in her third year among the Comanche, when she bravely challenged Pecos. While Quanah held the pain of his mother's loss inside, the younger brother struck outward, becoming something of a bully. Pecos was challenging the younger boys and giving them a hard time when they refused to fight him. He had backed several against the rawhide side of a lodge, refusing to let them pass unmolested, until Nalin could take no more of it. He was still her best friend, but his actions of late were becoming intolerable.

"If you want to wrestle so badly, Pecos, then wrestle me," she dared him. At this time the thirteen-year-old girl was six inches taller than her fifteen-year-old friend. The rugged life she was leading, competing in boys' sports, had made her lean; her figure had not yet been softened by gentle curves. Pecos had wrestled her playfully before, and each time found it increasingly difficult to get her down. He was not eager to try again, yet he didn't want to lose face either. "You're a girl, Nalin."

"Can't you whip a girl?" she shot back. "Or do you prefer little boys you know you can whip?"

That was all it took—Pecos charged like an angry bull. Without knowing quite how she managed the feat, Nalin swung around quickly so he was forced to grab her from the back. As his arms closed around her waist she ducked low, grabbing his neck, then, springing her backside upward, she flipped her boastful friend into the air to land in the dirt with a resounding thump. The gathered boys were gape-mouthed in awe, staring down at the bewildered Pecos still trying to figure out how his defeat had happened. Nalin, too, was struck with shock, never expecting the plan to work so well. Only one sound came from the sidelines. Quanah had watched the entire episode and was laughing.

Chapter 5

ALTHOUGH Nalin had once brought on Quanah's laughter, the occasions were rare. He seldom smiled and even less often engaged in any games other than the races. Intense and serious Quanah joined the warriors around the camp fires but never bragged about his deeds in battle. The others did it for him, relating the young warrior's large and growing list of coups. Any act of bravery over an opponent could be a coup, from striking him with a bare hand to killing him, though there was little honor in causing a death without just cause. To prevent bloodshed, a personalized stick might be used, with which the warrior could leave his mark on a defeated foe. Quanah's coup stick had touched enemy warriors more often than most of the seasoned veterans' sticks, and there were many he had laid coup on with his bare hands. His cunning had already increased his herd by a few hundred horses; his prowess as a hunter kept his father's wives and his half-sisters busy with the meat and hides he brought them.

After that day, while others noted his skill, Nalin, though taking his reputation into account, also focused on his striking handsomeness. She had never noticed before how dark and haunting his eyes were, and it was strange that she hadn't before seen his well-muscled shoulders.

She began to spend even more of her time with Pecos, now that she had seen his brother with the eyes of a maturing young woman.

Pecos had not missed the fact that though she spent her time with him, her attention was usually riveted on his older brother. In the winter, games by the fire in the warmth of the lodge were much preferred over freezing outside. Even the winter robes with the skin side turned out so the fur would be next to the body for more heat were not quite as snug as the inside of a winter lodge, when Nalin and Pecos could get away with staying indoors. Nacoma's lodge was one of the largest, a massive affair that had required all his wives, daughters, and several friends to erect, so there was plenty of room for Nalin and Pecos to play their game and remain out of the way of the rest of the family. But Nalin wasn't paying attention to the game anymore—Quanah had come in.

Pecos waited, and she still didn't take her turn, instead gazing lovestruck at his brother. Nalin had been much more fun to be with before she became so enamored of Quanah. Pecos scowled from her to his brother and back again. "It's your turn, Nalin."

"Hmm? Oh." Absently she took it, then returned to staring at Quanah. The older brother's back was turned to them as he ate a late meal, having only just returned from a hunting trip. He was quite used to Nalin's presence in their lodge and had not even bothered with a greeting when he came in. Nacoma was sitting across from him, quietly asking questions about the hunt.

Nacoma had always somewhat frightened Nalin. He had a gruff, serious manner, rarely smiling as Manatah so often did, and he held his children at a distance, never as openly affectionate as her own father. Still, he was chief of the Kwahadi, and perhaps that had a lot to do with his bearing. Usually Nalin avoided Nacoma, taking wide berths around him and making certain her behavior in his presence was impeccable. If he ever had occasion to speak to her, Nalin very likely would have fainted on the spot. He put up with her presence as though she were one of his own seven children. If one needed chastisement he told one of his wives and let her see to it. Only recently was Quanah, his eldest, treated like a man, and thus his father was interested in what he had to say. For that reason, Nalin and Pecos were playing their game as quietly as two mice sneaking crumbs.

"Nalin, it is your turn again," Pecos reminded softly, nudging her with a poke in the arm. She took her gaze off Quanah's back to glare at him.

"Do you want to play or stare at Quanah?" the impatient Pecos snarled in a low growl.

"I am not staring at Quanah . . . "

Her friend's expression changed to one of impending mischief now that he had found a way to irritate her. "Would you like me to tell Quanah that you love him? Perhaps he would like to know."

"I do not," she answered quickly.

"Yes, you do," he teased. "And I'm going to tell him."

"You tell him, Pecos, and I'll give you this." She threatened with a cocked fist.

Their argument became a bit too loud, causing Nacoma to glance toward them with a frown. Nalin noticed it first and paled. Pecos nudged her again with an elbow, then sprang to his feet. The game forgotten, both rushed out into the crisp January weather. There was a light blanket of snow on the ground. Their feet, encased in ankle-high boots of tough buckskin, made crunching sounds through the carpet of white as they wandered away from Nacoma's lodge.

For several minutes they walked aimlessly side by side, neither leading in a planned direction. Her friend's forehead became creased as a slow anger gradually built up pressure, then exploded. "You only come to see me because you wish to see Quanah," he accused, stopping suddenly and spinning about on her. "I thought that *I* was Nalin's friend, but, oh no, you only use me to be near him!" His tirade cut off suddenly as he turned about and struck off away from her.

Nalin was too stunned to move until he was fifty feet away, then she sprang to life, trotting after him. "Pecos, that is not true." She tried to stop him, but he pulled his arm roughly out of her grasp and kept walking. Nalin stayed alongside him. "Pecos, *you* are my friend . . . my best friend. You are my brother. You will always be."

"No, you only use me to be near Quanah—"

"That is not so. You were my friend before I ever knew Quanah. Am I back inside staring at Quanah now, or am I with you?"

The question stopped him. He pulled up abruptly, and Nalin took his arm, making him look at her. "You were my friend before Quanah. You will always be. Do I not see you every day? Do I not come even when Quanah is away? It is true, I do like him, but in a different way. *You* are my brother."

"Someday you will forget me. You will have time only for Quanah," he pouted, still hurt, but the anger was cooling.

"Perhaps someday I will marry and have children, but so will you. We cannot always be together as we are now, because we will be grown up," Nalin answered logically. "But you will always be my brother in my heart. That will never change."

Pecos gazed briefly at the intent look on her face, her whole bearing trying to convey how seriously she meant her words. The jealousy Pecos felt was not of a romantic nature. He and Nalin knew each other too well as friends. On the other hand, the young warrior thought, his mouth screwed up sideways as he peered at her, if Nalin's wish for romance with his brother came off and they eventually married, he and Nalin would be brother and sister forever. He would never have to worry about a brave from another band stealing her heart and taking her away. Instead Nalin would stay with the Kwahadi . . . with his own family even. The idea had merit. He nodded somberly, and Nalin smiled in relief, taking his hand and running off to join a group of their friends in an aimless ride on horseback, which accomplished no more than the passing of a winter afternoon.

Curiosity brought them closer to sounds of human activity issuing from the other side of a bluff. Their seven mounted Indian forms appeared on the top of the ridge, peering down on a small wagon train. The oldest at fifteen and then some was Red Fox; the youngest was a girl slightly younger than Nalin who also had an inclination for boys' games. Concealed in winter clothes, the distance between ridge and wagon train effectively hid their tender ages.

The problem below seemed to be that one of the wagons was stuck in snow-slushed mud. The Indian shapes on the bluff soon attracted the attention of a white woman who looked up, pointed in wide-eyed terror, then screamed.

Pecos was the first to realize the danger and spun his horse about, shouting for everyone to run. Nalin remained staring down in amazement at the sight of her own race. Whites, several of them, when she had seen none in the past four years of her new existence. She had seen a few slaves in the camp, those defeated and subjected humans whom she never spoke with and considered somehow different from both herself and her people . . . her people . . . who were her people? The whites in the ravine below her seemed strange and foreign to her now. Several of them were scurrying about, pointing at the ridge and yelling out to one another, and she could not understand a word they said. She should know. She *had* known what the words meant.

"Nalin!" Pecos shouted.

Nalin had once, long ago, told herself she would rejoin her race *if* she ever saw any whites. Later she had sworn she would fight and die rather than let them take her away. Both promises had been easy to keep while she never laid eyes on her own race. Here whites were as close as five hundred yards away. Her gaze turned from the settlers to Pecos and back again. The settlers were watching the ridge fearfully, fearful of her because from that distance she could have been a brave, a vanguard of attack for the Comanche nation.

"Nalin?" Pecos called again, a question this time, but she didn't seem to hear him as she still stared down intently at the whites' camp. Her tardiness was also causing the others to pause. Little Eagle and Red Fox had followed Pecos; the rest remained on the ridge.

Panic had set in below at the sight of the Indians. This was not a wagon train but only a small group of three wagons that hoped to cross the frontier without paying for the services of a guide. Knowing there could be danger from Indians, they were prepared for it, rifles ready and pointed upward at the threat.

"Nalin, run," Pecos shouted from below the ridgeline.

Now was her chance to rejoin her own race. Now . . . or never. If she went, she would forever leave behind all those she had come to love—Pecos, Quanah, all her friends, Manatah and Toppasannah. Simultaneous to the thought she made up her mind. She turned Blackie's head away from the whites, kicked his ribs, and dove for the safety below the ridge. An instant later shots rang out from the ravine. A small scream of surprise followed the rifle shots, and Desert Flower, the youngest girl in the party, fell backward off her mount, then took a rolling sprawl into the ravine.

"Oh, my God, Kincaid . . . it's a kid! It's only an Indian *girl.*" Jack Roberts stared at the unconscious form of the child.

Kincaid had already rolled her over on her back and was carefully examining her for injury. Thankfully, she wasn't shot, only stunned from the fall. A small trickle of blood stained the ebony hair at the back of her head. "Help me get her to the wagon." Kincaid picked up the girl, mortified at what he had nearly done. Thinking in retrospect, the Indians on the ridge had all been kids, far too small in size to possibly mean harm to them. Just seven curious Indian kids come out to watch. Kincaid cursed himself for his folly. He had damn near killed this girl, narrowly missing, and he had never shot at a human soul before in his life. He gently laid the limp form down on the bed within his wagon. Every one of the rest of the small party's members was gathered outside wondering what to do next. Jack Roberts was all for getting the wagon out in a hurry and moving on before the kids went back for the warriors.

"And what do we do with the girl?" Bill Baumann argued. "They'll come looking for her for sure. Better we stay and explain the situation."

"Explain what?" Roberts countered. "That we nearly killed her? You think they'll give us time to explain?"

Mary Roberts nudged her husband, interrupting his argument, then pointed at the ridge. This time there was only a single Indian form covered in buckskin, astride a black horse.

"It's one of the kids," Baumann said as the form slowly began to descend toward them.

"This time nobody gets stupid," Roberts warned the assembly. He started walking out to meet the rider.

His first surprise was over curly red locks in place of the straight black hair he expected; then he noticed a light, sunburned complexion and recognized a white girl in Indian dress. The girl stopped her horse five feet away from him. Her mouth hung open as though to speak, but she couldn't seem to find the words.

Nalin couldn't understand why she felt this way. She was terrified of the white man before her. The idea had been hers to go into the white camp and fetch Desert Flower. She had convinced Pecos and the others to let her try before resorting to riding back to camp for help. Now she couldn't think of what to say or how to say it. Complete non-use of the English language added to the difficulty, because she couldn't remember the words. The white man before her seemed just as flustered.

"Do you speak English?" he tried first.

Nalin nodded uncertainly. At least she had understood that much. Her forehead creased as she concentrated, dredging up the long-forgotten words. "I c . . . come for Desert Flower."

"The girl?" The white man cocked a thumb toward the wagon. "She's all right. Only knocked out. We're real sorry."

"I . . . take her now." That was the best Nalin could do. Her frightened mind refused to work properly. "I may have her?"

"Sure, of course, as soon as she's well enough to ride. Come on inside and see for yourself." Roberts was becoming increasingly curious over the strange white girl who had trouble with her own language. He would have immediately assumed she was one of the hostages he had read about in the papers back East, but this girl didn't seem to be a captive. He'd like to find out a bit more about this. "Come on down, and we'll see how your friend is."

The girl looked uncertain but complied, jumping to the ground but keeping her distance even as she followed him to the wagon.

All of them were staring at her now, and Nalin reddened under their scrutiny. Now she regretted insisting on this course, wishing she had let Pecos go for the warriors instead. All these strangers watching her, studying her . . . She wished fervently that she was back in Manatah's lodge, safe again with her own people. Now she was sure beyond doubt, she no longer belonged in the white people's world.

Desert Flower was groggy but awake and conscious enough to be frightened of the white woman hovering over her, trying futilely to bathe her forehead with a wet cloth. Desert Flower shrank away from her, pushing her hand away each time she approached. With Nalin's appearance in the wagon the girl squealed in joy and leapt into her friend's arms. The girls spoke in Comanche as Nalin gently stroked the younger girl's hair.

"We will go now." Nalin spoke to the one who had met her.

"Well, maybe you ought to wait a bit. Your friend had a bad fall . . . "

"No, we go." Nalin took the girl's hand, helping her down from the wagon.

"Wait, I'd like to talk to you a minute."

The girls paused.

"I want to know . . . to be sure." Roberts gazed from the white Indian girl to the dark one and back. "Well, what I mean is . . . do you need any help?"

The girl looked at him, her brow furrowing.

"I mean, if you're being held against your will, I can send help back."

"I need no . . . help."

"I mean," Roberts corrected again, feeling he was getting off his point. "Are you a prisoner?"

Nalin looked at him like he couldn't know what he was talking about. Why would the Comanche hold her against her will? Did he think she was a slave? The notion insulted her. "I am the daughter of Manatah . . . I am Kwahadi . . . I need no help," she spat back haughtily. As the dumbfounded whites watched, she turned on her heel, taking Desert Flower's hand again, and started to stride back to Blackie.

"Jack." Mary Roberts gripped her husband's arm. "Stop her. She's white."

Roberts glanced at his wife, who was watching the children leave with pity written clearly across her features.

"She doesn't belong there." Mary shook his arm, prompting him to go after the girl. He reached the pair as the white girl helped her Indian friend onto the horse's broad back.

"Wait, child." Jack paused as the girl turned bright green eyes up at him. Now he didn't quite know what to say. The child had denied wanting their help. Perhaps she had been among the Indians too long to remember where she came from. "Look," he began falteringly. "We can see you don't belong with these heathen. You're a white girl. You belong with your own kind. We can help you if you'll let us."

The girl's brow furrowed, then her head shook negatively. She turned away from him to make sure Desert Flower was well seated.

Jack Roberts was a God-fearing Christian; the girl's immortal soul was in jeopardy. She'd never learn Christian ways in the hands of these savages, and there was only one way to stop her. He grabbed the girl by the waist as she tried to mount, yanking her away from the horse. Startled, she barely had time to react, kicking the horse's flank and yelling in Comanche to the girl on the mount.

The horse started off, the Indian girl barely grabbing the mane in time to keep from being unseated as she started to ride for the ridgeline. Good God, what had he

64

done? He tried to hold the screaming, flailing white girl.

"Shoot her." Kincaid stepped forward, pointing at the child galloping for the ridge. Baumann was the only one who still had a rifle in his hands, but he didn't lift it. "She'll go for the warriors! We're all dead now!"

Panicked, Kincaid grabbed the rifle from the inertly staring Baumann. He lifted it, drawing aim on the girl's back, but his fingers refused to pull the trigger. Finally, as she disappeared over the hill he lowered the barrel, a cry of hopelessness issuing out as he watched the now empty ridgeline.

"Damn you, Roberts!" Kincaid threw the rifle down and stormed toward the man still holding the white child, who had ceased struggling and now watched them. "You goddamn fool!" Kincaid ranted. "Your stupidity has killed us all! She'll get the warriors. They'll slaughter every last one of us. Let the damn kid go."

Roberts stared at him numbly. "She's white," he murmured.

"So the hell what?" Kincaid screamed, red-faced. "Is it worth all of our lives? They'll kill us!" The last word came out almost in a screech as he grabbed the girl out of Roberts' grasp and tossed her to the ground.

Nalin fearfully looked from one to the other of the two men. Toppasannah's warning about the fate of Quanah's mother echoed through her head as if the woman was standing beside her. Whites had taken *her* back. She had died in the white man's fort. Toppasannah had warned that she must never be seen by the whites or they would take her back, too. They would force her to live among them. They would make her a prisoner, never allow her to leave. She would never see her people again. She, too, would die in the bluecoat fort among strangers. If she ever let herself be taken back there, surely she would die just as Quanah's mother had died.

"Child." A white woman leaned over her, reaching down to help the girl out of the snowbank where the man had tossed her. Nalin backed up, squirming out of the woman's reach.

"Child, we won't hurt you. You're safe now," the

woman murmured, but the girl continued to stare in wide-eyed terror.

"Let her go." Kincaid approached again. Nalin huddled further into the snowbank, too terrified to translate the words into understanding. Mary Roberts backed away, her thin hands twittering with uncertainty.

"Can't you see she wants to go back there?" Kincaid shouted. "She's scared of us. Not them, goddamn it! We're the ones scaring the hell out of her. Let her go."

"He's right." Ann Baumann placed a hand on Mary's trembling shoulder.

"But the girl's a Christian, Ann." Baumann looked at his wife.

"But it's us she fears, Bill. Lord knows how she came to be there . . . poor child." Ann looked down at the girl huddled as far into the snowbank as she could get herself. She reached down and took the girl's arm, prying the child to her feet. "Do you understand me?" Ann asked softly. The girl paused, watching her carefully, then nodded.

"Do you want to go back?"

Nalin glanced at each of the six faces before her, unable to believe the woman's question. Was this some trick? Some game? Or did they truly mean they would set her free? Her gaze focused on the blonde woman who had spoken, and she nodded again, tears misting the green eyes.

"We have to let her go." Ann turned toward the rest.

"She's right." Baumann spoke. "Besides, it's the only chance we have. If we don't let her go the whole tribe will be out here after us."

"Maybe they won't want her back," Roberts offered.

"And if they do?" Baumann shot back. "How are we going to fight them off?"

"I thought you'd understand," Roberts shouted at Baumann, who was going west to serve as a minister. "I thought you, out of all of us, would understand that the child's a Christian. Why should they care about getting a white girl back? She belongs here with her own people. . . ."

Nalin listened to his words, understanding most of

them. Would that be true also? Would her people come for her or would they let her be taken back? She *was* white—only an adopted daughter. Would they mind her loss? Risk a war party to save her? Tears she had sworn never to shed again began to roll down her cheeks. She wanted to go home . . . home to the warm lodge she shared with her foster parents . . . home to the friends she had shared a happy life with. Please, Great Spirit that Manatah talked about, oh please, He Who Watches Over Us All, please let them come for me. Please, please, let me go home and never, ever again, will I let myself be seen by whites. Never. Was this her punishment for disregarding her mother's warning? Was this retribution for her hesitation on the ridge—never to see her people and to be brought back to die in the white man's fort?

"I do not want to stay. . . ." For a moment she did not even realize she had said the words aloud and in English. Now all of the light faces turned toward her. "I want to go home," she continued murmuring, her face tightly screwed up with emotion. "I want to go home."

"You see?" Mary Roberts faced the others with a look of triumph. "You heard what she said. She wants to go home. She wants us to take her home."

"Mary." Ann Baumann gazed at the child, whose jaw had dropped open in astonishment. "I'm not sure that is what she meant—"

Kincaid's wife, until now watching silently, happened to raise her head for a moment and then shouted, stopping Ann in mid-sentence. The rest gazed up where her finger was pointing. Now there were dozens of Indian forms on the ridge, and all of these unquestionably adult.

"Oh, dear God!" Baumann uttered at the mounted shapes lining the ridge; there had to be thirty or more.

"Send her back!" Kincaid screeched. Quickly gripping the girl's arm he propelled her forward toward the Indians. "Go on," he shouted at her. "Get out of here! Go!"

Nalin needed no further encouragement as she darted out of the white camp and ran wildly toward the nearest riders. Panicked, she yelled, "Help me! Help!" in Comanche, flying toward them as fast as her feet could carry her. The first brave she reached was Crooked Thumb, one she had known since the day she first came to them, one who had taught her the trick of dropping below the horse to shoot arrows from beneath a galloping horse's neck. Aim was poor in such a position, but the trick had merit in showing off for other tribes. Now he tried no such theatrics; hearing her pleading cry he aimed true at the white man who had thrown the girl forward. His arrow buried itself deeply in the man's chest.

Nalin stopped, spinning about in time to see the attack begin all around her. The braves dashed off the ridge toward the white camp, arrows and bullets raining down on the three stranded wagons.

"No! No!" Nalin screamed, starting to run after them. "They *let* me go! They let me!"

No one could hear her as the attack continued. She ran wildly, trying to catch up to the horses, shouting to be heard above the war cries and screams. It was no use. They couldn't hear. She couldn't stop them. She saw the other one, Baumann, fall forward, the snow turning red beneath his body. The woman who had asked her if she wanted to go back stood over him screaming until a brave rushed by her, lifting her up and throwing her over his horse's back. Nalin rushed toward Crooked Thumb to tell him to release the captive. She was still running when her body was yanked up into the air, the breath pushed out of her lungs as she was plopped haphazardly in front, her legs barely straddling the horse's neck. It was the horse she recognized first—the black Appaloosa gelding Quanah rode into battle. She tried to turn her head against the speed of the full gallop to see if her eyes had betrayed her. They hadn't. It *was* Quanah, his handsome face set intently on getting her to safety, his strong arms wrapped around her to keep her from falling.

"Quanah, it's a mistake . . . a mistake. They let me go." She tried to force the words out, but he glanced down at her as if she were babbling incoherently. Perhaps she was. Perhaps her words had failed to come out clearly.

"You are safe now, Nalin." He spoke as the horse

slowed down on the far side of the ridge. He lifted her effortlessly again with one arm and gently set her on her feet.

"Quanah, I . . . I . . . " The handsome face she cherished, had feared she might never see again, swam before her. The trees behind him upended, taking him with them. The ground became the sky and the sky seemed to be beneath her as Nalin pitched forward, landing in a tumble at his horse's feet.

Chapter 6

NALIN had only fainted from the fear and exertion. She awoke to find herself still on the ridge where Quanah had left her, in the hands of the medicine man who had accompanied the thirty braves of the rescue party. Red Eagle Feather had used a foul-smelling herb to prod her into wakefulness, and Nalin rose to a sitting position, coughing and sputtering from the sharp scent that had assaulted her nostrils.

When she was sensible enough to ride, Red Eagle Feather helped her mount Blackie; they rode below to the wagon train. Nalin looked about in horror. The bodies of the three white men were scattered on the ground, the women nowhere in sight. Warriors were searching the wagons, pulling out supplies they could use.

Nalin was horrified by what had happened. Her choice to remain white or Comanche would have resulted in death any way she had chosen. Had she picked the path of the whites, the Comanche would still have come for her. She had chosen the Comanche path, and two braves had died in the effort to bring her out again. Their bodies were now laid out on travois to be returned to camp. Either way, some would have died.

"I am not so important as to cause such as this." Nalin turned to Red Eagle Feather, seeking an answer in the ancient, grizzled face of the medicine man.

"There are some, young Nalin, who will not agree with you. How *can* one person be worth the cost of another's life? Or of several lives, it is true, but it is also the way life is. Some die that others may live. We cannot let others take from us that which belongs to us—our land, our horses, or our children. They must know the Kwahadi will never accept such insult. You are not the sole cause of this. It was also to keep our pride so that all will know the Kwahadi cannot be defeated. They would have done the same for Desert Flower had you not rescued her. No woman or child shall be taken from us while our braves can ride to fight. Do you understand, daughter of Manatah?"

Nalin nodded slowly, still watching the dead men lying on the snow, their bodies stripped of anything useful, the heads bare where the hair had been scalped off. She had seen such sights before, but never this close and never against the whites. She knew there were always those who would take your possessions from you. She knew from the old storytellers that even before the whites came there were those who would steal your horses, take your possessions, run you off grassland and out into the desert if you were not strong enough to resist. The Comanche strength had come from kinship. Their supremacy was a result of the special gift of God-dog—and an unwillingness to compromise in matters of what was rightfully theirs.

Nalin knew she had faced the most important decision of her life: Either she would fight for the Comanche way of life or she would return to the white man's world. No, she could never do that. She was no longer part of the white world; she hardly understood their tongue, no longer comprehended their ways. She was Kwahadi now. She had chosen her path, and now she had to follow it.

In camp, Nacoma spoke directly to Nalin for the first time in the four years she had been there, telling her that she had done well in entering the whites' camp for Desert Flower. He counted her act as a coup, and, since she was too young to do so herself, he would recount the coup for her before the warriors. Nalin very nearly fainted again.

Though she had earned an honor, she remained one of the boys. She grudgingly spared time to learn what she

71

was expected to know, helping Toppasannah set up the lodge as well as pack it up again for moving. In the evenings she learned cooking and some sewing and beadwork, but when time came to tan the buffalo hides and work them into soft buckskin, or to gather vegetables from the prairie, or any of a dozen domestic chores girls were supposed to learn, Nalin would disappear like a wisp of smoke through the open flap of the tepee.

Several days had passed following the incident when Nalin again saw a sign of the white women taken from the wagon train. One of the three was never seen again, but Crooked Thumb had taken the blonde woman who had spoken on her behalf. Nalin was glad to find that this kind woman belonged to Crooked Thumb, who was a brave man and a good provider.

For the other woman Nalin felt sympathy. She now belonged to Two Feathers. He had already caused one wife to divorce him, taking her housekeeping tools along with her, even the lodge she had painstakingly crafted out of the few buffalo skins the hunter had managed to provide. Two Feathers was lazy and had a foul temper. No other woman would stay with him, but a slave had no choice. Such was the fate that befell the defeated. There were some good and some bad among Indians just as there were among whites.

It had not escaped Manatah's attention that Nalin had been unable to remember her own tongue the day she rescued Desert Flower. He realized that she was now thinking in the Comanche tongue; soon she would remember no more of the white man's language than Nacoma's white captive wife had known when she left them. On the rare occasions when he decided to improve his own English and asked her to teach him new words, she could no longer remember them without thinking very hard, and often failed to recall them at all. In exasperation, Manatah looked over the tribe's white captives. He could easily buy the woman Two Feathers had kept, but she was broken, her spirit fled; she went about her assigned tasks like an old pack horse. Besides that, the woman was

72

pregnant with Two Feathers' child. Manatah did not want the responsibility of caring for an infant from the loins of so dishonorable and lazy a man.

Instead his gaze finally fell on the blonde woman Crooked Thumb had taken into his household. He spoke to him about her and learned the brave would be happy to let her go—and for a fair price. She worked well, but often argued with Crooked Thumb's wife. She was resentful and uncooperative, and he warned Manatah that she would not make a very good love partner. Manatah replied that at his age that was unimportant, Toppasannah was all he could handle, and he purchased the woman. Part of his purpose was to lighten Toppasannah's burden of household tasks, but another part of his plan was to have the woman help Nalin relearn her own tongue.

For Manatah, knowledge of the white man's language was a decided advantage. Since he was one of the very few who spoke English, his presence during raids of white settlements was invaluable. One didn't have to make gestures and pantomimes to be understood when Manatah was along. He wanted Nalin to be able to perform this same function. She was fast approaching the age when boys would be allowed to accompany the warriors on hunts and raids. At first they were allowed only to watch the war camps and guard the loot; later they would be included in the war party. He was pleased that his daughter had shown such an affinity for the boys' games and had encouraged her in her desire to be a warrior. Among the tribes it was rare but not unheard of for a woman to become a brave. The Crow had such a woman, an able and fierce fighter called Woman Chief who sat on their councils and counted coups. She was so successful at her chosen way of life that she had become rich with her plunder and had "married" several women to tan hides and attend to her domestic chores. Nalin seemed to be destined for the same chaste fate.

Manatah had no son to look after him in his approaching old age, only this one daughter. Marriage could solve the problem for him, but it would be an unusual warrior who would decide to wed a hot-tempered woman who had

73

learned so little of a woman's place and duties. His remaining option, therefore, seemed to be to allow the girl growth in her chosen direction. She rode as well as the boys, was expert with bow or rifle, gave not an inch in rough-and-tumble games with them. Other seasoned warriors complimented Manatah on his daughter's prowess and talents, and the old man's chest swelled with pride. Soon, she would go along with the other boys on hunts, then raids. When she learned enough she could replace her father as the war party's translator. But first she had to relearn English.

Ann Baumann came fearfully, terrified at the prospects awaiting her in the hands of her new owner.

Manatah made her sit down before him and sent Toppasannah from the lodge. "I am an old man, long past any wish to wrestle with a woman." He spoke to her in a mixture of English and Comanche, which she was only beginning to learn. "Your duties shall be lighter here than in the lodge of Crooked Thumb. I have only one wife, one daughter, and our needs are less. You will have time to teach my daughter to speak her language again. If you fail I shall have the right to beat you, but I tire easily now, and I have no wish to waste my energy. See that she learns her tongue as well as she once knew it."

Ann nodded slowly, unable to quite fathom the sudden turn of her fortune. It was not exactly like being free again, but it was a definite improvement in her hostage status. Ann had pondered the idea of escaping. At first, grief for Bill had been too great for clear thinking, the terror and pain of being a slave and concubine too great a shock to her senses. Later, common sense prevailed—the vast prairie and miles of desert they passed through never gave a sign of civilization. Where could she go? How could she escape? She was sensible enough to realize she needed a workable plan to even hope to succeed. She had considered asking the white child for help, but she doubted the girl knew any better than she did how to find a settlement.

Her new owner stood up, signaling his adopted daughter to come inside. The child Ann had first seen six months ago appeared within the lodge, presenting as strange a picture as she had then. The dark red tresses were braided and covered in a layer of mud from a spill off her mount. The girl faced Ann almost resentfully, the green eyes glaring from her grime-encrusted face. Her father spoke to her in Comanche, too rapidly for Ann to grasp the words. The girl answered him just as quickly; her tone indicated she disliked her father's intentions. The father's voice became harsh with the sound of a direct order. The girl screwed up her face with displeasure but finally harumphed loudly and knelt beside the white woman.

"Teach her," Manatah ordered with a finger pointed in the girl's direction, then he turned and strode out into the warm summer sun.

For what seemed to be an interminable time, they sat side by side in silence. "What's your name?" Ann began at last in a friendly tone. The girl paused so long the teacher thought she might not have understood the question.

"Nalin," she replied, gazing down at the clean-swept ground with a bored expression.

"Nalin is your Indian name. Do you remember a name before that?"

The green eyes turned upward, glittering with defiance. "I have no other name," she spat in Comanche.

Ann paused, wondering if this might be harder than she had thought it would be. "Will you answer in English . . . as your father wishes?" She used the reminder that this entire affair was not her idea, but the father's. "How long have you been here?"

The girl's slow smile became mischievous. "Forever . . . I was born here."

She was lying; Ann knew it, watching her carefully. She had been a teacher for five years back East before Bill decided to take a mission in California. She had taught reluctant students before. "How did you learn English?"

"I do *not* know English. That is why Father wants you to teach me."

Ann translated most of the words in her mind, then continued in English. "But you do know it. How do you account for that?"

The girl dropped her gaze again and shrugged.

"You don't like speaking English, do you? Why?" she prodded.

"I do not *need* to know the white man's tongue." This time the thought was perhaps Comanche but the words were English.

"But you *are* white, Nalin."

The girl lapsed into silence, glaring daggers at her.

"What have we done to you that you hate us so?"

This time the girl paused to carefully pronounce the words she was unfamiliar with. "I do not hate whites. I do not like them also. They are evil . . . bad."

"Why?"

"I do not know why people are evil . . . because the Great Spirit made them so."

"Am I evil, Nalin?"

The girl seemed to ponder the question, looking directly into the teacher's eyes. "You tried to help me. You are different perhaps. Maybe you are not evil," she granted, leaning back to a more comfortable position.

Maybe she could make a friend of her yet, Ann hoped.

"Tell me." She tried a new tack. "I know you weren't born here, but how did you come to live here?"

"I do not remember."

Apparently she wasn't about to impart any knowledge of a previous life. Ann sighed.

Surprisingly the girl began to speak again, in English, the words becoming more faithfully pronounced. "If I tell you, you would tell them. They would come to take me. They would take me to the fort, and I would die there."

Ann's brows furrowed. "Nalin, what makes you say that? Who told you you would die if you went back?"

"No one needs to tell me . . . I know."

Chapter 7

NALIN uttered a war whoop, leaping in the air for pure joy as she raced back to her lodge to fetch her things.

"Mother, Mother," she cried, grabbing Toppasannah around the waist and swinging her in a circle. Ann Baumann looked up from scraping a buffalo a hide. She was learning more Comanche as the months passed, and Nalin's stock of English improved steadily, but still the girl refused to sit for lessons if she wasn't forced to do so by Manatah's gruff, no-nonsense stare. Ann had tried several times but had been unable to learn the girl's given name. No questions about parents or where she had come from had ever been answered.

"I'm going with them! I'm going with Father. . . . Father sent me for my things. I'm going! I'm going!" The half-grown girl danced in glee.

Toppasannah tried to smile happily, but the effort fell short. Nalin noticed her mother's sadness. "Don't worry, Mother. It's only a buffalo hunt. I only get to hold the horses with Broken Hand." She paused, sneering disdainfully. "Pecos gets to hunt with the men."

"Pecos is older," Toppasannah reminded, helping the girl gather what she would need for several days away.

"I know." Her nose screwed up briefly. "But I'm a better shot than he is. I hit the cactus right in the center more times than he does."

"Yes, you do," her mother agreed. She had often watched the games they played, mimicking the warriors' hunts. Toppasannah had watched these games with a mixture of emotions, with amusement at her child's antics and at the same time with a lump of fear in her throat, dreading the day when the game would become reality.

Manatah had confided to her his plans for Nalin. She did not approve, yet she could not defy her husband. She tried to teach Nalin what she would need to become a wife, but the girl far preferred her father's lessons. Toppasannah had already lost one child to the dangerous buffalo hunt. She didn't know if she could stand the loss of another. Her happiness would be complete if Nalin could remain with her in the hunting-party camp instead of accompanying the warriors. Toppasannah was also going along but for a different purpose. Her place would be to stand back from the action, coming forward only when the hunt was over, circulating among the dead animals and locating by the design of the arrows those killed by her husband. For Manatah now there were fewer than there had been, and she understood her husband's reasoning that if Nalin could replace him someday then there would be more buffalo, perhaps as many as he had brought down in his prime.

She had watched, too, her daughter's relationship with the boys of the camp. Though they liked her immensely, she was one of them. A white girl would be a prize any man might envy, but few would want Nalin for a wife.

In the case of Toppasannah's friend, Quanah's mother, she had been desired by all for her womanly ways and the pride of possessing her white skin. The chief had married her, and she had been a good wife. Cynthia Ann Parker had been obedient, faithful, and hard-working. She had known a woman's place. Nalin did not. Toppasannah doubted any of the boys now her playmates would want her for a wife no matter how white her skin or how pretty her face, or how desirable her body became as she began to show the unmistakable signs of approaching womanhood. There seemed no other choice for the girl but to become one of the extremely rare female warriors.

Happy beyond measure, Nalin scampered back to the

warriors. Toppasannah sighed deeply as she set about preparing for her daughter as she would have for a son.

Pecos rode beside her, chattering excitedly about their coming adventures, but Nalin hardly paid attention to him. Her gaze was locked on the tall, broad back in front of her, and the head with hair that shone sable in the sunlight rather than blue-black. His color was only slightly lighter than those around him, yet she would recognize that back from among all the others without a trace of doubt. He was five riders ahead of her, yet she kept her horse centered behind his, closer than to her father's on the right.

For the hunt the braves had stripped down to breechclouts and moccasins, sheath knives tucked into their belts. Many of the hunters carried repeating rifles, bought or stolen from the settlers. Though Quanah owned several rifles, he preferred to hunt as his ancestors had done. He carried only a short lance and a three-foot bow with a quiver of twenty iron-tipped arrows. He would decide which to use when they sighted their prey. Then he would dismount from the black and white horse he now rode and mount the back of a magnificent Appaloosa gelding that he led in reserve as his favorite buffalo horse.

A warrior employed several horses in various capacities. Almost without exception, each warrior rode one animal in daily use and then switched to the favored buffalo horse when the game was located. The buffalo horse had to be the finest animal their husbandry could breed. He had to be able to hold steady through a stalk and stay calm through the screeching and gunfire as they rode to their quarry. He had to be fast enough to overtake a stampeding herd and strong enough to cover miles of terrain at a gallop. The buffalo horse had to be brave enough to plunge into the pack of slashing horns and nimble enough to avoid injury. In return this prized animal was hand fed and groomed and fussed over with more care and affection than a warrior often gave his wife. He was accorded the honor of bearing no burdens or packs or riders until his special services were required. Thus

Quanah led this horse behind him by a short rope, as did the others, with the exception of those unfortunates too poor to own more than a single horse.

Quanah, due to his prowess in horse stealing from whites and neighboring tribes, had a large herd already, though he was only twenty. The pinto he rode and the Appaloosa he led were his favorites.

Nalin's place on the hunt now that she had attained the age of fourteen winters would be to hold her father's horse while he rode off on his buffalo horse and to guard any of her father's equipment he was not using.

After several miles, the scouts returned with news of buffalo. Nearing the herd, the warriors paused to change their mounts.

Manatah handed her the reins of his everyday horse, carrying his rifle and only a quiver of arrows to mark his kills for Toppasannah. Nalin had no more to do than hold the spare gelding next to her own Blackie and watch from the hillside. She was peering down at the herd of about fifty buffalo below, grazing peacefully on the lush grass. Even in her memory, the bison herds had once been larger.

She sensed someone behind her and turned. She was rooted to the spot in awe as Quanah stopped before her.

"Nalin, will you watch my horse for me?" She couldn't find her voice to speak and only nodded. Previously Pecos had always watched Quanah's belongings, but now he was old enough to join the hunt. She would have expected Quanah to choose from among the other boys, surely one of his own half-brothers, for to hold a warrior's horse was no small responsibility. It was a token of trust that the holder was sufficiently matured to handle the horse if it should shy or become excited. A holder who allowed his charge to break free lost face with all.

Choosing the bow and arrow, Quanah also held his lance out to her. "Will you take this also?"

Again Nalin only nodded, taking the weapon from him. As he turned away to mount the Appaloosa, Nalin was half inclined to leap into the air with a shout, but she couldn't move. To do so would have been awful, for she would have startled the buffalo as well as the horses and stampeded the whole lot. She couldn't have in any case. Her arms had lost their power and could barely hold on to the three sets of reins and Quanah's lance. *His* lance! He gave me his lance to hold! Normally she would have set her father's extra weapon down on the ground at her feet, but not Quanah's. It would never touch the ground while she had charge of it.

Hugging the lance, Nalin watched from her hillside perch as the hunters began in two columns, converging at a gallop on the massive prey. They shrieked, waving their arms to turn the lead buffalo back into the herd, and, with the animals swirling in circles, the warriors rode around them firing rifles and arrows with deadly speed and accuracy. Clouds of dust rose over the melee as the braves charged into the pack of frightened bison, which lashed out with their horns.

Nalin held her breath when she saw Pecos fall as his horse was gashed. In pain, the wounded animal fled away from the herd, but Pecos remembered to hold on to the trailing length of rope attached to the horse's head for just such emergencies. He let his full weight drag on the rope, slowing the panicked horse until he could pull himself back on top. She smiled, wishing Quanah could see his brother's bravery as the young warrior brought his injured horse under control and charged back into the fight. Later, she decided, she would ask Toppasannah for ointments and help him tend the animal.

The hunt was successful, and bellies would be full for some time to come, Nalin was just thinking, when the lead bull charged through the surrounding Indians, goring a horse to the ground and trampling a fallen warrior. The remainder of the herd followed the bull's lead, making a break for the hole in the circle. The pounding of their hooves echoed like approaching thunder as the lead buffalo stampeded the herd straight up the hill, racing in terror for the very spot where the youngest warriors waited with the spare horses.

Nalin knew she had only bare seconds in which to act. At least thirty terrified bison were heading toward her at top speed. Already panicked watchers had raced for the sidelines, making way for the buffalo at all costs, dropping reins, forgetting weapons as they fled.

Nalin dropped Blackie's reins, certain that the loyal horse would follow. She sprang on Quanah's pinto, knowing him to be faster than the other two, and held on tight to the reins of her father's horse as she dug her heels into the pinto's sides, galloping for the closest area of safety. A huge buffalo's head passed the pinto's flank by mere inches. She pulled the pinto to a halt and waited for her heart to stop pounding before assessing her performance. She had saved Quanah's horse from harm as well as her father's. Blackie, his nostrils flaring from the excitement, pranced about her. She had done well, lost nothing, except— She looked down at her lap in dismay. Quanah's lance was missing. He had entrusted it to her care, and it was gone, probably broken into small pieces beneath the bisons' powerful hooves. She fought back tears—she would not add that weakness to her failure.

She was still bemoaning the lost lance when a group of warriors gathered about her, racing circles around her and the horses she held, war-whooping her name in praise. Quanah rode through the group and reined in beside her, jumping to the ground in an easy leap. His strong arms came up and grabbed her waist, lifting her off the pinto and swinging her around in a circle before setting her down. "You did well," he beamed, smiling broadly. "I am proud to call you friend."

"Quanah, I . . . I lost your lance." Her chin trembled.

"Foolish girl." His eyes lit with amusement. "You saved more than all the others did." He pointed beyond the crowd of warriors. The braves' spare horses were scattered everywhere, the boys responsible for them running on foot to catch them. All of them had lost the weapons they were charged with and had deserted the horses as well. "You will be a fine warrior," he assured her, still smiling. "I will be honored when you ride beside me."

Nalin's heart pounded even faster than during her fright, and her knees felt suddenly weak and wobbly. She couldn't believe that Quanah was praising her. He gripped her waist again and set her back on the pinto. "He is yours, young Nalin. You have earned him. Warriors need more than a single horse. Let the pinto carry you home; the black one should be your war horse."

Nalin rode back to the hunting camp on Quanah's prized pinto like a warrior, back straight and proud. That night, Toppasannah did not even ask that she help with the slain buffalo.

After Nalin's feats on the buffalo hunt, Manatah could well understand why Quanah wished to take her. Though only fourteen she showed far more maturity and dependability than any of the boys her own age. Even Nacoma, chief of the Kwahadi Comanche, had spoken of it, twice praising her before the other warriors. Small wonder that Quanah should ask for her company on this quest.

The day before, when they made camp by the river, Quanah had seen a herd of wild mustang that contained a white stallion, young and full of spirit. He wished to breed it to his growing herd of mares. This one would not be used as a war horse, though certainly he would be capable. A stallion was too skittish to be trusted in battle, and this was too fine an animal to geld.

Quanah was an excellent judge of horseflesh. He was also, as Manatah well knew, a level-headed young man, several times having led raiding parties safely to victory. For a man so capable of leadership it was strange that he preferred to walk alone. To find the white stallion Quanah wished to take only one helper, Nalin.

Manatah was sure Quanah had earned his manhood somewhere along the line in twenty years; he was a much-sought-after bachelor, and any maids who had tried to win his heart in that manner would not be betrayed by the close-mouthed warrior. Manatah was certain that Nalin was only a child in the young man's eyes; a gifted, capable child, but she still looked like a boy. Manatah would have no fear if Nalin accompanied Quanah. Seduction of the fourteen-, nearly fifteen-year-old, would be far from Quanah's mind. He could be well trusted with the sub-chief's daughter. Manatah would not even ask for

Quanah's word that his daughter's chastity would not be violated. Knowledge of Quanah's reputation would be enough. Had Quanah been less than the honorable man he was or had Nalin been older, perhaps rounder, than she was, he would never have considered it.

"She may go with you," Manatah agreed solemnly, tapping his everyday pipe on a rock to empty its smoldering contents. The action also signaled the conclusion of the interview. Quanah required no more prodding than this action. He quickly rose to his feet, bid his thanks and farewells, and left without as much as a glance in Nalin's direction. As for Nalin, her adoring gaze fastened on the closed flap of the lodge entrance long after the warrior had departed.

Nalin was utterly content and at one with her universe; her universe was centered on the tall brave who rode slightly ahead of her through the woods. For most of the journey she saw only his back; she had memorized every contour, fervently wishing this excursion could last forever. Most of the time they were silent, Nalin's usually lively tongue stilled by his awe-inspiring presence. Every so often he seemed to feel obligated to say something to her, if only to acknowledge her presence. Usually it was only a comment on a certain bush they passed that had medicinal properties for healing a wound should she ever need it. Quanah spent much of his time with the medicine man and liked to share his knowledge. Many of his comments addressed facts that any novice brave should become familiar with.

"How *do* the hunters always know where the buffalo will be?" she asked.

"Our friends tell us." Quanah slowed his horse slightly to let her ride beside him. At her puzzled expression he pointed to the sky where a raven was circling, its wings spread wide to ride the air currents. "When the raven circles our camp four times then flies away, we watch the direction he takes, for he will always take us to the buffalo."

Nalin had seen Red Eagle Feather, the Kwahadi medicine man, do this many times, watch the animals and the skies and the earth for signs the spirits were showing him. Red Eagle Feather had once cured her of an awful rash, one that made her itch crazily until she thought she would lose her mind. His smelly ointment had worked, and her father had paid him one fine mare from his herd for the service. She had no doubts from then on about the medicine man's powers. "But sometimes the raven does not come."

"When our friend the raven does not come, then other of our animal friends will show us the way. The horned toad, if we ask him, will run away in the direction buffalo can be found."

For the Great Plains Indians it worked. When the method failed to produce the desired result, then it had to be the fault of men who had neglected some part of the ritual, or had dishonored or aroused the wrath of some spirit that had therefore punished them. As close as they lived to the nature around them, at the mercy of drought, flood, starvation, or many other natural occurrences that could threaten disaster, it was only sensible to appease all of the forces they did not understand. Spirits were everywhere. They lived in the sun and in the earth, in thunderstorms and in rainbows. Each river, each hill, had its own spirit within it, as did every creature upon the earth. The spirits had powers to grant success in hunting or war. They protected the young and the old, and they healed the sick. Nalin had learned much of this already. She had learned the significance of the number four, present in so many of their ceremonies. Four corresponded to the four primary directions, north, south, east, and west, and was very powerful. She had learned the reasons for the dances and to which spirits they appealed. She had learned the taboos and how to atone for them.

Quanah believed in the faith of his ancestors, as did Nalin. Manatah had taught her most of it, yet he always punctuated his explanations with "they say" and "people believe," never quite admitting that he accepted all this for himself. Father belonged to the Kaitsenko, the Society of the Ten Bravest, and was therefore known to be a deeply religious man, but he never spoke of his faith as openly as Quanah did. Father never forgot the daily offering to the earth spirit, cutting off a tiny morsel of his food and burying it in the ground to appease the earth spirit and bring bounty back to the tribe. Quanah, she learned as she traveled with him, never forgot it either, nor did he ever forget that the spirits had given this land and its bounty to the people, entrusting them with its proper care.

Sometimes, as they followed the trail of the white horse, Quanah would ask her about the sacred beliefs of the whites, but Nalin could not readily answer him. What she had learned of God and spirits had become as dim as the white language in her own mind. There was some Great Spirit over all who created the world and all things in it, but about lesser spirits she couldn't quite recall. There was something about a place called heaven that corresponded roughly to the Indian belief in a spirit world for the departed ancestors, where people went about daily lives much as they did here on earth. About hell she remembered fire and brimstone and that it sounded at least as bad as the Indian notion of bad spirits condemned to walk the earth alone forever.

On the third day of their outing Quanah finally saw the white stallion. He was fat in the late summer from too much grazing, just as Quanah had hoped. He would be easy to catch.

Nalin had been part of wild horse captures before and needed no further instruction. Since they were after only one horse, she and Quanah would face the white mustang alone.

Quanah waited until the hot afternoon sun forced the horses to water at the river. He watched from the concealment of high grass until the white one had bloated his stomach with water, then Quanah mounted his horse and began the chase. The white horse sprinted for the first fifteen or twenty minutes, then began to slow from the extra weight in water and body fat. The horses were territorial, having chosen this site as their own for as long as the sweet grass lasted, so the stallion, though he ran like the wind, continued to run in a miles-wide circle, always returning to his territory and his mares. After many circlings, Quanah gave Nalin the hand signal that told her to take his place. Watching for it, she took off at once on Blackie, giving the white horse no time to pause for breath as she took Quanah's place. For several hours they ran after the stallion in relays, wearing him down until at last Quanah threw his lasso about the horse's neck and brought him down.

The white one was half-trained before they started back to camp. Quanah tied him to an old mare they had brought along for that purpose and let the steady horse teach him by her manner that there was nothing to fear. Before setting out he had taken the stallion into the river until the water reached the horse's chest, then mounted him. The soft silt on the riverbed and the water's buoyancy made it harder for the mustang to buck, and when he did, Quanah's landings were softer.

With Quanah leading the mare, who in turn led the mustang, they at last set out for home.

About to make camp on the second night after capturing the white horse, Nalin was the first to hear voices rising from the far side of the bluff. She touched Quanah's arm to attract his attention then pointed to the bluff. Together they crept closer, until they could see over the rise without being seen. It was a Tankawa band of five warriors making camp for the night. Hands and feet tied together, a single brave was dropped on the ground near the camp fire they were making. The man was still alive, though he wouldn't be for long if the Tankawa had their way. Before very long the trussed-up brave would be their dinner. Quanah's immediate urge was to do something, anything, to try to help the captured warrior, whoever or whatever tribe the man belonged to. The Comanche despised the cannibal Tankawa, as did most of the Indian nations of the Plain. If Quanah had had a raiding party with him, the man-eaters would have been caught alive and tortured to death for their despicable crimes. But

Quanah had only Nalin, and he had guaranteed her safety to Manatah. She was capable as a hunter but had never been tried as a warrior. He couldn't take that chance with her life. Neither could he permit the Tankawa to get away with their plans. Nalin had assessed the situation as he had, recognizing the bound man's plight. Her expectant face gazed up at him, waiting for his plan.

"We are only two against five," he whispered.

"Are not two Comanche better than five Tankawa?" she whispered back.

He stared at her, wondering if she could accomplish the dangerous plan forming in his mind. Nalin was steady, brave, and sensible, when she did not try overhard to please—which she very likely could. There was an abundance of brush and trees near the Tankawa camp site below them. Quanah pointed to a Tankawa warrior gathering sticks for the fire a bit far off from the others. "Keep close to the shrub line." Quanah spoke softly near her ear. "Come around behind him and wait until you are sure he and you cannot be seen by the others. Do not wrestle with him for he will call out. Use your knife quickly and well. Strike here or here." He showed her two fatal places on his own body. "And plunge deeply. Can you do that?"

Nalin had never killed a man before. Her gaze shifted to the Tankawa she was assigned to assassinate.

"If you cannot, tell me now. There will be no shame."

Her head turned to look at the captured brave stoically awaiting his own horrible death. "I can, Quanah. I will not fail you."

"When you finish with him, I will have attacked from the other side. Be careful, but come forward and cut the ropes of the captive so he can help me."

Nalin nodded, then on his signal to start she crept down the hill, keeping close to the boulders and bushes. As she neared the wooded area where the Tankawa warrior had disappeared, she took her knife from its sheath. Quanah had already taught her to walk lightly on the balls of her feet, and to pass in silence; she remembered well the rules of stalking, though her skills had only been used for play and for hunting. This time her quarry was a man, a human being, even if he was a hated Tankawa.

Her assigned target was wearing a dark blue jacket, hard to see in the gathering darkness of nightfall. Either he had taken the jacket from a fallen soldier or else, like many Tankawas, he worked for the Army as a scout and translator. Indians of other tribes did not tell the white soldiers that the guides they often hired were cannibals. Let the whites learn of it for themselves.

Remembering their preference for human flesh made it easier for Nalin to follow her purpose. She finally located him by the flash of his silver buttons in the last gleam of the setting sun. Waiting until his back was turned, his arms full of the sticks he had gathered, Nalin moved forward, quickly putting the blade of her knife against his throat, then jerking backward. Warm blood gushed over her hand, and a gurgling sound in the severed windpipe made her suddenly sick to her stomach. She released her grip and the Tankawa fell forward, flat on his stomach, unable to cry out or even moan. In seconds he was dead. Nalin felt an irresistible impulse to vomit, but she fought the rising bile in her throat. She had done just as Quanah had asked her to, killed him efficiently and silently. She was now more than a girl who played at boys' games, more than a hunter—she was a warrior. Proudly she straightened her shoulders, ordered her stomach to be still, and set forward on the next part of her task.

Quanah had attacked from the far side, emitting a blood-curdling yell to divert their attention from her as he leapt the nearest Tankawa and plunged his knife into the shocked man's chest. While they were diverted, Nalin rushed to the captive and cut his bonds. The warrior was on his feet instantly, attacking the closest Tankawa with his bare hands.

Nalin gained her second coup as a recovered Tankawa aimed a rifle at the released captive. She plunged her knife into his back between the ribs, and he sprawled forward. By then the fight was over. Quanah had slain two, Nalin had slain two, and the prisoner had strangled the last one.

The brave they had saved was a Kiowa called Satanta, or White Bear. They left the Tankawa bodies to be plucked clean by the prairie scavengers as the Tankawa would have left the remains of Satanta. Sharing a small deer Quanah had brought down earlier, the new friends ate and shared jokes and conversation, then parted when the sun rose, promising close friendship. Satanta, a bit older than Quanah, was a Kiowa sub-chief and swore the aid of his people if Quanah ever needed him.

Returning to the Kwahadi with the mustang and news of their small war, Nalin was allowed to be present in the warriors' lodge when the coups were recounted. As one of them now, she stood slightly behind Quanah by her own choice and listened as he told them of her part in the adventures as he would never have bragged of his own deeds, feeling at last a full part of his raiding party.

Chapter 8

ALMOST two years later, Nalin crept silently behind Quanah, her moccasined feet making no sound on the ground. She could barely see his shadowy form as he moved stealthily from bush to bush under the sliver of moonlight from a cloudless sky. At this moment she was honored in her estimation above any of the others. Quanah led this raid, and he had especially sought out her father's permission to take her. Though she was now just sixteen, she had grown rapidly in both size and experience. A warrior with several coups to her credit after her success in the Tankawa attack, she was entrusted with more responsibility than others her same age. She had begun to follow the warriors of the Kwahadi band on every hunt and almost every raid of other Indian camps, and she was becoming quite proficient at each assigned task. If other Comanche bands made so bold as to laugh at Kwahadi warriors for having a woman among them they were soon silenced by a challenge to race—if she didn't win every time it was always close enough to prove her worth.

And she was becoming a woman now by almost every qualification. Her straight up and down body had rounded into soft curves. The hips were still in the process of widening; her waist was small and trim. Her pert breasts were almost but not quite as large as they would ever be. Nalin's face had started to lose the chubbiness of youth and showed promise of great beauty to come. Her green eyes had become even larger and more luminous, and her hair had darkened to a deep auburn that glowed with strawberry highlights.

Only one thing had failed to occur yet, and that was a source of fretful impatience to her. Her menstruations had not yet begun. Girls younger than she had already started, and until Nalin did, technically she was not yet a woman. Though her mother assured her the menses would soon start, Nalin continued to worry. She would not be courted until they came, since all would consider her still only a girl.

At the moment, however, her mind was far from the state of her body. In fact, she had been ignoring the slight cramping pain in her lower abdomen. Quanah signaled her to come up beside him. He pointed at certain staked horses from the group grazing in the darkness. Her eyes were not as sharp as Quanah's; he was more accustomed to staging raids on nearly moonless nights. She could barely make out the darkest horses, but she nodded assurance that she understood which of them she was to take.

Quanah moved off to the right as she moved left. Drawing her knife from her belt she approached the first horse and held out her free hand for him to sniff so he wouldn't be startled. She patted his neck, then moved her hand downward to the rope that tied him. She cut it and moved on to the next staked horse, continuing the procedure until she had freed the five horses assigned to her and held them by the cut ropes.

She led them to the place where Quanah had told her to meet him. She mounted Blackie and waited. Soon Pecos and Running Deer joined her, leading several more Ute horses. Others from the Comanche raiding party began to gather at the meeting place, but not Quanah. She couldn't see him but could well guess what he was up to. Quanah led this group of raiders because of the cunning he had shown repeatedly during the raids of other tribes and white settlements. Quanah would be going after the most prized horses, not those staked out on the outside of the Ute hunting party's camp but the well-trained buffalo horses they kept nearby. While the Ute braves snored on the ground, each holding the end of his favorite horse's lead in his hand, Quanah would creep past the posted sentries or perhaps bash them into slumber from behind. Then he would inch his way to the sleeping braves and cut the tethers without awakening the sleepers. Few had the daring to attempt it, much less the skill to succeed.

The insult to the warriors who lost their mounts would prove the Comanche reigned supreme here. The Ute might retaliate by staging a raid against the Comanche, but that was their right.

The ground both groups occupied happened to be within Cheyenne territory, but neither side would worry overmuch about that technicality. The Plains Indians wandered at will from far north to far south, ignoring borders the white men set up and only stopping in any direction when challenged by superior forces. For the Comanche, especially the numerous Kwahadi, that rarely occurred. They had been at peace with the Kiowa for generations, and they usually honored the pacts of friendship made five years before Quanah's birth with the Cheyenne and Arapaho, but everyone else was fair game. The Comanche had ranged all the way to the Rockies and down into Mexico so far that they reported having seen tiny men with tails and birds of colorful plumage. There weren't many who could stop them, and the only standoff in recent years had been against the Texans, who were, surprisingly, as aggressive as they themselves were. To steal Ute horses, however, was considerd child's play. Then why was Quanah taking so long? Worried glances began to pass from one face to another as they awaited their leader's return.

The shrill war cry they had been waiting for finally broke the silence; it was followed instantly by the pounding of hooves in the Ute camp. A dozen horses came over the rise, their severed lead ropes dangling as they ran. Behind them Quanah, on a stolen horse, was warwhooping them on, waving his arms to spook them forward. His band of warriors galloped after him, driving their own loot in with his and shouting obscenities over their shoulders at the hapless Ute who pursued futilely on foot. Arrows and bullets began to whiz over the Comanche heads, and the fleeing warriors still laughed, mocking their victims. Running Deer fell, his shoulder pierced by a Ute arrow. Quanah spun around, and, as he passed, the wounded brave leapt on in back of him. As they rode away, Running Deer turned about from the back of Quanah's mount to make faces at the Ute.

Their venture had been profitable, twenty horses gained and no losses suffered. Running Deer's wound was not serious; the arrow had pierced no vital spots. It was painful, but would soon heal.

Cheerful but weary as they returned to their own war camp, Nalin wondered why she was so extremely tired. Now as they prepared for sleep at their own camping spot she was more painfully aware of the distress in her lower abdomen and thought with disgust that this was a fine time to come down with a stomach ailment.

She passed the warriors gathered about in a group, congratulating themselves and each other and praising Quanah, rehashing over and over what had just occurred. Usually she joined them, but this time they got on her nerves, and she only wanted to ignore them and sleep.

Even if Quanah himself ordered her to sentry duty tonight she wouldn't be able to do it, she decided as she leaned over to roll out her sleeping mat. She flopped down on top of it, not even bothering to unfold her blanket.

"Nalin."

She heard Quanah's voice and for once was not at all glad to hear it. Wearily she forced her eyes open. "Quanah, I can't watch the camp tonight. . . . I can't trust myself to stay awake."

"Were you wounded, Nalin?" He knelt beside her, his handsome face creased with concern.

"No." She shook her head for emphasis.

"Are you certain you were not injured?"

"Yes, Quanah, I am certain." She had planned but now was reluctant to tell him about the stomach pains. She was absolutely certain she was not injured. "Why?"

Quanah stared at her silently for a moment, then broke

into an amused grin. "Because, Nalin, your backside is covered with blood."

"Oh!" Nalin shot up to a sitting position, her face turning quite pale before she blushed crimson at the sight of the many warriors watching her with amused grins. She jumped up, grabbed her blanket, and darted into the high grass, accompanied by the sound of their laughter. Quanah barked a harsh command for them to be silent.

Angry and burning with embarrassment she stomped to the spring where they had watered the horses. She ripped the soiled robe over her head, making out the dark stain across the bottom of the skirt even in the darkness. She plunged the dress into the water, scrubbing the stain furiously. She was angry with them all, every last one of them, for laughing at her. Even Quanah, especially Quanah, for telling her in front of them. It had not yet occurred to her that probably one of the others had first noticed and pointed the fact out to him.

This day should have been a happy one; she was at last a mature woman. Instead hot tears were spilling down her cheeks and dropping into the black water. Finished with a scrub that was meant to brush the soft buckskin shiny, she wrung the robe out and spread it over a bush to dry.

Normally at a time like this, her father would have been told of the occurrence and would have gone out to proclaim her new womanhood; thus all the bachelors would know she was of suitable age to court. His announcement would hardly be necessary now, she thought with a frown, striding out into the cold water to wash herself.

As Nalin stepped into the spring-fed pond, she couldn't see Quanah coming up behind her. He had come to apologize for her embarrassment and to convince her to come back among them. Instead, hesitantly, he watched the naked body glide into the water. He had never seen the soft curves her body had taken beneath the shapeless robe. He had suspected but had never quite known how arousing they might be. Where the robe protected her from the sun, her skin was pale white, smooth, and soft as calfskin. For a long while Quanah had been carefully observant of Nalin's growing beauty, watching without seeming to as the child grew into a woman. To some, Nalin's beauty would be overshadowed by her manner, but he knew that he was not the only one who saw her as far more than another warrior. Others too desired her, and only until now had they been held back from speaking. From among all the women he had seen, Nalin was the most desirable. Though several maidens had made clear their willingness for him to court them, he had avoided their advances, waiting for Nalin.

As she came out, her light skin glistening, Quanah retreated farther into the darkness so she would not know he had seen her. Still smarting from her embarrassment and with her robe still wet, she curled up in the blanket to sleep by the edge of the water.

She was slightly too far away from the warriors to suit him. He returned to the camp fire for his own blanket. "Nalin sleeps tonight by the pond," he told the nearest sentry while the others slept. "She is to take no watch tonight. I will be near her. Wake me for my turn."

The sentry nodded, and Quanah crept back. Silently he laid his own blanket down ten yards away, close enough if she needed him, far enough to avoid waking her near dawn when his own watch began.

"Mother, how can I make Quanah notice me?" whined Nalin, pouting heavily.

"He does notice you. Does he not ask for you each time he goes out?" Toppasannah regarded her daughter, who was huddled in a blanket. The raiding party had returned late the previous night, an uncomfortable day-long ride the day before for Nalin, and this morning her robe was not warm enough. The girl's lips were slightly bluish, and her body trembled with cold chills though the new spring day was warming the air pleasantly. "You should not have bathed yourself in the cold water, especially at this time. Washed yes, but . . ." Toppasannah frowned, returning her attention to the brew she was concocting for Nalin. The lining of a buffalo's stomach was tied to four upright sticks beside the coals of the breakfast fire, its center drooping enough to hold the water and the various herbs Toppasannah had added to it. Holding them with sticks, she dropped fist-sized hot rocks into the mixture to heat it.

"But I want Quanah to notice me as a woman, not as a warrior." Nalin fell to her knees, then leaned backward, resting on her calves. Toppasannah did not answer, drawing some of the broth out with a ladle made of buffalo horn and handing it to her. Nalin's nose wrinkled. "That smells awful."

"It will help to warm you and ease the pain in your stomach."

"And probably heal the cut on my toe as well." Nalin scowled at her mother's cure-all brew.

"Yes." Toppasannah smiled. "Now drink it."

Her whole face screwed up as she gingerly tasted the hot mixture. "It tastes worse than it smells," she complained loudly.

"Warrior or not, you do as your mother tells you. Now drink it."

Nalin gulped the contents down as fast as the mixture's heat would allow, her face wrinkling distastefully throughout the procedure. "Eeeyuk." She handed the ladle back. The brew was already spreading its warmth through her body, but Nalin wasn't about to admit it. Toppasannah always felt that if one did good, two would do better, and she wanted no more of that stuff. Her mother's cooking skills were exceptional, but Nalin wondered where she had learned that awful recipe.

"As to Quanah." Toppasannah was ready to reply now. "Do you want him to court you?"

"Yes," Nalin answered quickly.

"Then you must, perhaps, change your ways. You cannot expect a man to consider a wife who knows only how to ride and hunt. They look for wives who can prepare their lodges—"

"I can do that." Nalin jumped up eagerly.

Toppasannah narrowed her eyes at her. "Can you tan the hides?"

Reluctantly Nalin shook her head. "I can cook."

"Some," Toppasannah agreed. "And you can sew a little. But do you know where the roots grow? Can you find herbs that heal or only those that poison?"

Nalin's head lowered shamefully. "You're right. No one would want me." Toppasannah's warrior daughter was about to cry.

"Perhaps it can be remedied." She patted her daughter's knee. "You can learn these things."

"Now?" Nalin screeched. "I'll be old and gray before I learn all those things. Quanah will marry another, and I will die alone and unwed."

"Perhaps not," Toppasannah consoled, though her daughter had said exactly what she feared most. No young warrior would station himself in her path to speak with her. None would call at their lodge to visit or ask her to walk out with him, making clear his intentions. There would be no one to ask Manatah for her hand in marriage after a suitable time. Toppasannah could think of no words to comfort her. "Are you better now?" she finally asked. Nalin nodded. "Would you fetch water for me?"

Again she answered with a slow, despondent nod as she rose to her feet and soberly set off for the riverbank, her mother's water pouches slung over her shoulder. Each morning that Nalin was not away with the warriors she went soon after breakfast to refill her mother's water supply. Her step most mornings was brisk and spritely. This morning one foot trod slowly after the other, her gaze fastened on the ground. Thus she did not notice Little Eagle until he came up by her side.

"Nalin, are you going for water?" Little Eagle stepped up beside her. He was Pecos's age, eighteen, and often rode in Quanah's band. He was becoming a handsome young man.

"No, I'm going out to the desert to fill the skins with dirt," she answered grouchily.

He gazed sideways at her, sheepish. "May I walk with you, Nalin?"

She stopped still in her tracks, turning to look at him with a puzzled frown. "Why?"

He misread the question and wasn't sure what he had done wrong. "I just wanted to go with you. May I?" he asked again hopefully.

She continued staring at him, quite unable to believe her senses. Young men did not ask to accompany young women unless they were interested. Little Eagle's offer was the first step a young man made in courting. He would wait along the path for his intended to pass, hoping she would allow him to join her. Little Eagle wishing to court her? Impossible! He rode in Quanah's band with her; they all knew what a terrible wife she would be.

"May I?" Little Eagle prodded.

"Well, um, yes." She nodded, still not certain this was really happening. Five minutes ago she was sure she would die an old maid. Of course none of them would have courted her before she became a woman, but Manatah had not even announced it yet, and here was Little Eagle by her side already. He would be a good catch for any maid, a good hunter, a brave fighter, and from a good family. He would make a fine husband. Yet her thoughts strayed back to Quanah. She could not think of marrying any man while her heart belonged to him. For years now he had been her idol, her dream. Each time he had spoken to her was engraved on her memory. Certainly he was different from the rest, intense, serious, and driven, yet these were all parts of why she loved him so dearly. She gloried in the knowledge that he asked for her when he led the bands out to forage, but that he would ever consider her as other than a warrior was beyond her wildest hope. Quanah was the best catch in the Kwahadi camp, son of a chief and a sub-chief himself. He was rich, too, independently of his father's wealth. Quanah already had more horses than many of the chiefs. Any maid in the Comanche nation would be honored to be his first wife.

She glanced at Little Eagle. It would be unfair to allow him to believe he had a chance. She might die unwed, but she could belong to no other. "Little Eagle," she began, but he was looking up the path ahead of them with the same intent look he wore when he did not like the odds on a raid. She followed his gaze, and the blood suddenly drained from her head. Quanah was near the path, leaning against an upright pole, one foot cocked back against the wood. His arms were crossed over his chest, by his stance obviously awaiting someone's arrival, and he was looking straight at them. Nalin's heart began pounding again as it always did when he was near.

"Good morning, Nalin," he greeted without smiling.

"Good morning, Quanah," she replied, pausing uncertainly in her step. He was positively glaring at Little Eagle, who was becoming increasingly discomfited. Though brave enough in battle, Little Eagle had always been a bit afraid of Quanah, anxious to please him and distraught if Quanah spoke harshly to him. If Quanah said anything to him now, Little Eagle looked like he would vanish so fast he wouldn't disturb the dirt in the path.

Still glaring at Little Eagle, Quanah straightened, his crossed arms coming down to his sides. "I was waiting to join you, but I see you already have company."

Little Eagle looked sick as Quanah turned away and stalked off. Nalin swore silently, wishing she had the power to make Little Eagle disappear. Instead she started out again beside him. A short while ago she had no hopes, and now she had two suitors, one of them Quanah himself. She had to walk demurely by Little Eagle's side, yet she couldn't help glancing back over her shoulder, worried and dreading the thought that Quanah might not try again. Her fears evaporated as she caught sight of him. He, too, had glanced back, meeting her gaze, and he smiled.

On the following morning Nalin dressed carefully, selecting her best robe, the one with a long fringe and many small mirrors embedded in the soft leather. She combed her hair until it gave off sparks of red and gold in the sun. She didn't braid it; instead she parted the long waves in the middle and tied them behind her ears so the loose auburn curls would catch the sunlight. Satisfied with the effect, she tied her best band around her forehead and slipped her feet into new moccasins.

"Are you sure you want to go to the river for water?" Toppasannah watched her daughter's meticulous grooming suspiciously. Nalin had mentioned nothing of Quanah's waiting for her. Toppasannah had seen Little Eagle walk her back and was very relieved and happy about the event. Let her think the care was in expectation of Little Eagle, then Nalin would not have to explain if Quanah were not there. Of course, if he were not there, she just might keep walking straight into the river.

She picked up the water skins and started off briskly, but her step slowed as she neared the turn around the final lodge that would bring her into view of the place where he had waited yesterday. She paused, fearful of taking the step that might reveal his absence. Her pulse was racing, the familiar thumping back again. With a deep breath she steeled herself for the confrontation with the dreaded place and stepped forward, hardly daring to look. He was there! Oh Mighty Great Spirit, there he was just as he had been the day before, in exactly the same position. She tried to keep her gaze off him as she walked toward him, otherwise he would know the full measure of her love for him. Mother had warned her not to seem too anxious. She forced herself to hold her gaze on the ground before her.

"Good morning, Nalin."

She looked up as though somewhat startled. "Oh, good morning, Quanah."

"I see you have no company today," he said, still leaning on the pole, arms crossed over his chest as if he had never budged since yesterday.

"No, not today," she replied with a sweet smile. The care she had used in dressing herself was not lost on him; that she had dressed this way for him made her all the more desirable. "Would you rather walk alone?" He peered down at her with a strange half smile.

Her brow creased in a slight frown. She would rather he had asked, and now he had turned the burden around on her.

"I can . . . or not," she replied haughtily. "You may come if you wish." There now, it was back in his hands again. Nalin turned away, starting toward the river.

"I will come with you." He took the water skins from her hands, then grinned at her mischievously. "I would not want you to soil your new moccasins."

Nalin blushed as Quanah stepped on ahead of her.

Toppasannah's face was beaming as she leaned back on her haunches watching Nalin approach with Quanah beside her. Nalin had walked beside Quanah before, but only in the course of business. This time it was not Quanah standing outside their lodge calling Nalin to come with the warriors. A man only walked with a woman about the tasks of domestic chores if he cared for her. Quanah set the filled skins in their places, greeting Toppasannah politely, and just as properly bid them both farewell. He was an old-fashioned warrior. He would not stay and chat as Little Eagle had done yesterday, for such was not quite proper on the first day. Quanah would court her with the respect due a chieftain's daughter. Quanah would be an excellent match for her. Toppasannah could see by the light shining in her daughter's eyes that Nalin thought so as well.

"One day Little Eagle and the next day Quanah?" Toppasannah smiled broadly. "You do well, my daughter."

Nalin giggled delightedly, dropping to the ground by her mother's side.

"While you were away, Red Fox stopped by to call on you." Toppasannah returned to pounding the dried plums for the pemmican she was making. Nalin, who had never done so before, was watching her intently.

"Red Fox, too?" The girl broke into more giggles, her eyes dancing with glee.

"Two days into your womanhood and already three suitors. I shudder to think how many braves we shall have outside our lodge in a week."

"None but one, I think, Mother." Nalin smiled.

"Do not show too quickly that he is the only one in your heart," Toppasannah warned, though she remembered the same feeling when Manatah called on her, the urge to speak only with him. It had been difficult, but she knew it was necessary to keep him guessing for a while.

"Who is Father talking to?" Nalin changed the subject to the voices she heard from inside the lodge. She had no intention of keeping Quanah in too much suspense. He might change his mind.

"White men have come to trade with him."

"White men!' Nalin jumped in horror, prepared to leap in any direction to avoid being seen.

"Do not worry, Nalin. They are outcasts from their own people."

"Outlaws?" She settled down again but warily, casting furtive gances at the tepee entrance.

"I think they have broken white men's laws. They have guns from Mexico and have offered them for sale."

Nalin leaned closer to her mother, whispering conspiratorially. "We do not have to buy them. I could tell Quanah, and we could—"

"Nalin!" Her mother looked at her sternly. "Are you to be a wife or a warrior?"

Only slightly abashed, Nalin shrugged. "Maybe both?" She grinned impishly, and Toppasannah couldn't help but laugh.

At that moment Manatah stepped outside, followed by the two white men. One was about forty, the other closer to sixty. Both were bearded and scruffy. The older one glanced down at the girl who had joined the Indian woman since he went in. Her back was to him, but he immediately noted the hair sparkling red-gold highlights in the morning sun. He had seen the golden-haired hostage

103

earlier, Nalin's tutor, who had looked at him hopefully until she realized no help would come from him. In fact, she'd be better off with the Indians than in the hands of this scruffy lot. Here she worked hard at never-ending tasks, but at least Manatah was satisfied with his one wife and left her alone. The leering stares of the old one had warned her that he would not be similarly inclined. Now his stares were on the slim back sitting out front.

"Nalin," Manatah spoke, and the girl turned. "Bring our friends their horses."

"Yes, Father," she answered in Comanche.

Sam Sutton watched her walk away. The long glimpse of her when she turned around was naggingly familiar. This one was white like the one inside the lodge but apparently had a far different status than her sister in color. *Father,* no less; Sam kept the sneer off his face. He was well satisfied with the transactions that had just taken place. He would deliver forty guns stolen from the U.S. Cavalry shipment; the Comanche would pay for them in U.S. gold they had taken from raiding a white outpost.

Sam wondered briefly about the two white women. One was a slave, probably taken full grown, but the other, to be adopted, must have been taken as a child. Then he knew where he had seen the chieftain's "daughter" before. Red hair wasn't all that common. Sure, she had grown a mite, and in all the right places from the look of her as she walked up leading the two saddled horses. Jesse's little filly had grown into a fine mare, he appraised with a practiced eye. The little bitch! She had been the cause of Jesse Sutton's death.

Ever since he had first heard what happened he had sworn to get even with her and her old man. He had gone so far as to ride into North Fork looking for both of them, and the wife, too, if it came down to it. He found when he arrived that Thompson's kid had run off, and nobody knew where she had gone. Most were convinced she must have died out in the desert. Members of the posse had followed some tracks to where they disappeared on the hard, cracked earth. Nothing for forty or fifty miles to the other

side of them. She couldn't have survived the trek. Yet ol'
man Thompson wouldn't believe that. Right after returning to North Fork he had packed up his wife and belongings, quit his job as sheriff, and gone off to work as a
U.S. Marshal for the whole territory. That way he could
earn a living while he continued the search for his daughter. Covering all of the Arizona Territory and as far east
as Texas he could go about his duties and still keep an ear
pricked for any news of a lost girl with green eyes and red
hair. Marshal Thompson thought she might have been
picked up by Indians, but he had only sought her among
the Apache, the Navaho, and the Paiute. He had probably
never considered the Comanche, who lived far northeast
of where Lisa had been lost.

And now Sam Sutton was the only white man who
knew where Lisa Thompson was. The outlaw smiled as
the girl handed him the reins. She didn't recognize him,
not one bit, but then six years in a child's life was almost
forever. He hadn't changed all that much. His hair was a
bit grayer, the paunch thicker. The only other changes
had been inside. Six years ago he would have wanted her
death in revenge—hers and Thompson's. But the past few
years had mellowed his appetites. His grief was not as
sharp as it had been. He no longer cared for the complica-
tions of murder. His draw was not as fast; rheumatism in
the shoulder from an old wound had taken care of that.
Sam could be satisfied now with watching Hank
Thompson's face when he told him his precious only child
was a Comanche squaw. He'd probably even make him
pay for the information . . . and plenty. Sam mounted his
horse and set off behind his new partner. This had been a
profitable morning.

Chapter 9

NALIN'S friends among the women were few, since
much of her time was spent with the men. One of
her close friends since childhood had been Desert Flower,
the girl she had "saved" from the wagon train, and,
through her, she had come to know Day Moon, Desert
Flower's sister who was soon to be wed. The bride was
being prepared for her coming marriage, and Nalin had
gone with them to the creekside. More warrior than
maiden, she stood apart from the rest, watching the pro-
ceedings as the girls teased the bride-to-be. She felt out of
place with her own sex and only listened from the top of
the boulder beside the bank. The girls teased that Lone
Wolf would be a hard husband to please, a stern man who
would beat Day Moon often. Nalin knew better; he was
another raid leader nearly as brave and strong as
Quanah, but not a man for a wife to fear. Poor Day Moon
had known Lone Wolf all of her life yet hardly knew him
at all. They had never spoken, and the marriage had been
arranged by his parents and hers, then decided on by the
council. Day Moon had only known of his courtship when
he left five fine horses tethered outside her father's lodge.
She was a gentle girl of nineteen summers and would accept her father's wisdom. Without sparing a thought to
her future she had taken the horses to mix them with her
father's herd.

Tiring of standing, Nalin sat down on the rock that
jutted over the water's edge, placing her bow down beside

her. Part of Nalin's reason for being here was to guard the girls, and she took the duty seriously.

"Come, join us," Desert Flower beckoned with a waving arm. Though inclined to boyish ways, Desert Flower had never taken the path of a warrior. She stood now in the fresh blue water up to her waist.

Nalin smiled and shook her head. "I am the only warrior between here and camp."

"You take it all too seriously." Desert Flower waded toward her.

"The scouts have seen cold camp fires that are not ours."

"So if they are cold then they are far away from us by now."

"Red Tepee, *your* father, asked me to guard you."

"Then guard us from here, oh protective one." Desert Flower splashed a column of water at her solemn friend. Nalin squealed, scampering to her feet.

"Come in, come in, before we pull you in." Desert Flower danced about in the water, motioning Nalin to join her. "Will you *ever* be a warrior and never learn to laugh?"

Nalin thought about it for a moment. She had promised Red Tepee, but he had only asked that she bring her weapons with her as a precaution. He had not sent her solely to guard the girls. Had the warriors truly thought there might be trouble they would have sent a party of braves to protect them. Nalin already knew too little of a woman's ways. She hoped to be Quanah's wife. Why not?

Making her decision Nalin started to unfasten her leggings. Modest, even with girls, she turned away from them to undo her robe, her gaze idly falling on a line of bushes along the bank. Something moved there and did not belong . . .

Turning back to Desert Flower she was careful to keep her voice light. "I will put my clothing back here to keep it dry, then I will join you." She picked up the leggings and her bow, barely watching the bushes while she kept her form low to the ground, hoping the hider would not see the weapon. She had only started behind the bushes when a shrill war cry broke over the sound of the girls' laughter. A small war party suddenly jumped out, seemingly from nowhere, turning the gaiety into screams of terror. Naked, the girls were yanked out of the creek and carried squirming in their captors' arms.

Nalin dove for cover, but one of the raiders saw her, and she only had time to unsheath her knife and then bury it deeply in the man's bare stomach.

By now she knew that singlehandedly she could not hope to help her friends; the only chance would be to escape to camp and warn the others. As she started running she could already see several braves from the raiding party sneaking up on the Kwahadi camp five hundred yards beyond. Nalin ran as fast as she could, screaming a warning that was suddenly stifled as she was grabbed from behind and knocked forward to the ground. Struggling furiously, she tried to break the man's grip, fighting to bring the knife into play. He squeezed her wrist, twisting it until the pain forced her to release the weapon. By now more warriors had joined him, and further effort would be in vain. One held a lance against Nalin's throat, and she stopped struggling.

The raiders hit and ran quickly, making off with several fine horses, some supplies, and the five girls who had been taken from the creekside. Nalin and her fellow captives would not know how the Comanche had faired in the quick attack. A brave had thrown her over his horse's back, holding on to her tightly as they made a quick escape, finally dumping her to the ground when they reached their own camp site.

Wordless, the five girls were left to wait in the dark, wearing ragged robes provided by their captors. The band that had stolen them spoke a language unfamiliar to them, and they did not know where they were being taken.

There were fewer raiders than she had thought, and as she gazed about she noted that there were no women among them. They had set up tepees, sloppily made but sufficient, so this was not a war party merely making camp for the night. The prospects that fact opened to her did nothing to reassure her about her status or that of the four other girls.

"Who are they?" Day Moon whispered to Nalin. "I do not recognize their symbols or their tongue."

"I do not know," Nalin whispered back, her gaze trying to pierce the darkness beyond the camp fires for some means of possible escape.

"They are not Tankawa, are they?" Little Fawn said in a tight, frightened voice, her dark eyes as wide as those of her namesake.

"No, they are not." Nalin patted the girl's hand. Neither were they Apache, nor Ute . . . in fact, she couldn't discover what they were. They did not look or speak like any nation she knew. The men were holding some kind of council at a distance from the captives, only one of them left to guard the prisoners. Nalin dismissed the idea of jumping him, for even if she could bring him down, there were the rest to contend with. She knew she could count on Desert Flower to help her, but she couldn't be sure of the others.

Finally, as the girls worried over their fate, one of the warriors stood, shouting something to another man still seated on the gound. The man said something back to him, and the first one then strode toward the captives. He stopped before them, then began a slow stroll, looking them over. He looked at Nalin carefully, and she tensed under his gaze, but he continued his walk to the end of the line. He came back part way then reached for Day Moon, yanking her to her feet. The girl screamed, trying to pull out of his grip as he started to drag her behind him.

Nalin rose to her feet, but the guard pulled her down again, almost throwing her to the ground and shouting harsh words at her. Nalin could only watch in horror as Day Moon was pulled inside a lodge, her screams suddenly muffled. Desert Flower grabbed Nalin's arm tightly, her gaze frozen on the lodge entrance where her sister had disappeared.

"I am sorry, Desert Flower," Nalin whispered.

"It is not your fault. If blame belongs to any then it is mine. I asked you to set down your weapon." She looked at Nalin, trying to smile. "It is I who should ask your forgiveness."

Another warrior strode toward them, this one the man the first brave had spoken to. He did not pause as he marched straight to Nalin, gripping her arm and yanking her to her feet.

"Leave me alone." She fought for freedom from the viselike hold. "Let me go." He yanked harder, pulling her toward another shelter. He might have thought so, but Nalin was no mere maid to be treated like a slave. She waited, beginning to yield until he pulled her inside, then she grabbed for his knife, nearly unsheathing it.

He caught her arm, twisting until she let go, then threw her roughly against the rawhide wall, nearly knocking down the entire structure. He muttered a few coarse words in his own tongue, and Nalin glared at him, waiting for a second chance.

He tried a few more words, paused, waiting, then stepped forward. "*Comantica?*" he questioned.

Nalin started in surprise at the sound of her tribe's name in her own language. Her brows lowered in puzzlement as she nodded.

"You *are* Comanche then." He had finally said something that was intelligible. Again she nodded.

The man took another step forward, then knelt before her, leaning back on his haunches. "But you are white . . . a hostage?"

Nalin shook her head, her nostrils still flaring with unspent rage. Whoever and whatever he was, he spoke fairly fluent Comanche. "I am the adopted daughter of Manatah, a chief of the Comanche," she spat viciously. "He will see you tortured to death for this."

The man laughed, fueling her anger until Nalin's jaw tightened painfully in contained fury.

"I am Iron Bar, a chief of the Crow, and you are my prize now."

"I will die first." Nalin sat up, glaring at him. "But you will die before me."

"You speak bravely." He laughed again.

"And you will learn, Iron Bar of the Crow, that I also speak the truth." The tossed-back reply stopped his laughter. "You may have your way now, but sooner or later, sometime, you must sleep . . ."

He stared at her for a moment, silently. "You carried a warrior's weapons when we found you."

"When you *stole* me," she corrected. "I did not see you increase my father's herd with my bride-price. And had I been quicker then my weapons would have found their way to your heart!"

He regarded her a moment longer then broke into a smile. "There is only one woman of red hair that would speak so bravely. You are the Woman Warrior of the Kwahadi."

Nalin's brows raised in surprise that this stranger, a Crow, from a land far north, would know her.

"Yes, Woman Warrior of the Kwahadi, even we have heard of the woman who fights like a brave man. Satanta of the Kiowa has given us your name and told us that you saved his life from Tankawa coyotes . . . You need not fear me, Warrior Woman." Iron Bar backed away to prove he meant his words. "I have no doubt that you would do as you say and though you are most desirable, I would not lose my life to take you."

"Then let us go . . ."

"That I cannot do, little one . . . For you would surely ride back for your brother warriors." The Crow got to his feet and searched in a parfleche, not daring to turn his back on her. He withdrew dried buffalo meat and offered it to her. "You must be hungry . . . . Eat."

"I cannot while my sisters are being tortured."

"You can do nothing for them, Warrior Woman."

Nalin stared at him evenly. "I will see all of you die for this."

111

"Perhaps that is so." He set the spurned jerky on top of the parfleche. "Do you not wonder why Crow are so far from our land?" He looked at her but received no reply. "The white eyes have pushed us out. They chase us from the land of our ancestors. If we will live free as men we must flee—"

"Only cowards flee. Brave men stay and fight," she dared back, realizing she was trying to provoke his anger but unable to hold her tongue.

He was not to be baited. "You Comanche have not yet seen how the white eyes come, more in number than the great herds. You yourself are white. You should know this."

Nalin shook her head slowly. "I came to the Comanche as a child. I know nothing of the whites but their tongue . . . and I would learn nothing more of them."

The warrior nodded his understanding. "Then even you do not know how many there are. The Comanche will be pushed back as we were, as the Blackfoot were, as the Sioux are being pushed back even now."

"But there is a war between them, one brother against another. A trader told us so."

"No longer, Warrior Woman," the Crow responded. "The war that was between them is ended only a moon ago. There is peace in their camps now, and soon they will seek more land again."

"The Comanche will fight them," she said quickly, then despised herself for conversing with this coyote Crow.

"You will fight as we fought, and you will lose as we lost."

"Why are you here then? Why have you come so far? Surely you do not think to stay here in Comanche lands."

"Warrior Woman, those you have seen outside are all who remain of our village. We need wives if we are to live. Or, if no one will take us into their land, then we must all die. We have spoken of this, and each of us knows it."

"If it is your wish to live in peace among us, this is not

the way to seek it. You could have spoken to our chiefs, told them you would join us to fight the bluecoats. They would have listened to you."

"We asked this, just as you say, of the Cheyenne. They attacked us, and only we escaped. The rest are dead or slaves."

"Cheyenne are not Comanche. They come in the night and slaughter women and children and old men."

The warrior gave her a puzzled frown. "I had heard there was peace between Comanche and Cheyenne."

"There is, but we do not forget Wolf Creek and what they did to our brothers, the Kiowa."

"Tell me of this." He sat down cross-legged again, ready to listen to her story.

Without realizing she was actually doing it, Nalin began the tale she had heard from the ancient storyteller. She told him of the hatred that had existed between the Cheyenne and the Kiowa, how a Kiowa band had come across a party of Cheyenne and fighting had broken out. The Cheyenne were slain to the last man. Time passed before the Cheyenne ever learned of what had happened to their brothers. In retaliation, the Cheyenne attacked a Kiowa camp, killing the women and children in an ambush. From those acts began one of the bloodiest of Indian wars, the Battle of Wolf Creek. Though years later a pact of peace was made, neither side ever entirely forgot the incident.

When Nalin finished her tale it was nearly dawn. She had survived the night unharmed, but the Crow had said he could not set them free. His men needed wives . . . and they had taken them, but what of her? He still had to settle the problem of the Warrior Woman of the Comanche.

"Nalin of the Kwahadi, I must give you a choice." Iron Bar rose to his feet again, then reached down to urge her to stand up before him. "I cannot set you free, and I would not trust you as a slave. I will ask you to be my wife."

Nalin looked at him, thunderstruck.

"I do not mean as they have taken wives." He gestured toward the tepee entrance. "For to take you as such would make you no more than my slave. I ask for you properly, to be respected and honored as my wife. I will send horses and gifts to your father to purchase you."

"I . . . I cannot."

"Then you will force me to kill you."

Nalin took a deep breath, but there was no other answer. "Do as you must, Iron Bar, for I will never be your wife."

Loud shouts outside turned both of them toward the sound. They were shouts Nalin recognized, voices she knew. The Comanche had found them! Before she could begin the shout she intended in reply, Iron Bar locked his arm about her throat.

"I am sorry that you must be my shield." He started to pull her out of the lodge into the weak dawn light. The surprise attack had already ended. Thirty or more Comanche braves swarmed through the Crow encampment, half of the Crow band already dead or dying.

Iron Bar, gripping Nalin's neck in the crook of his arm, held his dagger between her ribs. For the first time Nalin knew real fear as the sharp point cut through her robe, digging shallowly into her skin. If she dared move, he would bury it to the hilt.

Nalin heard Quanah's voice before Iron Bar turned her around to see him. He was on his war horse, his lance poised and ready to throw.

"If you come closer the Warrior Woman is dead."

All activity in the defeated camp had stopped, watching Quanah as he lowered the lance. "You have lost, Crow, release her."

"Give me a horse and a start. I will release her in the woods."

"I would not trust your word. Let her go." Quanah's horse pranced before them, heated from the battle. The Crow dodged the hooves and buried the point deeper into Nalin's flesh. She winced but would not cry out. "I *will* kill her, now!"

Quanah saw Nalin's blood staining the buckskin robe crimson. His eyes flashing with anger, he trembled in his effort to keep himself from attacking the Crow warrior. "I will give you one chance," Quanah said tightly. "Fight me, you and I alone to the death of one of us. If you win I will tell my warriors now to let you pass from us unharmed."

"How do I know that I can believe *your* word? They may kill me if I defeat you."

"It is the only chance you have, for if you harm the woman I will surely see that you take days to die."

Nalin felt his grip loosen, the knife point withdrawn. "Tell them then."

"They have heard my words." Quanah continued to glare at him. "They will obey them."

Iron Bar released her, pushing her away from him.

"Choose what weapons you will." Quanah dismounted and faced him.

"I choose tomahawks, then knives, then bare hands."

"So be it." Quanah readied himself for battle, while Nalin was forced to watch from the sidelines. She could not interfere; neither could any of the others. Quanah had given his word, and it had to be obeyed by them all.

Broken Hand came forward, handing each contestant one knife to tuck in his belt, and a tomahawk. The contest began, and Iron Bar swung the tomahawk, missing Quanah's head by inches. Instantly Quanah spun about in retaliation, his tomahawk swooshing the air past Iron Bar's ear, but the Crow's weapon still managed to find blood, digging into the flesh of Quanah's forearm. The blow was not a good one, cutting the skin but failing to cripple him.

Locked in combat, they continued with the tomahawks until Quanah lost his when Iron Bar stepped on the handle, and only reflexes spared him from the weapon, which was nearly buried in his back. He drew out his knife, and Nalin felt a bit safer; she knew how capably he handled this weapon.

Iron Bar now used both, his tomahawk in one hand, his own drawn knife in the other. He charged forward with both of them cutting the air. Quanah leapt away from the furious onslaught, jabbing with the knife, which buried itself to the hilt in Iron Bar's thigh. The Crow brave screamed in pain and rage, and, quickly, before Iron Bar could move again, Quanah struck with the knife once more, the point entering this time beneath the ribs and piercing straight into the liver. In minutes Iron Bar was dead.

The remaining Crow warriors, from their new status as prisoners, watched the brave who had defeated their leader, until the other Comanche started herding them off.

Nalin's impulse was to run to him, throw herself into his arms, whisper words of love in his ear; but to do so among the warriors would not be seemly. Instead she went to him somberly and started examining the wound, asking Day Moon, who had come up beside her, to fetch pieces of hide to wrap it and staunch the flow of blood from the forearm. Day Moon cut pieces out of the Crow's lodge, handing them to her.

Nalin held the severed flesh together and began to wrap the strips around his arm. For a moment she gazed up at him, knowing the full measure of her love must be written on her face. He met her gaze stoically, then his eyes flashed in pleasure, and he smiled.

Chapter 10

"NALIN, you are the only one I can speak to of this. I must ask you to help me."

"Help you with what?" Nalin replied, looking up at Day Moon's worried face. She had been sitting on the ground a few feet from the night camp fire, pensively alone and pondering the fact that Quanah had engaged in life-or-death combat to save her. Never had she known before that he loved her so much. He was a man of few words and even less evident emotions. What he felt, even deeply, he kept well inside him. Where others might have spoken many words of love by now, Quanah only betrayed his feelings with occasional gestures or by the fact that he was near her at all. She resented her thoughts being interrupted but tried not to show it to Day Moon, the cause of her irritation.

"You must speak to Quanah for me. Please, Nalin, speak to him and to the other warriors. I would speak for myself, but I do not know them as you do. They will listen to what you say."

"What do you want me to speak of?" Nalin queried, genuinely puzzled by Day Moon's pleading expression.

"It is the Crow brave, Spotted Face. The one who . . . who took me." Day Moon's gaze lowered in embarrassment.

"Do not worry, he shall be punished," Nalin began, but the girl grasped her arm, her face fretful. "No, that is just it. I do not want him to be punished—"

"Day Moon!"

"They will kill him! They will torture him to his death, and I do not wish for that to happen!"

"After all he has done?" Nalin cried, incredulous. "He took you only hours before your wedding—"

"That is why, Nalin, that is why I wish his life to be spared. Lone Wolf has spoken to me." The demure gaze dropped again. "He says he no longer wishes to take me as his bride . . . because of . . . what happened. Nalin, no warrior will want me now. None of our people who know what has happened. Spotted Face was . . . was not unkind to me, Nalin. He was gentle. He asked to take me as his wife though he has no horses to offer my father. He would join our people if we would allow it. He would live among us and fight our battles against any but other Crow." Day Moon's gaze rose to her friend again, searching Nalin's face for a sign of hope. "Please, tell them of this, Nalin."

"Spotted Face would be poor. He has nothing."

"Then he will work all the harder. Nalin, please . . ."

The fire crackled, sending sparks and a small billow of white smoke up against the night sky, attracting Nalin's attention briefly. "Very well, Day Moon, I shall bring your request to Quanah. If he agrees it is wise, *he* will ask the council."

Day Moon grasped her hand, too overcome for spoken gratitude, as Nalin rose to her feet.

Quanah was out in the clearing, tethering Iron Bar's horse to the ground near his own.

"Quanah, may I speak with you?"

He nodded, still busy with the horse, currying him down with a rough-edged comb of carved buffalo horn. He continued working silently, listening as she related Day Moon's request. "Do you think Day Moon's father would allow such a thing? Would the council permit such a marriage?" Nacoma was no longer part of the Council of Chiefs. He had fallen in the buffalo hunt six months past now. Through ability as well as heredity, Quanah had taken a place on the body of men who governed the tribe. His words would not carry the weight of Nacoma's until, through his exploits, he had earned enough respect to have his words heeded. As yet he was too young, still too

118

inexperienced, but his wisdom grew quickly, and they listened when he talked. He rarely did speak until he had thought his words through carefully, and he did so now, still continuing the horse's grooming as he spoke.

"I think Day Moon's father may accept her decision. Her life is her own, and perhaps she is right. If Lone Wolf rejects her so might the others, whether their judgment is wise or not. If those are truly Spotted Face's words, that he would join us, then perhaps the council would consider it."

His words stopped, but Nalin could tell he was thinking again. She waited.

"Nothing he had is his own now. Not even his horse. He will need help to start again. I will give him two horses from my herd, and I will ask Lone Wolf to help them, too. He can give them the lodge he would have shared with Day Moon, since he is the one who has broken the marriage contract."

"Would Lone Wolf do such a thing?" Nalin stood closer when Quanah's hand dropped to his side, finished with the grooming.

"He will. I shall speak to him and convince him that his generosity would be wise for him." A bare smile crossed his lips. He gave the horse a few more swipes with the comb, then patted his neck and started back to the camp. On the way he grasped her fingers, giving them a tight squeeze before letting them rest in his hand.

"Quanah," she began, troubled as she strolled beside him. "I want you to know . . . last night with the Crow, Iron Bar . . ." She could hardly force herself to continue. "N . . . nothing happened. I swear to you. He never . . . n . . . never touched me. I swear it."

Quanah stopped, taking her by the shoulders to peer at her intently. "Nalin, I know that. You need never swear to me."

"I thought you might think he . . . that it . . . that . . ."

He silenced her by drawing her tightly against him. "You were meant to be mine, Nalin," he whispered against her cheek. "I will not allow it to be any other way."

* * *

"Toppasannah, you are sure Nalin made this?" Manatah still chewed the last of the deer meat, then sat back, licking the grease from his fingers.

"It surprises you, my husband, that your daughter can cook?"

"It surprises me that it is fit to eat if she did."

"Father!" Nalin squealed in pretended indignation. She had seen the teasing gleam in his eye.

"It was good, Nalin." He smiled. She beamed back happily.

"Nalin has had a visitor every day for a week now," Toppasannah informed him as she and Nalin began to clear away the remnants of supper.

"Little Eagle again?" He gave his daughter a sideways glance. Of the three of them he was the one least surprised by his daughter's sudden popularity in spite of her being considered a warrior. Of the five girls taken by the Crow, Nalin was the only one who had come back exactly as she left the camp, which might seem to prove her destiny would be the chaste life of the very few female warriors; instead, the men were speaking of her bravery in defying the Crow leader. One of the girls had heard her threaten him with a knife in his back if he tried to violate her, and the word had passed from household to household, from mouth to mouth, many of the eligible bachelors deciding it might not be so bad to have such a brave wife.

Attitudes were changing, and women's work would not be as difficult as it had been. The buffalo were quickly disappearing, and the people would have to find other sources of food and supplies. Since these changes had been wrought by the white man, it was he who would have to pay for changing the Comanche way of life. Why tan buffalo hides when whites could provide leather and canvas? If the whites slaughtered Indian food and let the carcasses rot in the sun, then why not steal the white man's food from the herds they drove through Comanche land? Beef was not as tasty as buffalo meat, but eating it was better than starving. Manatah already had it in mind to take back an iron kettle for Toppasannah from the next wagon train they raided. The men had discussed this recently, and that was why Manatah had been commissioned to buy the rifles. Soon Red Fox, Broken Hand, and Quanah would be sent out on raiding parties all the way into southern Texas. Not that they had not raided whites plenty of times before, but their needs were becoming greater. They needed food for the coming of winter, and their usual sources had been diminished or driven away. They would not find enough buffalo to see them through the winter. If whites thought they had Indian trouble before, it was little to compare to what they would soon have.

Toppasannah had not yet answered Manatah's question, however, when she was interrupted as the tall bearer of the name she was about to mention stepped inside. As was Manatah's custom of an evening, he had left the lodge flap open for any to enter as they desired. Had the flap been closed, Quanah would have called out his presence.

Manatah completely ignored the conversation he had been having with his women, indicating that Quanah was welcome and should sit.

Quanah crossed his long legs, lowering himself to the ground, and Manatah began talking at once, telling the fellow sub-chief all about the trade made that day in the purchase of guns, for he was sure that was what Quanah had come about. He was telling him how the white outlaws had delivered as promised and didn't see his daughter's shy smile of welcome, neither did he notice that his audience of one was paying attention only to his child. Toppasannah knew but dared not interrupt her husband, so she consoled the two would-be lovers with sympathetic glances. Ann Baumann, too, sat far back in the lodge watching the pair exchange glances with each other. Nalin's English lessons were progressing admirably, her pronunciation of her mother language becoming almost perfect, since she only needed to remember forgotten words. In the interim, though, Ann had been steadily increasing her own vocabulary of Comanche, and she knew enough of the language now to realize that the young brave who had just come in was practically the only subject spoken of since Nalin's return.

Quanah, only half listening to the older man's account of how he had bested the whites in the trade, watched Nalin as she took up pieces of soft hide and stitched them together for a new robe. What a wonderful woman was this, the one he wanted for his wife. An able and trusted warrior, as brave as any man, and yet gentle and soft as a woman should be. His eyes never left her, though hers remained lowered to her work. He knew that she knew he watched her because a blush had spread over her cheeks and remained there. He loved the way her fair skin betrayed her emotions. His mother had also been fair skinned, but hers darkened in the summer sun. Nalin's never did, only reddened so the blush would remain for several days and make her itch crazily, then it would whiten and flake off in little specks like snow. His mother's hair had been golden, like Manatah's white captive's, and her eyes had been as blue as the sky above them. Nalin's tresses were coppery red, waving wispily over her breasts, while her eyes were the color of new spring grass. Never, he decided, had there been any woman like Nalin. Manatah had finished and was waiting for some comment. "You have done well, Manatah. The chiefs will be pleased."

"Um," the older man grunted, lighting his everyday pipe with a stick of burning wood. He puffed quietly for a while, wondering why Quanah remained if he wanted neither to hear more nor to engage in the conversation. His brow furrowed as he followed the young warrior's gaze that was fastened on Nalin, a slight smile on the usually somber lips. The girl had the silly, lovestruck look of a fawn on her face, big eyes gazing back at the young man. Slowly the whole thing began to dawn on him.

"Manatah, may Nalin walk with me?"

So he had found his voice at last. Manatah was pleased, but would not show it to either of them. "Nalin!" he

122

called out gruffly. The startled doe eyes turned to him. "Do you wish to walk with Quanah?"

The eyes lowered, the cheeks turning pink. "If you wish it, Father."

Manatah was impressed. Nalin of the sharp tongue did not always answer so humbly. She must care a great deal to behave so properly.

"Go then." He waved them out as though anxious to be done with them both. Quanah waited for Nalin to pass, then followed her out into the warm summer night. "Do not be long!" Manatah shouted after them. "Wife, why did you not tell me Quanah was courting Nalin?"

"When was I to tell you, my husband? While you were still talking?"

Manatah frowned. Sharp tongues must be contagious he thought.

Nalin walked silently by Quanah's side, their steps taking them to the quiet edge of the camp. Dogs barked within the village, and sounds of people laughing and talking could be heard. Children were still at play inside the lodges, while parents tried to settle them down for sleep. In the distance, wolves and coyotes could be heard faintly answering the dogs in the camp. Reaching the last rim of tepees, Quanah's pace slowed to a stroll. Nalin was content with the warm night, the thousands of stars, the bright full moon, and Quanah's presence by her side. Her knuckles brushed his wrist and sent a bolt of lightning through her. Quanah's fingers wrapped lightly around her hand.

"Nalin." He spoke at last, still walking and not looking at her. She peered at his face; it looked vaguely troubled. "Red Fox will be waiting for you tomorrow when you go to the river."

"Will he?" She paused, waiting for the effect. It came quickly. He stopped and faced her, his look questioning her silently.

"Then I shall go to the river by another way." She smiled.

123

His hands gripped her waist, drawing her a bit closer. "Then there will be no other while I am away?"

"How can there be if I am with you?"

"Nalin, I take the war party south—"

"To the settlement of the Texans, I know."

"I have never taken you on raids of the white man's lands. I would not ask you to fight your own people."

"The Comanche are my people!" Nalin retorted quickly.

"Nalin, you are white."

"I am Comanche!" Her temper flared quickly, even at him. "I am Manatah's daughter, and I am a warrior."

"You would kill a white man?" he asked slowly. "Even if he might be your true father? Would you kill the friends you knew there?" Quanah knew the whole story of Nalin's betrayal by the people of her town. She had spoken of it often enough when the warriors talked around the camp fires on the war or hunting parties. The raids she had been on had only been against other Indian tribes. She thought she wanted revenge, but Quanah did not think her hatred was strong enough to strike at her own people. He couldn't allow her to go, no matter how strong her feelings for her adopted people. Though half white himself, Quanah owed that half of his heritage nothing for having stolen his mother away and letting her die rather than returning her to the family she loved. He owed them even less for putting a bounty on buffalo in efforts to starve the Indians into submission.

Nalin did not answer him, her quick temper cooled by his logic. "Would you truly be able to kill a white man?" he prompted, drawing her closer yet.

Nalin's chin lowered to her chest, unable to answer him. Quanah's hand touched her chin and gently raised her head. His handsome face was only inches from her, and all her disappointment evaporated. She stretched to the tips of her toes, pressing her lips against his. Since she had only kissed Hank and Maureen Thompson and, once, Hugo Brady, she wasn't too good at it. Quanah's brow wrinkled questioningly. "I have seen whites do this."

"It's a kiss. A token of love."

"A white man's token." He pretended disapproval, though his smile remained.

"Did you not just remind me that I am white?"

Quanah laughed. "Then show me again. What whites can do, Comanche do better."

Quanah's war party was away for two months, returning at the beginning of autumn. Losses had been light and the expedition highly successful, as they now had food and supplies for the coming of winter. They drove in beef cattle just as the whites did, urging them forward on horseback. Quanah had made an excellent deal with a cattle drive they ran across on their homeward journey. The Comanche chieftain decided the cattle drive required his services as an escort. In exchange for his undesired protection on their trek, Quanah demanded two longhorn steer for every day of the journey. In return Quanah would let them live. By the time they parted company, the Comanche had a sizable portion of the herd. The warrior's name was quickly spreading throughout the southwest at the very moment he was returning home, watching anxiously for Nalin among the cheering greeters. Manatah was the only one he saw.

"Quanah," the old warrior began, his face wrinkled from worry. "While you were away the bluecoats came."

"Because of the raids?" Quanah tensed, looking over the village for signs of retaliation. The main encampment looked just as it had before.

"No, not the raids. They came a moon ago. I do not think they had yet heard of the raids so far south."

"What did they want then?" His gaze returned to the old man.

"A trade. They would return all of our warriors held in their prisons if we gave them our white hostages."

Quanah grabbed the man's arm tightly. "Nalin?"

"No, Quanah, we did not give her to them. The yellow-haired one went, but Nalin came to us willingly, thus we could tell them truthfully we had no more hostages."

Quanah's eyes closed briefly in relief. "Where is she?"

"In my lodge. We have seen bluecoats watching the village. We keep her hidden from their eyes."

"Then I will drive the bluecoats away."

"No." Manatah held the warrior back from starting out right away. "The chiefs have decided to move. When the war party is rested we shall go farther north. The day approaches when the Comanche bands meet together. Then we shall also discuss the retaliation the whites will surely send against us now."

Quanah nodded, satisfied with the sense of the plan. "Manatah, I would like to see Nalin."

"She waits for you inside my lodge." He had barely spoken before Quanah set out. "*With* her mother," he shouted after him.

"I'm sorry, Marshal, but this is all the captives they returned." The captain pointed in general to the throng of about twenty dirty people shuffling about making beds for themselves in the cleared supply room. Hank Thompson looked them all over carefully for the second time. They were incredibly dirty and tattered, much of it perhaps due to the long ride to the fort. There were no men, but a few boys between six and twelve years of age. The rest were women and girls of widely varying ages and descriptions, but not one of them even remotely resembled Lisa.

"Sutton, you swore to me Lisa was there!" The U.S. Marshal spun about angrily.

"She was. I know I saw her."

"I'll save the judge hanging you and shoot you right here!" Thompson's face was livid, his hand clenching reflexively over his gun handle. The recently released captives looked up, startled by the outburst. Their weary faces reflected fear they had learned to live with if not conquer. They were still not fully cognizant of their new freedom, even here in the safety of the fort. They expected and waited to be told what to do, afraid, too, of how their own people would accept them now that they had been Indian slaves. A few of the women cradled half-Indian babies in their arms. For them, all hope was gone; they knew how they would be viewed, simply because they had chosen surrender rather than death. All the pairs of frightened, tired eyes were now fastened on the two civilians standing amid the soldiers.

"Look, Marshal." The captain stepped between him and the manacled outlaw. "Are you sure she isn't here?"

"I'm sure, goddamn it! I'm sure!"

"Girls change a lot from ten to sixteen."

"She's not here!" Thompson shouted in the officer's face. "This lyin' son of a bitch—"

"Now, wait . . ."

"I ain't lyin' to ya, Marshal. She *was* there. They prob'ly just didn' give her back is all. You know how them schemin' redskins are."

Thompson was ready to hit him. Captain Nash held him back. "Get him out of here!" he ordered the two guards, who began to drag Sutton out backward.

"You broke our deal!" the outlaw screeched. "You gave your word."

"We had no deal, Sutton. You came with an offer, and I turned you down. Because you opened your mouth anyway don't mean we had a deal."

"It is possible they held out on us," the captain said slowly, looking over the captives. "I never have trusted Indians, and Comanche are the worst of the lot. After what that Quanah has done . . . did you hear what that damned half-breed did to Whiteside on the cattle drive?"

Thompson nodded. He had heard about that and the raids in Texas, and right now he couldn't care less about any of it.

A single head rose from the crowd of released captives and looked up at the two men at the sound of the Comanche's name. The captain noticed it and stepped over a body or two to reach her. "You know Quanah?"

Wide-eyed at the officer's attention, she nodded.

"He come from that camp where we found you?"

127

She nodded again.

Captain Nash glanced at the marshal then back to her. "M'am, would you mind coming with me a minute?"

She rose and followed the man out to the next room.

"What's your name, m'am?" The officer offered her a chair. She sat down rather unsurely. She was still dressed in Indian buckskin, her blonde hair disheveled from the long ride.

"I forgot what it is like to sit in a chair," she murmured, her fingers running over the armrests as if she was unsure such luxury still existed.

"How long you been with them?" Captain Nash leaned over the table near her. Thompson was still smarting from the disappointment. He walked over to the window, gazing out at the darkness.

"A little over three years. We were on our way to California, my husband and I. I was going to teach there and Bill was . . . was . . ." Her voice began breaking, long-held-back tears welling up.

"Take it easy, m'am." Nash touched her shoulders. He could well sympathize with her plight, whatever horrible atrocities she had been subjected to.

The woman got herself under control. "Bill was to be a minister. We were told to take the Oregon Trail, but Bill was sure it would be easier going straight through northern Texas by the Santa Fe Trail."

"That's straight through Comanche Territory," Nash interrupted.

"We didn't know that. We thought . . . it was safe now."

"Never *be* safe with them on the loose."

"The, uh, the Comanche attacked the wagon train we were with. Bill was . . . killed. They took me and two others who survived."

"The others are in there?" Nash pointed to the back room.

"Yes, one. The other killed herself the first night."

"M'am, you never did tell us your name." He smiled encouragingly.

"It's Ann, Ann Baumann. My husband was William Baumann from Philadelphia."

"Pleased to meet you, Mrs. Baumann. You said Quanah was in the camp you came from?"

"Yes, sir."

"All the time, or did you just see him once or twice?"

"Oh no, he's there. Unless he's on raids or hunting."

"You're sure it's Quanah? Not just—"

"No, Captain. I know it was Quanah. I've seen him many times and heard his name mentioned frequently. Far *too* frequently among the family I came from."

"M'am, I'll have to ask you some sort of personal questions, about the circumstances . . ." Nash wasn't quite sure of how to put it.

"If you are wondering why they kept me, it was not what you think. I was luckier than most. The man who eventually bought me only wanted a teacher. I had to work hard, but there was no . . . no . . ." She began blushing. There had been her original captor, but that was several years past now; she could almost pretend that part of her nightmare had never happened.

"Why would he want a teacher?" Nash's brow furrowed.

"Though I had a thousand other occupations in a day, my primary responsibility was as a tutor for his daughter." The woman was gradually losing her fears. She was speaking like a schoolmarm again, almost ridiculous in the Indian dress.

"Why would he want that?" Nash leaned forward, unable to hazard a guess.

"He wanted his daughter to learn English. That's what I taught her . . . when I could. It seems she had forgotten most of it."

"Wait, hold on a minute." Hank Thompson spun around from his place by the window, suddenly interested in the turn of the questioning. When the subject had been the much-sought-after Comanche brave, he had hardly listened. Quanah was a matter for the military. "You said she forgot?"

"Well, yes, you see she isn't his real daughter. She's adopted. She's—"

"White?" Hank blurted.

"Yes, very," Ann sneered, remembering with clarity Nalin's contempt for her.

"Is she in there?" Hank pointed to the back room.

"Oh, no, not that one."

Hank was too excited to hear the sarcasm in Mrs. Baumann's voice. "You mean she's still back there?" He fired the question at her.

"Yes."

"What does she look like?"

"Oh . . ." Ann paused, puzzled at the marshal's anxiety. "She's very light complected. Never tans, just burns." She grinned slyly, as if that fact was a source of vengeance to her for the girl's repeated snubs. "She's a bit taller than me. Um, green eyes and high—"

"Red hair?"

"Yes." Ann looked up at him. "A dark red, very wavy."

"Lisa," the marshal murmured, gazing at Nash. "Is her name Lisa?"

"I don't know what her true name is. They call her Nalin. Do you know her?"

Marshal Thompson looked down at the woman. "Yes, m'am, I do. She's my daughter."

"Oh my!" Ann Baumann's face paled.

"What? What is it?"

She covered her mouth with her hand.

"Mrs. Baumann?" he prodded.

She looked up at him pityingly. "Is that . . . Quanah, is he wanted very badly?"

"I'll say he is!" Nash answered with venom. "Ask anyone in Texas how much they'd want his hide."

"Mrs. Baumann, what does Quanah have to do with my Lisa?" Thompson frowned.

"Oh, dear." Her gaze turned back to the lawman. "She's going to marry him."

Chapter 11

"ARE you sure you know which tepee is his?" Thompson asked for the third time to assure himself. Mrs. Baumann had been very reluctant to ride anywhere near the Comanche camp. She had told them how to distinguish Manatah's tepee from all the others and had hoped never to see it again. It was Thompson who had insisted on her going with them. Ann could feel sorry for the man, his daughter disappearing six years ago and then his wife dying not long after, leaving him alone on his desperate search. Still, it wasn't fair making her come along. Even if he located Lisa, she wouldn't come with him. Ann had told him that, but the man just didn't listen. "I lived with them for three years. I know which one it was by the markings on the outside, no matter where we set up camp. I saw them every day." She couldn't quite keep the irritation out of her tone. It was all well and good to take a detachment of soldiers out here to the camp and demand Lisa's return, but Ann knew these people. They wouldn't give her up without a fight. Nalin, or Lisa, would not leave Quanah, and most likely Ann Baumann was going to be killed, if not in the fighting then as soon as the Comanche knew she had led the whites here.

"The encampment is just over this rise." She pointed to the hill before them. Even as she said it she paused to wonder why everything was so quiet, so still. Usually from here one could hear children laughing, playing at their games, the dogs barking. Some of the colts even

131

grazed up this far. There was no smell of smoke in the air, and no wisps of it drifted over the rise.

On a signal from Nash, a soldier dismounted and crept up to the edge of the crest. The cavalry was already spreading out to follow Nash's plan for a quick surprise attack. Thompson only wanted Lisa, but Nash wanted Quanah.

The scout leaning over the precipice straightened, presenting himself to full view below. "They're gone, sir," he called back.

Nash rode to the crest, Thompson right behind him until they pulled the horses to a stop. Below them was evidence of where the Kwahadi Comanche had been but no trace of where they had gone. Blackened areas remained where camp fires had burned. Paths were worn in the grass leading from where one tepee had stood to the next bare patch of ground, but of the Indians themselves there was no trace remaining. Thompson's heart sank in his chest, thinking of his daughter. He pictured Lisa now looking much like Maureen Brannigan had looked when he met her, but on her face was the worn, frightened expression of the captives he had seen at the fort. In his thoughts he pictured his cherished child traded off to the renegade Comanche chieftain with every possible vision of the horror stories he had been told by white captives burning through his brain. He saw her terrified expression as she gazed up at a faceless brave, cornered by him, with no salvation from her plight other than the one Ann's friend had taken—suicide.

Nalin was laughing, watching her father play the button game. He was always so good at it, his wrinkled face impassive, even his eyes expressionless as he faced the other team without a hint of the button's presence in his gnarled brown hand. As the laughing, bantering, and wagering went on, she sought out Quanah's notice. He was standing behind the Kwahadi team, arms folded across his lean chest. She caught his eye and smiled. To her surprise he cocked his head toward the grove of trees beyond the nighttime camp fires. She nodded slightly so

Toppasannah would not see. He moved off, slowly strolling toward the treeline.

Nalin looked down at her mother, sitting with the other women, engrossed in a game of their own. She slipped off quietly, keeping a wary eye on her mother's back. Quanah had not yet asked Manatah for her hand, though the whole band knew he soon would. He was waiting for the proper amount of time to pass. During the months of their courtship it was always he who insisted everything proceed according to custom. Though Quanah now outranked Manatah in a position on the chief's council, he politely asked the old man's permission to escort his daughter, always taking her home again in the right amount of time. After the first time he never again let it be said they were not well chaperoned, confining their strolls together to within the limits of the camp, or visiting with Nalin in the presence of her famly. That was why Nalin was so surprised when he gestured for the meeting. There might be talk of their meeting alone in the darkness.

Nalin peered once more behind her. The sky was nearly as light as day, so numerous were the camp fires. Almost all the Comanche bands were represented, and some Kiowa, Arapaho, and Cheyenne had also joined the tribal gathering. Dancing and games surrounded each fire as the bands and the visitors from other tribes renewed old acquaintances. For tonight no one wished to bring up the topic of the encroaching whites. The tribal reunion would last several more days, and there would be time to speak of it later.

She slid quickly behind a tree, plunging herself into near darkness as the firelight from the camp was cut off. She stepped forward, straining to make out his form in the dark. "Quanah?" she said quietly. Only the rustle of leaves and the sound of the drums and voices beyond could be heard. "Quanah?" She peered about, frowning now. She was brave enough everywhere else, but in the dark, completely alone, goose bumps began to appear on her flesh. She was about to call when something touched her arm and a triumphant "Ha" sounded in her ear.

133

She jumped and almost screamed in fright as she spun about to face the danger. Then her mouth curled into an angry snarl. "Quanah, you scared me!"

He was laughing.

"That was not funny." She frowned, still feeling the startled fright.

"The way you jumped was funny indeed."

She turned her back on him, arms folded crossly.

"I am sorry, Nalin. I did not think I would scare you so badly."

She remained offended.

"Nalin." He reached for her, and at his touch she was off, sprinting through the trees, laughing herself now, teasing him into the chase as he started after her. At first her giggles betrayed her whereabouts as he plunged through the trees and brush in pursuit, then she fell silent, and Quanah lost the trail. He slowed to a walk, ears listening. He stopped, gazing about in the darkness, sure that at any moment he would hear her step.

A twig cracked behind a large tree, and Quanah knew he had her. Confidently he crept up on the spot, ready to spin in front and grab her. His fingers touched the bark of the tree, muscles tensing.

"Ha!" He was grabbed from behind. Quanah leaped around, stance ready for combat, as Nalin nearly doubled over with laughter in front of him. "You jump well also," she said, then broke into laughter again. He had only himself to blame for teaching her to creep so silently.

"You," he grinned, reaching out for her. Her eyes opened wide, playfully fearful, and she started to run. Quanah caught her in two strides, turning her around by the arm. She was still laughing as his mouth closed over hers, his arms pulling her body tightly against his. She molded herself to him, her arms entwining around his neck. His lips traveled over her cheek to her neck, then he backed away far enough to see her. "I love you, Nalin," he murmured.

"And I love you, Quanah . . . my Quanah." She drew her face into the crook of his neck, standing on tiptoe to reach him.

134

Quanah's hand came down to her buttock, then pressed her tightly against him. She could feel the male hardness of him as his muscles tensed. He kissed her again, and, as the kiss held, his other hand inched up her back to her shoulder, bearing pressure there, pulling her downward. Yielding, Nalin knelt, then allowed him to lay her back on the grass. The ground was cold with the coming of winter, but she hardly felt it as another kind of warmth spread through her. His lips brushed over her cheek to the tip of her ear. "Will you be my wife?" he whispered, his breath hot against her cheek.

"Yes, oh yes."

His body pressed against her, driving her wild with passion. She wiggled a leg beneath his, wanting to be taken this very moment. She could hardly breath for the desire pounding through her. Quanah kissed her once more, his thigh pressed between her legs. She moaned his name, then suddenly, through the buckskin shirt, she felt the muscles of his back beneath her hands tense even harder. He stiffened and pulled himself away with effort.

Her eyes darted open, puzzled as he drew himself up to his knees. "I will speak with your father tomorrow," he said with proper Comanche solemnity.

She couldn't believe her ears. "Quanah!"

He smiled down at her, watching the anger flush her cheeks. "Not yet, my Nalin. When you are my wife!" He bent down to kiss her again, this time careful not to touch her with anything but his lips. If anything, his reserve was hurting him more than her. Never had he wanted anyone so badly. Only strong determination held him in check. Though he knew she wanted him now, Nalin was special. He would not take her until she was rightfully his.

The column of mounted soldiers halted, Nash giving the order to turn back. They had picked up the trail farther north and followed it for several days, but now they could go no farther. The pursuit was officially ended.

"Rest your horses, men," Nash called, his gaze fastening on Thompson with pity. The man was still watching the trail of the tribe, passed beyond their reach. The marshal dismounted, even remembering to help the lady, Ann Baumann, from her horse, but his eyes always returned to the trail. Nash walked up beside him. "I'm sorry, Thompson. Truly I am."

"I'm going after her. You can stop if you must but—"

"Marshal, I can't allow you to do that. You know we can't go inside Cheyenne lands without putting the treaty in jeopardy. You go in there alone, and you'll never get her out. I can't let you break the treaty."

Thompson glared at the captain with hostility, his thin lips set in a firm line.

"I know how you feel, and I'm sorry."

"I won't let it happen." Thompson's gaze fell back to the trail. "I'm not gonna let her be taken, forced into . . ." Thompson couldn't bring himself to say it, his mind replaying the vision of a faceless warrior cornering his daughter, forcing himself on her. He couldn't stand it. "I won't let it happen."

Nash was envisioning the same thing. He didn't know how to console Thompson, thinking of his sixteen-year-old daughter at home. It could have happened to her.

As the men stood silently looking down the trail neither of them noticed Ann Baumann. "You haven't heard a thing I've tried to tell you, have you, Marshal?"

Thompson turned his gaze on her.

"I've tried to tell you as gently as I know how that your Lisa is not being *forced* into anything. She's not like the rest of us. She *wants* to be there. No one makes her stay. You wouldn't believe—" Ann stopped, remembering the girl she talked about with such hostility was the man's child. Her voice softened. "Mr. Thompson, Lisa wants to marry Quanah. By whatever heathen rites they use." She shook her head, wondering if it could be called a marriage. Nevertheless, "Your daughter loves him."

"You can't be tellin' me the truth!"

"I am, Mr. Thompson. I don't know what sort of Lisa you remember, but she isn't the same now. She's a woman. One who knows what she wants . . . and she wants to be there, and she wants to be Quanah's wife."

Ann paused, surveying the marshal's expression. She was beginning to reach him, but doubt remained. "You are thinking of her as the girl you knew. Picturing her, perhaps, as like us, the other hostages. She's not! I guess there is no other way to say it, Mr. Thompson. Your daughter *hates* whites. She refuses to think of herself as one. She treated us, the hostages, no worse or any better than her people did. Her adopted father had to make her listen to my English lessons or she never would have. She prefers speaking Comanche. She's a . . . a . . ." Mrs. Baumann couldn't continue. Why hurt the man worse than he had been already by telling him his daughter was a full Comanche warrior. "I lived with them," Ann said gently. "I know her as she is now, and, believe me, Mr. Thompson, your quest is futile. If you found her, she would never consent to going back."

Thompson stared off over the prairie to where the endless grass gave way to streams and trees. Somewhere behind them Lisa might even now be wedding herself to the Indian. "You say she loves him?" he said, staring.

"Yes, Mr. Thompson, she does." She could see his confusion, wanting to believe his little girl could be happy. Ann decided to tell him the rest of the truth about the arrangement, only omitting the parts about Lisa's warrior activities. "Mr. Thompson, Lisa is a respected member of the tribe, not a slave. Her father—*adoptive* father—is a chieftain and the band's translator. Believe me, Quanah is courting her with all the respect due a chieftain's daughter." Nash harumphed, and Ann glared at him. "Lisa is happy, Mr. Thompson. I don't know what Quanah has done elsewhere in Texas and the like, but I can tell you how he is with her. He loves her."

Thompson and Nash both looked at her as if she'd gone crazy.

"He does!" she asserted. "I don't know his reputation here, now, but I know what he is like there and with her." She looked directly into Thompson's eyes. "He comes to see her in the evening and calls for her properly. He walks with her under the chaperoning observation of the camp, only holding her hand. He *does* love her. Any

137

fool can see it in his eyes . . . and she loves him. He's good to her, and I assure you, Marshal, if he's half as fierce as the U.S. Army seems to think he is"—she shot a glare at Nash—"then your daughter will never be harmed. Not as long as Quanah can prevent it." In truth, Mrs. Baumann did like the young chieftain, finding the blossoming romance one of the high points of her stay there. Quanah had never spoken harshly to her, even excused himself for accidently stepping on her foot while his gaze was locked on Nalin.

Henry Thompson's eyes lowered, considering the painful decision he had to make. "Best I leave her alone then," he murmured, choking back the emotion caught in his throat.

Ann remained silent, sure she had said enough. Only Nash stared out beyond the trail, an idea taking form in his mind. The best way to strike an enemy was to find his weakness and use it against him, and Mrs. Baumann had just told him Quanah's. A slight smile spread over the captain's face.

Chapter 12

NALIN was ceremoniously called before her father. Toppasannah waited outside the lodge, pretending to be about her work while her ears strained to overhear.

Sitting beside her father, Nalin's legs were tucked primly to the side. Manatah's expression was sober and serious, as if weighing most important matters within the graying, wrinkled head. "Quanah has come to speak with me this morning." He paused dramatically. Nalin knew that! She had been sent out on an errand when he appeared, going about her chore joyfully as he spoke to her father. "He has asked if he may have you for his wife." Again a pause. Father was dragging this out for all it was worth. "I refused," he stated.

Nalin's eyes widened in horror, her face paling as she stared at him. For once, his sharp-tongued child had no voice. At last the sun-weathered features crinkled, eyes dancing at her dismay. "I tease you, my daughter. I have given my permission."

Relief flooded over her in waves. "Oh, Father!" she scolded, smiling broadly. She was about to spring at him with a bear hug, but his upraised hand held her back, his expression becoming serious again. Now that he had had his fun the whole thing would proceed properly. Nalin dropped back to her place, her mouth screwed up impatiently while Manatah carefully explained, in detail, how it had been discussed before the chiefs' council and decided that the match would be a good one. Manatah gave her all the reasons they had thought of for why she should seriously consider accepting, but she knew all of that, too. Never mind the logic that the marriage would unite two good families, Manatah's and Nacoma's. Never mind that she could marry no finer than the famous Nacoma's son; that Quanah, already a seasoned warrior and a wealthy man, would be an excellent husband and provider. She didn't need to know why she should accept; she only wanted to be up and out so she could meet Quanah approaching with the string of horses that would seal the bargain.

Again Manatah's dark eyes sparkled with mischief, watching her suppressed excitement, deliberately prolonging the lecture. For a love match, detailed explanations were hardly necessary, but he droned on and on as though he had to convince her of the wisdom of his decision. Had the pairing been only an arrangement between two families, she still could refuse, but he had known her heart was Quanah's, and it pleased him that she had the good sense to love a man he would have chosen for her anyway. Finally the old man ran out of words. He could hear the horses outside and knew Quanah waited. She had not missed the sound either, and her gaze traveled to the entrance, anxious to be out. He smiled once more and dismissed her.

Nalin sprang to her feet, only slowing as she stepped into the sunlight, waiting for Quanah's approach. He led five horses in his own hand. Pecos, behind him, led five more. She smiled inside, letting no trace of it show on her face for this solemn occasion. She had fetched a good price, ten of Quanah's finest horses.

As those from the nearest lodges watched, grinning broadly, Quanah held the reins of the horses out to Nalin. The moment of truth was at hand. She could refuse by simply turning her back on him or she could take the reins from his hand and lead the horses to mix with her father's herd, thus sealing their engagement.

Nalin's fingers brushed his hand as she took the reins. Wordlessly, she walked away, leading the horses toward her father's. The occasion was broken by a single loud "Eeyaa!" from Pecos, overcome by his emotions. All eyes turned on the impulsive younger brother, who suddenly bowed his head sheepishly. Nalin began it, and everyone joined in the laughter.

Pecos was now allowed to accompany his soon-to-be sister-in-law to the stream. The water, barely more than a deep mud hole, was over a hill and nestled within a thin layer of trees. After Nalin had accepted Quanah's proposal, the Kwahadi band had moved off from the reunion place, renewing their endless wandering trek southward into the hundreds of square miles of Comanche land. Winter was quickly approaching, and they wished to be on familiar ground to make their winter camp.

Pecos couldn't have been happier if it were his own wedding taking place tomorrow. He and Nalin had not forgotten their close friendship, and now she would be part of his family forever. He adored his older brother, and, as he walked to the river beside Nalin, he chattered excitedly about the wondrous event. The Kwahadi had stopped at this spot for several days because the dwindling buffalo had been spotted nearby. Until the hunting failed, they would stay awhile, which would give the couple a chance for a honeymoon.

"I know where Quanah plans to take you after the ceremony," he revealed with boyish glee. Sometimes, for an eighteen-year-old, Pecos could be so childish.

"Do you?" She grinned, glancing sideways at him through the newly matured eyes of a soon-to-be wife.

"He's taking you far off from the camp for the honeymoon. I helped move supplies there this morning."

"Then why aren't you helping him now?"

"He wants to do the rest himself." Pecos shrugged, as if that really didn't make much sense to him, to refuse an able pair of hands.

"Maybe because you talk too much, and he does not wish to listen," she teased.

He answered her seriously. "Probably." He shrugged again.

Pecos was the opposite of Quanah in almost every way. Where the elder brother was tall and lean, the younger was short and compact, built like a small bull. Though both were only half Indian, Pecos reflected more of the Indian side of their heritage. His skin was coppery, his hair wispy and blue-black. Only their eyes matched exactly, both pairs dark and piercing. Though as fierce and aggressive as Quanah in battle, Pecos was too impulsive, too emotion-charged for leadership. Instead he was content to follow his older brother. Where Quanah was quiet and introspective, Pecos was an extrovert, frequently given to laughter and ready for any game or mischief. The brothers were close, and where Quanah was, Pecos was usually not far away.

The younger brother now felt it was his obligation to escort his brother's bride in his absence. As they neared the creek bank, two unwed young ladies were just finishing the same chore of fetching water that Nalin was engaged in. One of them had previously caught the ever-roving eye of the young bachelor. The girls were starting back to camp, furtively glancing and giggling at the handsome warrior.

Pecos greeted the one he had his eye on. She replied and kept walking while he, reluctantly now, followed Nalin, glancing over his shoulder at the maidens.

"Pecos, go with them if you wish," Nalin offered.

"Um." He still watched regretfully as the girls trod up the hill. If a pebble came into his path he would trip on it. Nalin laughed quietly. "No, I promised to walk with you," he replied.

"I release you from the promise."

"I don't wish to leave you at the river alone." He looked about. No one else was around at the moment.

"We aren't that far from camp. I shall be fine. Go ahead, catch up with them. Go on." She tossed her head in the direction the girls had taken. Pecos grinned broadly and trotted after them. Soon all three disappeared over the hill as Nalin wandered into the grove of trees by the minuscule river. Emerging on the other side of the treeline, she saw what the two maidens had seen and thought no more of it than they had. Twenty yards downstream a pair of scruffy white men watered their horses. Pecos, more attuned to possible danger, wary like his brother, might have read more in the appearance of the white men. But Nalin knew very little about the people she had come from.

She was afraid of soldiers, fearing they might recognize her as white. Cowboys, she had learned, would mind their own business if she asked no help from them. These two, however, did not look like cowboys wishing to pass through unharmed. There was a frightening aura about them, as the pair gazed at the attractive figure of the lone Indian maid. In shadow, beneath the trees, Nalin's hair did not give off its usual sparkle of red and gold. It occurred to neither of them that the girl might be white. It would have made no difference.

Nalin didn't see this in the visitors, and thus had no hesitation about kneeling at the creek's edge to fill her container. Had the strangers been Apache or Pawnee, she would have been more on guard, but even then she would have felt relatively safe with the Comanche strength so close behind her. She would just have watched them carefully. But white strangers were no threat to her, since they were only two in number. Their horses satisfied, the strangers moved off into the trees.

Completely unimpressed, Nalin looked down, concentrating on filling the containers. Beneath the shade of the tree she had no warning of the form creeping up behind her. The man struck quickly, stifling a scream with a hand thrust tightly over her mouth, an arm encircling her waist and dragging her backward. Nalin released the containers, which began to sink into the shallow water.

The man, however, had also misjudged his victim. Nalin was not a simple Indian maiden startled into helpless terror. She drew an arm forward, then jabbed back hard with her elbow, catching him dead center below the ribs. The man's breath went out of him as he staggered backward. Nalin wiggled out of his loosened grasp and spun about, drawing her knife from her waistband. She followed through with a kick at the man's head as he doubled over from the first blow. Her kick caught the side of his head and sent him sprawling onto his back. Had she screamed in that moment, Pecos would certainly have heard her beyond the hill, but it was not a warrior's way to scream; the thought never entered her mind.

By now the second man had appeared, and she threatened him with the knife. He grabbed for it, and Nalin slashed his arm. The first one had regained his feet and rushed at her from one side while the second, ignoring his bleeding arm, came at her from the other. She fought, kicking and trying to bring the knife into play, but one had her by the wrist and bent it backward until her fingers lost their grip on the hilt. She struggled like a fury, and it took both of them to even begin to hold her.

"Jesus Christ, I don't believe it!" the first one muttered, trying to hold an arm down to her side.

"Let's forget it." The second tried to ignore a well-placed kick to his shin. "They'll hear in a minute." He glanced up the path along which at any moment another Indian might appear.

"Cain't now. She'll bring the whole bunch of 'em down on us." Nor could he afford any more lost time. Fist clenched, he spun her around and quickly jabbed a hard right into her jaw. Her head snapped back, nearly breaking her neck, then she slumped silently forward.

Pecos waited at the edge of camp, the girls safely delivered to their father's lodge. He had wandered back a short way to wait for Nalin, wondering what could possibly be taking her so long. He gazed up the path that disappeared over the hill, his brow creased not in worry as much as in curiosity. She should be back by now. Slowly he began treading his way up the hill. Probably I won't see her until I am all the way up, he grumbled silently. He called her name from the outward edge of the trees, then waited for an answer. When none came, his brow wrinkled again, this time in worry. "Nalin?" he called more loudly. The grove was silent, his voice hushing the birds and insects. Emerging on the far side of the woods, his step quickened. There was no Nalin to be seen, but her water containers were half submerged in the creek bed. The sandy bank showed signs of a struggle, blood was spilled, and four booted foot prints were visible on either side of her small moccasined imprints. Nalin's bloody knife lay in the sand.

He backed away in shock and an overpowering sense of guilt. For a few seconds his feet were rooted to the ground in horror at his failure. Forcing himself into action, Pecos tore down the trail. Instead of running directly for the village, he sped five hundred yards down the river through the trees. Quanah must be told first, then together they would fetch the warriors. He never ran faster in his life, ignoring the branches and thorns that struck out at his passage, thinking only of reaching the place Quanah readied for his bride. He emerged in a clearing hidden on all sides by trees. Quanah looked up, startled by his sudden appearance.

"Quanah," Pecos panted. "Forgive me. . . . Two white men have stolen Nalin from beside the river bank."

Quanah dropped the blankets and sped without question into the lead, toward the encampment.

The Comanche braves followed the river, certain the whites had taken it upstream into the hills, where trails were more easily covered. Silently, the braves of the war party carefully studied the banks of the river for signs of leaving the water. Pecos pushed his guilt to the back of his mind, refusing to brood over the fact that this would not have happened had he not left her. He was too well trained in matters of war to center his thoughts on anything but finding the trail.

Quanah, too, betrayed no emotion, riding in front on his war horse, gaze fastened intently on the banks. For hours they had followed the river, not a single shoulder sagging, not a word being spoken as the afternoon sun began its descent in the western sky. He spotted broken branches off to the right, then hoofprints in the soft mud. Two horses, one bearing an extra burden. Without a word he turned his horse up the embankment. The trail was hard to follow in places, the process excruciatingly slow. The whites had been able to lope their horses and were hours ahead as night began to fall.

145

White minds were filled with misconceptions about Indians; they did not know that the customs of one tribe might not be those of another. Because some Indians didn't war at night, they figured that all of them didn't, and that the Indians probably would not mind the loss of a "squaw" at any rate. Even if they did, the white men were sure they would search for a few hours, until darkness fell, then give up and go home.

But the two men didn't know the girl they had taken belonged to the Comanche. Few if any of the Great Plains tribes would have dismissed her loss so easily. Most would continue the hunt wherever it led, even into other territories. For the Comanche, nothing would stop their determined pursuit, especially not the simple approach of nightfall.

"You know, Injuns don't track at night . . . 'gainst their religion," Mike assured as he set about camping for the night. Frank, the dumber of the two, wasn't so sure.

"Believe me," Mike stated with certainty. "They ain't gonna track no futher after nightfall. *If* they's even out there. Prob'ly went on home already. Injuns don't give narry a damn 'bout a squaw. Even a young 'n' purty one like this'n." Mike gazed at the still form he had dropped to the ground. She hadn't moved all day. Mike moistened his lips as he stared, then hurried through the rest of his unpacking.

"You sure you ain't kill't her?" Frank watched the motionless form. The slow rise and fall of her chest had not quite convinced him.

"Well, we're gonna find out real quick, ain't we?" He leered.

"Mike, you know she's a white woman, don' cha?"

"Do tell?" His eyes raised, checking his partner's claim. The leering grin broadened. "Well, danged if she ain't."

"You couldn't see her, hung over your horse like she was, but I could. I don' know, I don' mind havin' us some fun with an Injun squaw but a white woman . . ." He scratched his beard, rustling the lice in it. Both men were

146

rank from bathless weeks on the trail. Any money they had had was already spent on booze rather than baths. Broke, at least until they found a lone saddle tramp to pounce on and rob, the fun seemed ended for a while, until the supposed Indian squaw crossed their path. Taking her was Mike's idea, and Frank had gone along with it, though he had a cut arm to nurse for his trouble. Frank's minister father had assured him that Indians, like niggers, were Cain's children, somewhere just below being human. Frank believed that lesson as firmly as he believed most of the others his father beat into him with a rawhide strap. He knew for a fact he was going to hell anyway, so what difference did it make what other sins he committed? But this was a white woman.

"So she's white!" Mike countered. "Prob'ly some hostage they took. You can bet she's done been well worked over by 'em anyhow. She'll prob'ly 'ppreciate some good white stuff fer a change." Mike stood over the limp form, unbuckling his belt.

"Mike, she ain't even awake," Frank said.

Mike picked up his pocketknife, leaning over her as he slit the buffalo dress down the middle from throat to hem. She moaned softly, awakening as Mike's rough hands began to move across her body. Rank breath, smelling strongly of sour-mash whiskey filled her nostrils, and Nalin started, fully awake. He was slobbering over her, running his wet, foul mouth over her neck and shoulder. She felt his groping hands reach between her legs. The man backed away to turn toward his partner, the crooked, black-toothed smile broadening.

As he looked away, the girl beneath him moved quickly, her knee jerking reflexively, and her foot connected, an unaimed blow of sheer panic that struck Mike in the stomach. The grin changed to an open-mouthed scream. Mike's face paled as he fell off her, gasping.

The girl tried to stagger to her feet, still weak from the blow she had received earlier. "Stop her, Frank!" Mike screamed as she regained her feet.

Frank could only stare in shock, his inertia causing a further rage in Mike, who forced himself up, grabbed her

147

by the arm, and swung another blow into her face. She would have fallen if Mike had not been holding her arm. Again and again his free hand struck, forcing her head first to one side then the other.

"Mike, stop it! You'll kill her!" Frank came forward, but his enraged partner was beyond hearing him.

Chapter 13

SHE awoke to terrible pounding pain. As she tried to focus, she was aware only of the agony between her legs and the awful, overpowering stench filling her nostrils, then of a sickening grunting and the feel of naked flesh against hers. Her eyes opened, and Nalin screamed. The man who had brutally beaten her was now covering her with his filthy body, raping her unmercifully. The excruciating pain as he pounded against her would not allow for clear thought. She screamed again and again. The man stopped his awful hammering against her insides only long enough to snap, "Shut up, bitch!" She screamed again, and he backed off, hitting her across the face several times until, dazed, she could do no more than whimper at the edge of consciousness. Mercifully, she passed out again.

Only unbearable, agonizing pain dragged her out of the darkness. Her swollen, bruised face hurt almost as much as her body. One eye was swollen solidly shut, her lips a single bruise from repeated slaps, but she could hear. Both men were talking a few feet away.

"Mike, I'm tellin' ya, its diff'rent with a white woman."

"She ain't no better'n a lousy squaw," Mike countered. She recognized the voice of Mike—he was the primary cause of her pain. The other she had seen watching her agony, offering pity but no aid.

"Law might not look at it that way." The other

sounded worried. "You reckon she speaks only Injun like some of 'em?"

"I don't know, and I ain't gonna find out."

"We gonna kill her?"

"I ain't takin' no chances. I would'a done that by now if'n you hadn't a' butted in."

"Yeah, Mike, but murder . . ."

"Shee-it! White or no, she's a Injun whore now. Lousy savages, all of 'em. She ain't gonna have no tales to tell come mornin'. Now get some shut-eye. We gotta lot a' ridin' ta do tomorrow." She heard him settling down.

"What about the girl?"

"She ain't no girl, she's a goddamn squaw! She ain't goin' nowheres with the workin' over she got. 'Sides, if she's still alive in the mornin' I'm gonna teach her a thing or two more about appreciatin' a white man's lovin'."

Mike rolled over in his bedroll, signaling that conversation, for now, was ended. Frank sat up before the camp fire, casting glances toward the girl's battered body. Somewhere along the line, after Mike had finished his rape and was spending the rest of his fury in kicking the unconscious body, he had managed to pull Mike off short of killing her. Now he kept staring at the girl's broken form, his conscience for once bothering him deeply. That part of his psyche hadn't stirred in ages. Aside from his father's occasional lessons with a strap, violence was rather new to Frank—but he was learning—fast. He had learned to rustle cattle and rob saddle tramps and lone prospectors, but rape and murder was an entirely new experience and one, he discovered, that he didn't have the stomach for. When he had heard the sickening crunch of the girl's ribs beneath the onslaught, he had finally been unable to stomach any more. Mike was crazy, just plain dumb crazy. But maybe Mike was right now, and they would have to kill her to keep her from going after her redskin friends. But what difference would that make? By the time she got back they'd be long gone anyhow.

Frank's quick-changing though slow-moving mind began to sort through the possibilities. Once Mike was awake in the morning there'd be no stopping him from killing her. On the other hand, Frank could drag her off into the bushes and tell Mike she had died during the night so he had buried her. Maybe that wouldn't be too far from the truth, since he couldn't quite tell if she was still breathing or not. Still undecided, he stood up and began moving toward her.

Nalin had waited through several long minutes of silence before forcing the less damaged eye open. One of the men was asleep before the camp fire, the other still staring into the flames. Thanks to Ann Baumann, father's captive white teacher, Nalin had understood every word they had said. With practice she had learned to speak English again as well as she had ever known it, perhaps better. Her decision, however, would have been the same had she understood their plans or not. Language was not necessary to know what Mike's plan had been, nor what he would do to her tomorrow morning.

The other one had gazed in her direction, and now he was rising, coming toward her. He had only watched before, but now she didn't know what to expect from him. Were his plans the same as Mike's? Had he seen that she was awake and would he now call out to Mike to finish their aborted plans? Panic wanted to set in and cause her to betray herself, but she held it in check. Carefully she let her fingers trail along the ground by her side, blocked to the awake one's line of sight. Her fingers touched an object and felt it over: a rock, a very solid rock.

Nalin's eyes closed, feigning unconsciousness. She heard his boots treading over the gravel as he approached. Hardly daring to breath, she willed herself to remain motionless.

The footsteps stopped, and she felt a blanket being spread over her. "Least I kin do for now, I reckon," the man said softly, only a few feet, maybe two, above her. He must be kneeling or leaning over. Judging her aim by sound as Quanah had taught her to, her eyes opened at the very instant her fist connected with his skull. The rock crunched the bones of his temple with a sickening sound. The one called Frank no more than grunted once as he toppled sideways over her body. She wanted to throw his weight off her and run, to escape from this nightmare, but by sheer willpower she remained motionless beneath his weight. Slowly, when the other showed no signs of awakening, she rolled Frank onto his back and silently freed her legs. She stared down at the hated face; the eyes were open and rolled upward, a small trickle of blood oozing from the temple near the hairline where she had struck him. His mouth was agape in an expression of surprise.

She rose to her feet, steeling herself to prevent crying out in pain. Manatah, and Quanah, had taught her well to bear the pain of wounds in silence, to do what she had to do in spite of the agony of forcing her legs to support her. Her insides felt as though they might spill out over the ground, a sharp pain knifing through her chest, but she made herself stand straight and endure. Under control now, she leaned down and took the dead man's gun. She was dizzy as she rose again, wobbling slightly before she could make her feet obey her and step forward. Silently she crept toward the vicious creature who had begun her attack. She aimed the revolver at his back, then paused. No, not good enough. He should suffer for what he had done, for what he had wanted to do. He would be tortured before he died, as he had tortured her.

She had him to thank for the horrible beating, for the fact that her body was soiled now, dirty beyond cleansing, that she could not marry Quanah now, after this filth had touched her.

"Mike," she called out. He stirred beneath the blankets then jumped to a sitting position, his jaw gaping open like the other one, his eyes wide with fear when he saw the gun aimed at his head. "Put the blanket around you and put your hands on top where I can see them."

His gaze shifted to Frank's limp form, then back to her. "Sure, girlie, whatever you say." He had recovered somewhat from his initial surprise. One hand came from beneath the blanket, the other bulged under the cover near his gunbelt. Nalin sighted down the barrel, quickly changing her aim, and fired. The one called Mike screamed in agony as he drew the remains of his hand out from beneath the blanket, staring at the jagged stumps of two fingers severed at the third knuckle and spurting blood.

"You will watch your death, savage!" she spat in flawless hate-filled English. The gun was aimed at his forehead. He was now frozen in terror, holding the wrist of his injured hand, which continued to spurt blood onto the blanket. Slowly, Nalin started to move the gun downward over the blanket-covered form, stopping where his outline told her the place she sought was located.

"N . . . No! Oh, please! Oh, God, no!" The remaining hand flew to cover his crotch, where the gun was pointing. "Please, kill me quick but not there! God no! Not there! Have mercy, please—"

"Mercy? I am only a lousy redskin whore. Savages don't show mercy . . . no more than you did!" Nalin began to increase the pressure on the trigger steadily until the gun exploded. The bullet shattered both hands before finding its target. His screams echoed over the canyon wall as the blanket was quickly dyed red.

"Die slowly, *savage,* as you would have had me die."

Both of his hands were broken, and she had little fear of his reaching for his gun. He was quickly weakening anyway and would not live much longer, but she still took the gun from his holster and tossed it into the darkness.

She returned to the one she had killed first, removing his gunbelt and slipping it around her waist to close the front of the ripped dress. It was far too large to buckle, slipping down over her hips, so she tied it around her, then tucked the gun into the belt.

The saddles and blankets were near the camp fire, and she had no desire to return there or to touch their things. Instead she freed one horse and used the rope he was tied with to fashion a bridle for the other. Quickly forming a war bridle, a slip knot over the horse's lower jaw, Nalin tried to jump up, but her weakness and the pain wouldn't allow it. Finally she dragged herself up by her arms to mount. She looked back once more. The camp site was silent now. She kicked the horse in the sides and sped off at a gallop.

To expedite their search in the darkness, the warriors had split into smaller groups within hailing distance of each other. Pecos and Quanah formed one group that followed what might be the trail they sought, but it began to branch off in two directions. Quanah signaled Pecos to take the left branch while he took the right. He had followed it five hundred yards when he saw a piece of something fluttering in the pale moonlight at the edge of the woods. He pulled up near it and dismounted for a closer look. It was a piece of cloth but old and weathered; he tossed it to the ground in disgust. He was about to remount when a sound distracted him. Something pounded through the brush at breakneck speed. He stayed to watch. A horse galloped into the clearing, and he instantly recognized the rider.

"Nalin!" he called. She pulled the horse up so quickly that the animal reared and bolted, sending the rider over his rump to the ground.

Quanah ran to her. She was sprawled on her back like a broken, abused straw doll. It took only seconds to assess the full damage in the moonlight. Her face was bloodied, grotesquely disfigured from the beating. The dress had opened again in the fall, and her chest was a solid mass of purple. Dark splotches of blood and blue-black bruises marred the fair white flesh of her legs. Gently Quanah pulled her limbs together and lifted her in his arms. The darkness forbade doing any more for her tonight. He carried her into the edge of the woods, then sat on the ground, leaning against a tree trunk, her limp body cradled in his arms. Keeping her warm with his own body heat, he ignored the calls of the warriors when they passed.

Dawn broke through the leaves of the trees above him. Quanah was still awake, motionless, Nalin cradled against him. At first she began to twitch, then thrash in his arms. "Nalin," he called softly. She began to fight harder at the resistance of his arms. "Nalin, I am here. Quanah."

Half screaming, she awoke with a start, staring at him for several seconds without recognition. "You are safe. I am here now."

First she moaned, her arms reaching for him, then suddenly she stiffened and backed away from him. "No! No! Don't touch me!"

"Nalin." He grabbed her, holding her against him. Her body shook with tremors of hysteria, but no tears would come to wash away the pain and horror. "Nalin, who did this to you?"

"They are dead . . . both dead!" Her voice was flat, emotionless; her arms had gone limp at her sides. He gripped her shoulders to hold her away from him. Her damaged face made him want to strike out at someone. "You killed them?"

"Both of them. They are both dead!"

He had never heard her voice so cold and filled with hatred. It would have given him relief to kill them himself. His fingers clenched in repressed anger until he noticed they were biting into her flesh. Amazingly she seemed insensitive to the pain. She stared, not at him, but off into space as if she saw nothing, felt nothing. He frowned with worry. "Come, we will go home now."

He picked her up effortlessly. His horse was grazing in the pasture beyond their secluded woodland shelter. Quanah set her on the animal's back then sprang on behind her. She made no effort to resist him when he leaned her backward to rest against his chest.

Quanah stopped by a creek and helped her to wash. Her muscles were so stiff now that her legs would not support her, and she had to be carried to the creek. Her fair skin remained purplish and red beneath the dirt he cleaned away. Both cheeks were still swollen, her lips puffy, and the lovely face he cherished was a solid mass of purple. Large finger marks disfigured her slender throat, standing out harshly against the pale skin. Placing her in the shallow water to ease the pain for her, he made her lean against him as she soaked. Nalin never once whimpered or cried as he ministered to her, though the washing must have hurt. Her eyes remained dry, staring sightlessly beyond him. Quanah cursed himself silently.

Most of this was his fault. He blamed himself for what had happened. Not for the evil intentions of the men but for her reaction to them. He was the one who had taken a girl-child interested in boy's games and made of her a warrior. Manatah had given her riding lessons, taught her to shoot rifle and revolver and even how to make a bow, but it was Quanah who had taught her to take the harmless play of youth and turn it into the deadly aggression of a Comanche brave. Had she been left to be a woman she would have called out when the men grabbed her by the river. She would have screamed and brought the wrath of the Comanche nation on the two men's heads. They would have been tortured to death, and Nalin would not now be suffering.

While Manatah had taught her only the games of youth, Quanah was the one who had taught her never to cry out. He had taught that braves fought; they did not scream like women. The thought that had Nalin not fought she would at this hour have been hurt far worse or would be dead did not as yet occur to him. His self-blame did not reach far enough to realize that he taught no more than Nalin wished to learn, that her choice to fight her attackers would have been the same, though less effective, if not for his teachings.

Gently he picked her up again, clothing her in the torn dress he had tried to mend for her while she soaked. He set her on the horse's back and sprang on behind her. The cool water of the creek must have eased her pain because her head began to nod then dropped back against his shoulder. He cradled her sideways over the horse's back.

Pecos spied the lone rider and shouted for the others. He kicked his horse to a fast lope and started out ahead of them. "Quanah, we found two white men, both dead." The younger brother rode up from behind. His words failed on his lips when he saw the still form in Quanah's arms. Quanah stared straight ahead.

Pecos saw the bruises and winced. Nalin had not moved. "Is she dead, Quanah?" he finally asked slowly.

"No, the Great Spirit has given her sleep," the older brother answered, glancing down at the closed eyes.

Pecos emitted a low sigh of relief, then looked at his brother again. "Then she must have killed them, Quanah. We found the bodies. We left them for the buzzards and coyotes. She shot one right in the . . ." Pecos fell silent at a harsh glance from Quanah. The warriors had caught up, and Pecos gestured for them to be quiet, pointing and motioning that Nalin was sleeping. He prodded his horse closer to Quanah's to whisper, "Was she . . . did they?"

Quanah glared at him hotly. "No! They did not! She killed them first."

Pecos backed away like he had been scalded. Never had Quanah spoken to him so harshly. He let his horse fall back, giving Quanah the lead alone with his burden. He dared not ask if he might take the precious cargo for a while to rest his brother's arms. Quanah sat straight, Nalin's still head resting on his outstretched arm as they rode.

Only Toppasannah ever learned the full extent of Nalin's injuries. Quanah stuck to his story, telling Manatah she had killed the men before they had been able to rape her, and the old woman loved him all the more for it.

The bruises began to heal, but there was something still badly wrong with Nalin. It was her spirit that was damaged far more than her body had suffered. The usual perky laughter and teasing back-talk full of gaiety and recklessness were gone, replaced by a huddled, saddened figure who sat before the fire in her father's lodge, knees drawn up to her chin, rocking slowly back and forth day after day and week beyond week while the bones of her ribs healed. She hardly ate or slept. And she refused to see Quanah. She would talk to no one, ignoring them all, her gaze fixed on the fire, but if he came near she would beg them to make him go away. Six weeks after the incident, Quanah came in the morning as he had done every day that he was not away. No mention was made of the postponed marriage. Nalin's parents sat outside enjoying an unusually warm winter day. He knew without asking where Nalin would be.

"She still will not see me?" He sat down beside Manatah.

"She says she will not." Manatah cast a glance backward to the open flap of the tepee. "But if my mind does not fail me it is still my lodge. *I* say you may enter."

Quanah paused, half rising.

"Go to her, Quanah." Toppasannah nodded at him.

He stepped inside, his eyes taking a few seconds to adjust to the dim light. The fire was out and cold, yet Nalin sat in front of the ashes, knees still drawn to her chest, just as Pecos had described to him. "Nalin?"

"Go away." Her voice was soft and sad, the words coming out like a moan.

His sense of guilt returned that he had failed to help her when she needed him. "Nalin, let me speak with you." He knelt beside her. She had turned her face away from him. Gently he reached to take her chin in his hand and turned her around to face him. "The bruises are gone now." He held her chin lightly. She still refused to look up at him.

"I will have Father send back your horses."

He searched her face. "You do not mean that."

When she finally did look up, there was a hardness and bitterness in her eyes that startled him. "You asked me once if I could kill a white, and I could not answer you. I can now. I *have* killed two, and I can kill many more. When you next ride into Texas I want to go with you."

She was waiting for an answer, but he didn't know what to say. If he refused she would ask another and another of the raid leaders until she found one who would take her. Failing that, she would strike out alone. He read all of it in the green eyes burning with hatred. "If that is your wish," he finally replied.

Satisfied, she turned away. "They bring nothing but death and misery." Her voice was harsher than he had ever heard it. "First Jesse, now this. They kill our people for sport . . . the old ones, the children, it makes no difference to them. Thieves and murderers! I hate them all!"

"If you truly wish it then I will take you to Texas." He could not deny her the right of vengeance, yet what had that to do with their marriage? "We can still be wed, Nalin."

She glanced at him once more then turned away, huddling into a small ball. "Noooo," she moaned, at the edge of tears.

"Why not?" He wanted to touch her but could not bring himself to; his hands remained poised in the air.

"I will not disgrace you. They . . . he . . . I have been touched by them." The memory still remained fresh of her clothing being cut off her, of dirty, filthy hands on her body. Though she washed daily, scrubbing hard, the filth of the memory would not leave her. "I will not bring shame to you."

"Nalin," he said softly, this time taking her by the shoulders to turn her around. "What happened is not your fault. You are not to blame for it. It is my shame that I did not come sooner to help you, but you have given yourself to no one but me."

"Quanah, I never . . . we never . . ." She looked up, eyes bright with moisture.

"The night by the meeting place, Nalin. You gave yourself to me then . . ."

"But we never . . ."

"We wanted to. In our hearts it is the same. I am the first who has touched you, and the evil men mean nothing."

Slowly, as she looked at him, the held-back tears began to come. Quanah urged her into his arms, and she began to sob, huge wracking sobs that should have come weeks earlier. "Cry, my Nalin, cry." He gently rocked with her.

Chapter 14

SOLEMNLY Nalin walked behind her father, followed by Toppasannah and then by various relatives of the family. She was dressed again in the same fine buckskin robe she had worn the first day Quanah courted her.

Quanah's father, Nacoma, having died a year before in the dangerous buffalo hunt, was represented by a tribal elder distantly related to the orphaned brothers. He greeted Manatah at the entrance to Quanah's lodge with a joyful cry of "There you are," as though he had thought they might never arrive.

Standing beside Quanah's elder, Pecos smiled broadly, at times ready to laugh in happiness. The groom's relatives bid the bride's family enter, and Nalin's gaze immediately sought out Quanah's. She loved him so much her heart seemed about to burst. Only the cloud of that day Quanah promised they would never remember stayed over her like a shadow, marring the occasion. Yet he was so handsome, sitting in the center of his, now her, new home. For the first time since the incident Nalin smiled slightly as she was led to sit beside him. Her knees brushed his thigh as she folded her legs beneath her, and the lightning shock passed through her again, the cloud lifting even further away.

Each elder of the two families seemed obligated to add some word of advice about wedded life and their promises to each other before Quanah's surrogate father at last presented him with the gift that sealed their vows.

Manatah stepped forward, taking his place by his

daughter's side as Quanah turned to her, offering the present. "Do you want me for your husband?"

She met his gaze with longing. This was the day she had dreamed of for almost as long as she had known him. "I do, and I am happy; love me as I love you for I shall love only you."

Quanah held the gift over Nalin's head as ceremony prescribed. "I love you, and that is why I asked you to be my wife. Here is that which I give to your parents to purchase you." He handed the present to Manatah.

Nalin then placed her left hand in Quanah's left hand as he said, "I am your husband."

"And I, your wife."

There was one last gift to be presented, and that was the wife's first offering to her husband. Nalin took the knife her father handed to her and lifted handfuls of her long auburn tresses, cutting through them carelessly to just below her ears. As every Comanche wife had done on her wedding day, she gathered the mass of severed hair and presented it proudly to her new husband.

Escorted by both families, the newlyweds were taken to the honeymoon lodge Quanah had prepared. The place he had selected was well secluded, a beautiful, peaceful spot nestled in a grove along a riverbank, far enough from the tribe to give them total privacy. For three full days they would remain undisturbed.

Quanah had decorated the honeymoon lodge, strewing wild flowers, the first to bloom in early spring, about their lodge to celebrate their joining. The family left them inside, and as their laughter and conversation drifted farther away down the path, Nalin found herself totally alone with Quanah at last.

He gazed at her for several moments, soaking in her beauty and the fact that she was entirely his, properly and forever. He would never give her cause to divorce him, never give her reason to seek a new husband. To him the thought of taking a second wife was unthinkable. He would buy slaves if necessary to help with the work, but he wanted no one but Nalin. Gently he touched her face with his fingertips, then ran them through the short hair that had already begun to curl about her face.

"Oh, Quanah, I love you so, my husband. At last I can say, 'my husband'."

He let her see his smile before bending to kiss her. She responded, molding against him as she had done before. He led her to their marriage bed, prolonging every moment as he removed her clothing and then his own. Her light skin blushed under his gaze, and he loved it. Lying down beside her he began to caress her in places he had never trusted himself to touch before, cupping her breasts, brushing the sweet, firm nipples tenderly. "Nalin, my wife," he murmured against her cheek as he eased his body over hers. Almost immediately she stiffened beneath him. He went no further, easing her fears by softly stroking her, kissing her gently, but she couldn't relax. Instead her flesh began to tremble in memory of the awful night and the severe beating. She wanted him; she loved him. Her eyes squeezed tightly closed, trying to block out the illogic of the memory surfacing now, wanting the love of the man she cherished, yet afraid, terrified, remembering the awful men and the terrible pain.

She held him, her fingers digging into his bare back, desperately wanting to return his passion, yet her body rebelled against her will, her muscles flinching. Finally Quanah backed away and lay down beside her.

"Oh, Quanah, I'm sorry. I am so sorry . . . I love you . . . I do . . . I want you." Her voice broke into sobs of grief.

He forced her gently to put her head on his chest. "We can wait. The day will come."

"I want you, Quanah . . . believe that I do! I just . . ."

"Hush," he soothed, stroking the soft red hair. "We have the rest of our lives. We will wait until you are ready."

"I have failed you."

"No, you have not." He felt hot tears drip onto his bare chest. "We will wait . . ." He continued stroking until the soft weeping stopped and the change in her breathing told him she slept. He burned with resentment he would not let her see, for it was not directed against her but was focused in unfulfilled vengeance on the two dead white men who had done this to her. A few short weeks ago, Nalin had been unafraid, even anxious for lovemaking, her mood as gay and light as the breeze that heralded spring. Now she had only partly overcome her experience, only begun to respond to a touch or a gesture without trembling. Her lasting depression covered everything, even this night, in a fear she had never known before.

For the three days of their honeymoon, he tried several times to consummate their marriage, but each attempt was met with the fear-filled wall of unconscious resistance. She tried, too, never asking him to stop, but the moment he felt her tension he could proceed no further. Her body's failure to release the fear did nothing to lighten her despondency. The three-day seclusion both had so looked forward to became a travesty of the happiness they should have been sharing.

"No!" Nalin straightened suddenly from bending over to fold the bedroll. "I won't go back!"

Quanah looked up. They were in the middle of packing their gear for the return to camp. The lodge was still up, but they had dragged everything outside to be cleaned and aired, then folded.

"I am not going to return when I am not yet a wife!" She began rewrapping the bedroll too loosely for carrying, just shoving it together.

For a moment he was too stunned by her determined speech to say anything. She picked up the roll and started for the lodge. "They will expect us to return this morning," Quanah began. "If we don't, they will worry. Perhaps even begin to search for us."

"I am not going back if it takes forever. Not until I am your wife in more than name only!" She disappeared inside, bedroll and all.

His eyes rolled heavenward for patience; she picked a fine time for stubbornness. "We must go back. . . . Do you hear me?"

No answer came from within. With an exasperated grunt he walked over, then leaned inside to fetch his wife. Instead he was grabbed off guard and tugged inside, practically knocked off his feet. No trace of her injuries remained, and she was in healthy shape for a wrestling match.

Her first maneuver was a tackle, trying to knock him the rest of the way over. Both of them laughing, he allowed himself to be sprawled to their marriage bed, pulling her down with him. He tickled her fiendishly until she squealed for him to stop.

He settled on his back as Nalin snuggled against the crook of his arm, her chest heaving to catch her breath. Recovering, she flipped onto her side toward him. "*My* husband," she said possessively, running the tip of her finger down his nose, over his lips, and to his chin. "I love you. With my heart and soul, I love you."

His hand touched the back of her head and pulled her down for a kiss. This time, as his hands began to explore, there were no tremors, no stiff fear. Her desire began to match his as she leaned above him, stroking him back, running her fingers over his bare chest, kissing him there. She sat up and removed her dress without blushing or shame, then came to him, kissing him in mounting passion as he rolled her onto her back. He took her then, and though she cried out once in pain, she held him tightly, urging him to go on.

Sometime later, as they slept in each other's arms, Quanah awoke instantly to the sound of twigs breaking on the path. He slid his arm from beneath her and found his knife. Footsteps continued to approach, then a male voice called out, "Quanah?" He recognized the voice and thrust the knife back into its sheath, donning his loincloth quickly. Nalin awoke and gazed about, startled.

"Brave Bear and Red Fox," he assured her.

"Quanah?" Brave Bear called again.

"I am here." Quanah stepped partially out, blocking the entry while Nalin peered over his shoulder.

"We thought when you failed to return this morning that something might have happened."

Quanah continued to frown from one to the other of his life-long friends.

"We came to rescue you." Red Fox grinned, seeing Quanah's bride behind him. "But I don't think you want to be rescued just yet." The two warriors broke into peals of laughter as Quanah scowled at them.

"And if you need us," snickered Brave Bear, another raid leader, "just call. We will come." His words were cut short as Quanah took a few steps toward him. The braves turned and fled down the path, snickering and laughing.

Quanah re-entered his lodge, watching his wife with clear disapproval. Nalin was doubled over on the ground, howling with laughter.

"What is so amusing?"

Nalin looked up, tried futilely to explain, then lost the effort in more laughter. He began to smile at her helpless glee in spite of the fact that he didn't know what she found so funny.

"Quanah." She finally controlled herself enough to speak. "They think, after three days, still you are not satisfied. You will be a legend in the tribe when they return."

Quanah's smile broadened into laughter. She began laughing again with him until their sides ached. Finally he pulled her close to him. "Then they shall have more to wonder about. We will not return until tomorrow."

"Surely they will sing about you, oh man who never has enough."

Their prolonged honeymoon ended, their return was greeted with knowing grins from all sides, directed mostly at the new husband of such astounding virility. For most, three days were more than enough to have nothing to do but break in a new wife.

Manatah greeted his new son-in-law with a broad smile, pleased that he had indeed given Nalin a good husband. They would give him many grandchildren before

165

his days were ended. The old man, inspired perhaps by his son-in-law's heroic feat, seemed to take on a new youth himself, plainly evidenced by his wife's fatigue in the days that followed.

The couple set up housekeeping as the band continued their wandering trek through their vast domain.

A month into their marriage, Quanah returned from a short day's hunt in disgust. So many of the bison they depended on for food had been killed by the whites that the rest had been driven off to safer pastures. The hunters would have to go farther for game or raid a farm or settlement for provisions to carry them through the remaining springtime, until the grass grew high enough to lure the buffalo back from their hiding place. The hunters would have to be away for several days. Nalin had not been parted from Quanah for more than a few hours since their wedding and did not intend to begin now. She started to pack for two.

"You are not going," Quanah told her as soon as he noticed.

"Why not? I always have before."

"You are my wife now," he answered, as if the statement explained it all.

She turned to him, green eyes flashing. "Quanah, you promised. I have earned the rights of a warrior. Do you deny that?"

"No." He knew full well the status she had earned before their marriage. Her revenge on the two white men had proven her, and no one would argue her place if they raided a white settlement. No one but Quanah. "I promised you could come on raids, not hunts." He defended his position weakly, fully cognizant of the fact that she had been taking part in hunts since she was fifteen. That was different. That was before.

"And if you do raid a settlement?"

"You are *not* going now!"

"I am!"

First he tried to stare her down crossly, but a cool Comanche was no match for a hot-tempered Irish lass. "You will disobey me?" he shouted.

"Only if you forbid me to go."

Red Fox called from outside. "Quanah, are you ready yet?"

No respectable Comanche would ever think of striking a woman, but at this moment the thought was tempting.

"Quanah?" Red Fox called again.

"We are coming!" he shouted back. "Well, don't just stand there, woman. Hurry!" Quanah stormed out, retrieving his dignity by letting her carry all the provisions.

Chapter 15

SOMEHOW, every time they now went on a raid, she always seemed to wind up on this side, like a mere boy. Quanah's band of raiders, unable to find buffalo clear into the summer season, had settled more often for wagon trains, rich with supplies and oxen.

She could hear the gunfire from the other side of the hills while she remained, as Quanah had ordered, holding the extra horses. She might try disobeying him at home, that was one thing, but never as chief of a raiding party. He told her to hold the horses, and that she must do, in spite of her feet that wouldn't stay still as she paced, waiting for them to return.

The gunfire stopped, and Nalin ineffectually stood on tiptoe trying to see over the hills, which were far too high. What was going on? Had the wagon train surrendered?

Minutes dragged by as she resumed her pacing. The war camp was silent behind her, disturbed only by an occasional whinny or snort from the grazing horses tied to stakes. Still pausing occasionally to look out in that direction, a single warrior appeared over the hill, galloping back toward her.

Broken Hand reined in short in front of her. "Get your horse, Nalin, and your weapons. Quanah wants you to come with me."

"Quanah?" Her face drained to pasty white.

"He is not hurt, Nalin, but hurry."

168

It took only a minute to pick up her bow and quiver and sling a rifle over her shoulder then mount Blackie and ride off with Broken Hand. Past the hills she had wished she could see over, she found her people circling the wagon train out of gun range. She saw in a moment that Quanah's surprise attack had gone awry, resulting in a standoff, the wagon train forming an effective shield for the settlers, while the overwhelming Comanche force could not move in without heavy losses. Quanah would not sacrifice needlessly.

She and Broken Hand slowed their mounts as they approached. "Quanah needs you to talk to them. Tell them we will leave them in peace if they give us supplies."

By now Quanah himself had come up to meet them.

"Is that all I am for?" she shot at him angrily. "You only want me to talk to them?"

"Manatah is not here to speak for us. You know the language. No one else among us does."

"Oh, so at any other time Nalin is useless. Simply to hold horses and guard war camps. But *now* you need me?"

"Nalin, go and speak with them!" he ordered, both as her husband and as her chief. She glared at him before kicking Blackie into a canter. The warriors stopped circling the trapped wagon train, giving them time to realize they were ready to parley. Nalin walked her horse through the warriors, approaching slowly.

"What in hell is that?" The wagon master peered carefully over the edge of a wagon hitch. As she came closer, there was no room to doubt she was female: full, firm breasts and a tiny waist noticeable even beneath the loose buckskin shirt and leggings.

"It's a woman," McGee answered from beside him.

"I know that, but what kinda' woman? She ain't even Indian."

Indeed it was a strange and unexpected picture she presented as she neared them. Nalin's femininity precluded her dressing as the other warriors did for battle. While they stripped down to only a breechclout, she also wore full leggings and a buffalo-hide shirt that wrapped around her torso, bound by the leather belt that held her knife. Over her back was her quiver filled with twenty steel-tipped arrows, her bow over the other shoulder, while she held the rifle that was pointed upward and resting on her thigh, her hand over the trigger and ready. The auburn hair, now cut to her shoulders, framed her face in wispy curls held back from her eyes only by the leather band across her forehead. Two braves flanked her on either side and only slightly behind.

"We would speak with you," the undeniably feminine voice called out.

Wagon master John O'Halloran stood up. "We're listenin'."

"Leave us food, blankets, the oxen, and spare horses, and you may pass in peace."

"Whose side is she on?" McGee piped up, staring at the obviously white female.

"Theirs, dumbass!" O'Halloran turned back to the warriors. "We can't do that."

One of the warriors moved up beside her and spoke to her briefly before she shouted, "It is a small price to pay for your lives. We are many, while you are few."

O'Halloran considered his chances, betting on his position. "Well, we're enough I reckon."

The warrior spoke with her again, then spun his horse around as she called out, "So be it!"

As they turned, one of the settlers fired, the bullet hitting the ground, splattering the dirt in front of the woman's horse. In an instant, gunfire exploded from everywhere. Nalin lowered her rifle, firing and missing O'Halloran by inches as he ducked behind the wagon. Instead of turning about and retreating, she screamed a blood-curdling war cry and charged the wagons. Seeing her action, the brave beside her turned and charged as well. O'Halloran had only seconds to ponder his fatal error. As Nalin leaped the hitch, he aimed at her, but the brave behind her brought down his rifle and fired. O'Halloran's chest shattered.

The remainder of the warriors, taking courage from

170

their leader, also charged the defenses, and from there the battle was a short one. Within five minutes most of the settlers were dead or wounded, and only five braves had been hurt, one killed. The women, children, and wounded men were gathered together, ready to be taken back as slaves, while the wagons were searched and supplies drawn out.

"Burn all of the wagons but one," Quanah ordered. "Leave two oxen behind to pull it."

"For what, Quanah?" Red Fox looked at his chief, puzzled.

"Put the women and children and the wounded in it. Leave that one to help them." Quanah pointed at McGee, nursing an arrow-pierced shoulder.

"We are not taking them?"

"No, our days of taking slaves from our raids have ended. We have all we can do to feed ourselves now. We do not need their burden."

"Then we can kill them."

"No." Quanah turned on him sharply. "We will leave the slaughter of women and children to the whites."

Red Fox acknowledged this, while Quanah turned at last to his wife. His dark eyes flashed so angrily that she involuntarily gave a slight jump. "Stupid woman! Did I tell you to charge the wagons?"

"But that was the only way, Quanah. They fired on us."

"*Did* I tell you to?"

"No," she answered meekly. She had seen him angry before but never quite this angry. The ebony eyes had sparks in them.

"Never again do you attack until I tell you to!"

"Yes, Quanah."

"You stay behind me, and you tell them what I tell you to say!"

"Yes, Quanah," she mumbled.

He turned from her and started to walk away. Nalin fell in behind him. "But, Quanah—"

He spun around, furious. "Do not speak to me until I tell you you may!"

171

She didn't even dare answer "Yes Quanah" this time and just numbly nodded.

All the way back to the war camp he would not allow her to speak. Darkness fell, and still his anger had not abated. He would have been angry and shown his displeasure with any warrior who had usurped his position and perhaps jeopardized the war party. For one as young and inexperienced as she, temporary ostracism by the warriors was fit punishment for her failure to know her place, but, coming from him, to be totally ignored hurt far deeper. Her two coups, when she killed one enemy and wounded another, counted as nothing, and not yet would anyone praise her for them, not while Quanah consigned her to exile.

She wished to ask his forgiveness but didn't dare; instead she attended her duties, helping the others as they prepared food and ate. While they laughed and recounted stories of their bravery, she sat quietly, casting furtive glances at her somber and still angry husband. When Quanah at last stood up to go to their shelter, Nalin followed. She cursed herself solidly for her impulsiveness. Perhaps it would be a long time before he forgave her, before he would trust her again. He had asked only one thing of her, *talk* to them—just that. Not make a foolhardy charge that jeopardized her life and his as he turned to follow her dash. No matter that it had come out well, she had put all of the warriors in danger by provoking them into following her. The price in lives could have been high if not for the surprise of the whites at the suicidal charge. It had been stupid, just plain stupid!

Nalin knelt on the ground, putting away the weapons. They had built a small lean-to shelter a close distance from the others. Leaves and branches over buffalo hides gave them a roof and privacy on one side and hid the light of a small fire burning beneath for warmth in the cool summer night. Quanah stretched out on the bedroll Nalin had laid when they made the war camp. Finished with her chores, she rose, standing uncertainly, afraid to look at him.

"Nalin, come here."

172

She obeyed him silently, unwilling to gaze on those dark eyes if they were focused on her in disapproval. She knelt at the edge of the bedroll, removing her belt then her leggings as Quanah watched. She pulled the shirt over her head, revealing the smooth, firm flesh beneath. Quietly she lay down beside him as he pulled the blanket up over them both.

He lay on his side, facing her. "Nalin." He touched her cheek, turning her face toward him. "My foolish girl," he whispered softly. "You were nearly killed today. Do you know what it would do to me to lose you? My life would be worth nothing."

"I'm sorry, Quanah, I did not mean—"

His mouth covered hers, effectively silencing her. "I love you, woman. Do not lose a life so precious to me."

Nalin's arm encircled his back, holding him close as she basked in the warmth of his embrace. "Always love me." She snuggled deeper underneath his chin. "For I will always love you." She repeated the words of her marriage vow, meaning each one with every fiber of her being.

She promised him then to always use care and caution with her life, and for the next two years of their marriage she did, at least reasonably well. Eventually, Quanah, too, learned to speak the language of the whites, and instead of being his speaker, she rode only slightly behind him, silent as her husband spoke for himself. She was close beside him in every encounter, whether to trade or to fight, and now had many coups to her credit. She was almost as adept at stealing horses as he, and both had become an irritating thorn in the sides of the Cavalry trying to protect settlers and wagon trains from the marauding Comanche band.

As the buffalo dwindled, they took more and more to raiding to provide the necessities. McGee, spared by Quanah after the wagon train attack, was the first to carry back tales of the white woman warrior. The long locks of red hair Quanah carried on his battleshield, at first thought to be the tresses of some unfortunate lass,

173

were soon matched to the short red hair of the woman warrior, and the whites learned of her as Quanah's woman, nameless except for her connection to him. Quanah refused to come to, or even discuss, peace terms with the bluecoats. He would make no promise he did not intend to keep, and he intended no peace with the invaders of their domain. Thus, Nalin never learned of the plot conceived to bring her husband in by declaring her wanted for murder and treason.

Chapter 16

MAJOR PARKER didn't often leave the confines of Fort Smith. In his capacity as legal counselor, his services were rarely required elsewhere. Thus, when an opportunity to defend a soldier in a neighboring fort presented itself, Parker took the case as counsel for the defense, if only to get out of the four timbered walls that outlined Fort Smith.

He was enjoying the ride beside Sergeant Ryker, who was as uninclined to chat as he himself was at present. The day was warm and cloudless, with a slight cooling breeze from the northwest. They rode fifth in the column of mounted soldiers, the line punctuated only by occasional wagons of supplies destined for the fort. Knowing the heavily laden wagons would be a likely target, twice the usual number of escorts accompanied them, and Tankawa scouts combed the hills searching for signs of possible raiders.

As they passed, unharmed, through several places likely to be used to launch an attack and nothing happened, attitudes began to relax, though they were still prepared for trouble. They made camp by the river. Dawn began to break on a clear sky, heralding another warm late-summer day. The soldiers awoke refreshed, washed, ate, then began to saddle up and pack, and in that moment of near-security, while everyone enjoyed the fact that they had only three more hours of riding before reaching their destination, the Comanche forces descended on them while the soldiers still held their saddles in their hands.

Harrison Parker was caught in the process of tightening the girth on his saddle. He made a four-yard dash back to his rifle, just as a Comanche warrior swooped down on him, the rifle firing inches from his head as he fell to the ground and rolled to safety. The warrior turned for another try, but by now Harrison had the rifle ready. He lifted, pointing more than aiming, and fired, striking the Indian in the chest. The man seemed to hang suspended in mid-air briefly as the horse galloped out from beneath him, and he sprawled to the ground on his back.

Instantly, another warrior was upon him. Harry grappled with the man, who still managed a well-placed stab into Harrison's shoulder. The knife buried itself into the soft flesh, missing bone by inches. Ignoring the searing pain, Parker managed a kick to the warrior's groin that brought him to the ground. Desperately, he followed through with another kick to the head that snapped the Indian's neck.

Pure luck so far, Harry thought as he raised himself to his feet. He cast about, looking for another foe or something to do to help the situation that was fast becoming a major defeat for the soldiers. He saw Ryker flat on his back, grappling with an Indian. Harrison stepped forward to help, and in that moment his bleeding, punctured shoulder was grabbed and he was swung around to face a new enemy. Before Harry could move, Quanah had hit him with the butt end of a rifle, sending the lawyer to the ground into oblivion.

Ryker's own circumstances were desperate, yet he had seen the major fall. Disarmed by his opponent, Ryker flinched, ready for the slash the brave was about to administer that would cut his throat. The brave had Ryker by the hair, ready to end his life, and the army sergeant couldn't figure a way out of this one. What he was sure would be his last sight on earth was of Quanah, standing over Major Parker, knife upraised in his hand, ready to claim another white man's scalp.

"No! Don't kill him!" Ryker shouted, ignoring his own precarious predicament.

Quanah stopped and looked up. "With a knife at your own throat, you ask for this one's life?" He dropped Harrison's head into the dust and came toward Ryker. The other Indian waited, still holding the knife at the sergeant's neck.

Ryker glanced at the Indian above him, then back to Quanah. "It's just that I wouldn' want ya ta kill a blood relative."

"You lie badly," Quanah spat, beginning to turn away.

"He's your cousin," Ryker shouted after him. "Name's Harrison Parker, son of Isaac Parker. That's your uncle, Quanah."

The Comanche stopped again, staring at the unconscious form of the hated bluecoat. Ryker had only seconds to convince him, maybe for both their sakes. "I swear it, Quanah. He's your ma's cousin . . . an' yours."

"If you lie—"

"I ain't lyin'. He's Harrison Parker."

Quanah spoke a few quick words in Comanche to the brave holding the knife at Ryker's throat, and the blade was miraculously removed. Roughly, the Indian pushed Ryker to his feet. Quanah stepped forward until he was only inches away from the sergeant's face. "You will live, but only until I find out if you speak the truth. If you have not, you will wish you had died here."

Ryker was taken to the camp and guarded in one tepee while Harrison was taken to another. Once a day, a meager ration of food was tossed in front of him; Ryker thought it a generous gesture since the Comanche themselves had almost starved through the winter and were doing little better now. As days adding up to a week passed, he saw neither Quanah nor anyone else who spoke a word of English. There was no way to discover how Major Parker was faring, but Ryker knew, if Parker died, he'd know it soon enough. Since his own fate hadn't yet been settled, the major must be in pretty bad shape and unable to talk. *If* and when, hopefully, pray God,

177

when Parker answered, Ryker could only hope he'd go along with being Quanah's cousin and not argue the matter, since the major didn't have the slightest notion of the blood tie either.

A single face manifested itself through the half-awareness of the days that followed for Harrison Parker. His delirium was broken for mere seconds of wakefulness in which the woman, known to him only as Quanah's wife, leaned over him, spooning weak broth down his throat. When the fever broke at last, he slept in complete oblivion for a day and a night; by that time the face of the one who had nursed him was engraved on his memory.

He awoke a few minutes before she appeared, having already assessed that he had, somehow, been saved from certain death, and completely at a loss as to why. Quanah's wife knelt beside him, startled to find him awake and fully conscious.

"Hello," he said, in surprising strength for one who had been so near death. She did not reply as she offered the spoonful of broth to his lips. He accepted it gratefully, ravenously hungry after the long siege. Silent and stoic, she shoveled several mouthfuls of broth down his throat, as if anxious to be finished with the loathsome chore. "I've been told you speak English. Is that true?"

If she understood a word of it she was not letting on, continuing to shove the spoon into his mouth mechanically.

"Do you have a name?"

The last mouthful went in. She set the bowl down and prepared to rise.

"I'm very grateful for what you've done for me."

The hostility in her gaze took him aback, reflecting not only that she had understood him, but that his salvation was not at all her idea.

"Why *am* I still alive?"

She started to rise again, and Harrison touched her arm. She wrenched it from his grasp. "Your life was spared by my husband," she answered in concise, cold English. She rose far more slowly and clumsily than she apparently wanted to. Harrison looked up to see the large mound of her belly. The fort residents had been wondering why Quanah's wife had not been seen since the raids last fall; now he knew. She was very pregnant; about due any day, he guessed. She waddled out with the gait only a pregnant woman can assume, and Harrison smiled in amusement. Must be hell for a warrior, he surmised silently—grounded for the duration.

Of course he had heard all the tales Ryker knew about the half-breed Quanah and his white wife. With her glaring coldness he no longer had the slightest doubt that she was among the Comanche by choice. It was ironic, though, that the baby the rebellious pair had created would be three-fourths white and only a quarter Indian.

Harrison had little time to muse over the irony, however, as a few minutes after her departure, Quanah himself entered. Though he had never met him, the man's bearing left little doubt about his identity. Harrison remained quiet as the Comanche chief squatted beside him. His last glimpse of those features had been his closest brush ever with death.

"What is your name?" Quanah's English was nearly as good as his wife's. The speech was clipped into the short halts Indians were used to, but carefully and flawlessly pronounced.

"Parker." The white held eye contact with the warrior. "Harrison Parker."

Quanah paused, still staring, almost searching Harry's features. His eyes narrowed. "Who is your father?"

The question puzzled Harry. "Isaac Parker."

"He had a niece?"

"A niece?" Harry was totally perplexed now. So much so, in fact, that he had to think about the answer. "Yes, he had several."

"One named Cynthia?" Quanah had trouble pronouncing the name, but it was comprehensible. He had eased all the way to a sitting position, cross-legged on the ground, a mere foot from Harry's shoulder.

"No, I don't remember a Cynthia." Harry couldn't figure out the Indian's interest in his family tree. Thoughts

179

were jumbling through his mind too quickly, then a memory struck. "Wait, I think there was a Cynthia."

The chief gave him time to form an answer. It was difficult with the elected leader of the Comanche nation hanging over him. This *young* man, who couldn't have been over thirty, was the single unifying force behind the entire Comanche power. Since Medicine Bend, many of the young warriors, dissatisfied with their chiefs' agreements, had fled their own bands to join Quanah and the Kwahadi. It was rumored Satanta, of the Kiowa, who had signed at Medicine Bend, was now deserting his word and joining forces with the Comanche. Before Quanah they had been scattered into several small bands, ineffectual under so many chiefs. With him, they had been united into one of the most aggressive fighting units the U.S. Cavalry had ever faced. Concentrating on childhood memories was not easy under the circumstances, since Harry had never met his cousin Cynthia, only heard of her.

"My father did have a niece named Cynthia Ann. She was captured by Indians long before I was born. He used to tell me about her though. She was his favorite . . ."

The Comanche accepted the information without a trace of expression. "Go on," he urged when Harry stopped.

"I remember Father writing to me when I was in school back East. He told me Cynthia Ann had been taken back. That he had seen her again. He was upset about the incident though, because she wanted to go back. She wanted to return to the tribe where her . . . sons . . . were . . ." His voice trailed off as the words started to form a picture. Long-buried memories, almost entirely forgotten, were coming back. The single letter mentioning Cynthia had been of little importance other than to provoke passing sympathy for the cousin he never knew anyway. Pa had said she was taken by Indians, but he never said which tribe. And that she had given birth to two sons, left behind when she was recaptured. Two half-white sons, and now half-white Quanah wanted answers to questions about the Parker family. "Why am I still alive?" Harrison asked in the ensuing silence. He was fairly sure he knew why now.

"Cynthia Ann was my mother." The half-breed rose to his feet, looking down once more on the cavalry officer. "For her, you live." He turned on his heel and walked out, leaving Harry to ponder his strange kinship.

He was still pondering some time later. Naturally it was a surprise, although he should have considered that he did have two Indian cousins back in the West somewhere. He was also slightly surprised at his reaction to the knowledge. Technically, he and his cousins were sworn enemies, and yet he found himself a bit proud of the relationship to the awe-inspiring chieftain. Isaac Parker had married late in life, putting Harry very near the age of his second cousin.

He regarded Quanah much as he regarded Robert E. Lee; perhaps they were on opposite sides, but that fact could not lessen his admiration. Harrison's father, a soldier and statesman, had taught him that a man, even one you were at odds with, had his own point of view to consider and should be treated accordingly, not judged as right or wrong, but of a different persuasion.

Now Harry was bursting with curiosity about his newfound relatives, though he doubted the same could be said for Quanah, who had allowed him to live only in memory of his mother. Harry closed his eyes, more in an attempt to rest them than in any effort to sleep. The wound he had suffered still hurt, but, as long as he didn't move too much, it was bearable. He heard the sound of someone pattering about in the tepee, probably keeping quiet, thinking him asleep. He kept his eyes closed, feigning just that.

Then there was the soft murmur of voices deliberately kept low, a man's and a woman's whispering in Comanche. Harrison peered through the slit of one eye. It was Quanah and his wife; she was handing him packages. In profile, her belly was enormous. Apparently, Quanah was leaving on a trip of some duration, at least several days it

181

seemed from the size of the packages. From his pretended sleep Harry watched the pair, spying on the relationship of Quanah and his woman.

He didn't know quite what he expected. Perhaps stories heard in the fort had left impressions that were not accurate, but he found himself surprised at the obvious tenderness expressed by the dreaded Comanche chief; it was as if there were two Quanahs, the warrior Harry had so painfully met in battle, and the husband, concerned about leaving his pregnant wife.

Harry couldn't understand a word of their whispers, but the gestures were plain enough. First, as she clumsily bent to lift a parfleche, he teased her by pinching her bottom. When she pretended anger, he took her in his arms and held her for a long, lingering moment. Plainly read on each face was concern for the other. The warrior backed away, cupping her head in his hands, gazing at her as if to burn her features into his memory, then he leaned down and kissed her tenderly. He placed a hand over her distended abdomen and whispered something, grinning broadly. Harry couldn't help a smile creeping over his face at the domestic scene before his spying eyes. Finally, as though forcing himself, Quanah gestured for her to stay and left. She watched from the open flap, apparently until he was out of sight. When she turned back to check on her bluecoat patient, his eyes were open.

"Guess I must have dozed off." He faked a yawn so she would not know of his spying. The soft, gentle gaze of a few minutes before was replaced instantly with hostility. She *hated* him, and he wished he knew why.

Barely a moment later, another figure entered. This brave was shorter than Quanah and as stocky as the chieftain was lean. The Indian noticed Harry's wakefulness and actually smiled at him. The brave walked over, crossed his legs, and sat facing the white man.

"You are Har'son," he said, still smiling broadly.

The question was needless, since there were no other white men present. Harry looked at him and nodded. The man was dark, handsomely Indian-featured, blue-black straight hair loosely bound by a headband and hanging well below his shoulders. He wore breechclout and leggings but no robe or shirt, only a few layers of beads and colored quills about his neck. "I am Pecos." He pointed at himself. "Pecos Parker."

Harry's brow lifted, not expecting the use of the name. He held out his hand, and his cousin grasped it, giving it a shake that was a bit too strong, then backed off, still grinning. Where Quanah showed some signs of his white heritage, his younger brother showed none. Nor were they, obviously, of the same temperament. This one was friendly, as eager as Harry was to satisfy his curiosity about his new relative.

Pecos confessed that he had been left behind to help guard the camp and to protect Nalin from Harry, should he try to escape. Harry was also informed by the younger of the Parker brothers that he was to remain until Quanah returned. Pecos chattered on about "the other," whom Harry finally figured out was Sergeant Ryker, who had been spared with him. Quanah had taken him along and would presently set him free within distant proximity of the fort. Pecos did not explain why Quanah was freeing Ryker unharmed, nor could Harry coax out of him why or where Quanah was going. He was also told with a friendly smile to remain within Quanah's lodge, because more warriors than Pecos remained to guard the camp since the bluecoats occasionally came in the early dawn, and if Harry stuck his head out for air, one of them might take it as a sign he was attempting escape and shoot him.

As for Nalin, as he had learned her name was, she spoke to him rarely and then only to inquire about his needs. When he asked her a question, it was usually answered with a gesture, a monosyllable, or not at all.

Once, while Nalin was out on her daily stroll—a ritual, he had learned, of all pregnant Comanche women—Harry tried to find out from Pecos why his sister-in-law hated bluecoats so much. Pecos had replied that it wasn't necessarily bluecoats she hated, but all whites. Beyond that he would say nothing more, cheerfully changing the subject.

Seeing her daily, Harrison was struck anew each morning by how beautiful she was. Even her swollen belly enhanced her loveliness, lending a serene charm to her features.

When Pecos was not present, and sometimes even when he was, Harrison would watch her going through her daily chores and routines. Gradually what began as curiosity and infatuation became desire and hopeless obsession. He was falling in love with another man's wife—Quanah's wife.

Chapter 17

HARRISON awoke, not certain what had awakened him. He could see the first light of dawn through the edges of the tepee flap. Pecos was stretched out before the entrance. Nalin was on the farther side, directly across from him. He felt a twinge of pain in the healing shoulder; the wound was mending nicely enough. Then he heard it again, the sound that must have awakened him, a low moan from Nalin's side of the lodge. He called her name softly, but either she didn't hear him or was again ignoring him.

Harry sat up, then made his way over to Pecos. "Pecos, wake up." The words were hardly out of his mouth before the brave spun about. "I think Nalin is having the baby." At the same moment, she groaned again, and Pecos needed no further inquiry. He had been anxious and fretful for days over the coming of his brother's child; he was taking the place of Quanah, who, had he been home, would have been the one to fetch and carry and fret. Rough Comanches, when their women were due, took oversolicitous care of them, not allowing them to lift any burden and waiting on them in a manner that would be unbefitting a warrior at any other time. Pecos had been his brother's proxy. He was up on his feet and off in a hurry, to find a midwife, Harry assumed.

Harry watched as Pecos ran across the encampment, searching out a particular abode. As he did, his eyes caught a gleam in the dawn light from the ridge above the camp. Instantly he recognized its meaning. "Pecos, get down!" Harry shouted, and he was almost immediately answered by the loud, jarring boom of a cannon.

Pecos had heard him and dove for the ground, rolling himself against the edge of a tepee. Gunfire started from atop the ridge, and the resulting pandemonium was a scene from hell.

Startled awake, the Indians, men, women, and children, staggered outside to be met on all sides by the constant cracking of rifles, while the cannon intermittently exploded around them, bringing their homes crashing to the ground. The warriors who had remained behind tried to hurry their families to safety while preparing a defense. Bodies were falling everywhere as Harry, gapemouthed, watched in horror. As a lawyer he had never accompanied the soldiers on these raids though he had heard of them. Never had any been described like this. This wasn't war; it was slaughter.

The braves tried to reach their horses; some made it, many more died in the attempt as the soldiers moved down the ridge closer to the camp. As they fired indiscriminately, women fell, smothering their babies beneath them. Old grandfathers picked up weapons, attempting a last vain effort to ward off the attackers. Children fell in the onrush, and Harry couldn't believe they were hit deliberately until he saw a mounted soldier ride down a boy of about seven and shoot him in the back. He turned away, ready to vomit, but his mind was already set to a different task. Forcing the bile down his throat, he stepped over to Nalin, wide-eyed with fear but unable to rise. He reached down to help her to her feet, but she began to fight him.

"We can't stay here." Harry held her flailing arms. "We have to get out."

His use of the word "we" was so surprising that she stopped fighting him.

"Are there any weapons in here?"

"Only a knife," she said tightly, trying to keep from doubling over. The baby was coming, now of all times! Harry cursed under his breath as he found the sheathed knife where she had pointed and stuck it into his belt. He grabbed Nalin's waist tightly, pulling her up and putting her arm around his shoulder. He released her again only long enough to slit the back of the tepee, then helped her through, hurrying toward the far ridge, where the survivors were running for cover.

Nalin began to moan louder, half weeping as she stepped over the fallen bodies of friends. Harry pulled her toward the safety of the hills. Had he been Indian, they never would have made it. Soldiers swarmed everywhere, pulling old people and children out of the tepees. Mounted and on foot they passed him, noticing only his blue uniform and figuring he was taking the woman prisoner.

Progress would have been faster if he could have carried her, but he tried once and his shoulder wound opened, sending a searing pain through his arm until he was forced to set her down. He passed the farthest corner of the encampment, weighing briefly the possibility of escape on one of the frightened horses still tethered to the ground. But Nalin was doubling over now, barely able to walk, much less ride. On foot, he started to climb the ridge, pulling her along with him, ignoring the blood that was now seeping through his sleeve.

Indians on all sides were disappearing among the rocks and crevices above and below him; hell still reigned with the screams and wails of those caught in the death trap below.

The warriors who had managed to escape and mount their horses were trying to form a line of defense to at least protect the hills where the people had fled. Harry made out the form of Pecos among them. They charged, and the suicidal act seemed to surprise the soldiers into drawing back. Harry closed his mind to it; there was nothing he could do for them now, promising himself, though, that if he survived and reached Fort Smith, the truth would be known. Nalin stumbled and fell, groaning. She couldn't go much farther. He left her briefly to search the ridge, finding a place that would have to do. He helped her into a crevice between boulders that formed a three-sided room where they could be hidden from view. Gently he laid her down; she was gasping now, her arms clutched over her abdomen. He looked frantically about for a woman, any woman, to appear. There was no one around; only the confusion below.

"Oh, God," he mumbled as Nalin's arm clutched her body in another spasm. "This is a fine time to have a baby."

"I can't help it!" she retorted through clenched teeth.

"What am I supposed to do now?"

"Join your murdering friends down there!"

Harry stood over her, helpless as the spasms came closer together and harder. "I think you're holding it in. You're not supposed to do that."

"How would you know? Get out of here! Get out!" she shrieked as he knelt beside her. Harry's hand covered her mouth. One look was sufficient for her to realize the hand was a warning. There was complete silence now, no voices, no gunfire, nothing. Nalin stifled her cry as another spasm shook her body. Harry signaled her to be quiet with a finger over his mouth, then crept to the nearest boulder to peer over.

Amongst the smoke and dust swirling below, the bluecoats were wandering through the now-deserted village. The warriors had fled to parts unknown, as had those who had survived the raid by running for the hills. Prisoners had been gathered into a circle on the far side of the camp, and a few soldiers were being ordered into the hills to search for more. Harry hurried back to her. "They are combing the hills for survivors. Don't make a sound."

She was perspiring now. Her legs had begun to spread apart in spite of her efforts to hold them closed. The baby was coming, whether the time was right or not.

"Goddamn! Oh, goddamn!" Harry muttered in a whisper. He had no faith left in the humanity of his fellow soldiers, not out of this pack, not after what he had seen below. It wouldn't take them long to figure out who the redhaired squaw was, and for Quanah's wife there would be no mercy. "Don't scream!" he warned, leaning down close to her ear. "Don't make a sound." Her face reddened under the strain, but she held it in. "Here." Harry removed the knife from the leather sheath and stuck the rawhide in her mouth. "Bite down hard!"

Nalin's teeth dug into the leather, her face pinched and bright red.

Once more Harry checked over the boulder. The soldiers were still climbing, but only a few. Without realizing what he was doing, his hand was gripping the knife hilt, holding it ready. Two soldiers scattered to the left and two to the right. They would pass on either side a few feet away. Don't come yet, baby . . . please, God, don't let it come yet, he prayed silently. He had chosen this spot because the boulders gave the appearance of one piece of solid rock without a hint of the crevice between unless they passed it. Please God! His hand clenched the hilt tighter.

A shout from below echoed up over the hill. The soldiers stopped within five feet of the hiding place. They were signaled to come down, and they started off at once. Harry wanted to edge closer to see why they had turned around, but a stifled moan turned him back. Nalin was thrashing wildly on the ground, her teeth dug deep into the leather sheath. The baby's head was out, but was going no farther.

With another whispered "Dear God," Harry rushed back. The baby's head was sideways; the shoulders seemed to be stuck in his mother's small pelvis. Praying that he was doing the right thing he gently gripped the infant's head with one hand and squeezed his fingers inside, feeling for the baby's spine. Nalin was rigid with pain, not helping his task as he slowly began to ease the tiny body around and outward. In minutes that felt like hours, the baby finally burst into the world, whole and intact, dropping into Harry's hands.

Nalin had gone limp with relief as he held the tiny form in his hands like a porcelain doll, not sure now what to do with it. The baby squirmed but didn't cry. Harry fleetingly thought that he was supposed to spank it, then was horror-struck at the idea. If the infant cried here, now, the sound would echo out of the rock formation and bring the soldiers back. "Hush, baby, don't cry, please. For your ma's sake and for your pa's sake, please don't cry!" The baby's mouth opened, the body squirming from the uncomfortable position. Tiny blue eyes seemed to peer at Harry closely. "For *my* sake, baby, don't do it!"

The small mouth opened wider, and the baby yawned like a tiny old man who'd lost his teeth. The mouth opened and closed again, several times.

"Harrison," Nalin whispered weakly. She was looking at him fearfully, beads of sweat still clinging to her face. Harry smiled to reassure her, then held the tiny form up for her to see. "A boy," he whispered. Nalin smiled back, the first time he had ever seen one on her. Gently Harry placed the baby belly-down on his mother's stomach, and Nalin touched the wet head lovingly.

"The cord," she whispered to him, then made a cutting motion with her fingers. Harry's brow furrowed as he looked at it. "How?"

She showed him how far with her finger and thumb, just as the women had told her. Harry scrubbed the knife on the cleanest part of his jacket and made the cut as if fearing the blood of mother and child might spill out, then Nalin motioned for him to take the baby again. He pulled off his uniform coat and wrapped it around the doll-like form, then turned away as Nalin struggled to get up. While she did whatever women were supposed to do, Harry concentrated on rubbing the tiny limbs clean. As he rubbed with his coat, the baby's skin started to show pink and healthy, and still the little bugger hadn't made a sound. Harry smiled at him. "You're something, baby. You sure are," he crooned just above a whisper. "Brave, just like your folks. Born in a battle, and you don't make a sound. Hey . . ." Harrison was suddenly struck with the idea. "You're my cousin, you know that?" He would have sworn the baby smiled at him. By now, he was working on the tiny head, drying the baby fluff, which began to lighten.

"Hey, Nalin?" he said quietly. She came up beside him. "This fellow's a Parker all right. Parkers are always born blond."

"I'm telling you, it runs in the family," Harry argued, louder now that he was sure the soldiers were gone. They still rested in their hideout between the rocks. Nalin was lying down now on her side, the baby sleeping against her, still wrapped in Harrison's officer's coat. Harry's open wound continued to ooze blood that Nalin watched in concern. As for Harry, he didn't seem to feel a thing, sitting against one of the boulders, long legs spread out before him. He was beyond pain at the moment, too inebriated with excitement at his part in the birth. "My father was blond when he was born, I was—"

"You are not blond." Nalin grinned.

"No, it darkened." He touched the unruly mop of sandy hair. "But when I was a baby it was blond, just like his. And blue eyes, they run in the family, too."

"Babies are always born with blue eyes."

"Oh." Harry was disappointed but sprang back rapidly. "I bet his stay blue. Mine stayed blue. I'm telling you, he's strictly a Parker. See? Parker nose, Parker eyes . . ." He pointed out each asset on the sleeping face.

Nalin giggled. "He is too young yet to know."

"No, I'm right." He folded his arms with finality. "You can't argue with a godfather. Godfathers just know."

Nalin still smiled but was puzzled. "Harrison, what is a god . . . father?"

He had to think about the answer. "Well, a godfather is someone who would take care of the baby, look after him, raise him, if something happened . . . if the need ever arose," he corrected. She didn't need reminders about the horror below them or the fact that Quanah could still be in danger.

Her smile was gone as she looked at him. "You would do this . . . for him?"

He didn't have to think about the answer. "I would be proud to be his godfather, Nalin."

"But he is Comanche, part Comanche . . ."

"And I'd make sure he knew it and was damn proud of it."

The main body of the Comanche warriors rode in slowly, as there was no need for speed now. The desertion in the camp told them no one remained alive there. The soldiers had gone, probably leaving the moment their scouts spotted the warriors coming back. The raids on white settlements had been victorious, until now. The braves had been met by some of those who had survived the massacre, Pecos among them, who now rode by his brother's side. If Quanah and the main force of the Comanche nation had not been away, this would not have occurred. They had not been there to defend their people, and Quanah felt the brunt of it. For his failure, the Spirits had punished him. For the second time in his life he rode into a camp destroyed by the soldiers. The last time his mother and baby sister had been taken, and this time Nalin and the baby she carried. Either she had been taken back to the bluecoat camp or she was out of his reach forever. . . . He dismounted before the ruins of the lodge they had shared. The skins were scorched, the lodge poles broken by a direct hit from the cannon.

"Quanah, I couldn't reach her." Pecos stared at the burned tepee, his eyes moist with tears. Quanah could bring no tears to his own eyes; the shock and grief were too great.

"The bluecoat . . . Parker," Quanah began. Instead of finishing he began angrily sifting through the ruins on the side the soldier had been sleeping on, kicking the scorched skins roughly aside.

"He was awake when they came," Pecos started.

"He knew!" Quanah shouted, ready to bring blame down on any head. His usual cool logic failed him utterly now, not realizing that there was no way Harrison, or even the other soldier captured with him, could have known. Quanah had released him only a day ago, and for the soldiers to reach here the plan must have been set long before.

"Quanah, he saved my life. When the bluecoats came Nalin was . . . the baby was coming. I ran out to get the midwives. Parker saw the soldiers. It was he who warned me—"

"Then where are they? Where is Nalin?" He kicked through the rubble, venting his anger on the inanimate pieces. "He took her! He took her back to them! I'll kill him!" Quanah stormed back to his horse, ready to ride to Fort Smith with or without his warriors. Most were of the same mind and, seeing his action, began to remount.

"Hey! Hey down there!" The sound echoed over the camp from the hill above. Quanah turned to see a wildly waving Harrison Parker in only his shirt and trousers. The man's stupid face was grinning. Quanah saw no reason now, only blind grief and rage. He charged up the hill on foot, his hand already clenched over the knife hilt. Pecos recognized the look and started after him.

"No, Quanah, listen to him . . . Quanah!" Pecos was no match for his longer-legged brother, who quickly outdistanced him.

Harrison still stood looking at them, the stupid smile on his face. Quanah stopped in front of him. "Where is Nalin?"

"Right in there." The nonchalant Texan gestured toward the boulder.

"She is—"

"She's fine." At the last moment Harrison had recognized the murderous hatred in the man confronting him, so he enjoyed himself with the last dig as Quanah started toward the hideout. "Your son is fine, too."

Quanah froze in his tracks. Just then, the baby began to wail.

Chapter 18

SLOWLY, the scattered band began to re-form; women and children who had fled into the hills made their way back. Quanah set the braves to work, some to constructing a makeshift camp for survivors, others to searching the rubble for items still useful, and the rest to locating the dead amid the ruins.

The men helped the women reconstruct lodges for the coming of night out of pieces and scraps. Long ago, in the days of their ancestors, the work had been divided due to necessity and the biological makeup of the sexes. In their nomadic existence, the women, the child-bearers, carried the packs to leave the men's arms free to carry weapons. The men's place was to hunt and to protect the tribe, while the women took on the tasks of daily living. For centuries they had been content with that way of life. The ways were changing now, and the braves were forced to help the women retrieve belongings and set up camps. The once plentiful food supplies had dwindled, and no longer would parfleches be filled for the coming of winter. The venerable traditions could serve no longer. The Comanche had to keep pace with a world that was turning upside down.

Quanah returned to the shelter they had hastily constructed for Nalin and the baby. He had helped in the search through the rubble for the bodies of the slain, and his heart was heavy.

"Har'son," he called. The bluecoat soldier was helping an old woman construct a tepee from patched hides. He wasn't handling the logs too well, in spite of the old woman's gestured instructions. As a result, each time he had the logs almost right, one dislodged and the structure collapsed. Harry Parker looked up toward his cousin, letting the whole thing go when Quanah gestured to him.

"I have sad news for Nalin. You wait, I will bring the baby to you. You hold him."

As Quanah entered the lodge Harry nodded, grinning in pleasure that Quanah trusted him enough to leave his new son in the soldier's care. He couldn't understand the words they used within, but his grin faded while he wondered what it was Quanah had to tell her.

"Quanah." Nalin greeted him, beaming. "Has Toppasannah returned yet? She must see her new grandson and give him a name."

"No, Nalin, she has not." Quanah knelt beside her and reached for the child, asleep in his mother's arms.

"Isn't he beautiful, Quanah? Harrison says he looks just like a Parker."

Quanah soberly lifted the infant out of her arms. She made no protest, but her eyes questioned him. Silently he straightened, cradling the infant, and took it outside to Harry, placing the squirming baby in the soldier's arms. The look in Quanah's eyes told Harry all he needed to know; he took the baby from Quanah. He sat down on a stump outside, wrapping the blanket tighter around his godson.

Nalin was propped on an elbow, watching Quanah's face as he came back to her. "Is Toppasannah outside? Did you show her her grandson?" Her look was halfway between hope and nameless despair.

"No, Nalin, she is not." He knelt again beside her as she sat up. He took both of her hands in his, holding them in his strong grip. "She will never be. . . ."

Nalin's face, pale enough after the ordeal of birth, became even whiter. "She's . . . she's . . . Father! Where is he? I must go to him . . ." She struggled to rise, but her husband still held her hands.

"Manatah has been taken captive by the whites. He is their prisoner."

The struggling ceased as she looked up at him wide-eyed and stunned.

"We will get him back, Nalin. We will find where they have taken him. We will trade Har'son for him if we must, but we will get him back," he promised, offering her the only hope he knew.

"Who will name my baby?" Her voice broke, tears beginning to well up.

"I will," he offered softly as her shoulders began to tremble and she gave in to her grief. He touched her, and she propelled herself forward, sinking against him with bitter, wracking sobs. "I want my mother to . . . ," she moaned against his chest. "I want my mother." The warrior thought his heart would break as he felt his beloved wife's despair.

"I will tell them they may have you back when they return our people." Quanah spoke gruffly, but something in the warrior's face told Harry he didn't mean it. Harry was not being treated as a prisoner. He was no longer guarded or even watched; he went wherever he wished through the decimated camp. For days now, he had been helping them rebuild, disposing of the bodies of the slain, including Nalin's mother. They had learned that her father was being held at Fort Smith awaiting trial.

"Let me go now, Quanah, and I'll do everything I can to have him sent to the reservation."

Quanah's dark eyes spewed fire for a moment. "Manatah is a warrior! He will not spend the rest of his days *kept* by the white man." Quanah spat the word venomously. "We are Kwahadi. We do not live like women and children, to be fed, clothed, and sheltered. We are men!"

The words betrayed all of what Harry's peers could not seem to fathom, why the Great Plains tribes fought and starved and ran rather than submit to the white man's beneficence. Quanah stood up suddenly, motioning for Harry to follow him. He led him outside into the warm summer afternoon and began to walk through the slowly reconstructed camp. "Look, what do you see?" Quanah gestured with an upraised hand.

Harry did not understand the question. On his last raid, Quanah's band had taken the canvas that was now being used to construct lodges. Their own clothing damaged or burned beyond salvage, many were dressed in at least some article of white man's clothing, a plaid shirt here, blue trousers there, an occasional jacket that had been taken from a fallen soldier. The women were cooking over fires, putting their meager fare of buffalo meat, stolen beef, and prairie vegetables into iron kettles, stirring the contents with metal spoons. A little girl played with a blonde-haired doll, the china face cracked down the middle, the doll's dress scorched from a fire, but these flaws did not detract in the least from her enjoyment.

Quanah stopped briefly to watch her play, and the child gazed upward at the warrior, smiling. As he again began to walk through the camp, Quanah started to talk, though without a glance in Harry's direction. "Once the buffalo served all of our needs. He provided meat to fill our bellies and his hide covered our lodges and our bodies. Once our children played with toys made from the buffalo, and our women used even the bones to sew our clothing and to stir our pots. All that is ended now. The whites come and kill them, leaving meat to rot in the sun. Their only use for the buffalo is to take the hides and keep us from our food."

Harry's face reddened under the truth of Quanah's words. He had seen for himself: Bison were shot only to remove the Indians' food source and thereby bring them into submission. Profitable bounties had been put on the animals; a hunter would stand on a bluff and shoot down as many as he could manage before his trigger finger tired. Passengers going through on trains brought down bison for sport. Harry could say nothing to him. The vast herds of bison that had covered the plains were nearly gone; there was no way to bring them back. A way of life for the Great Plains Indians was becoming extinct—and so were they.

"Soon the buffalo will be no more." Quanah's steps had taken them to the edge of the camp. "Like the buffalo, soon the Comanche will be no more."

"That doesn't have to be, Quanah."

"Have you not seen what I have shown you? The ways of our ancestors will soon be forgotten, as the buffalo that fed us and kept us warm will be forgotten. My people, those who live on, will not be Comanche as I have been Comanche, as our fathers have been. They will be Comanche who live in the world of the white man, by the white man's ways. If they are not all to die like the great herds, it must be so." Quanah glanced once more about the camp, then turned to face Harry again, his face intent and troubled. "You can bring Manatah back to us?"

"I can't promise, Quanah. I'm not that big a chief in the Army, but I do swear I'll try. I'll try every way I know to get him freed and returned to you."

"I have known the pain of losing a mother and then a father. I know what Nalin suffers now. To lose Manatah also would make much grief for her."

"I will try, Quanah. That I do promise you."

"Promise me one more vow then, Har'son Parker."

"If I can."

"You can, and I have seen in your eyes that you will want to promise me this. I do not know the future of the Comanche. Perhaps we will all die, perhaps we will become as white men. I am not a medicine man who can see these things that must happen. For me, I do not know that I can live in the white man's world. But for my son, I see that this is how it must be. You must promise me this, Har'son Parker. If I do not survive this new world, you will see that my son does. You will teach him to be white."

For a long moment Harry was silent, staring at his younger cousin. Quanah was entrusting the care of his only child to Harry, a white man, a bluecoat. Harry was moved beyond anything he had ever felt before. His blue eyes misted with moisture as he met the gaze of his dark-eyed relative. "I promise you that, Quanah. Whatever happens, if he ever needs me, I'll be there, and I'll move heaven and earth for him."

"I knew you would do this." Quanah smiled faintly. "And for Nalin? Will you care for her also? She, too, will not fit in the white man's world. She is Comanche, like me. But you would help her to try?"

"Quanah, wherever you will be she will be, too. You know she'd never leave you."

Quanah understood thoroughly what Harry meant, that if Quanah was destined to die in battle, Nalin, his warrior wife, would die beside him. His smile broadened knowingly. "I pray that you are wrong, Har'son Parker, but in my heart I know you are right. Should this not happen, should I die and Nalin live, I will still ask that you take her."

"I would, Quanah, you know that," Harry pledged just above a whisper. He already loved her; it would be a promise he would keep without being asked. Or did Quanah already know that?

"Do not promise so quickly," Quanah chuckled lightly. "Nalin will not be easy to teach. Her mind is like the bull bison. She sets her feet and will not budge even when prodded with lances. I give you fair warning, Har'son Parker, sometimes you will want to strike her." The brave glanced sideways at him. "But do not do so, for surely she will strike you back."

With promises of undying friendship, Harry prepared to leave. After he set off for Fort Smith, the Comanche would break camp and follow their own direction. Many of the survivors had gathered to see the bluecoat on his way. He had been with them through the dawn attack and then through the weeks of counting losses, deprivation, and the restoration of some order to their lives. They no longer saw his white face and blue uniform; they saw a friend.

Harry shook hands with several of the warriors he had come to know in the past few weeks. At last it was time to bid farewell to his new-found family. Nacoma's one remaining wife, a proud, beautiful woman of nearly sixty, also held her hand out for the soldier's grasp. Harry took the proffered hand, a small one, dainty and smooth over the back but rough and calloused on the palm. Gallantly he bowed over it, kissing the top. "Farewell, lovely lady, until we meet again." Nacoma's widow, though she understood not a word of it, giggled girlishly.

Pecos bestowed a present on him, a well-honed knife of fine steel with a carved buffalo-horn hilt. Harry had refused his cousin's offer of a string of horses to take back with him, explaining that he needed no more than a single horse and that the U.S. Cavalry wouldn't let him keep them anyway. Pecos thought it foolish to refuse such wealth and unreasonable of the Army to make a man remain a pauper. Harry accepted the knife gratefully and reciprocated by giving his cousin his pocket watch. Pecos never had fathomed the telling of time, thinking the sun a more reliable device, but loved to listen to the watch's ticking noise. Harry demonstrated how to wind it and warned not to be overzealous lest the spring break. Pecos answered that he would care for the spirit within the watch properly and would not turn him around too many times.

Then it was time to part from Quanah and his wife.

"You will remember our words to each other, Har'son Parker." It was more a statement than a question, and Harry nodded silently.

"I'll send word back about Manatah as soon as I reach the fort. If I can't do any more for him, I'll at least let you know where he is. If he's held on a reservation I'm sure you'll be able to . . . settle the problem." Harry winked. He offered his hand to his cousin, and Quanah grasped it firmly.

"What does this mean, this touching of the hands?" Quanah asked him.

"A handshake? It's just a custom," Harry explained as their hands held briefly. "See, when the right hand is held in friendship, it can't have a weapon in it, meaning we can only be friends."

"It is a good custom." Quanah gave his hand a final

squeeze. "We will meet again, Har'son Parker, and always in friendship."

"Always in friendship," Harry repeated, smiling. Then he turned his gaze to the baby Nalin held in her arms. She had no material yet for a backboard to carry the infant. The one she and Toppasannah had worked on so painstakingly, decorating it with small beads and bits of shell and quill, had been destroyed when their lodge burned. Harry watched the infant's sleeping face, afraid to look up at his mother, knowing his gaze would betray his emotions. He loved Nalin as he had loved no woman. It was wrong—dead wrong—to feel this way! Nalin belonged to another man. What was more, she belonged to a man he respected and to whom he had sworn undying friendship. He meant it, of course, but he had to still the jealousy that lifted its head when he pondered the fact that she would always love Quanah as she could never love him. "Goodbye, Nalin." He tried to make his voice sound natural, but it was a forced croak; he wished as he said it that Quanah had not been there to hear.

His gaze was still fastened downward, no longer quite on the baby as he had hoped, but rather on the blue edge of the blanket Nalin had made for him out of Harry's coat. How he wished for a moment of solitude to tell her that he loved her and would always be there if she needed him . . . that he didn't care if her love was for another man, he would be content only to be near her. Yet he could say nothing of his forbidden feelings with her husband right beside her. Studying the baby's blanket, he was about to turn away when Nalin startled him by darting forward to plant a quick kiss on his cheek. As he looked up at her, her face blushed suddenly crimson. "It is not permissible to kiss the godfather of my son?"

Harry grinned, sure that his face, too, must be reddening. "Yes, it's permissible." He glanced at Quanah, who had given his unspoken acquiescence to his wife's gesture by only slightly smiling his approval. Quanah knew that he was safe with Nalin's love and that no one, including Harrison Parker, could take her away. The green monster reared its head again, and Harry forced it back. His gaze shifted once more to the infant. "Bye, White." He rubbed the light fluff of blond hair. As part of Quanah's pact with himself that his son would learn to live in the white man's world, he had named him White to always remind the child of the way he must learn to live. The baby opened his eyes and peered at him sleepily.

Harrison looked once more at Nalin, engraving her features on his memory, then turned away to mount the single horse he had accepted from Quanah's herd, looking back only one more time as he rode away. Quanah had come to stand beside his wife, his arm around her as they watched him go. Harry pried his eyes off them, told the green monster to leave him alone, and prepared to nurse his depression in peace.

As Nalin finished nursing the baby, Quanah continued to watch her, his expression troubled.

"What bothers you, my husband?" she asked as she laid the infant down then came to sit beside him. She took his hand from his lap, holding it in her own to prod him to speak.

"I have no wish to burden you, Nalin."

"Are your burdens not mine also?"

Quanah's dark gaze flickered to her face. He was disturbed by the things he had discussed with Parker, but Nalin had already been through so much that he hesitated.

"I would prefer to know your mind, Quanah, so mine also would be at rest."

Quanah sighed heavily, his hand gripping her fingers tightly. "So much has changed for us. This time of our son's birth should be filled with rejoicing. I look outside our lodge and all I see is how I have failed our people."

"No . . . no, you have not," she said quickly.

"Nalin, I am their chief! To me falls the safety of the Comanche. It is my wisdom they seek in council. It is *I* who have brought them to this."

"You are wrong, Quanah. It is the whites who have brought this change to our land. But, had they not come, I would not have found you here among my adopted people." She smiled at him playfully, trying to lighten his mood.

"Yes, that is true." He grinned back faintly. "They brought you."

"Harrison said we can live in peace. He said many whites wish for peace to come. Only some want war."

"But those are the bluecoat chiefs!" Quanah spat back venomously. "They want peace at the price of our manhood. They would take from us all that is ours. If we will live as children begging bluecoat fathers for crumbs they will let us live in the peace they tell us they want."

"But the Comanche are not as children, are they? They are warriors who will give the bluecoat chiefs no rest until they allow us peace by our terms." Nalin peered upward at his solemn face. "Is that not the wish of your people, my chief? Have they not so spoken in council? Even the women, even those widowed or made childless, have they not given voice in the council lodges for war, not peace, until peace is granted that we can live with? A wise chief follows the path his people wish to take. Have not your people spoken?"

"But our son, Nalin . . . can I give him a world full of war?"

"Your son, too, is *Comantica*. He will grow to manhood listening to the storytellers boast of his father's deeds."

"And if there are none of us left to tell him?"

"Then the bluecoats will know Quanah's name so well their old men will speak it in awe around the camp fires. They will tell of Quanah who would not surrender. And our son's children and grandchildren will also know of him. They will speak with pride of Quanah who led his people to victory."

"Not victory, Nalin. That I know cannot be. The whites are too many, the Comanche too few. We cannot win."

"Then we will lose victoriously!"

Quanah stared at her for a moment, then broke into laughter. "Nalin, my life, what would I be without you?" He still smiled as he pulled her into his arms.

"Very lonely, my husband, as I will let no other woman near you," she returned, leaning into his embrace.

"Perhaps I should take another wife," he teased, holding her too tightly to allow her the jab that would no doubt come if she could free her arm. "It would lighten your burden," he explained playfully.

"I would lighten her head by knocking her brains out!" Nalin countered, renewing his laughter. When it subsided, he backed up, peering into her face with only the remnants of a smile. "There can be no other woman for me, beloved," he said seriously. "I love you as no man has ever loved a woman."

Nalin stared back, her gaze growing passionate. "Prove your words, Comanche chief," she whispered.

Quanah kissed her, easing her back on the bedroll as he stretched out beside her. "Is it not too soon?" he asked huskily, near her ear. For the several weeks he had been away and since his return with the baby's birth, his desire had been held in check too long.

Nalin could only shake her head. She, too, had been without him far too long. Her fingers traced the outline of his bare back as Quanah's lips traveled over her. As he mounted her, she felt a twinge of pain from the recent birthing, but it was quickly overwhelmed by her own rising needs.

Chapter 19

COLONEL RONALD MACKENZIE stood over him, glaring down ominously. Unperturbed, Harry remained in the chair the colonel had ordered him to sit in.

"What do you mean you don't know, Parker? You have to know!"

Harry put on his most boyishly *innocent* expression. "I'm sorry, sir, I have no idea where they moved the camp." That part was true. He had been sent off before they moved on, and he had made it a point not to ask the direction they would head in. Then he could truthfully claim not to have the slightest idea where they were.

"I don't understand it." MacKenzie stalked off to the open door then back again. "She had to be there. I don't understand how she got away."

"Maybe she was killed, sir," Harry suggested, glad the colonel had his back turned so he couldn't see the contempt. "Surely you didn't see *all* the bodies."

MacKenzie spun about, his thin lips set in a grim line. "We didn't get her, Parker. You *know* we didn't, and I'd still like a better story about how you and Sergeant Ryker got back here." He came around and sat at the desk. "Ryker says Quanah is your cousin. That true?"

"Of course not. He also told you he made it up because Quanah's mother and I have the same last name. Quanah believed him and spared our lives. That's all there was to it . . . sir."

"Yeah, and he also changed his story only after he

talked to you." MacKenzie's green eyes squinted, focusing on the major. "I can find out if you're lying, Parker."

"Why would I do that, sir?" Harry smiled again.

"To keep from telling me what I want to know." MacKenzie slammed an open palm on the desk top. "To keep from telling me where your redskin relations have made off to!"

Harry issued a slow sigh. "I really can't help you, Colonel . . . sorry."

"All right, Parker, you're dismissed." MacKenzie glared. "But I'm going to be watching you."

"Yes, sir." Harrison saluted briskly and left. Ryker was waiting for him on the dusty parade field before the officers' barracks.

"He give ya a bad time, Major?"

"Naw, not so bad." Harrison trod slowly beside the sergeant. "He *thinks* he gave me a rough time, but what the hell can he prove?"

"But if he fin's out 'bout Cynthia Ann—"

"*What* Cynthia Ann, Ryker?"

"But ya tol' me!"

"I didn't tell you anything, Sergeant." Harry smiled crookedly at him. "I never told you a thing, did I?"

"Nope." Ryker nodded, slowly getting it. "Ya ain't never tol' me a thing."

They walked in silence for a few more feet, then Ryker stopped, a perplexed look on his grizzled features. "But I can't see how come ya don' want him to know."

"Sergeant Ryker, at this moment I wouldn't tell Colonel MacKenzie to get his boots if Noah's flood was coming. . . ."

The old man sat with his back pressed against the cold stone of the barrack's dungeon. The only light was a feeble ray through the small window high above his head. Only if he stood on the cot could he see outside, and then the only view that would meet his gaze was that of high black boots and blue trousers crossing a dusty yard past his window. He could no longer see the hills, the vast grasslands, nor the mountains far to the north from which he had once gathered his personal strength. The parade ground outside no longer held his interest. Now he simply sat with the knife, hidden beneath his leggings, that an unknown friend from the bluecoat scouts had passed to him through the window. He could feel the firmness of the steel, warmed by his own body heat, and its presence gave him comfort. For several hours, since dawn, he had been sitting this way, cross-legged, unmoving, expressionless, his clothes torn, his face wrinkled and wizened, his white hair, like cotton twine, stringy and left loosely bound to his shoulders. He had seen seventy years of freedom; to be imprisoned in this dark corner was more than his mind could bear.

This morning, a bluecoat who called himself Manatah's lawyer had come to see him. The bluecoat had promised in slow, carefully articulated English that charges against him had been dropped and that he would be sent to a reservation. The bluecoat, who called himself Harrison Parker, a name which seemed to mean nothing to the old man, had tried to explain more to him in a hushed whisper, but the appearance of another bluecoat officer behind him had stopped his speech. Manatah cared not at all for what the bluecoat might have wanted to say to him. He was Kaitsenko; he would settle his problems in his own way.

An hour ago, he had begun to chant, a low, doleful sound. The soldiers guarding his door had regarded it only as the soulful mourning of an old man.

Manatah had watched Toppasannah die and had been powerless to help her or prevent it. Bare seconds later, he had witnessed Quanah's lodge crumble into a heap of ruin, not knowing if Nalin had escaped the exploding destruction. With the vision of what he had seen before him, the old man's life force had gone. In his seven decades of existence he had been through wars, plagues, and starvation, but hope for the future had always been his closest companion. Now, even that friend had deserted him. The clinking sound of the key turning in the lock failed to rouse, or even interrupt, the slow wail of the "senile" Comanche brave.

"I wish to hell he'd stop that racket," Kawalski muttered, pushing the door open. "He's settin' my nerves on edge."

"You won't have to listen to it much longer." Prather scowled at him briefly. The least they could do was leave the old man his right to mourn his dead in his own way. Prather stepped past Kawalski and gently grasped the Indian's arm. "Come on, old man, time to go." He exerted a bit of pressure on the arm he held. "You're only going to the reservation. You'll like it there. You'll see."

The old man droned on in his chant, his gaze still fixed straight ahead as he got to his feet. Corporal Prather kept a light grip on the Comanche's arm more in an effort to catch him should he stumble than from an effort to hold him or force him forward. The old man was moving under his own power, following Kawalski up the steps and into the bright light of midday.

"Why the hell we gotta move him when the sun's hottest, I'll never know," Kawalski complained loudly to be heard over the Indian's chanting. He spun about suddenly, snarling, "Shut up, damn you! Stop that whining!"

"Leave him alone, Kawalski," Prather warned.

The Indian continued his mournful song, oblivious to the arguing soldiers on either side of him. "Come on," Prather prodded again. "We'll get you to the reservation. All your friends will be there. It's going to be all right."

"Quit baby-talkin' the old bastard, Prather. Just get him up here." Kawalski had climbed into the wagon and leaned over to grip the man's manacled hand. On the way to the fort, the old man had tried three times to escape or arm himself with a weapon. He wasn't to be released from his bonds until safely within reservation bounds.

"Careful with him," Prather warned sharply. Kawalski didn't answer, but his pull on the Indian to get him aboard was only firm enough to be of assistance.

Horace Jones, an Indian fighter from way back and now the fort's interpreter, stepped toward them as Prather got in behind the Indian. "You'd better watch that old man," Jones warned. "He means trouble."

"Trouble . . . how?" Kawalski laughed. "From a senile

old man? I don't even know why they still got manacles on him. He's through fightin'. The old goat's half crazy anyhow."

"I mean it," Jones answered seriously. "Watch him."

The driver, who had been waiting for them to board, now signaled the horses forward. The wagon lurched as the wheels started to turn. Horace Jones watched the wagon join the rest of the Fourth Cavalry that was beginning to move out. He could still hear the distant, fading sound of the Indian's chant. Jones had met members of the Kaitsenko before, the Society of the Ten Bravest, as the Indians called them. An elite group of an elite nation, only the bravest in battle, the best warriors, were permitted within the ranks of the society. This old man was one of them. He had seen a Kaitsenko brave tie himself by the ankle to a stake in the ground and single-handedly stave off an attack by a warring tribe. For him the war was not over until it was won, or until his life had ended.

Jones replayed the chant in his mind, translating it silently into English as the warrior's voice drifted out of the wagon. "Oh, Sun, you remain forever, but we Kaitsenko must die. Oh, Earth, you remain forever, but we Kaitsenko must die." Over and over, the old man sang his song, working himself up some powerful medicine, just like the warrior did that day, repeating his death chant until the enemy came.

Jones shook his head as the wagon disappeared through the wide open gates of the fort. Two columns of mounted soldiers fell in behind. Kawalski and Prather were dead wrong. The old Indian wasn't senile; he was Kaitsenko. He knew damn well what he was doing.

"Are you cold?" Prather leaned forward, touching the old man's hand. The wind had shifted in late afternoon, coming out of the northwest and bringing colder air with it. The man's withered hand felt chilly beneath his palm, so Prather opened a blanket and stretched it over him. For a few hours, the Indian had been quiet, his chanting falling off until he did no more than stare straight ahead. Prather looked at him, frowning. The old man had seemed to put himself into some kind of trance, immobile, impassive. What Prather couldn't figure out was how he could stay like that for so long.

"Kaitsenko ana obahema . . ."

"Oh, Jesus Christ, you started him up again!" Kawalski shouted above the Indian's lament. "Here he was quiet, and you had to go rile him up again!"

"I only covered him up," Prather defended, none too pleased himself that the reprieve was over. Talking became an impossibility over the Indian's loud chant. Both soldiers contented themselves with trying to ignore it, avoiding even glancing at each other. Suddenly the Indian's head ducked down beneath the blanket that Prather had spread over him. Prather's eyes barely had a chance to narrow before the white, grizzled head popped up again, staring sightlessly, and took up the chant where it had left off. Prather relaxed until the next cadenced chant ended and the Indian again ducked beneath the cover.

"What the hell is he doing?" Kawalski asked after the Indian had done it several more times.

Prather shrugged, still watching the white head as it bobbed beneath the blanket then popped out again to repeat the chant.

"Must be some kinda crazy Indian hoo-dah." Kawalski grinned.

"Yeah, I reckon," Prather answered, then turned away to leave the Indian to his magic.

Again and again Manatah's head ducked beneath the blanket, a punctuation mark of each finished song. He was beyond pain now, feeling nothing as he stripped the flesh from his forearm with his teeth. He focused on the chant, putting every fiber of his concentration into the repeated words, just as he had done when he hung from the lodge poles by strips of his own flesh during the sun ceremony in his young manhood. The scars of the ordeal were still on his back and chest, marred flesh that he wore proudly. He blocked the signals of pain his torn wrists were sending up to his deliberately numbed brain, centering his mind solely on the song. A few more and he could slip one hand through the handcuffs.

Finally his left hand pulled out of the confining metal circle. He was free. Still chanting, he reached for the knife hidden beneath his leggings.

Prather's eye caught the movement of the blanket being thrown back as his prisoner stood up, knife upraised, and gave an ear-shattering war cry. He spun about in time to see the completion of the metamorphosis from senile old man to Comanche warrior.

Prather drew back in shock as the ancient brave slashed at him, cutting the front of his jacket. A thin red line of blood began to ooze out of the tear. Kawalski had also stood in surprise, and as the Indian slashed the air in front of him, he jumped back, his legs hitting the edge of the buckboard, and he spilled out, rolling into the dusty wagon tracks. Prather was right behind him, tumbling head over heels into the dirt. The Indian had picked up one of the carbines, left unloaded just in case, and was trying to load a cartridge into the chamber. His injured left arm was refusing its cooperation, and he fumbled with the bullet.

The cavalry behind the wagon stopped just short of trampling the two soldiers, and panic set in. No one had expected trouble at all, much less from within their midst. Carbines were raised, and firing began indiscriminately, those in back not even sure what all the confusion was about. A wagon driver was hit, shot by a cavalry bullet in the melee.

The lone warrior ceased trying to fit the bullet into the chamber. He screamed, pointing the empty gun, and leapt off the back of the wagon. Bullets flying unaimed tore into him, and his body jerked convulsively beneath their impact. He went down but rose again, staggering now, pointing the useless gun in a last gesture of defiance. More bullets struck him. He staggered forward, pushing against the force of the lead pellets hitting his body, then fell for the last time, the gun still clutched in his bleeding hand that had been gnawed to the bone.

When they were sure he would not rise again, the soldiers stepped cautiously forward. Prather and Kawalski reached him first, their expressions numb with surprise. The blood-spattered body that had sent the cavalry into a panic was once again just that of an old man, one old man who had conducted a lone war against the entire Fourth Cavalry. Prather was not at all certain it was the cavalry that had won.

"Is that what we've come to?" Parker shouted. "The U.S. Cavalry now conducts war on old men and helpless kids! We don't fight like men! We're butchers, lousy murderers—"

"That's enough, Parker," Beaumont warned. The lawyer stopped his ranting in mid-sentence, trying forcefully to put his rage under control. Until the last few moments the general had let him vent his anger. Word of the Fourth Cavalry incident had just filtered back to Fort Smith, and Beaumont didn't like it either: seasoned soldiers panicking like rookies, firing on one old man bearing an unloaded rifle in his self-mutilated hand. Corporal Prather had revealed the entire episode without embellishment or excuses and nearly in tears. In fact, once excused, he had broken down into open weeping, finishing with, "He looked so frightening. I never saw an Indian like that! Powerful! Fierce! I really thought he'd kill every last one of us. And then, after . . . he just looked like a crumpled old man again . . . skinny. Covered in blood . . ."

Kawalski had been more specific, reporting that twenty-nine bullet holes had been counted in the old man's body. He, too, was somber, soberly reporting the facts of the skirmish that had emotionally defeated the cavalry.

All this had followed on the heels of Major Parker's report of the Comanche raid he had witnessed. Beaumont felt sick at the descriptions Parker had given him. "I know it doesn't look good, Parker, but war never is," Beaumont began.

"That's a hell of an excuse," Parker interjected, still fuming.

The general decided to ignore the breach, sympathizing with Parker's feelings. "Look, damn it! I don't care for MacKenzie's methods any better than you do, but he's in charge of the Comanche surrender, and that's on orders from back East! I can't do anything about them, and *you* can't do anything."

"We'll see about that . . . sir," Parker answered tightly.

"Parker," the general sighed, raising up the last of his patience to deal with the impertinent junior officer. "I am not trying to be your enemy on this thing. I'm trying to be your ally . . . *if* you'll let me. Now will you cool off and listen to reason for a moment?"

Parker's gaze suddenly dropped to his lap. "I'm sorry, General. I'm listening."

"Good." Beaumont settled back, the chair squeaking in protest. "Now, like it or not, the politics of the situation are these . . . yes, politics, young man, so don't look at me like that. You've lived in the world long enough to realize that politics have a hand in everything. The popularity of our judges and legislators rests with what the vocal majority wants. And right now, the vocal majority wants the West opened up to progress. You've been back East. You know people are anxious to come out here, settle on a piece of land, and raise their families. Most think they'll strike it rich here, and that's what they're coming for. Now they can't do that with the Indians running loose, burning them out, stealing their wagon trains—"

"They only do that because we've left them no choice," Parker defended, interrupting the general again. "We've killed off their food sources. It was their land first! *We're* the invaders here!"

"Slow down, Parker, I know that. We're not much different from the Huns or the Romans taking over Gaul and Britain. Technically, we are invading their land and stealing it away from them. But face facts, they've been doing the same thing to each other since long before we came here. The Cherokee were chased off their land by their red neighbors. Your precious Comanche ran the Apache into the desert. Small tribes are pushed out or

213

slaughtered to make way for larger, more aggressive rivals. Blackfoot harass the Crow and so do the Sioux. Back when I came out here thirty years ago I would've just dared you to try to get a Kiowa and a Cheyenne in the same tepee. They'd kill each other on sight. Some Indians starved before we came along because stronger tribes wouldn't share the land with them. That's the way it is, Parker. Man, be he red, white, yellow, or black, always beats his fellow man out rather than share with him, and the strongest is the one who wins. Right now, we are stronger than our red brothers, and we need, or we *want*, what belongs to them—so we take it. If that means breaking the backbone of the Comanche tribes, then that's how it will be done, and right now their backbone is your cousin, Quanah."

Parker looked up sharply. "He's not . . . Quanah's not . . ."

"I know he is, Major. I was here when Cynthia Ann was brought in. I was with your father when he identified her as his niece. I saw Cynthia Ann Parker starve herself to death rather than take up the white man's ways. Our people just can't understand how a thing like that can happen. They can't think how a girl brought up as a Comanche could have her whole racial heritage altered by just being raised differently. I've read these damn dime westerns put out by writers who've never been west of the Mississippi. They like to tell how awful it is for white women to be captured and raped by Indians. Guess that's what sells. The shock. The atrocities. And for some of them, it's true. I saw a girl, only fourteen, nearly dead with shock after her family was massacred in front of her. She was raped and taken captive, then, when she wouldn't speak, or eat, or even move of her own accord, they left her to die in the desert. Far as I know she still hasn't said a word and might still be locked in that sanitarium. It happens like that sometimes. And sometimes, you see a case like Cynthia Ann's. Nobody could believe she really loved that Indian husband of hers. She was his first wife, and I guess that's an honor of some kind to them. Anyway, she was damn proud of it. She was proud of her two sons, too. She didn't talk much, and we needed a translator to understand most of it, but she really wanted to go home again. To where she considered home—back to the tribe, to her people, to the man she loved and the children she bore him.

"That daughter she had, the little one." Beaumont smiled sadly. "Prettiest little girl I've seen. Only three or four, I think. Big brown eyes, real quiet. She died in her mother's arms, of the fever. I've hardly ever shed a tear in my life, but I did that day. Your father did, too, when that little girl died. We tried to save her, but it wasn't any use. Know what she died of?" Beaumont looked at Harrison with one brow upraised and didn't wait for an answer. "Chicken pox. Yes, that's right. Just plain old chicken pox every kid gets once in a lifetime, only Indian kids never got it until the white man brought it here. She didn't have any resistance to it—so she died.

"Our good intentions, all our high plans for them." Beaumont paused, shaking his head as he remembered the past. "We gave Cynthia Ann a piece of land. Just *gave* it to her. And she still ran off, four, maybe five times, trying to rejoin her family. We kept finding her, bringing her back, trying to teach her to live the way we wanted her to. Then that little girl got sick and died, and Cynthia Ann just gave up. She wasn't more than thirty or so herself. She wouldn't eat, hardly slept. Just sat all day, waiting for death to come. Your father was with her when it happened, and the last words she spoke were in Comanche."

Harrison had never heard the full story of Cynthia Ann's return to the world of her heritage. Isaac Parker had never explained the entire story as Beaumont had just described. Like the general said, Isaac Parker hadn't been able to comprehend how his mission of mercy had gone awry.

"We do a lot of things in the name of Christian charity that we shouldn't ought to do," Beaumont continued finally. "We had no business forcing our way of life onto

Cynthia Ann. Nor do I think we have any right to judge the white woman Quanah's married to. . . . You've met her now, Parker, haven't you?"

Harrison nodded.

"What's she like?"

"Well, her case would be very similar to Cynthia Ann's, sir. She was brought up Comanche. She learned English from a teacher her father bought for her, a white woman. Her brother-in-law, Pecos, told me she came when she was barely ten and was adopted by a couple in the tribe. He also told me she felt her own people, the whites, had betrayed her, though he didn't explain how. He only said that every contact she has had with her own race has caused her heartbreak. Even this last one—her adopted mother was killed in the raid. Her father, well, you know now what happened to him. She truly loves Quanah, General, and they now have a son."

"And I imagine if MacKenzie succeeds in this plan of capturing her, she'll go the same route as Cynthia Ann." The general pondered.

"I don't think so, sir. Nalin—that's her name, sir—would be hard to take alive. She's trained as a warrior and would fight to the last. I'm afraid she'd go more like her father did—fighting to the very end."

"MacKenzie is going to try again, you know that, don't you, Parker?" Beaumont gazed at him.

"Yes, and I wish I knew some way to stop him."

"So do I, but for now I don't know of one. Quanah keeps foiling him, eluding him, and MacKenzie can't stand to fail. He's promised to bring about the surrender of the Comanche, and the top brass have given him full control to do it. They don't care about the atrocities you've seen, Major. They care about those voters back East who want the Comanche problem solved. They care about the opinion of the Texans who want Quanah, *and* his woman, stopped at any cost. Your fellow Texans don't share your sympathy for Quanah's woman, Parker. They hate her even more because they can't understand her. Men, and women, can't forgive her for being in love with an Indian. You know how it's been even for these women released from Indian bondage with their half-white babies. They're outcasts, too, and they don't deserve it. Perhaps the Texans have some cause for their hatred, as she's been responsible for reducing their numbers. They'd love to see her captured, convicted, and hanged."

"That's hardly fair, sir." Parker was starting to redden with anger again. "Her husband isn't wanted for murder—"

Beaumont cut him off. "Her husband is considered a Comanche with just cause to resist our encroachment. Even the Texans see it that way. They want his surrender and will be satisfied with that. But this . . . what's her name? Nalin? She's born white, and they see her as a traitor. As with Cynthia Ann, they just can't see how she could take to the Indian way of life rather than ours. They want her *hide*, Major Parker, and if MacKenzie and Major Nash get their way and capture her, I think the whole thing might get out of hand so even they can't control it. They don't want her death. Not really. They only want the threat of it to bring Quanah in. But it's the civilian authorities who will judge her if she's brought in. They will go with the will of the people. And we both know what that will is going to be . . ."

Chapter 20

NALIN had taken the news of Manatah's death well, as if she had half expected it all along. Many times in the weeks that followed, Quanah would see her eyes red-rimmed, but she would not let him find her crying. Guilt for his failure to protect his people hung heavily over him, and she would not add to his burden.

Moving quickly, frequently at night to keep the soldiers from learning of their movements, the Comanche had gone south to where the winter would be less harsh, but food also would be less plentiful. They might yet be forced by starvation into breaking their cardinal rule against eating the flesh of God-dog, for there would be nothing else.

In the spring, for those who survived, Satanta of the Kiowa would join them in an effort to regain a hold in their own land. He had signed the treaty at Medicine Bend but had not fully understood its meaning until Quanah explained it to him. He had not known he was signing away his right to the land forever. He had thought he would only be permitting them use of it also, as the pact between the Kiowa and the Cheyenne had once granted. He couldn't understand how anyone could own land anyway, since the Great Spirit had created it for all men to use. It could not be a possession; like the air and the water, land was only lent to man. But Quanah had told him that the white men drew up pieces of paper and felt that by the writing upon them the Great Spirit of the whites had given the land to them to own forever. When this was explained, Satanta decided his word had been gotten by false pretenses and there would be no shame in breaking it. In the spring, they would make their combined strike. For the autumn and through the winter they would merely try to survive.

"Is Nalin again not to be trusted against the Texans?"

"I did not say that."

"Then is Nalin no longer capable as a warrior?"

"I did not tell you so." Quanah looked up disgustedly at his wife, standing over him, her hands stubbornly planted on her hips.

"Then why can I not go to Texas with you?" She finally knelt beside him in front of the small fire that warmed their home. The baby, White Parker, slept, blissfully unaware of his parents' discussion. Even Quanah was getting quite used to his wife's badgering about the raids. She would shut up, for a while, if he ordered her to, but sooner or later she'd bring it up again. During the months of her pregnancy he had been granted relative peace about the war parties she was missing. Nalin would take no chance of losing his son. Now that White was several months old and able to stay in the care of his grandmother, Quanah's stepmother, the days of peace were ended.

Since he had not answered, Nalin started again. "The medicine man says that the omens are good. We will win easily—"

"I know that, woman. Leave me be! I never forbade you to go along!"

Nalin's mouth was still open, ready for the next retort, but his words stopped her cold. Come to think of it, he never had said no. "I can?" She fairly leaped into the air toward him, nearly knocking him over as she squealed in delight. That sound did wake the baby, who began to wail in fright until his mother picked him up, cooing at him to quiet him again.

Barely a week later, Quanah watched from the shelter behind the rocks. Already sixteen braves were dead, more wounded, lying on the ground and moaning for help that couldn't reach them. He couldn't tell how many of the whites within the trading post had been killed or injured; probably few since they had all managed to get inside and the bullets and arrows had done little good against the shuttered windows. He would have to find another way. A frontal attack was losing braves needlessly. There was no chance that he could give up and leave the trading post unentered. Winter was starving his people. White and the other children cried from hunger. Many of the elders had already given up their portions to feed the grandchildren, and they soon wandered out onto the prairie to be seen no more. Nalin had lost so much weight now that her robes were hanging on her. If they did not succeed in taking this post, many more would die. Already they had been forced to kill and eat the younger foals from their herds, but some of them, too, had to live to help the warriors hunt. Without horses to carry them to their food, all would die.

Red Eagle Feather, this time, had failed them. The medicine man had assured them that a raid now would be favorable. Instead, Quanah had lost almost a third of his warriors in the first few fruitless attacks. Their families would still be at the winter camp, waiting. If he could not give them their men back, then at least he had to return with food.

He studied the trading post layout carefully, looking for some means of entry. There was a slim chance that someone small enough might make it to the large oak tree beside the post. From there he could climb the tree and reach the roof. If he carried burning green wood he could drop it into the chimney. Green wood would make a great deal of smoke and little fire. It would force the Texans to open the doors, but there would be little chance of it burning the structure or the precious supplies within. The brave had to be light enough to not fall through the flimsy roof; Little Raven was the smallest among them. Quanah signaled him forward and hastily explained the plan.

"I am smaller than Little Raven." Nalin interrupted from behind him when he was nearly finished. Both warriors turned to look at her. She was right; she was inches smaller and several pounds lighter than Little Raven. "I can do this, Quanah. Let me."

Quanah was about to automatically deny her proposal, then stopped himself before he spoke. How could he ask Little Raven to do what would be too dangerous for Nalin? Were not they both warriors and his responsibility? Little Raven had seen only nineteen summers, had been married only a year before, and already had a small daughter at the winter camp. How could he ask this of a husband and father if he would not ask it of his wife? Then it was a bad plan. . . . But no, it was the only plan that might succeed. Nalin had proven her worth as a warrior. She *was* lighter and smaller and thus the most likely to succeed at the task, and yet he could not bring himself to say the words that would send her off in Little Raven's stead.

When she fought by his side he could worry enough for her safety, but to send her out alone and watch from the sidelines was more than he could ask of himself. "Nalin, Little Raven is the best tree climber among us. He will have to carry the burning wood."

"Yes, and then he will fall through the roof when his foot is set upon it. I can climb the tree and carry the wood."

Nalin was as easy to reason with as an eagle that has sighted the same prey as the hunter. One might ask, they might listen, but both would then do as they pleased, to follow or not what was asked of them. Little Raven might crash through the roof; Nalin probably wouldn't.

"I will go, as you would choose, my husband, if I were any other warrior. And I will come back, if only because I will let no other woman have you." She touched his cheek lightly, then ran off.

"Red Eagle Feather," Quanah called to the medicine man. "Atone for some of your failure this day and make strong medicine to keep Nalin safe."

Red Eagle Feather hurried to his parfleches, pulling out ingredients and talismans. He stuffed several items into a leather bag then ran after Nalin with it, hanging it about her neck with a hastily mumbled prayer.

Quanah dared not approach her again, certain that his heart would win out over his head and make her stay. Instead, he watched from the shelter of the rocks as Nalin crept as close as she dared, with the dash still before her. She would have to run like the wind in a zigzag pattern to keep their aim from flying true. When she was ready to start, she signaled Broken Hand behind her, who began firing to keep the whites occupied. At his first volley, the rest of the braves started shooting to cover her dash.

Bullets whizzed by her, several close enough for her to hear their passage, more hitting the ground and throwing up chunks of dirt into her path, but she reached the tree with the green wood sticks in her hand, her other tightly clutching the medicine man's magic pouch strung about her neck. She only released the leather bag with its wealth of talismans to free her hand for climbing. Making her way up the stout branches, her progress was slowed even further by the sticks she carried. The smoke kept getting into her eyes, making them burn and tear, and she was unable to see clearly or concentrate on her footing. Twice she slipped and only caught herself in time. When she was high enough to see the roof a few feet beneath her, Nalin tried to step down. Her foot touched the thin board, her body following, then stopped. Suddenly she was strangling and nearly thrown into panic. She dropped the greenwood sticks onto the roof and grasped for her throat. It was the medicine bag, caught on a branch and now choking the breath out of her. Nalin's foot began to slip on the slanted roof. Frantically she used both hands to yank the leather cord. It broke, and at last she could breathe again, as she reached the roof and safety. She sat down, panting from the exertion and near strangulation. Her gaze rose upward over her head to the medicine bag still tangled in the branches. She wanted the bag and the safety of spirit protection it afforded, but not at the cost of her success. Already the burning wood was scorching the boards of the rooftop. If the roof caught fire, all their efforts would be in vain.

Forgetting the bag caught in the tree limb, she snatched up the smoldering wood, stepping lightly over the rooftop. She had been right. Even under her light weight the boards were sagging; Little Raven would never have made it. The whites below were too busy returning gunfire to hear the boards protesting as she moved toward the chimney. She tossed the torch down into the blackness, then waited.

Smoke billowed out of the hole, some perhaps escaping into the room, for she could hear a few sputtered coughs begin below, but most of it was escaping through the chimney place. This would never succeed in forcing them out. She needed something to cover the hole and keep the smoke inside, but what? All she had was her own clothing, her leggings and her robe. Nalin's gaze fastened on the leggings. Quanah would not like it at all, her coming down again only half-dressed, but he would like even less returning to camp empty-handed. Quickly she removed the leggings; her robe would cover her at least to mid-thigh. Rolling them into a ball, she stuffed the leather leggings into the hole, and the reaction was immediate. Coughing, shouting, and moans of protest issued from the trapped and choking whites inside. Running for the tree and the safety of its concealing branches, Nalin heard the doors thrown open. Quanah no longer needed her to understand the shouts of surrender. The gunfire almost immediately stopped as the men threw out their weapons, then followed them out with their hands held high over their heads.

She stayed in the foliage, listening as her people came down from the hills to swarm over the captured post.

"Nalin?" Quanah's voice sounded worried, calling from beneath the tree.

"I am here, Quanah."

"Are you safe?"

"I am safe," she answered quickly, feeling a hot flush spread over her as she remembered her half-naked condition.

"Why do you not come down then?" he called up to her.

"I am . . . I am coming." She started down the tree, trying to pull the robe down, wishing it were inches longer.

Quanah could see one bare, slim leg coming out of the branches. "Woman, what are you doing?" he called in amazement.

"As you told me, I am coming down."

"Nalin, where are your—" He was shouting, and he realized it. He lowered his voice. "Where are your leggings?"

Nalin's pert face peeked out at him from the branches, grinning broadly. "In the chimney, my husband."

"Stay there!" he shouted upward, pointing a warning finger at her. "Do not move one step farther!"

She muffled her laughter as he ran off to find her covering.

In her years of riding with the Comanche, Nalin had grown used to being stared at by prisoners. Her coppery hair was impossible to hide, as was her light skin. Most stared at her in curiosity, as if she had just grown two noses. Some, a few of the prisoners she guarded, had tried to seek help from her, beseeching her to give them aid in escaping. Usually, a hard glare and a pointed rifle were enough to stop their wagging tongues.

Quanah had found her a pair of spare leggings, and she was fully dressed again as she leaned against a table, watching the trading post survivors, her rifle balanced against her knee ready to be lowered quickly. Broken Hand and Little Raven helped to guard the five white men clustered in a circle on the floor. Quanah had not yet decided their fate; whether or not to let them live. One of them, a young man of perhaps nineteen or twenty, kept returning his gaze to the oddly attired white woman holding the rifle. Nalin tried to ignore his appraisal, but it was irritating. Adding to her annoyance was the commotion she was hearing from outside. The loot had been taken, supplies packed and ready, but now argument had ensued. She could not hear clearly but recognized Quanah's voice arguing with the others, and frequently the name of Red Eagle Feather was mentioned. She was straining to hear, then finally pushed herself off from the table edge and started toward the window. Her movement brought her closer to the rudely staring prisoner. Nalin leaned partially out the window to hear.

"Miss . . . young lady . . ."

She gazed down at the man trying to get her attention. He was looking up at her hopefully. As was her custom when dealing with members of her own race, she ignored him, turning back to the window.

"Young lady, listen," he whispered. "If you'll help me, I promise I'll help you. I'll get you out of this. I swear it."

"Shut up, you damn fool!" the man beside him snarled aloud. "You're wastin' yer breath. That ain't a 'young lady,' " he mocked. "That bitch would as soon have yer scalp as any of 'em."

Nalin turned to stare at the speaker, who glared defiantly back. Still trying to hear the argument progressing outside, she turned back to the window.

"Lousy redskin whore," the man continued with venom. "Injun coyote bitch!"

Broken Hand and Little Raven understood no English, but the sound of the words propelled Broken Hand forward, his rifle butt rising to strike the cursing man's shoulder.

"No." Nalin motioned him back. She was used to such name-calling by a few of the whites who dared vent their anger when they knew they had little to lose. Often that anger fell on her. Names could not hurt her; their opinions were worth little in her own mind. "Let him rave, Broken Hand."

Broken Hand lowered the rifle, stepping back to his place by the wall.

"You goddamn fool, yourself, Jensen!" A third prisoner spoke. "There's no sense to rilin' them more—"

"What diff'rence is it gonna make? They'll kill us anyhow."

"Mebbe if they was goin' to, they would've by now. Damn it, shut yer mouth!"

. "Isn't she a captive, like us?" the youngest member prompted, his gaze still fastened on Nalin's back.

"Ain't you heard, boy?" her name-caller responded. "She's Quanah's woman, the white Comanche. She'd kill ya soon as look at ya. Murders her own people. I heard tell she killed her own pa to run off with that redskin bastard."

This time Nalin turned from the window to focus on the speaker with a hard glare. Name-calling rolled off her unfelt; against Quanah it was a different matter. "Silence, Heavy Whiskers," Nalin said in concise English. "Or I shall cut out your tongue with a dull knife."

"See what I mean, boy? A white redskin. Sure is a curiosity, ain't it?"

Nalin was tired of listening to Heavy Whiskers's useless chatter, primarily because he was drowning out the sounds she had come to the window to hear. She moved to the door, finding Voice Like Thunder on guard duty outside. She spoke to him about trading places, and he went in to guard the prisoners while she stepped out into the sunlight. Now she could hear what the arguments were all about. It was soon apparent that the heated discussion was over Red Eagle Feather. Several of the braves, disappointed and angry that the hard-earned victory had produced such scanty supplies, wanted to vent that anger on the medicine man. Red Eagle Feather had failed them. He had prophesied easy victory and a wealth of plunder. Instead many had died and for what? Only a few pounds of food, several blankets, and a roll or two of cloth and canvas. Red Eagle Feather must have offended the spirits he consulted. Not lost to their argument was the fact that Nalin had lost her talisman, was almost choked to death by it, in trying to reach the roof. Red Fox, at one time a would-be suitor of hers, was vociferously complaining that the medicine man's magic had nearly killed her. He was useless as a medicine man. He should die for his failure. Perhaps that sacrifice would appease the spirits.

Nalin looked over to Red Eagle Feather in pity. She knew him to be near Manatah's age; the two men had grown up together. Red Eagle Feather had become the medicine man taking the place of his own father when the older man's infirmities caused him to seek the desert. Until now, he had guided them well. He sat on a rock now, his shoulders hunched, stringy locks of hair hanging limply in front of his sun-weathered face as he listened to the younger warriors. This man she had known and respected since her childhood. She remembered when he walked tall and proud among his people, when the force of his power drove evil spirits away as he danced, when his knowledge of the roots and berries made the sick well again. They had forgiven him when his potions and dances, his charms and talismans, could do no good against the sickness brought by the whites. They had excused him when his magic could not bring the vast herds of bison back to the plains. But this last failure was more than they could bear. He could no longer protect his people against five men holding a single one-room post.

"Red Eagle Feather's death will not bring back our warriors," Quanah argued against the braves who wished to torture the old man to death. "It will only reduce by one more the number of our own people. Have we not lost enough already? Will we add to that number and kill one of our own?"

"He is useless, Quanah," Red Fox shouted in anger. "He fails us again and again. His magic no longer works against the whites—"

"Perhaps the white man's magic is stronger than that of the Comanche," Quanah answered evenly. "Perhaps it is the will of the Great Spirit that Red Eagle Feather's magic shall work no more. Perhaps it is time the Comanche were no more . . ."

Nalin could not believe her ears. She had heard Quanah's words, but her mind wouldn't accept them. Quanah, who had always been so certain . . . his faith in the spirits of their ancestors had nurtured her belief. Could he now tell them that the Comanche were deserted by their God?

"Every summer more whites come," he continued. "There is no end to their number. They build their lodges. They cut the trees and clear the land and plant what the Great Spirit never put there before. The land of the Comanche as our fathers once knew it shall be no more. Soon there will be no room for us. Already our brothers the Cheyenne and the Arapaho, the Nawkoni Comanche and the Penatukha Comanche, have given up their fight and live as the white men wish them to—"

"Do you say we stop fighting them, Quanah?" Red Fox still shouted in his anger. "Do we sit as children and let them have their way?"

For several moments Quanah failed to answer him, and Nalin held her breath, waiting for his reply. "No, we do not lie down as children and let the whites take what is ours. We will fight them as Kwahadi Comanche, as warriors, until we can fight no more."

"You say that they will whip us, Quanah?" This time the question came from Pecos, and there was infinite sadness in it.

Again he took a long time to reply. "Perhaps . . . but if we are to die we shall do so as men!" He turned away and stalked off, leaving a silent gathering of his followers to stand in the sun pondering his words.

Nalin watched him go to where the horses were tethered. She could not leave him alone at a time like this and half ran after him. Catching up, she only touched his arm from behind him. Quanah's hand came about to grasp hers, then he turned and pulled her into his arms, hugging her desperately. "Nalin, my life, lend me your strength," he whispered against her ear.

"We will win, Quanah."

He backed away, cupping her face in his hands. "No, Nalin, we will lose. We no longer have even the faith of our forefathers to guide us. Never again shall I believe in the omens of the medicine man. Never again shall I ask

228

our animal friends to guide us to our food. What was true for our forefathers is true no longer."

Nalin's eyes burned with held-back tears. "You will surrender, my husband?" Her voice broke as the hot tears escaped to run a course down her cheeks.

"Not yet." Quanah smiled down at her, rubbing the tears away with his thumbs. "They shall win. But we shall cost them for their victory."

She could think of nothing else to say to him to give him comfort. "I love you, Quanah," she whispered.

He smiled again, pulling her head against his chest. "And I love you, my heart," he said softly.

Travis Jensen, Heavy Whiskers, stretched his spine to attain the height necessary from his position on the floor to peer out the trading-post window. The shutters were drawn back now, and he had no trouble seeing the several braves conversing in a semicircle outside. Near them, but alone, an old white-haired warrior sat on a rock, his face down between his knees, his gaze focused on the ground before him. Jensen's gaze lifted farther and saw the white woman warrior locked in the embrace of the redskin. The sight made him sick. In silence his mouth tightened, jaws clenching, his nostrils flaring slightly outward as he watched them. Damn sickening! Unnatural, that's what it was. He lowered himself to a more comfortable position. Sick, that's what it was . . . sick for a white woman to throw herself at one of them savages.

Sullivan, the young man who had appealed to Nalin for help, had managed to work his hands out of the rope that tied them behind his back. The Comanche were almost ready to leave; a delay had been caused by the old man who had stood up a half hour ago and walked off. No one could find him though they called his name. He did not answer them. Very soon they would give up the search, decide the fate of the prisoners, and be on their way. Sullivan had to act quickly, though he had no idea as yet of what to do with his new freedom. He wasn't an Indian fighter, only a cowboy from Dodge City. He had been on cattle drives that had been attacked by Indians and had fought them off successfully, sometimes, at least managing to escape the skirmishes with his scalp intact. But what to do as a captive was quite beyond him. "Travis," Sullivan whispered. "I'm loose—"

"Well, don' waste time, boy. Back up ta me and undo my ropes." Jensen wiggled around to the young man's reach. There were only two Indians now, one half-asleep in a corner, the other trying, as the woman had, to peer out the window.

The door pushed inward again, and the white woman warrior entered, speaking briefly to the Indian by the window, then her gaze fell on Sullivan, nearly back-to-back with Jensen.

"You! Move away!" she ordered.

Sullivan's eyes widened. He hadn't half undone Jensen yet, but if he moved as ordered they would see that his hands were free.

"I tell you to move!" she ordered again, stepping forward. The other brave was right behind her. Sullivan panicked. He was more afraid of the brave behind her than of the woman. Pushing himself to his feet, he charged, pitching himself and the Indian to the floor. Nalin raised her rifle and brought it down hard on the base of Sullivan's skull. A sickening snap later, Sullivan sprawled over the brave beneath him.

Nalin instantly had the rifle turned, pointed at the other prisoners. As Voice Like Thunder crawled out from beneath the white man, it was obvious there would be no more fighting from him. Sullivan was dead. Eyes wide open and staring, his broken neck flopped his head around to an ungainly angle.

"Ya killed him!" Heavy Whiskers glared, full of hatred. "You lousy redskin-lovin' bitch! Ya murdered him!"

"Silence!" Nalin pointed the rifle at Heavy Whiskers.

"I'll see you hang for this! I swear on the boy's dead body."

Nalin had done no more than Voice Like Thunder would have done for her if the positions had been reversed. She had acted instinctively, stopping the white man in the easiest workable manner. True, she had not meant to kill him, but there had been no time to judge her aim carefully. She would not repeat this coup before the warriors, for there was no honor in missing the blow you intended to strike. But neither was there shame in saving the life of a friend. Heavy Whiskers called it murder, but what would he have called it if the white man had won? He would have proclaimed his friend's coup for all to hear had the white man killed Voice Like Thunder. The ways of the world were indeed strange to comprehend. What is murder to one is not to another, but is victory instead. With the pointed rifle, Nalin motioned Heavy Whiskers to move back to the wall.

"She's been seen again, sir."

"Where?" MacKenzie shot to his feet, leaning over the desk anxiously.

"Northern Texas," Major Nash answered for the soldier, who quickly assumed he was dismissed and gave a brisk salute before turning on his heel and marching out. Nash was capable of telling MacKenzie anything he would need to know. "Word's spreading through the fort from the wagon train that just pulled in here. She was right beside that half-breed throughout the attack. They've raided settlements as far away as San Antonio. Taken enough provisions to see them through to spring."

"Where are they now?"

"Last reports have them headed to Oklahoma. They aren't going to be easy to catch unawares this winter, Colonel."

MacKenzie glared at him, wanting no reminders of the last winter. General Beaumont had been all over after that paper pusher, Parker, told him what he had seen. In the final tally of the fall raids, few Comanche warriors had fallen; the rest had been women, children, and old people. That had given Beaumont enough to write Washington about and start an investigation into MacKenzie's procedures. If the East had not been so set on settling the Comanche problem to allow settlers to move through the territory unhampered, they might have listened to the weak-livered general. As it stood, however, the politicians would clamor for only one thing, peace at any cost. If the Comanche would not be subdued without war, then war it would have to be. MacKenzie's orders had not been retracted: Bring the Comanche in, stop Quanah and his raiders, make the Southwest safe for settlers.

"You got any more bright ideas, Major Nash?" MacKenzie scowled.

"I haven't given up on the last one yet, Colonel. Sooner or later, they have to be separated again. Until then, we wait."

Chapter 21

NALIN was finally learning what Toppasannah had tried so often to teach. She had just finished gathering wild roots and a few other scattered vegetables not yet ruined by frost, which would have to serve as their supper. There would be no meat; all the game had long ago departed, and no more foals could be spared from the herds. The supplies they had taken during the summer would never see them through until spring.

She had spent the whole morning gathering even this tiny portion. Added to some of the stolen supplies, it would barely be enough. She would feed White, then give most of her portion to Quanah, hoping he would believe her again when she told him she had already eaten. He needed his strength more than she did. He would go out tomorrow to try to find food. Since she was two months pregnant, she would not be going with him. Red Eagle Feather had been right about one thing before he walked off into the Texas desert; the only way she had brought her son to term was by staying off horseback. The Comanche birth rate had always been lower than that of other tribes whose women walked. Nalin had stayed off Blackie from the very moment she suspected her condition, and, so far, the pregnancy had been normal. In the past two years since White's birth, she had become pregnant twice, both times losing the baby within the first few months. This one she was determined to keep, even though it would be harder if she did not gain more weight. She glanced over at Blackie, tied with the other horses near their lodge. He was pawing through the snow, trying to reach the frozen grass beneath. He, too, was showing signs of the lack of food. In pity for her faithful animal, Nalin spared a wild plum from her basket, putting it under the soft black muzzle on an outstretched palm. Patting his neck, she whispered a few words of nonsense in his ear, nuzzling her face against his mane. She looked up to see Quanah approaching their lodge. He had not seen her yet, and an idea for mischief began to form.

It was an old game, one Comanche women had played with their mates for as long as anyone could remember. Other women who had also been out gathering vegetables and roots were coming in behind her, and she had little doubt they would readily join in the fun. Once the weapons had been buffalo chips, baked dry in the sun. Those were scarce now. Instead, Nalin set down her basket, lifted a handful of snow, and rolled it into a ball. He had almost reached the flap of their tepee.

"Quanah of the Kwahadi!" she called out, challenging. "Prepare to defend your life!"

He looked up, and, whap, the snowball hit him dead center in the chest. His surprise gave her time to form another one, but this one sailed over his head as he ducked.

Desert Flower, behind her, saw the game start and gave a war whoop, grinning broadly when her own mate poked his head out of their lodge. Quickly she had picked up a handful of snow, and the hastily formed ball met his head soon after he emerged. She ducked behind the lodge, then followed Nalin's lead as they retreated to form a line of defense behind a small hillock. Desert Flower's war whoop had alerted the others to the beginning of the game, and the women dropped their parcels, quickly forming snowballs and stockpiling the ammunition as the men stopped their tasks to join the fun. The women would be the invading war party, their husbands the enemy defending their camp.

Quanah lobbed a snowball at Nalin that struck her shoulder, and Nalin threw one back that he deflected with a rawhide bag held up as a makeshift shield. Snowballs began to fly back and forth between the men

234

"guarding the camp" and the women holding their line of defense.

The melee spread throughout the camp, women against the men, snowballs flying in both directions. Children and grandparents had come out to watch, and stray pellets of snow struck them by mistake. Some of them, too, began picking up handfuls of snow, tossing them at both sides.

Quanah, using his rawhide-bag shield to ward off the flurry of snowballs she was throwing at him, began to advance on Nalin's position. He reached her, threw down his shield, and tackled—gently so as not to injure the child she carried. He pushed her carefully onto her back as she gave up on snowballs and picked up handfuls of snow, pelting his back with them. "You lose." Quanah sprawled over her, careful that his weight did not bear down on her.

"Not yet," she tossed back mischievously, stuffing a handful of snow down the back of his shirt. Quanah yelled as the cold snow melted under his shirt and backed off as she squirmed out from under him then let him have it again with handfuls of snow, plucking the meager grass out with them in her haste.

He picked up a handful and stuffed it down the front of Nalin's shirt. While her mouth was still open in surprise, he lifted her up in his arms. In the last mock battle, months ago, he had thrown her over his shoulder like a sack of cornmeal and paddled her rump all the way to their lodge. This time he dared not be so rough and had to suffer her pounding on his back as he carried her home.

"Surrender, woman." He set her down on the bedroll within the lodge. "You are captured! You are my slave now."

Nalin stopped struggling, her arms still around his neck. "I will always be your slave, my Quanah," she whispered huskily.

White was in the next lodge with his grandmother and his aunts. The sound of the snowball fight still continued outside as she drew Quanah down toward her.

He kissed her, and Nalin arched her back to mold her-

235

self against him. His hand slid down to cup her buttocks for a moment, then he pulled up the hem of her dress, caressing the smooth, bare flesh. She had nearly stopped nursing White, but with the new pregnancy her breasts were heavy. Quanah softly kissed each one in turn, then raised himself to mount her.

"No," Nalin whispered. Reading her provocative smile, he turned over on his back, letting her lead their lovemaking.

Sometime later she lay in his arms, nestled against his shoulder, motionless as he slept beside her. She was unwilling to move and disturb him, content to stay and enjoy his nearness. So often of late, Quanah spent restless nights, sometimes rising in the darkness to pace the small space within their home. Sometimes, to keep from disturbing her, he went out and walked through the darkness, and she could hear his soft footsteps crackling through the snow. At times like these she realized his need to be alone with his thoughts and stilled her impulse to be with him. He was unwilling to worry her with his burden, but she knew what troubled his sleep. His people. The Comanche bands were his now—all that had not surrendered and gone the way of the white man. Now they were not *just* the Kwahadi. Mutsani, Nawkoni, even the more hot-headed of the Penatukha had deserted their chiefs to follow Quanah in his resistance. Some Kiowa and Arapaho and even Cheyenne had left their chiefs to the white man's peace talks and gone off to follow her husband. The weight of their welfare lay heavily on his mind. Most of them still believed they could regain their land, unwilling to listen to the facts.

Quanah knew them. He had heard from his long talks with the bluecoat, Parker. The East was filled with whites. More than a man could count in many days and nights. More kept coming from a faraway land across the water. Parker told him of their strength, of the places he called factories where they made guns and rifles by the hundreds each day. He told him of the war fought years ago, one white man against his brother, and even that

236

had not seriously reduced their number, and now that the war was long ended the whites had again turned their attention to the West. Quanah knew his people would lose, that the fight was futile; yet could not bring himself to surrender their lands. More died, almost daily, but he could not face bringing his people in.

For a short while, Nalin's game had turned his thoughts from his troubles and had given him a few minutes of much-needed rest. She would stay quietly in his arms and give him each precious second.

Quanah stirred in his sleep, his free arm coming around her waist, and she kissed the portion of his neck brought into her reach, snuggling even deeper against him. He awoke slightly and increased the pressure, pulling her closer yet.

Suddenly, a loud, jarring boom shattered the quiet of the village. Nalin jumped to a sitting position, startled, and Quanah sprang instantly to his feet. Another ear-shattering explosion followed, this time the sound of a cannon shell hitting the ground just outside their lodge. As Quanah dressed hurriedly, grabbing his weapons, rifle fire started. The bluecoats had found them again.

Nalin started to pick up her own rifle, but Quanah stopped her, grabbing her wrist. "No, Nalin, not this time. Our son needs you. Go to White. Find him in his grandmother's lodge and run to the hills with the women. You must live . . . for our son."

Her eyes smarting with sudden tears, Nalin made a grab for his arm, but he was out of her reach, running out of the lodge and across the encampment. A sudden, overwhelming fear took over, telling her she might never see him again. She would have no life without Quanah . . . but she would have his sons. The son she had and the one she carried. His words were true. She must live for them, if only to raise them to avenge their father.

She sprang to her feet, leaving her rifle behind as she ran from the lodge. The fighting that met her emergence was unbelievable. Already the bluecoats were swarming through the camp. Feeling fairly safe here by the Red River, their precautions had been light, not thinking the

237

whites could or would attack in the middle of winter. They were wrong! Wrong as they had been so often in their decisions, misjudging the strength and determination of their enemy. Nalin ran for the shelter where her son was, hoping they had not fled so that she couldn't find him.

Desert Flower passed her, running in the opposite direction, her tendencies, like Nalin's, to fight. She had a rifle in her hands and raised it at a mounted soldier. The bluecoat saw her and charged, his horse knocking Desert Flower to the ground and trampling her. Then, to be certain, the soldier turned and fired his revolver into Desert Flower's chest.

Nalin forced herself to turn away, running for her mother-in-law's lodge. She entered and found Quanah's stepmother sprawled on the ground. Her throat had been slashed, nearly severing her head. Quanah's sisters were gone, fled or killed outside. Frantically, Nalin searched for her baby. A muffled cry drew her to a pile of buffalo skins. Quanah's stepmother had hidden him beneath the pile. She pulled him out, lifting him to her shoulder, and started outside again.

Holding White closely against her, she ran for the hills. A mounted soldier blocked her path, galloping his horse straight toward her. He had a sword raised in his hands, ready to bring it down. Wild with fright, Nalin held up her child, showing the soldier she was a woman and unarmed.

Miraculously, the soldier lowered his saber, turning the horse away just in time. He passed just to her left, the horse's flank brushing against her, knocking her to the ground. Several blue uniforms surrounded her instantly, most on foot, as she lifted herself up to a sitting position. She had dropped White in her fall, and the baby was crying but uninjured a few feet away.

A soldier reached White first, and Nalin stared in terror as he lifted the crying child, but he only picked him up and started to hand him to his mother.

"Hey, looka here," a soldier said from behind her.

Still sitting where she had fallen, Nalin spun around.

238

He was staring at her loose red hair and grinning. "We done caught Quanah's woman, men." The grin broadened. He started toward her ominously. Nalin turned to the soldier holding White. "Give me my baby," she pleaded. "Please . . ." She held her arms out to take him, and the soldier seemed like he was going to hand him over, but the one behind her grabbed a handful of the short red locks and yanked her backward.

"You murderin' Injun bitch!" He held her by the hair and slapped her across the face.

"Hey, stop it!" One of the soldiers started forward.

The soldier holding her by the hair spun about on him furiously. "Her band a' murderin' savages burned my brother out! Far as I know this bitch held the torch!"

"Leave her be, O'Hara," another soldier warned.

"I'll leave her be!" O'Hara turned back on her, yanking her head upward. "I'll leave her be awright!" He drew back his foot and kicked her in the stomach, the force of the kick loosening his hold on her hair. Nalin doubled over and fell into a fetal position, clutching her stomach.

"Goddamn you, you shit-eatin' Injun whore!" He started to grab her again, but several soldiers came forward to pull him away. Nalin couldn't move through the pain. Her eyes blurred the sea of blue uniforms surrounding her.

"Let 'im have her," a soldier called out.

"Goddamn it, shut up!" another answered.

The world had turned into waves of pain as she clutched her agonized abdomen. She knew she was losing the baby. There was a dark blur, larger than the rest, fuzzy and indistinct, coming toward her. She was beyond caring, or even trying to defend herself. Let him kill me, her numb brain responded. Then at least they couldn't hurt her anymore.

"What's going on here?" MacKenzie reined his horse in sharply. "What is this? Leave this woman be!"

"Colonel, it's Quanah's woman." A soldier stepped forward, and, to prove it, he, too, grabbed Nalin's red hair, yanking her around to face the officer.

"What the hell are you doing?" The colonel jumped off

239

his horse and marched toward them. The soldier released her, backing away from MacKenzie's anger.

"Goddamn it, you don't have to torture her to prove it!" He glared at all of them, one face at a time. "Get your asses in motion and prepare to move out of here. Quanah's gotten away, and you can bet he's preparing a counteroffensive. Now get on outa' here and *move!*"

The soldiers scurried off, all but the one who held the wailing baby in his arms. "Sir," he asked sheepishly.

MacKenzie spun about. "What is it?"

"It's hers." He held the child up like an offering. "The baby's hers . . ."

Colonel MacKenzie glanced down at Nalin's crumpled form then back to the soldier. "Well, thanks to your friends there, she is in no condition to take him. *You're* in charge of the child until its mother recovers."

"Yes, sir." The soldier gulped heavily.

"And I'm warning you." The colonel stuck his finger in the soldier's face. "You let one of them harm this child—if *any*thing happens to this kid—I'll nail your hide to the Fort Smith stockade. You got that, soldier?"

"Yes, sir, Colonel MacKenzie, sir!"

"Now you get some men together and help her up. Then you see that she gets to Captain Stanley for medical attention. You're in charge of her, and you make goddamn certain nobody else lays a hand on her. I want this woman alive! You hear me? She's to reach Fort Smith in one piece. She's the only bait I have to bring Quanah in, and it took me too long to get her to let it all be spoiled by a bunch of fools!"

"Yes, sir," the soldier responded quickly.

MacKenzie turned to the crumpled form on the ground. She had passed out, still in a fetal, rolled-ball position, lying on her side. MacKenzie had seen her only once before, when she and a handful of warriors had penetrated the fort's supply room, stealing whatever they could carry in their arms. Then it had only been a fleeting glimpse. On closer inspection now, he hadn't expected her to be so young. Maybe only twenty or so. But then Quanah had not yet turned thirty, had he? That constant thorn in his side was only half his age and had so far beaten him at every turn—until now.

Now Ronald MacKenzie was holding the aces. He had his wife and he had his child—a boy, probably, from the look of him. From what Nash said, Quanah loved this girl, though he couldn't much imagine an Indian brave being able to feel real love for a squaw. Their women were possessions, weren't they? Hardly much better than slaves.

The woman moaned, turning slowly onto her back, her knees still drawn up over her stomach. MacKenzie knelt down beside her. Even through the pain contorting her face, he could see that she was pretty—strikingly so. He hadn't quite expected her to be.

The green eyes opened, looking at him, but without any recognition in them. "Quanah," she murmured softly, her hand grasping the sleeve of his jacket. "Quanah is . . . he is . . ."

She couldn't force the rest of the words out, but her expression told him plainly what she asked. "He's alive, young lady," MacKenzie answered her quietly. "Your Quanah's alive. You, soldier! Get her some help . . . on the double!"

Chapter 22

HARRY was still fretting and stewing and griping to himself, occasionally out loud, over the arrest and internment of Nalin. They wanted a Comanche surrender, but this was not the way to do it.

"Ridiculous!" Harry muttered aloud to the empty room. If Quanah gave himself up, if he brought the Comanche bands in, he'd be granted full amnesty. The war with the United States ended, Quanah, as an Indian, would not be held accountable for acts of war. But his white wife was held, imprisoned, and due to stand trial. In her case, Nash had made an exception and called it murder. She had recovered quickly from the miscarriage, but all through her recovery they had kept her locked in the guardhouse, taking no chance of losing their prisoner. The trial would be held in a few more days, and Harry had appointed himself her lawyer. All he had to do was convince Nalin that she should allow him to represent her, and so far no one had been able to get a word out of her. She sat in the barrack's cell each day, her face impassive, staring straight at the wall and refusing to talk or to eat, or even to move. She had been that way ever since they took the baby away. They had done so only for White's protection; a jail was no place for a toddler. He was safe and healthy, cared for by Nash's wife. This was the third day of Nalin's refusal to eat. Harry could see the Cynthia Ann Parker incident happening all over again.

"Damn!" he swore, getting to his feet. He'd have to get her to eat something, or she wouldn't live long enough to go to trial. He started out across the parade ground, heading toward the stockade, but was intercepted by Ryker trotting out to meet him.

"Major, there's a man at the stockade says he wants to see Quanah's woman."

"Yeah?" Major Parker barked. "Well, tell him if he wants to see her, he'll have to wait for the trial. We aren't conducting tours for curiosity seekers."

"That ain't it, Major. This one's a U.S. Marshal. Says he knows her personal."

Harrison stopped, a puzzled frown on his face. "How would a U.S. Marshal know her?"

"Says he thinks she's his young'un." Ryker shrugged.

Harry quickly changed direction for the guardroom.

Sometime later, as he entered her cell, she was exactly as he had seen her the last time, sitting on the cot, her back against the wall, arms and legs lifelessly still. All hope seemed to have fled. Nalin, the fierce warror, the able fighter, had given up.

Harry signaled the guard to leave them alone. He glanced down at the untouched plate of food as he stepped toward her. Her gaze never strayed from the opposite wall.

"You have to eat something." Harrison stood over her, watching in concern. She hadn't answered him once during her captivity. She didn't now. "You need your strength."

She didn't move, didn't flicker, and Harry was beginning to lose his patience about the whole thing. "How can you do this to Quanah?" he began angrily. "It wasn't enough that he lost his mother this way, you're going to do it to him again! Go on, starve! Die! Let the army win, but how's he going to feel when he knows what you did? You told me yourself what his ma's death did to him. How do you think he'll feel when he knows you did it, too? I thought you were a warrior, Nalin. I thought you were Kwahadi, not Penatukha." Harry had stalked off to the far wall, his back to her. When he turned around, the green eyes were glaring hotly at him.

"Where is my son?"

243

"Major Nash's wife has him. She's taking good care of him."

Her gaze started to turn back. He was losing her again. "Lisa?" he tried experimentally, calling the name out softly. "Lisa Thompson?"

At first her expression was blank, then slightly puzzled, as though memories were stirring from long ago. "Does that sound familiar to you? Lisa Thompson." He pronounced the name distinctly, letting every syllable sink in. "Your name was Lisa Thompson from North Fork, Nevada. Your pa is Henry Thompson?" Harry pronounced everything slowly. "You were barely ten years old when you left, Lisa . . ."

Her puzzled expression hardened. "I am Nalin, daughter of Manatah, wife of Quanah."

"*And* you are Lisa Thompson, daughter of Henry and Maureen Thompson of North Fork, Nevada . . ."

"I do not remember this."

"Try, Lisa." Harry came back toward her. "Try to remember . . . Lisa Thompson. She wore pretty dresses and bows in her hair—"

"No!" She glared at him. "I am Nalin, daughter of—"

"Lisa!" Harry grabbed her shoulders and shook her once. She stopped, staring at him mutely, and Harry's voice softened. "Your pa's here, Lisa, he's just outside. He wants to see you."

She didn't protest, didn't move, just stared at him. "Now, I'm going to go out and get him and bring him in here." Slowly, Harry took his hands off her shoulders and backed away. She watched him as he went to the door calling out for the guard.

"Mr. Thompson, you want to come in now?" Major Parker motioned him forward. Hank Thompson started out hesitantly. For over ten years he had followed this quest, hoping someday to find his missing child.

He knew, now, far more than Ann Baumann had told him. He had heard the tales that circulated throughout the West of the Comanche warrior woman with red hair. Texas hated her, probably worse than they did Quanah.

His were acts of war, but she was white, a traitor to her own race. It was the celebrations and joyful tidings in Texas that had caused him to drop his prisoner off hurriedly in Houston and rush here to find her. He had always stayed close, hoping someday she might need him, and now it seemed she did.

Faced with the sight of the thick wood door of her cell, though, Hank Thompson paused uncertainly while Major Parker waited. Ann Baumann had once warned him that she wasn't the Lisa he once knew. She wasn't a just-barely-ten-year-old; she was a woman, full grown, with a husband and child of her own.

Major Parker was letting the marshal take all the time he wanted. Hesitantly Thompson glanced at him, then strode resolutely through the doorway. At his first sight of her, Thompson's breath caught in his throat. She was very nearly the spitting image of Maureen. Her hair had darkened, but bleached strawberry highlights made it shades lighter than her mother's had been. Her face, like Mo's, was sculpted perfection, the eyes exactly the same, long-lashed, large, and luminous green. For the rest of her, though, Hank was taken aback and shocked. He had been told but had never quite pictured how she would be now. The buckskin dress, moccasins, and headband made her look foreign to him. Her expression as she gazed back at him was without recognition, like a hostile stranger's. This wasn't . . . couldn't be his daughter. And yet, the resemblance told him she was.

"Lisa?" Thompson stepped timidly forward. The aloof glare hardened, warning him to stay back. He stopped. "Don't you remember me, Lisa? I'm your pa. Don't you remember?" Hank's eyes misted with tears that he hadn't shed since Mo died. "Lisa, I'm your pa . . ."

She huddled even farther back against the wall, spitting out a few rapid words in venomous-sounding Comanche.

"Stop it," Harry chastised her roughly. "She speaks English, Marshal. Her name is Nalin now."

"Nalin," Henry repeated, trying to smile. "That's a pretty name." Again, he approached cautiously.

If it was possible she backed even closer to the wall, rambling on, still in Comanche.

"Speak to him in English, damn it! He's your pa. He's only here 'cause he wants to help you!"

She turned to glare at Harry, but he was staring right back. "Quanah's right about you!" he stormed. "You're stubborn! *Mule*-headed!"

"Quanah never said that." She had forgotten her pa's presence, that she didn't speak English, and focused on glaring at Harrison.

"Yes he did!" Harry railed back. "He told me you're like an old bull bison. You just plant your feet and won't move no matter how many times you're prodded with the lances. And I'll tell you something else he said. He told me to take care of you if the day ever came when he couldn't. And I intend to keep that promise whether you like it or not!"

"I do not need your help."

"You don't, hey? You're so weak you can't even get off that cot. You can't even show decent Comanche manners to your pa, who's come a long way to see you. Did Manatah bring you up to behave like that?"

This time her chin set stubbornly, but her mouth stayed closed.

"Now, you're either gonna eat that food there, or I'm gonna sit on you and stuff it down. Take your pick!"

Nalin still glared as Harrison approached, picking up the slice of bread and offering it to her. She wouldn't take it.

"I'll make a deal with you," he continued, holding the bread out. "You eat, and I'll get White back to his pa."

The hard glare softened several seconds before she spoke. "You would take him to Quanah?"

"Nash's wife is okay, but I won't let Nash raise *my* godson. Eat the bread, and we'll talk about it."

Still watching his face distrustfully, Nalin took the bread from his hand and began nibbling at it. Satisfied with his progress, Harrison sat down on the cot right beside her. "Have a seat, Marshal." Harry magnanimously offered the cell's single chair to him.

"I don't know," Thompson began. "Maybe I best go . . ." He started to turn away.

"No, sit down. Nalin wants you to stay and visit, don't you, Nalin?"

Chewing the bread dryly, she glared at him again.

"Don't you, Nalin?" Harry poked her with his elbow. "It's bad manners to refuse a guest shelter and food, no matter how bad things are. No *proper* Comanche would turn a relative out. Bad medicine to turn your back on a relative. I found that out when I lived with them for a few weeks. Quanah said Comanches always help their brothers. I'm his cousin, did you know that?" Harry told him brightly.

Thompson shook his head, but slowly lowered himself into the chair as Harrison Parker prattled on.

As they strolled back across the parade ground, Harrison was pleased with himself for his accomplishment in getting Nalin to eat. He was doubly pleased for having her father beside him to help in his newly hatched plot. She still would not speak with Thompson but was at least responding with yes and no answers to Parker. Thompson was walking along beside him, lost in thoughts of his own. "Is that true, Major Parker? You're Quanah's cousin?"

"I sure am," Parker answered. "Second cousin, I guess."

"Then you know him, you've met him."

"Yes, sir, I suppose you could say I know him very well."

"Then you know what he's really like?"

Major Parker kept walking but gazed sideways at the marshal. "You mean with Lisa? What kind of a husband is he?"

Thompson's return look was apologetic. "I've heard so many stories, Major, tales . . . I don't know how many are true. The way they talk about him in Texas—"

"Oh." Harry laughed. "I guess Texans wouldn't have a lot of good to say about him. Whiteside tells everybody who'll listen what Quanah did to him on the cattle drive a few years back. He made a fool out of MacKenzie, which isn't hard to do, and you won't hear good from that direction either."

"Someone told me once that Quanah is good to Lisa, that he loves her."

Harry's step slowed even farther. "That's true," he answered seriously. "Quanah loves her. He's a good husband and a good father."

"Then Lisa is happy with him?"

Harry kept his gaze fastened on the ground, forcing his step to pick up again. Sure Quanah loved her. And she loved him, and Harry had no more hope than a spitball in a duststorm. "Yes, sir, she's very happy with him."

They stopped before a large frame house painted white with yellow shutters. Harry halted before the walkway. "Marshal, you said back in the guardroom that you wanted to help Lisa, that you'd do anything if it would help her. Do you still mean that?"

"Course I do." Harry looked perplexed.

"All right, follow me and just agree with everything I say, will you do that?" Without giving Thompson a chance to reply, Harrison started up the walkway. He rapped on the yellow door and waited. A few moments later, it opened on an attractive middle-aged woman who gazed out at them curiously.

"Mrs. Nash, m'am. I'm Major Harrison Parker. I think you remember me?"

"Oh, yes, the lawyer." she smiled broadly, standing back. "Do come in."

Harry stepped through the doorway, Thompson behind him. "M'am, this is Marshal Henry Thompson."

"How do you do?" Mrs. Nash closed the door, then offered her hand to him. Nash might be a low-down varmint, as Ryker termed him, but his wife was an angel. "Please sit down." She led the way into the drawing room and gestured for them to sit. "I'm sorry that Major Nash isn't here."

"Well, we know that, m'am. We haven't come to see him. It's about White . . . um, the baby," Harry corrected.

"Oh, is that his name?" She smiled, sitting down prettily in the chair across from them. Sure was the opposite of Nash. Harry wondered how this attractive, gentle woman could stand the man she was married to. "Roger never said what his name was, so we've been calling him Butch. He's such a sweet child. Never cries, always laughing . . . but I feel so sorry for his poor mother, locked in that jail. The poor dear. I wanted to visit her, tell her that Butch is well, but Roger absolutely forbids it. He says she's allowed no visitors."

"That's true, m'am," Harry interrupted, not wanting to stay too long for fear Nash might come home. "She's only been allowed one visitor. This is her father." He gestured toward Thompson.

"Oh." Her gaze darted to the marshal. "Oh my . . . then you're young Butch's grandfather, aren't you?"

Thompson was staring back at her amazed. He had heard Lisa had a baby. He *knew* that, but it hadn't registered on him yet that that made him a grandfather.

"Oh, you must be dying to see him." She stood up quickly, fluttering off to the stairway in the hall. "Jenny," she called upstairs. "Jenny Sue, bring Butch on down here."

"He's asleep, Momma," a girl's voice called down.

"Well, wake him up. His grandpa is here to see him." She came back in, standing uncertainly in the middle of the room. "He'll be right down . . . um, would you care for brandy? Coffee?"

"No, Mrs. Nash, thank you. But we haven't come to visit White. We've come to get him. The marshal here is his closest blood relative, and he'd—"

Mrs. Nash sank into the chair, disappointment evident. "Oh, yes, I understand. I suppose I knew I'd have to give him up sooner or later—to his momma when she's cleared of these ridiculous charges. I was sort of hoping I might keep him longer, though. All mine are grown. No more babies, and I do love them so when they're tiny."

"Yes, m'am, but his grandpa would like to take care of him now."

"I see . . . certainly." She glanced briefly at the marshal with a look that clearly said she didn't think

249

him capable of caring for the youngster. "I suppose it's only a matter of a week or two till his momma's freed, isn't it?"

"We hope so, Mrs. Nash."

"Oh well, surely they can't convict her. She's no more guilty of murder than the Confederates were a few years back. War is war, as Roger has said." She was interrupted by the appearance of a girl of about fourteen carrying a covered, wiggling burden in her arms.

"Jenny Sue, don't cover him up like that in the house. Lord, girl, he'll sweat, then catch the chills." Mrs. Nash took the child away, pulling the blanket down. Harrison had not seen his godson since he was a newborn, and Thompson hadn't seen him at all. White Parker was almost two now, a thin but healthy looking boy. The light blond hair was turning to a dusky brown, straight and wispy, and, for his age, he had plenty of it. When Mrs. Nash turned him about to face his visitors the boy broke into giggles, peering at them. His eyes were dark brown, just like his father's. Harry had lost the bet on the Parker eyes.

"Isn't he precious?" Mrs. Nash hugged him. "Oh, but of course you know that. I'm going to miss him terribly." She gave the boy a final squeeze, then offered him out to his grandfather. Thompson stared like his eyes were going to fall out of his head.

"Take him, Marshal," Harry prodded in amusement.

Thompson took the child gently, cradling him with both arms. He hadn't felt like this since the midwife placed a newborn Lisa in his arms. The child leaned on him, giggling away happily as he began to tug on his grandpa's sideburns.

"He says some things over and over again," Mrs. Nash continued with tears in her eyes. "I think they're words, but they must be in Comanche. You will take good care of him, won't you?"

"Yes, m'am, excellent care." Harry got up, hurrying for the door. A glance at the chime clock on the mantel told him Nash might be home soon.

"Oh, my goodness." Mrs. Nash's hand fluttered as she

turned away, hurrying toward a chest in the hallway. She took the opportunity to wipe at her eyes with the back of her hand. "I nearly forgot his things. I washed them and put them in here for safekeeping till his momma came." She came back with a small robe made of buffalo calfskin, a small Indian blanket, and a highly decorated and ornate backboard that looked like it wouldn't fit the growing child much longer. She handed them to Harry since Thompson's hands were full with a squirming grandson, bored with the sideburns and anxious to be set down.

"Bye, bye, Butch." Mrs. Nash wiggled her fingers at him as they went through the door. She caught the baby's attention, and he moved his whole arm up and down at her. She began to cry again, the tears squeezing through. "Major, tell me his real name once more, so I'll remember it if I ever see him again."

"His name's White, m'am . . . White Parker."

Her body remained as motionless as when Parker had left her. Only her thoughts were straying past the bars that surrounded her. Harry's visit had, perhaps unknowingly, given her a bit of hope. Not hope for herself, but for White. And for Quanah. For the child Harry would bring to him, Quanah would live. The only thing left to Nalin were hei memories, and they helped her to pass the endless hours of confinement.

At the moment, her thoughts were straying to the morning White must have been conceived. She had been fitfully sleeping, her arm wrapped about her husband's waist. The moment he stirred, she awoke, yet she wasn't quite ready to rise if he was only changing position. Her eyes remained closed, resting awhile longer. She wasn't sure how she knew he was staring at her. She felt his eyes upon her, and opened her own to peer at him through sleepy lids.

He was propped on his elbow; his gaze slowly travelled over her body. By the time he reached her face, Nalin was still feigning sleep, but a slight smile had appeared.

When he noticed it, Quanah smiled, too, with the look of a boy caught at mischief. Nalin reached up to touch his cheek, and he leaned over her, kissing her forehead, then her brow, then her lips, the kiss becoming a long and lingering one.

Quanah could prolong passion far more than she could wait. He did so again, backing out of her embrace, urging her to lie still while he traced with his hand the contours he had studied so carefully. His touch was light, teasing, and intoxicating. She closed her eyes, enjoying the exquisite torture. She could only feel it when he changed from using his hand to using his lips, again feather lightly, trailing a course upward with excruciating slowness. When he at last reached the nape of her neck, Nalin embraced him, pulling him closer. This time their lovemaking had been as lingering as the foreplay, every cherished moment deeply engraved in her mind. Out of such love surely White must have come, their prayers at last answered.

The loud clang of the cell door intruded into her thoughts. A guard deposited a dinner tray on the table and left.

By now, Harrison Parker must have picked up White. He might, even now, be handing him to his father. With that hope in mind, Nalin lifted a slice of bread and began to eat.

Chapter 23

THE backboard was giving him blisters, and Harry couldn't help but wonder how a woman, especially one as slight as Nalin, could carry a two-year-old child around like this all day long. White was large enough now to stand on tiptoe on the bottom of the backboard and play with Harrison's sideburns as they rode.

"Cut it out, White." Harry brushed the child's fingers out of his ear.

"Want I should take him awhile?" Thompson offered.

"No, it's all right. We should be getting close now. Nalin said they'd meet up at Tule Canyon, and we're nearly there. The scouts should have seen us by now. They usually don't miss much." Harry winked, smiling, then grimaced as White again yanked on a lock of hair. "Damn it, White, stop that!" He pulled the hair free, and the baby giggled. "I sure wish Nalin could have seen him for a minute before we left. It would have done her a world of good. I just didn't dare stay that long."

Thompson was peering at him curiously. "You've done an awful lot for my daughter, Major Parker. I been meaning to tell you I appreciate it."

Parker grinned sheepishly. "I'm doing it because I want to. I feel like it's the right thing to do. I guess you can say I'm doing it as much for myself. I think I enjoy making MacKenzie miserable." The grin broadened.

"Even so, thank you." Thompson rode on in silence for a while. "Major," he started again. "Won't you get yourself in a heap of trouble? Running off like this with the baby?"

"Not really." Harry shrugged indifferently. "What can they say about it? White isn't under arrest. And he's with his grandfather. *Your* rights, Marshal, precede those of the U.S. Government. He's your grandson, and if you want to take him back to his father, there isn't a hell of a lot they can do about it. I'm just helping you out, that's all. You *do* want to do that, don't you, Marshal?" Harry gazed at him. "I mean I don't have the right to make you . . ."

Thompson stared straight ahead for a long moment, pondering his own feelings. He hadn't known what Parker was up to, but, in retrospect, he'd have to agree it was what he might have done if he'd thought of it. "I know the pain of losin' a child, Major. Any way it happens, it's a hard thing to bear. If this Quanah is the man you say he is, if he's the man my Lisa chose to love, then I ain't gonna be the one to put him through that."

Harry wanted to say thank you, or something, but words seemed inadequate. The marshal had told him about how he came to lose Lisa, the years he had spent in search of her. He had bared his heart to the army major, revealing his decision to leave Lisa to the kind of life she wanted, free to stay with the Comanche without his interference. Now, after all these burdens, the fate of his only child still rested on the outcome of the trial.

Harry knew full well it was not going to be easy. Someone had to pay for the damages and the heartbreak Texans had suffered at Comanche hands. Since the government would deny them Quanah, that retribution could only fall on the white girl who chose to be Indian. Maybe her enemies could find some sympathy or compassion if they understood her cause, but to do so, the story would have to come from Nalin herself. If the wild rumors of every conceivable reason for her actions could be dispelled and the truth be known, if they could hear why Nalin turned on her own kind, they might be able to forgive. Nalin would have to tell them, and Harry seriously doubted he could get her to do it.

Approaching Tule Canyon, where Nalin had said the Comanche would re-form in case of attack, Harry was surveying the ridges, looking for some sign of them. He could guess his untrained eye might miss the signs of their presence, but he was equally certain the Comanche scouts would not miss them, two lone white men riding out in the open.

"What's that smell?" Marshal Thompson's nose wrinkled in distaste as he looked up, facing the direction the wind was coming from. Harry had noticed, but his brain had been too preoccupied to register fully until the marshal mentioned it. Then his nose, too, wrinkled.

"God, it's awful!" Harry proclaimed at the sick-sweet smell assailing his nostrils.

"That's the stink of rotting carcasses." The marshal prodded his horse into a trot. The smell was getting stronger, carried by the wind as they approached the canyon. Stronger than the odor of only a single, or a few, dead bodies, this odor was one of a great number of carcasses rotting in the sun. The December day was a warm one, melting the layer of snow on the ground and aiding the decomposition of whatever it was that lay in Tule Canyon.

Harrison, worried about riding any faster with the baby strapped to his back, finally caught up with Marshal Thompson, who had reined in short at the canyon entrance. "Oh, my dear God!" Harry exclaimed in a soft whisper as he saw what the marshal was staring at. His eyes widened in disbelief, his jaw dropping open after his short pronouncement.

The canyon was filled with the dead and rotting corpses of several hundred, perhaps a thousand, horses and mules. Had he been able to count, there would have been, roughly, 1,400 of them, all bearing in some manner a mark that proclaimed them part of the Comanche nation. Each also bore the mark, those still intact enough to show it, of having been shot once in the head.

"Good God Almighty!" Harrison found his voice at last,

fighting the nausea that was welling up as much from the sight as from the smell, still unable to believe the slaughter before him.

"Your MacKenzie has won."

Harry spun about to the sound of the voice. Quanah was standing behind him, on foot, a few of his braves beside him. They were carrying rifles but held them at their sides when they recognized the visitor.

"MacKenzie did this?"

Quanah walked forward, surveying the shallow canyon filled with bodies. He didn't look at Harry as he spoke. "We were not ready for the attack when they came," he said slowly. "Many warriors reached their war horses, but we could not free them all. As we prepared to attack, the bluecoats entered our village. Many of our people could not escape them. The bluecoats knew our needs—that God-dog brings us to our food, and so they took them. Because they could not hold so many, they killed them.

"We heard the sound of their rifles but could not see what the sounds meant until they had gone. Then we found this." Quanah at last turned around to look at Harry. His expression was that of a beaten man. He had lost his war, and his means of protecting his way of life. The full impact of the fact was there in the somber black eyes brimming with moisture. "You have come to tell me that Nalin is dead?" His voice was almost matter-of-fact, lifeless, as though no more pain could possibly enter.

"No, Quanah, she's alive. She's captured, but she's not dead." Harry dismounted awkwardly under the added weight of the baby squirming on his back.

"Then why is White not with his mother?"

"Nalin wanted him back here with you. She's being held for trial. They won't let her keep him in the stockade. Nalin was afraid he might get sick . . . like your sister did. She sent a message with us, too, Quanah. She said to tell you, to remind you rather, that you said one must live, for him."

Quanah's gaze traveled to his son on the major's back. The small child's hands were reaching out, recognizing his father. "We cannot care for him, Har'son Parker. We have no food, and no horses now to take us to our food. Many of our women were killed or taken. He would die here."

"Warm Summer Day?" Harry's brow furrowed, referring to White's grandmother, the lovely widow of Nacoma.

"She has joined her husband. She is at peace."

"Goddamn!" Harry murmured softly. "Oh goddamn, I'm sorry, Quanah."

"You must take him back. He must live in the world of the white man now."

"And what about you? What about your people?"

"We can fight no more." Quanah gazed back over the sickening sea of rotting horseflesh. "The Great Spirit has turned away from the Comanche in anger. He has taken back the gift of God-dog. Perhaps it is the will of the Great Spirit that the Comanche should all die as the buffalo have all died."

"Quanah, MacKenzie wants to make a deal with you. You bring the rest of the Comanche in, and he'll release Nalin."

The warrior's gaze turned to him. "He will release her to live with your people, or with mine?"

"With yours, Quanah. Whichever way she wants to live. As long as you surrender she'll be freed."

"He promises this?"

"He does," Harry answered, but his mind was still bothered by the fact that MacKenzie, perhaps seeking to share the blame should anything go awry, had turned Nalin over to be tried by civilian authorities, directly for the murder of Peter Sullivan, the cowboy killed in the trading-post raid. They had four witnesses lined up to testify to the fact that she, and only she, had killed the young man without provocation. Since the military had relinquished their claim to the prisoner, he wasn't sure MacKenzie would be able to keep his end of the bargain.

"It is not my decision to make. My people must decide to follow the white man, or to die here. I will not speak to them of my own decision. I will tell them only that

257

MacKenzie offers them freedom, on the reservation, for their surrender. The choice will be theirs."

Quanah had turned away, but Harry stopped him. "What about you? What will you do?"

"I do not know yet, Har'son Parker."

White was starting to squall, protesting his confined position. Quanah reached out and touched the small cheek. He smiled weakly, then dropped his hand and moved away. In a moment, Quanah and the braves had disappeared behind the rocks. Harry stared after them long after they had gone.

"What you think they'll do, Major?" Thompson interrupted his thoughts.

"I don't know," Harry answered in contained anger. Had MacKenzie been here before him, the least Harrison would have given him was a hard punch in the mouth. "They'll probably give up. What the hell choice do they have?" He remounted his horse. "I didn't introduce you, Marshal. I'm sorry."

"Forget it." Marshal Thompson climbed on his own horse and turned the beast away from the sight of the slaughter. "I reckon we'll meet another day. Want me to take the baby awhile?"

"I'd appreciate it." Parker prodded his horse forward. "Let's get away from here first." Harry maneuvered his horse around the half-rotted body of a black gelding.

When he told her what had transpired, Nalin accepted the news with the same hopeless stoicism she had displayed throughout her capture. They had returned White to Mrs. Nash. Major Nash gave him a harsh glare of disapproval but said nothing about the child's temporary disappearance.

"If someone so much as sniffles, they won't get near him," Lillian Nash promised them faithfully, after hearing the reasons for Harry's reluctance to leave the child.

In the hands of this capable lady, White would be fine; Harry was not as certain of his mother's welfare. She couldn't weigh more than a hundred pounds now; skinny as a post, the once well-rounded form was only a shade, almost a shadow, of her former self. Losing the baby and the bleeding it had caused had given her a sickly pallor. Only her cheeks were pink, and that was an unhealthy fevered flush. She kept her promise and ate, but so little it couldn't possibly keep her alive for long. Nalin was dying . . . of hopelessness. She might not live long enough for the court to hang her.

Chapter 24

HARRY had no choice left but to call her to the stand. The prosecution had rested its case on the four witnesses who had seen Quanah's woman commit an act of murder. Harry was sure she had not just clubbed a man to death without a reason, but cross-examination of the hate-filled Travis Jensen and his cohorts would not reveal a motive for the crime.

Major Parker had no defense unless he proved to the jury's satisfaction that Nalin's actions were for the protection of her people, who *she* felt were her people, the Comanche. He had to try to make them see past her light skin and red hair. Make them see her as just as Indian as any of those she had fought with. He had used up all the witnesses he could gather for the defense. Hank Thompson had taken the stand, telling the story of Jesse Sutton's death and how the Indians must have found her out on the desert when she was no more than a child. Ann Baumann had volunteered and returned from Denver to testify to the differences between her captivity and Nalin's. Mrs. Baumann had tried to help, but as she related the way that Nalin had treated her—as any Indian would treat a white slave—the jury's feelings against the girl were strengthened. In her testimony Ann had only wanted to prove Harry's point, that Nalin didn't remember her white heritage. The jury, all Texans, didn't want to see it that way, and Mrs. Baumann left the stand in tears, certain she had helped seal Nalin's fate.

"The defense calls Nalin to the stand," Harry called out.

"I object." Flynn Mailer, the prosecutor, stood up quickly. "We've heard Marshal Thompson identify the defendant as his daughter, so the witness should be called by her real name, Lisa Thompson."

"Very well," Harry acceded with a frown before the judge moved on the motion. "Then I call Lisa Thompson *Parker* to the stand."

Flynn stayed on his feet. "She's not legally wed to that Indian."

"She's as married as you are, Mailer!" Harry retorted. "Your Honor. Are we going to tell Indians that they aren't legally wed because their wedding customs differ from ours? Are we going to tell people from foreign lands that their marriages are not valid in the United States because they were not wed by our customs? Our way?"

"All right, Major, you've made your point, don't belabor it. Objection overruled." The judge banged the gavel down sharply. "*Mrs.* Parker will please take the stand."

Harry turned to his unwilling client. Major Nash's wife had offered her daughter's clothing for Nalin to wear into court today, but Harry had taken a chance and refused it, thanking her. He wanted Nalin to appear as she was, dressed as she was used to dressing. He had sent for some clothing from the reservation, and now she was wearing a clean buckskin dress and fresh moccasins, and Harry had fastened about her neck a necklace of silver and bear claws that had cost him half his week's pay to purchase from a passing Navaho. The short red hair had been brushed to a gleam by Lillian Nash, then they had tied a beaded band around her forehead. Nalin had done nothing for herself. He was worried about her, in health and in spirit, and the worry expressed itself on his face as he waited for her to rise.

"Mrs. Parker." The judge leaned forward. "Will you please take the stand."

"One moment please, your Honor." Harry stepped toward her, his hand outstretched. "Nalin?"

Her gaze turned slowly toward him. Finally, she placed her hand in his and let him pull her to her feet. Harry had to put her hand on the Bible.

"Do you solemnly swear to tell the truth, the whole truth, and nothing but the truth, so help you God?" the court bailiff asked.

Nalin looked at Harry.

"She does, your Honor," Harry answered.

"Let her speak for herself, Major Parker."

The clerk repeated his question. Nalin stared at him in silence.

"Major." The judge leaned forward again. "Doesn't your client understand English?"

"Yes, she does, your Honor." Harry nudged her arm gently. "Answer him, Nalin. Just say 'I do.' "

"I cannot swear by God," Nalin said solemnly, prompting a murmur of voices from the packed courthouse. Even the judge was shocked into a moment of silence.

"Young lady." He leaned even closer to her. "You are telling this court that you cannot swear an oath of truth?"

"I cannot swear by this god if the god you speak of is a white man with a long, flowing beard such as I heard of in my childhood. He is *your* god, not mine."

"Then do *you* have a god by whom you can swear?" the judge asked gently.

"It is not the way of my people to tell false words. I will not lie."

"That's good enough," Judge Simpson proclaimed, banging the gavel to quiet the still-murmuring throng in the courtroom. "The clerk will record that the witness has sworn to tell the truth, the whole truth, and nothing but the truth . . ."

"So help her what, your Honor?" The court stenographer turned a puzzled face upward.

"So help her *god*, Bailey. *Her* god, whatever the hell that may be. Now just write it!"

"Yes, your Honor." Bailey meekly sat.

Harry was smiling, pleased that Judge Simpson was a fair man. He'd need him, with the jury stacked against his case.

"Nalin, I want you to tell the court, in your own words, how you came to live with the Comanche."

He waited.

"Nalin, tell the court—"

"They have been told this." She turned to him, the green eyes shining with fevered brightness.

"But we want to hear your side of it. How did they find you?"

"It is enough that they found me."

"Nalin," Harry pleaded.

"The witness will answer the question," Judge Simpson ordered, frowning.

Nalin ignored him, staring straight in front of her as Harry stepped closer. "Nalin, please . . . you have to tell them. You have to help me."

"I have done what I have done, Harrison. I will not ask the pardon of my enemy."

She had said it just loud enough to be heard in the now hushed courtroom. The prosecutor leapt to his feet. "Then you admit that you regard the United States as your enemy." He beamed triumphantly.

"It's not your turn, Mailer. Sit down!" the judge barked.

Harry moved near her to whisper, "Please don't do this, Nalin. You're taking the case away from me."

"I will not answer your questions, Harrison, for I will not make excuses for what I have done. I fought for the Comanche. I would do so again. I ask no one's pardon for this."

Harry gave his summation, knowing it would be futile. He tried to explain, using her own testimony to prove Nalin knew little of her own race. He tried to prove she thought just like any Comanche protecting their lands, but his efforts were in vain, undermined by her statement that she regretted none of her actions and would repeat

them if necessary. With the Comanche still not surrendered it was as good as saying she would return to them
immediately and continue her war with the United
States. He was defeated and knew it, and the knowledge
reflected even through his emotion-packed summation.
Whatever sympathies might have been ignited had been
stifled; the jury was out for less than an hour, returning
with a verdict of guilty.

"Parker, the best I can do is life imprisonment." Judge
Simpson sat back wearily. Waiting for the cheering to
calm down, he had not yet passed sentence on the prisoner, reserving it for the following morning. Even then he
wasn't sure the courtroom would bear his decision without a riot. They were in the judge's chambers now, Major
Parker, Henry Thompson, and Colonel Ronald MacKenzie. "You heard the verdict. The jury found her guilty of
murder. I can give her prison or hanging. That's all the
choice I have."

"Surely there must be some way to declare a mistrial."
Colonel MacKenzie spoke. He had good reason to. Word
had come a half hour after the verdict. The Comanche
had decided to surrender. Quanah was leading them in.
Had the news come earlier the judge might have been
able to postpone the trial, pending a change in the girl's
attitude if her people no longer fought.

"Now, Colonel, if the Army had seen fit to hold this
trial here, this might have been helped. But you, sir, had
to go and hand her over to the state of Texas for trial.
You've washed your hands of it, Colonel MacKenzie, and
now just what the hell do you expect me to do?"

"We can claim a prejudiced jury," Parker interjected.
"Lord knows, that's true enough."

"And you want me to claim my own court was unfair?
Sorry, gentlemen, I'm not taking the brunt of this. Not
alone, anyway. You can go ahead and petition for a new
trial. She still has the right to appeal. You'll probably get
one if public opinion is stilled by then. But *till* then my
decision stands. I'm not going to hang a woman and a
mother no matter what she did—or why! I'm sentencing

264

her to territorial prison for life. Or until you win an appeal or a pardon from the governor."

"Those procedures would take time, your Honor. Months for the case to be reviewed. Nalin doesn't have that kind of time. She's ill. Prison, even a week of it, will kill her."

"Maybe she'll feel better when her husband gets here."

"Judge Simpson, when Quanah learns she's been convicted, he's liable to turn right around and fight. I told you, his mother died being held at Fort Smith. He's not going to trust us to keep it from happening to Nalin. When he shows up we have to be able to hand her over to him, right there."

"You all should have thought of that before you gave her over to civilian authorities." His gaze rested harshly on MacKenzie. "You went along with the people in handing her over to them, and now you want me to put my career on the line to save your hide. My job rests solely with carrying out the will of the people of Texas. I'm not jeopardizing it to get your neck out of the noose. You want the girl returned to her husband, you find another way to get her freed. The people of Texas already spoke in my court, and I'm their servant, but I'll go only so far even there. *They* want her hung. I'm sticking my own neck out already by giving her prison instead. Now, you want anything more than that, you see the governor about it. He can grant her a pardon, *if* he will."

"Please, sir," Harry pleaded. "Can't we have a temporary release pending a decision by the governor or a new trial? One for medical reasons. Her health, sir—"

"Her health won't matter a bit, Parker, if I turn her loose, and you know it, or ought to. If these people see her walking the streets in spite of the conviction, they'll hang her themselves and probably you and me along with her. The safest place for her is far out of their sight until they start to forget the raids of last summer. People don't stay hot all that long. When they've cooled off, they might change their opinions, but, if I turn her loose now, she's as good as dead."

* * *

Judge Simpson's words kept sticking in Harry's mind like a burr against his skin, irritating and causing no respite, because they were so true. "The safest place for her is far out of their sight," he had said. The summer raids, though not very productive for the Indians, had cost the settlers just as dearly. Lives had been lost; supplies that the Indians had stolen might have comfortably filled settlers' bellies until spring. As it was, some Texans were having a hard time seeing it through until the end of the winter of 1878.

Perhaps with the coming of spring, when seeds were planted, when births increased the cattle herds, when supplies from the East at last reached their destination, people would be more inclined to forgive. As it stood, though, Judge Simpson was right. If he set her free, it could only be into the arms of the vigilante groups certain to override the judge's decision. Pardons, appeals, or retrials would all take time. Time that Nalin didn't have. In spite of his hope for a change in attitude by spring, he knew Nalin would die in prison while awaiting that change. Without Quanah and the baby her will to live was gone. If she couldn't be with him, she'd surely die, and soon.

Harry walked past the civilian jail where she was now being held. There were already circles of protesters around her cell window, screaming that if the judge didn't have the guts to hang her, they would do the job. A women's group from the church also stationed itself around her cell window, carrying placards that said it was against the will of God for whites to breed with inferior races. The group chanted Bible passages, preaching at her through the cell bars to reform her ways and reject the unnaturalness of her union with the Indian before she was called before her maker.

Harry had asked, and been given permission, to meet Quanah alone to tell him what had happened. He knew neither MacKenzie nor Nash had the guts to face him.

He walked past the protesters, feeling it would be useless to try to talk to Nalin again. She was quietly sitting on the cot in her cell, staring into space, exactly as she had done since her capture. It was only a matter of time until she died, just as Cynthia Ann Parker had done. Nalin's own worst fears had been realized.

Harry hadn't ridden far before he saw the remnants of the once proud Comanche nation treading slowly to the fort, almost every one of them on foot. Quanah, on a pinto, was leading them in; Pecos was on a bay mare beside him. Harry recalled sadly that warriors never rode mares.

Quanah greeted him soberly as Harrison stopped before him. "My people have chosen. They chose to live."

"Quanah, I must . . . I have to tell you something," Harry began falteringly. Quanah pulled the pinto to a halt while his people filed past him. Dirty, sick, beaten, they only wished to reach their painful journey's end quickly. Quanah waited.

"It's Nalin," he began. The warrior's hand reflexively clutched the leather reins. "The trial is over. She was convicted." Harry tried and failed to meet the dark-eyed stare. "The judge gave her prison. She won't be hanged, but . . . but I couldn't get her freed."

He half expected anger, or some explosive reaction. Instead Quanah prodded his horse with his heels, starting forward again. Harry turned his horse around to follow him. "Quanah, we'll keep trying to get her pardoned. There are a few things we can try. In time . . . in a few months at most. Quanah, will you listen to me?"

The warrior kept his gaze fastened on the horizon, the horse's pace slow and steady.

"Quanah—for Christ's sake, say something! Hit me for failing you. *Do* something! Pecos, make him listen to me."

Pecos, too, kept his gaze fastened forward. "He knows already, Har'son Parker. The Kiowa passed close to a white trading post. They were told of the celebrations of Nalin's defeat. They told us also that she is ill and will not live another moon."

"Well, she might if she has a reason to." Harry kicked his horse a few steps faster to catch up with the chief.

"She doesn't have any hope left," Harry argued. "And you won't help her a bit like this. Just accepting it? Is that the way of the Comanche? I thought you said you'd fight till the bluecoats came and whipped you—"

"They have done so," Pecos stated flatly.

"So you'll surrender Nalin to her fate? You'll let her die in the white man's prison without trying to save her? Tell me, Quanah, what did you try to do to save your mother?"

This time Harry received his response. Quanah swung his horse about, the black eyes flashing sparks again. "Hold your tongue, Har'son Parker, or I will forget that we are friends!"

"*Did* you try to save her?" Harry challenged. "Did you try to get her back?"

"We knew not where they had taken her. We knew too little of their ways then to find her again!" Quanah was angry now.

"Well, you know where Nalin is!" Harry retorted.

"And on foot we shall fight the soldiers?" Quanah stormed back. "We would be slaughtered as our horses were, and still Nalin would die. I would give my life for hers, but I cannot ask that of my people."

"No? Why don't you try asking them? You are their chief, Quanah. They heed your words. But now is when you fail them. You did the best you could all these years. You advised them, guided them, led them to many victories. There is no shame in trying to win and losing. There *is* shame in deserting your people when they need your counsel."

"Parker, you speak as a fool!"

"Do I? Let's see who's being the fool." Harry's voice raised to a shout. "People of the Comanche! Ladies and gentlemen." He rose in his stirrups to get their attention. The people stopped, turning about to face the bellowing soldier. "Listen to me. Your chief has remained silent these last weeks. He has not been giving you the wisdom of his mind and has not told you why. Nalin, his wife, your sister, is being held at the fort. She is not being given the chance to return to you, her chosen people, to live on the reservation with you. She will go to prison as Satanta of the Kiowa once went to prison. You remember the words he told you of what that was like. Satanta has told you he will die before he ever goes back there. Nalin of the Kwahadi will also die if she goes there. But you can save her, all of you. I don't mean by fighting. That will cost more lives. I mean by staying out a bit longer. Hold out, just awhile longer. Go back to the hills and stay there. Tell the bluecoats you will only surrender on one condition—if Nalin is returned to you. They will listen. The bluecoats will make the governor give her a pardon if you, her people, demand it! The Comanche must put down their weapons and fight no more, but you can still insist on your rights. Show them the Comanche are as one family and will not give over even one of their own."

Harry doubted most of them knew what he was saying, but he could already see his speech being translated by those who did understand English. Several groups were gathering about the translators, listening to them, then discussion began.

"I should cut out your tongue for this," Quanah began furiously.

"Nalin's your wife, Quanah, but she's also one of them. The Kwahadi are her people. Wait and see what they want to do."

The wait was a short one. Quanah and his brother were excluded from the conferences as the situation was discussed. Most began to turn back toward the hills before the elected spokesman reached them with the news of the decision.

"Each man and woman has chosen, Quanah. The bluecoat Parker's words are true. Nalin was of the brotherhood of the warriors. She fought as one with us, and we will not see her die. Even our women will not desert her in her time of need. We will stay out, and with what weapons and horses we can find or steal we will continue our fight. We will fight until all Comanche are returned to surrender with us. The bluecoat Parker may tell his people this, that the Kwahadi people will surrender only when we may all surrender together. Or we shall fight until the last of us is dead." He looked up at Quanah almost apologetically for usurping his leader's place. "That is our will, Quanah, as we have chosen."

Chapter 25

"THEY can't do this!" MacKenzie stormed in fury, rising to his feet to begin pacing his office.

"They've done it." Parker was sitting back, trying not to gloat. "They mean it. They won't come in until Nalin and every other Comanche held in our prisons is set free and pardoned."

"That's blackmail!"

"Yes, sir." Harry grinned. "You want the Comanche problem solved by spring then you better get off your ass and go personally to see the governor . . . sir." Harrison was beyond any concern for his own career. He had already stuck his neck in the noose, and what he still planned to do was only going to pull the rope tighter.

MacKenzie marched back to the desk, leaning across it to face Parker. "I wonder who taught them the fine art of blackmail?"

Harrison's answer was another broad grin.

"Next you'll be teaching them highway robbery—"

"No, sir, they already have that down pretty well."

MacKenzie frowned at him. "All right, you and your Comanche friends win. I'll leave today to speak to the governor. As you well know, he'll have no choice but to go along with it. You're damn lucky he isn't up for reelection for a couple of years."

"I'd say *you* are damn lucky, sir."

"You're impertinent, Parker!"

"Yes, sir, Colonel, it runs in the family."

"Get out of here, Major."

"Yes, sir." Harry rose.

"Wait a minute." MacKenzie pointed a finger at him threateningly. "One more thing before I go. I'm putting you in charge of our prisoner. I know she's held in the civilian portion of the jailhouse now, but I'm making you fully responsible for her welfare. You make goddamn sure she eats. In short, you make goddamn sure that girl is alive when I get back with that pardon. You hear me, Parker?"

Another smile appeared. "Yes, sir, Colonel, sir, exactly what I'm planning to see to."

MacKenzie's heavy brows furrowed. "What the hell does that mean?"

"Just obeying your orders, Colonel." Parker smiled nonchalantly, giving him a quick salute as he left.

Determined footsteps took him straight to the civilian portion of the jailhouse. Nalin was asleep. Good, she would need her rest. Harry looked down at her. The cheeks were flushed too pink; her skin was pasty. He still worried about her health, her ability to go through the coming ordeal, but perhaps once she had hope again . . . And now he *did* have direct orders from the colonel to see to her welfare. Another smile crept across his face. It would only be a few weeks before MacKenzie returned with a pardon. The governor wouldn't have any choice; he would have to make peace with the Comanche on their terms or face the spring, when the Kiowa would be able to join them in a combined effort that would cost settlers dearly.

Harrison leaned over and gave the flushed cheek a gentle kiss; one that didn't even stir her sleep, then he went out as quietly as he had come in. There was a lot left to do before nightfall.

"Why are you doing this, Major? You're throwing your whole career away." Hank Thompson peered up from the blanket he was rolling. Parker was on the far side of the barn's tack room, stuffing supplies into an already bulging saddlebag. For a long moment he couldn't answer the marshal, at least not truthfully. "Well, Quanah's my friend . . . as well as my cousin. In a way, I owe him my life—for sparing it, anyway." Harry chuckled.

The lighthearted answer wasn't quite satisfactory, and Thompson continued to stare at him. They were preparing for an extended trip; even Parker didn't know exactly how long it might take to find them. The packing was being kept secret in the back part of the stable. "I can see why *I'd* do it," Thompson stated. "She's my daughter. But you're risking everything—"

"It's something I have to do, Marshal." Harry kept busy, not turning to look at him, afraid of what his expression might reveal.

Thompson continued to watch the Major's preparations, his brow furrowed. He suspected he knew why. He had seen Parker with Lisa, seen the undeniable adoration on the young man's face. "How much trouble will you get into?"

"Don't know, Marshal." Parker shrugged, finally turning about with a nonchalant smile pasted into place. "Guess that depends on whether or not MacKenzie gets that pardon. If he doesn't, I'm hung—careerwise, anyway. If he does, who knows? They just might give me a medal for winning the Indian wars for them."

"MacKenzie will get the medal, you'll get court-martialed."

"Maybe." Parker shrugged again. "But then I'll still be a lawyer. They can't take that away. I'll get along."

"Will you, Major?" Thompson frowned at the young man now tying the saddlebags in place across the horse's back. Harry stopped in mid-motion. "What do you mean by that?" he asked curiously.

"Nothing." Thompson returned to his own share of the packing. "You're just a better man than I think I could ever be."

As planned, Harry entered the cell first while Thompson lagged behind, deliberately slowing until the guard stepped by him to open the cell.

"Evening, Nalin," Harrison called out cheerfully while the guard unlocked the door. "Your pa's come to see you

273

again." He had hardly stepped inside before he heard the sound of the thump. The deputy slumped forward, almost knocking into Harrison as he fell. Nalin looked up, startled, as the two men entered.

"Here, change into this, quick." Harrison drew a rolled-up piece of cloth out of his jacket and tossed it toward her. "Come on, hurry!" Harry stepped outside the cell, peering down the hallway. Thompson had already gone to the door at the end of the corridor to watch.

Nalin started to unfold the cloth. "This is a *white* woman's dress." Her nose wrinkled.

"You think you'll get out of here in buckskin?"

"I will not wear it!"

"You damn well will!" Harrison stormed back toward her. "You'll put it on, or I'll strip you and dress you myself!"

Still holding the dress as if it had lice in it, Nalin rose to her feet and began to remove her clothing. "Your people will punish you for this . . ." She paused to frown at Harrison worriedly.

"Never mind. Get dressed. Hurry up."

Harry turned away to give her privacy to change. In a few minutes he heard her grumbling softly. "Harrison . . ."

He turned around to find she had stuck the dress on all right—backward. "Oh, for chrissake!" He pulled the dress half down, yanked it around right, and started buttoning her up. "There now." Harry surveyed the completed task. "You look damn near like a white woman."

Nalin glared at him. "There is no need to make insults."

Harrison laughed in spite of their predicament, turning back to the marshal. "You got that hat?"

Thompson trotted back, drawing a folded-up bonnet out of his shirt. Harry straightened it, at least passably, stuck it on her head, positioning it to conceal the shortness of Nalin's hair, then tied a bow beneath her chin.

As Caucasian as she was, the dress and bonnet looked strangely foreign on her. Perhaps because he had never seen her that way before, he decided, wondering at the same time how things might have been different, for both of them, if she had never left North Fork . . . if she had never met Quanah. She would have been a marshal's daughter. She might have passed through Fort Smith . . . or he might have passed through her town . . . anything might have happened. But none of it had.

"Let's go," Thompson prodded, setting Harry into motion. Grabbing her arm, he started forward, leading them to the back of the cells, where the locked door entered onto an alley. "Christ, I forgot the key." Harrison dropped her hand to hurry back to the fallen guard, searching his pocket until he found the key to the back of the cellblock.

"Where do you take me?" Nalin asked.

"To Quanah." Harry hurriedly opened the door, and all three stepped out into the night.

Chapter 26

WITH Harry on one side and the marshal on the other, they strolled casually out of the alley and down the sidewalk toward the stables where the horses were saddled. The wide brim of the bonnet and the dark night concealed Nalin's face from those who might recognize her; the whiteness of her skin where the dress didn't cover provoked no curiosity. Still weak and feverish, her knees buckled twice, but Harry or the marshal caught her, holding her up and helping her forward.

Reaching the stable, Harry briefly entertained the thought of letting her ride the third horse alone. In her present condition, she'd never stay on. He mounted first, then Thompson helped her on behind him.

"Can you hold on to me tight?"

"Yes, Harrison, I can hold very tight." Nalin's eyes squeezed shut behind his back, remembering a similar experience over ten years ago. "Harrison, please be careful."

"We'll make it." He turned the horse around and headed out into the street with Thompson leading the third horse behind. Keeping to the shadows, they rode casually to the outskirts of town.

Thompson had no doubt they were being pursued by now, though his eyes couldn't begin to pierce the blackness of their second night out. They had ridden as hard as they dared through the first night, only stopping near dawn to rest the horses and allow them to graze. After another full day's riding, Thompson warned that they might lose the horses if they didn't stop for the night. He had taken the first watch while Parker rested, and then he woke him to change places.

"Parker, have you thought about what you're going to do if they catch up with us?" Thompson rolled out his blanket while Harrison sparingly dabbed water on his face from the canteen.

"No, I haven't, Marshal. I'm hoping they won't catch us."

"The name's Hank. Ain't no point in calling me marshal now. I don't know if Texas will take me for one after last night."

They grinned at each other, then Thompson settled into his bedroll and turned over. Harry checked on Nalin. She had fallen asleep almost immediately after eating heartily. Harry wished he could have heated a decent supper for her, but Thompson had warned that they didn't dare light a fire, so they had had to make do with canned beans and beef jerky.

A light snow started falling, and Harrison drew the blanket up to protect Nalin's head. She awoke and turned onto her back to look up at him.

"Are you warm enough?"

"I am warm enough." Nalin snuggled gratefully beneath the blankets. She looked much better now. There was still a trace of fever in her eyes and in the pink cheeks, but hope of seeing Quanah again had encouraged her appetite. Harry knew she would make it now.

"You are a good and kind man, Harrison Parker."

"Sure." Harry smiled. "I'm a saint." I must be, he thought silently, to return the woman I love to another man—a saint or a fool.

"He has told you of Jesse Sutton's death, has he not?" Nalin's gaze drifted briefly to the slumbering marshal, then back again to fasten on him with worry.

"He told me, Nalin." Harry smiled reassuringly. "And don't worry . . . it won't happen again."

"I could not bear to live with your life also on my conscience."

277

"Everything is going to be fine . . . you'll see."

"Harrison, there is something I would have you know."

Harry paused, waiting for her to form the words properly. Finally she began, looking up at him from her cocoon of heavy blankets, the snow falling and melting on her face to mix with the tears slowly rolling down her cheeks. "You know that my heart will always belong to Quanah. But I wish you to know there is room there for you, also. After Quanah, I will love you best of all forever."

"Nalin," Harry murmured, touching her cheek lightly. His fingers came back wet with tears—tears shed for him.

He was still kneeling beside her as Nalin impulsively sat up and kissed him on the lips. Before the kiss could fully register she had lain down again, turned on her side away from him, and pulled the blanket up to her neck.

Harry backed away silently, moving back to the lookout spot, watching until dawn.

Rifle fire cracked over the sound of the galloping hooves as the fugitives tried to outrun the soldiers behind them. There were only twenty, but they looked like fifty to Harrison's unpracticed eye. Another volley of shots exploded, coming nowhere near them. Riding over open prairie, they should have made excellent targets for the soldiers, who seemed inclined only to run them down with an occasional volley aimed high over their heads.

Suddenly, Harrison heard a small, half-stifled scream and turned his head. Nalin's horse had stumbled, pitching her to the ground. He reined in sharply and spun the horse around. She had struggled to her feet, dazed, a trickle of blood oozing from a small cut on her forehead.

"Give me your hand. Jump up!" Harry pulled the horse to a stop.

"No, Harrison," Nalin backed away.

"Come on! Jump!" he screamed at her.

"No! It is finished. I will not have your death on my conscience, too. We must stop!"

"Nalin!" he shouted in rage. The soldiers had caught

up with them, and further flight was out of the question. Thompson had returned and dismounted, waiting as the soldiers surrounded them. Major Nash was leading them. He stopped a few feet away and climbed off his horse.

"You're not taking her back, Nash." Harry had jumped down, too, putting Nalin behind him, and pulled out his gun.

"Parker, for chrissake . . ." Nash kept approaching.

Harry lifted the revolver waist high, pointing it at Nash's chest.

"Parker, don't be a bigger jackass than I already have you figured for. Put that goddamn thing down," Nash scolded in the same tone he might have used on a misbehaving child. "I ain't taking her away from you. In fact, I'm only out here to give you this before you get in any more trouble." Major Nash held out a slim scrap of paper. "If you'll put that gun down before you shoot somebody by accident, you can read the damn thing. It's a telegraph sent from the governor's office. Nalin has been pardoned, and every last mother's son of Comanche blood in our prisons along with her. Read it for yourself."

In an expression of disbelief, Harry lowered the revolver.

"You best hurry up, Major," Nash prodded, "before your friends on the ridge get it into their heads that you and the girl are in trouble."

Still in shock, Harrison turned in the direction Nash's gaze had traveled. Half a dozen mounted braves had appeared, and more were joining them. Quanah was in the front.

"Put the gun down, Major, so it looks like we're having a friendly chat."

Harry stuck the revolver in his holster, then waved at Quanah to signal him all was well below. He took the paper from Nash and read it through twice.

"She's free?" he asked in disbelief.

"Completely," Nash stated. "Providing the Comanche come in as promised."

"They will . . . Quanah gave me his word."

"Then you best send the girl on up there to tell her husband about it before he gets nervous about what's taking so long."

Harry turned to Nalin. She was turned toward the ridgeline, gazing up with a look of longing on her face, a look that could never be for him. "Nalin," he said softly, approaching her. "You're free. It's all over."

She turned back to him. "My baby?"

"You can pick him up on your way past Fort Smith."

She gazed back to the ridgeline. "I wonder what our life shall be like on the reservation they send us to?"

"I don't know, but Quanah only promised to come in. If he doesn't like it, he never promised to stay there."

Nalin smiled faintly. "And what of you?"

"Don't worry about me." He smiled, trying to make it a cheery one. "I'll be fine. Come on . . ." He helped her up into the saddle.

"We will see you again, Harrison?" She picked up the reins and held them.

"Sure you will. I have to visit my godson now and then, don't I?"

For a moment she looked at him sadly. "I know you will not come." She held out her hand, and Harry grasped her fingers in a tight, brief squeeze. "You will remember my words to you?"

"I remember them, Nalin." He stepped away. She turned the horse about, then stopped in front of Hank Thompson. The marshal looked up at her.

"Will you come with me, my . . . father?" She smiled. Hank was momentarily stunned, then hurriedly pulled himself into the saddle. He paused before Harrison to take off his badge and hand it to him. "Turn in my resignation for me, will you, Major?"

For the first time since Harry had known him, Thompson was smiling. "I won't have time now to chase down outlaws. I got a whole family to learn all about. Think I'll make a good Indian?"

"Be happy, Hank." Harrison smiled. "I know you will be."

280

Nalin had waited for him and kicked the horse's side into a trot as he came up beside her. Harrison watched them ride at a lope toward the ridge where Quanah waited. He wasn't even aware of it when Nash walked up beside him.

"Tell me something, Parker." Nash, too, watched the figures in the distance. "I already know you're an idealistic jackass, but you must have another reason for all you've done. You in love with that girl?"

Harrison ignored him until Nalin reached Quanah's side. He finally turned around to answer. "Who, me? That's the craziest thing I ever heard. Everybody knows she's Quanah's woman."

"That right?" Nash eyed him suspiciously. "Well, then, you just might want to know I have a daughter coming home this spring just about the right age—"

"Nash." Harry stopped in his tracks. "You just said I was a jackass."

"No, I said 'an idealistic jackass,' and so's Mary. You two should get along fine."

Parker stalked off laughing.

On the ridge, the noonday sun beat down on the figures of Quanah and Nalin. Nalin reached Quanah's side, his gaze momentarily straying to the man who rode up with her. Later there would be time for explanations. For now, she barely reined in beside him before he lifted her in his arms, transferring her to his own horse, pulling her up in front of him. With a victorious cry uncharacteristic of him, Quanah spun the horse around, riding at a gallop down the ridge and out of sight.

This is the special design logo that will call your attention to new Avon authors who show exceptional promise in the romance area. Each month a new novel—either historical or contemporary—will be featured.

CAPTIVE OF THE HEART
Kate Douglas   October 1982
Set in the American Southwest in the mid-19th century, this big, romantic novel is about a courageous white girl who has chosen to live with the Comanches, and the young chieftain who falls in love with her.
81125-1/$2.75

DEFIANT DESTINY
Nancy Moulton   November 1982
While on a dangerous sea voyage to deliver secret information to the rebellious colonies a young English beauty is captured by a notorious American privateer who soon captures her heart as well.
81430-7/$2.95

LOVE'S CHOICE
Rosie Thomas   December 1982
A lovely newspaper reporter finds herself torn between her desire to remain independent, and love, when she is caught in a passion for two different men. They are rival winemakers, and as Bell tries to decide between them—a debonaire, aristocratic Frenchman and a warm, vibrant Californian—a dangerous competition for her love arises.
61713-7/$2.95

Avon Paperbacks

Available wherever paperbacks are sold, or directly from the publisher. Include 50¢ per copy for postage and handling; allow 6-8 weeks for delivery. Avon Books, Mail Order Dept., 224 West 57th St., N.Y., N.Y. 10019.